PRAISE FOR THE CRIMSON SHADOW

"A fine adventure, filled with memorable characters and compelling action."
—Terry Brooks, *New York Times*–bestselling author of *The Fall of Shannara*, on *The Sword of Bedwyr*

"Salvatore describes and choreographs battle scenes better than any other contemporary fantasist." —*Publishers Weekly*

"A worthy, entertaining addition to fantasy literature."
—*Starlog* on *The Sword of Bedwyr*

"An epic blockbuster." —*Cryptych*

"Swordwaving, magic, and banter." —*Kirkus Reviews* on *The Dragon King*

"Salvatore tells a story with exciting action scenes that contain great bantering dialogue reminiscent of Indiana Jones." —*Voice of Youth Advocates (VOYA)*

"I admire Bob Salvatore tremendously . . . He gives us a world of depth and humanity, filled with color and sound and feeling and with heroes we can't help but admire."
—Tracy Hickman, *New York Times*–bestselling coauthor of the Deathgate Cycle

"Packed from cover to cover with high-spirited derring-do and the ring of crossed steel." —James Lowder, author of *Prince of Lies*

THE SWORD OF BEDWYR

ALSO BY R. A. SALVATORE

Forgotten Realms

The Dark Elf Trilogy
Homeland
Exile
Sojourn

The Icewind Dale Trilogy
The Crystal Shard
Streams of Silver
The Halfling's Gem

Legacy of the Drow
The Legacy
Starless Night
Siege of Darkness
Passage to Dawn

Paths of Darkness
The Silent Blade
The Spine of the World
Sea of Swords

The Sellswords
Servant of the Shard
Promise of the Witch King
Road of the Patriarch

The Hunter's Blades Trilogy
The Thousand Orcs
The Lone Drow
The Two Swords

Transitions
The Orc King
The Pirate King
The Ghost King

Neverwinter
Gauntlgrym
Neverwinter

Charon's Claw
The Last Threshold

The Sundering
The Companions

Companions Codex
Night of the Hunter
Rise of the King
Vengeance of the Iron Dwarf

Homecoming
Archmage
Maestro
Hero

No name trilogy
Timeless

The Cleric Quintet
Canticle
In Sylvan Shadows
Night Masks
The Fallen Fortress
The Chaos Curse

War of the Spider Queen
Dissolution
Insurrection
Condemnation
Extinction
Annihilation

Stone of Tymora
Stowaway
The Shadowmask
The Sentinels

The Legend of Drizzt Anthology
The Collected Stories
Corona

DemonWars
The Demon Awakens
The Demon Spirit
The Demon Apostle
Mortalis
Ascendance
Transcendence
Immortalis

Saga of the First King

First Heros
The Highwayman
The Ancient

The First King
The Dame
The Bear

The Coven
Child of a Mad God
Reckoning of the Fallen God (2019)

Other series

The Spearwielder's Tale
The Woods Out Back
The Dragon's Dagger
The Haggis Hunters

Chronicles of Ynis Aielle
Echoes of the Fourth Magic
The Witch's Daughter
Bastion of Darkness

Crimson Shadow
The Sword of Bedwyr
Luthien's Gamble
The Dragon King

Star Wars
Star Wars Episode II: Attack of the Clones

Star Wars: The New Jedi Order
Vector Prime

Novelization
Tarzan: The Epic Adventures

THE SWORD OF BEDWYR

THE CRIMSON SHADOW

R. A. SALVATORE

Cover illustration by Amanda Shaffer

ISBN: 978-1-5040-5560-4

This edition published in 2019 by Open Road Integrated Media, Inc.
180 Maiden Lane
New York, NY 10038
www.openroadmedia.com

To Betsy Mitchell, for all of her support and input,
for showing me new potential and new directions.
Enthusiasm truly is infectious.

And a special thank you to Wayne Chang,
Donald Puckey, and Nancy Hanger.
In a business as tough and competitive as this,
it's comforting to be working with
such talented and dedicated people.

Avon Sea
Dorsal Sea
N
Isle Marvis
Clywyd
Isle Caryth
Gybi
Bae Colthwyn
Hale
Dun Varna
Isle Bedwydrin
Rrohlwyn
The Diamond Gate
Mennichen Dee
Land's End
Eriador
Fields of Eradoch
Bronegan
Colonsey
Chalmbers
MacDonald's Swath
Felling Run
Felling Downs
Port Charley
Monfort
Dun Caryth
Glen Albyn
Malpuissant's Wall
The Five Sentinels
Bennybeck
The Iron Cross
Princetown
Baraduine
Glen Durritch
Eornfast
Dulsen
Berra
Bangor
Lemmingbury
Bonny Fowddwy
Mannington
Warchester
Deverwood
Speythenfergus Lake
Avon (Elkinador)
Ogniac Dee
Corbin
The Straits of Mann
Evenshorn
Lake Tummel
The Saltwash
Beachyhead
Darthemoor
Carlisle on Stratton
Darthemoor Wood
Stratton River
Newcastle
Gascony

THE SWORD OF BEDWYR

PROLOGUE

THESE ARE THE Avonsea Islands, rugged peaks and rolling hills, gentle rains and fierce winds blowing down from the glaciers across the Dorsal Sea. They are quiet Baranduine, land of folk and Fairborn, land of green and rainbows. They are the Five Sentinels, the Windbreakers, barren peaks, huge, horned sheep, and multicolored lichen that grows eerily when the sun has set. Let all seafarers beware the rocks of the channels near to the five!

They are Praetoria, most populous and civilized of the islands, where trade with the mainland is the way and cities dot the countryside.

And they are Eriador, untamed. She is a land of war, of hardy folk as familiar with sword as with plow. A land of clans, where loyalties run as deep as blood and to fight a man is to fight all his kin.

Eriador, untamed. Where the clouds hang low over rolling hills thick with green and the wind blows chill, even in the height of summer. Where the Fairborn, the elves, dance atop secret hills and rugged dwarves forge weapons that will inevitably taste of an enemy's blood within a year.

The tales of barbarian raiders, the Huegoths, are long indeed, and many are the influences of that warlike people on the folk of Eriador. But never did the Huegoths hold the land, never did they enslave the folk of Eriador. It is said among the clans of both Eriador and the barbarian islands that one Eriadoran was killed for every slain Huegoth, a score that no other civilized people could claim against the mighty barbarians.

Down from the holes of the Iron Cross came the cyclopians, one-eyed brutes, savage and merciless. They swept across the land, burning and pillaging, murdering any who could not escape the thunder of their charge. And there arose in

Eriador a leader among the clans, Bruce MacDonald, the Unifier, who brought together the men and women of the land and turned the tide of war. And when the western fields were clear, it is said that Bruce MacDonald himself carved a swath through the northern leg of the Iron Cross so that his armies could roll into the eastern lands and crush the cyclopians.

That was six hundred years ago.

From the sea came the armies of Gascony, vast kingdom south of the islands. And so Avon, the land that was Elkinador, was conquered and "civilized." But never did the Gascons claim rule of Eriador in the north. The great swells and breakers of the Dorsal Sea swept one fleet aground, smashing the wooden ships to driftwood, and the great whales destroyed another fleet. Behind the rallying cries of "Bruce MacDonald!" their hero of old, did the folk of Eriador battle every inch for their precious land. So fierce was their resistance that the Gascons not only retreated but built a wall to seal off the northern lands, lands the Gascons finally declared untamable.

And with Eriador's continued resistance, and with war brewing among some of the other southern lands, the Gascons eventually lost interest in the islands and departed. Their legacy remains in the language and religion and dress of the people of Avon, but not in Eriador, not in the untamable land, where the religion is older than Gascony and where loyalty runs as deep as blood.

That was three hundred years ago.

There arose in Avon, in Carlisle on the River Stratton, a wizard-king of great power who would see all the islands under his rule. Greensparrow was his name, is his name, a fierce man of high ambition and evil means. And evil was the pact that Greensparrow signed with Cresis who ruled the cyclopians, appointing Cresis as his first duke and bringing the warlike one-eyes into Greensparrow's army. Avon became his in a fortnight, all opposition crushed, and then did he turn his sights on Eriador. His armies fared no better than the barbarians, than the cyclopians, than the Gascons.

But then there swept across Eriador a darkness that no sword could cut, that no courage could chase away: a plague that whispers hinted was inspired by black sorcery. None in Avon felt its ravages, but in all of free Eriador, mainland and islands, two of every three perished, and two of every three who lived were rendered too weak to do battle.

Thus did Greensparrow gain his rule, imposing a truce that gave unto him all the lands north of the Iron Cross. He appointed his eighth duke in the mining city of Montfort, which had been called Caer MacDonald, in honor of the Unifier.

Dark times there were in Eriador; the Fairborn retreated and the dwarves were enslaved.

That was twenty years ago. That was when Luthien Bedwyr was born.

This is his tale.

CHAPTER 1

ETHAN'S DOUBTS

ETHAN BEDWYR, ELDEST son of the Eorl of Bedwydrin, stood tall on the balcony of the great house in Dun Varna, watching as the two-masted, black-sailed ship lazily glided into the harbor. The proud man wore a frown even before the expected standard, crossed open palms above a bloodshot eye, came into view. Only ships of the king or the barbarians to the northeast would sail openly upon the dark and cold waters of the Dorsal Sea, so named for the eerie black fins of the flesh-eating whales that roamed the waters in ravenous packs, and barbarians did not sail alone.

A second standard—a strong arm, bent at the elbow and holding a miner's pick—soon appeared.

"Visitors?" came a question from behind.

Recognizing the voice as his father's, Ethan did not turn. "Flying the duke of Montfort's pennant," he answered, and his disdain was obvious.

Gahris Bedwyr moved to the balcony beside his son and Ethan winced when he looked upon the man, who appeared proud and strong, as Ethan distantly remembered him. With the light of the rising sun in his face, Gahris's cinnamon eyes shone brightly, and the stiff ocean breeze blew his thick shock of silvery white hair back from his ruddy, creased face, a face that had weathered under the sun during countless hours in small fishing craft out on the dangerous Dorsal. Gahris was as tall as Ethan, and that was taller than most men on Isle Bedwydrin, who in turn were taller than most other men of the kingdom. His shoulders remained broader than his belly, and his arms were corded from a youth spent in tireless work.

But as the black-sailed ship drifted closer to the docks, the coarse shouts of the brutish cyclopian crew urging the islanders into subservient action, Gahris's eyes betrayed his apparent stature.

Ethan turned his gaze back to the harbor, having no desire to look upon his broken father.

"It is the duke's cousin, I believe," Gahris remarked. "I had heard that he was touring the northern isles on holiday. Ah well, we must see to his pleasures." Gahris turned as if to leave, then stopped, seeing that stubborn Ethan had not loosed his grip on the balcony rail.

"Will you fight in the arena for the pleasure of our guest?" he asked, already knowing the answer.

"Only if the duke's cousin is my opponent," Ethan replied in all seriousness, "and the fight is to the death."

"You must learn to accept what is," Gahris Bedwyr chided.

Ethan turned an angry gaze on him, a look that might have been Gahris's own a quarter of a century before, before independent Eriador had fallen under the iron rule of King Greensparrow of Avon. It took the elder Bedwyr a long moment to compose himself, to remind himself of all that he and his people stood to lose. Things were not so bad for the folk of Bedwydrin, or for those on any of the isles. Greensparrow was mostly concerned with those lands in Avon proper, south of the mountains called the Iron Cross, and though Morkney, the duke of Montfort, had exacted rigid control over the folk of the Eriadoran mainland, he left the islanders fairly alone—as long as he received his tithes and his emissaries were granted proper treatment whenever they happened onto one of the isles.

"Our life is not so bad," Gahris remarked, trying to soothe the burning fires in his dangerously proud son. The eorl would not be shocked if later that day he learned that Ethan had attacked the duke's cousin in broad daylight, before a hundred witnesses and a score of Praetorian Guards!

"Not if one aspires to subservience," Ethan growled back, his ire unrelenting.

"You're a great-grand," Gahris muttered under his breath, meaning that Ethan was one of those throwbacks to the days of fierce independence, when Bedwydrin had fought against any who would call themselves rulers. The island's history was filled with tales of war—against raiding barbarians, cyclopian hordes, self-proclaimed Eriadoran kings who would have, by force, united the land, and even against the mighty Gascon fleet, when that vast southern kingdom had attempted to conquer all of the lands in the frigid northern waters. Avon had fallen to the Gascons, but the hardened warriors of Eriador had made life so miserable for the invaders that they had built a wall to seal off the northern province, proclaiming the land too wild to be tamed. It was Bedwydrin's boast during those valorous times that no Gascon soldier had stepped upon the island and lived.

But that was ancient history now, seven generations removed, and Gahris Bedwyr had been forced to yield to the winds of change.

"I am Bedwydrin," Ethan muttered back, as if that claim should explain everything.

"Always the angry rebel!" the frustrated Gahris snapped at him. "Damn the consequences of your actions! Your pride has not the foresight—"

"My pride marks me as Bedwydrin," Ethan interrupted, his cinnamon eyes, the trademark of the Bedwyr clan, flashing dangerously in the morning sunlight.

The set of those eyes forestalled the eorl's retort. "At least your brother will properly entertain our guests," Gahris said calmly, and walked away.

Ethan looked back to the harbor—the ship was in now, with burly, one-eyed cyclopians rushing about to tie her up, pushing aside any islanders who happened in their way, and even a few who took pains not to. These brutes did not wear the silver-and-black uniforms of the Praetorian Guards but were the house guard escorts kept by every noble. Even Gahris had a score of them, gifts from the duke of Montfort.

With a disgusted shake of his head, Ethan shifted his gaze to the training yard below and to the left of the balcony, where he knew that he would find Luthien, his only sibling, fifteen years his junior. Luthien was always there, practicing his swordplay and his archery. Training, always training. He was his father's pride and joy, that one, and even Ethan had to admit that if there was a finer fighter in all the lands, he had never seen him.

He spotted his brother immediately by the reddish tint of his long and wavy hair, just a shade darker than Ethan's blond locks. Even from this distance, Luthien cut an impressive figure. He stood two inches above six feet, with a broad chest and muscled arms, his skin golden brown, a testament for his love of the outdoors on this isle, which saw more rain than sun.

Ethan scowled as he watched Luthien easily dispatch his latest sparring partner, then pivot immediately and with a single thrust, twist, and leg-sweep maneuver take down the opponent who rushed in at his back, trying to take him by surprise.

Those warriors watching in the training yard gave a cheer of approval, and Luthien politely stood and bowed.

Yes, Ethan knew, Luthien would properly entertain their "guests," and the thought brought bile into the proud man's throat. He didn't really blame Luthien, though; his brother was young and ignorant. In Luthien's twenty years, he had never known true freedom, had never known Gahris before the rise of the Wizard-King Greensparrow.

Gahris walked out into the training yard, then, and motioned for Luthien to join him. Smiling and nodding, the eorl pointed to the docks. Luthien responded with a wide smile and ran off, toweling his corded muscles as he went: always ready to please.

"My pity to you, dear brother," Ethan whispered. The sentiment was an honest one, for Ethan knew well that Luthien would one day have to face up to the truth of their land and the cowardice of their father.

A shout from the dock stole Ethan's attention, and he looked that way just in time to see a cyclopian smash an islander fisherman to the wharf. Two other cyclopians joined their comrade, and the three punched and kicked the man repeatedly, until he finally managed to scramble away. Laughing, the three went back to their duties tying up the cursed craft.

Ethan had seen enough. He spun away from the balcony and nearly crashed into two of his father's own one-eyed soldiers as they walked past.

"Heir of Bedwyr," one of the cyclopians greeted through smiling, pointy yellow teeth.

Ethan did not miss the condescension in the brute's tone. He was the heir of Bedwyr, true enough, but the title rang hollow to the cyclopians, who ultimately served only the king of Avon and his wizard dukes. These guards, these "gifts" from the duke of Montfort, were no more than spies, Ethan knew as everybody knew. Not a soul on Bedwyr mentioned that little fact openly though.

"Do your appointed rounds normally take you to the private quarters of the ruling family?" Ethan snapped.

"We have only come to inform the nobles that the cousin of the duke of Montfort has arrived," the other guard replied.

Ethan stared at the ugly creature for a long while. Cyclopians were not quite as tall as most men, but were much thicker, with even the smallest of the burly race weighing nearly two hundred pounds and the heavier brutes often passing three hundred. Their foreheads, slipping out of a tight patch of stringy hair, were typically sloped down to the bushy brow of the single, always bloodshot, eye. Their noses were flat and wide, their lips almost non-existent, offering a perpetual view of those animal-like yellow teeth. And no cyclopian had ever been accused of possessing a chin.

"Gahris knows of the arrival," Ethan replied, his voice grim, almost threatening. The two cyclopians looked at each other and smirked, but their smiles disappeared when they looked back at the fiery Ethan, whose hand had gone to the hilt of his sword. Two young boys, human servants of the noble family, had come into the hall and were watching the encounter with more than a passing interest.

"Strange to wear a sword in one's own private quarters," one of the cyclopians remarked.

"Always a wise precaution when smelly one-eyes are about," Ethan answered loudly, taking strength in the appearance of the two human witnesses. He more than matched the ensuing scowls of the guards.

"And not another word from your mouth," Ethan commanded. "Your breath does so offend me."

The scowls increased, but Ethan had called their bluff. He was the son of the eorl, after all, an eorl the cyclopians had to at least maintain the pretense of serving. The two soldiers turned about and stomped off.

Ethan glanced at the boys, who were running off, but undeniably smiling. They were the youth of Bedwydrin, the eldest son thought. The youth of a proud race. Ethan took some solace and some hope in their obvious approval of the way he had stood down the ugly cyclopians. Perhaps the future would be a better time.

But despite the fleeting hope, Ethan knew that he had given his father yet another reason to berate him.

CHAPTER 2

TWO NOBLES AND THEIR LADIES

A CYCLOPIAN SOLDIER, shield emblazoned with the bent arm and pick design of Montfort, entered the audience hall of Gahris Bedwyr's home a short while later. It was a large rectangular room, set with several comfortable chairs and graced by a tremendous hearth.

"Viscount Aubrey," the one-eyed herald began, "cousin of Duke Morkney of Montfort, sixth of eight, fourth in line to . . ." And so it went on for several minutes, the cyclopian rambling through unimportant, even minuscule details of this viscount's heritage and lineage, feats of valor (always exaggerated, and still seeming not so tremendous to Gahris, who had lived in the tough land of Bedwydrin for more than sixty years) and deeds of generosity and heroism.

A viscount, the island eorl mused, thinking that practically every fourth man in Eriador seemed to hold claim to that title, or to one of baron.

"And his fellow, Baron Wilmon," the cyclopian went on, and Gahris sighed deeply at the not-unexpected proclamation, his thoughts proven all too true. Mercifully, Wilmon's introductory was not nearly as long as Aubrey's, and as for their female escorts, the cyclopian merely referred to them as "the ladies, Elenia and Avonese."

"Ellen and Avon," Gahris muttered under his breath, for he understood the level of pretension that had come to the normally level-headed people of the lands.

In strode the viscount and his entourage. Aubrey was a meticulously groomed, salty-haired man in his mid-forties, Wilmon a foppish and swaggering twenty-five. Both wore the weapons of warriors, sword and dirk, but when they shook Gahris's hands, he felt no callouses, and neither had a grip indicating that he could even swing a heavy sword. The ladies were worse yet, over-painted, over-perfumed creatures of dangerous curves, clinging silk garments, and abundant jewelry that tinkled and rattled with every alluring shift. Avonese had seen fifty years if she had seen a day, Gahris knew, and all the putty and paint in the world couldn't hide the inevitable effects of nature.

She tried, though—oh, how this one tried!—and Gahris thought it a pitiful sight.

"Viscount Aubrey," he said politely, his smile wide. "It is indeed an honor to meet one who has so gained the confidence of our esteemed duke."

"Indeed," Aubrey replied, seeming rather bored.

"May I inquire what has brought such an unexpected group so far to the north?"

"No," Aubrey started to answer, but Avonese, slipping out of Aubrey's arm to take hold of the eorl's, interrupted.

"We are on holiday, of course!" she slurred, her breath scented by wine.

"We are come now from the Isle of Marvis," added Elenia. "We were informed that none in all the northland could set a banquet like the eorl of Marvis, and we were not disappointed."

"They do have such fine wines!" added Avonese.

Aubrey seemed to be growing as tired of the banter as Gahris, though Wilmon was too engaged with a stubborn hangnail to notice any of it.

"The eorl of Marvis has indeed earned his reputation as a fine host," Gahris remarked sincerely, for Bruce Durgess was a dear friend of his, a common sufferer in the dark times of the wizard-king's rule.

"Fair," Aubrey corrected. "And I suppose that you, too, will treat us with renowned leek soup, and perhaps a leg of lamb as well."

Gahris started to reply, but wasn't sure what to say. The two dishes, along with a multitude of fish, were indeed the island's staple.

"I do so hate leek soup," Aubrey went on, "but we have enough provisions on board our vessel and we shan't be staying for long."

Gahris seemed confused—and that sincere expression hid well his sudden sense of relief.

"But I thought . . ." the eorl began, trying to sound truly saddened.

"I am late for an audience with Morkney," Aubrey said haughtily. "I would have bypassed this dreary little island altogether, except that I found the eorl of Marvis's arena lacking. I had heard that the islands were well-stocked with some of the finest warriors in all of Eriador, but I daresay that a half-crippled dwarf from the deepest mines of Montfont could have easily defeated any of the fighters we witnessed on the Isle of Marvis."

Gahris said nothing, but was thinking that Aubrey's description of Bedwydrin as a "dreary little island" would have cost the man his tongue in times past.

"I do so hope that your warriors might perform better," Aubrey finished.

Avonese squeezed Gahris's arm tightly, apparently liking the hardened muscles she felt there. "Warriors do so inspire me," she whispered in the eorl's ear.

Gahris hadn't expected a morning arena fight, but was glad to oblige. Hopefully, the viscount would be satisfied with the show and would be gone before lunch, saving Gahris the trouble of setting a meal—be it lamb or leek soup!

"I will see to the arrangements personally," Gahris said to Aubrey, smoothly pulling free of Avonese's nailed clutches as he spoke. "My attendants will show you to where you might refresh yourselves after the long journey. I will return in a few moments."

And with that he was gone, hustling down the stone corridors of his large house. He found Luthien just a short distance away, dressed in fine clothes and freshly scrubbed after his morning workout.

"Back to the yard with you," Gahris said to his son's confused expression. "They have come to see a fight and nothing more."

"And I am to fight?"

"Who better?" Gahris asked, patting Luthien roughly on the shoulder and quickly leading him back the way he had come. "Arrange for two combats before you take your turn—at least one cyclopian in each." Gahris paused and furrowed his brow. "Who would give you the best fight?" he asked.

"Ethan, probably," Luthien replied without hesitation, but Gahris was already shaking his head. Ethan wouldn't fight in the arena, not anymore, and certainly not for the entertainment of visiting nobles.

"Garth Rogar, then," Luthien said, referring to a barbarian warrior, a giant of a man. "He has been in fine form of late."

"But you will defeat him?"

The question seemed to sting the proud young warrior.

"Of course you will." Gahris answered his own question, making it seem an absurd thing to ask. "Make it a worthy fight, I beg. It is important that Bedwydrin, and you, my son, be given high praise to the duke of Montfort."

Gahris stopped then, and Luthien bounded away, brimming with confidence and with the sincerest desire to please both his father and the visiting nobles.

"How embarrassed will Luthien be to fail before his father and his father's honored guests?" the huge man bellowed to the approving laughter of many other fighters. They sat in the low and sweaty chambers off the tunnels that led to the arena, testing the feel of their weapons while awaiting their call.

"Embarrassed?" the young Bedwyr replied, as though he was truly stunned. "There is no embarrassment in victory, Garth Rogar."

A general, mocking groan rolled about the chamber as the other warriors joined in the mood.

The huge Rogar, fully a foot taller than Luthien's six feet two inches, with arms as thick as Luthien's legs, dropped his whetstone to the floor and deliberately rose. Two strides took him right up to the still-seated young Bedwyr, who had to turn his head perpendicular to his body to see tall Garth Rogar's scowl.

"You fall this day," the barbarian promised. He began a slow turn, shoulders leading so that his grim expression lingered on Luthien for a long moment. All the room was hushed.

Luthien reached up and slapped Garth Rogar across the rump with the flat of his sword, and howls of laughter erupted from the warriors, Garth Rogar included. The huge northman spun about and made a mock charge at Luthien, but Luthien's sword snapped out quicker than the eye could follow, its waving tip defeating the charge.

They were all friends, these young warriors, except for the few cyclopians who sat in a distant corner, eyeing the play disdainfully. Only Garth Rogar had not been raised on Bedwydrin. He had floated into Dun Varna's harbor on the flotsam of a shipwreck just four years previously. Barely into his teens, the noble young barbarian had been taken in by the islanders and treated well. Now, like the other young men of Bedwydrin, he was learning to fight. It was all a game to the young rascals, but a deadly serious game. Even in times of peace, such as they had known all their lives, bandits were not uncommon and monsters occasionally crawled out of the Dorsal.

"I will cut your lip this day," Garth said to Luthien, "and never again will you kiss Katerin O'Hale."

The laughter became a hush; Katerin was not one to be insulted. She was from the opposite side of Bedwydrin, raised among the fisherfolk who braved the more dangerous waters of the open Avon Sea. Tough indeed were the stock of Hale, and Katerin was counted among their finest. A leather packet soared across the room to bounce off the huge barbarian's back. Garth Rogar spun about to see a scowling Katerin standing with her muscled arms crossed atop her sword, its tip resting against the stone floor.

"If you say so again, I will cut something of yours," the fiery red-haired young woman promised grimly, her green eyes flashing dangerously. "And kissing will then be the last thing on your small mind."

The laughter erupted once more, and Garth Rogar, red with embarrassment, knew that he could not win this war of insults. He threw up his hands in defeat and stalked back to his seat to prepare his weapons.

The weapons they used were real, but blunted, and with shortened tips that might pierce and sting, but would not kill. At least, not usually. Several warriors had died in the arena, though none in more than a decade. The fighting was an ancient and necessary tradition on Bedwydrin and in all of Eriador, and deemed worth the potential cost by even the most civilized of men. The scars that young men and women carried with them from their years training in the arena taught them well the respect of weapons and enemies, and gave them a deep understanding of those they would fight beside if trouble ever came. Only three years of training were required, but many stayed on for four, and some, like Luthien, had made the training their life's endeavor.

He had been in the arena perhaps a hundred times, defeating every opponent except for his first, his brother Ethan. The two had never rematched, for Ethan had soon left the arena, and while Luthien would have liked to try again his skills against his undeniably talented brother, he did not allow his pride to blemish his sincere respect and love for Ethan. Now Luthien was the finest of the group. Katerin O'Hale was swift and agile as any cat, Bukwo of the cyclopians could take a tremendous amount of punishment, and Garth Rogar was powerful beyond the normal limitations of any human. But Luthien was a true warrior: fast and strong, agile and able to bring his weapon to bear or to parry at any angle in the blink of a cinnamon-colored eye. He could take a hit and growl away any pain, and yet he carried fewer scars than any except the very newest of the warriors.

He was the complete fighter, the shining light in his father's aging eyes, and determined now to honor his father this day, to bring a smile to the face of a man who smiled far too little.

He brought a whetstone singing along the side of his fine sword, removing a burr, then held the weapon out in front of him, testing its balance.

The first fight, two cyclopians beating each other about the head and shoulders with light clubs, had already commenced when Gahris led his four visitors into the seats of honor at the front of the balcony directly opposite the tunnels that opened onto the circular fighting grounds of the arena. Gahris took his seat in the middle and was promptly sandwiched between Elenia and Avonese, squeezing in tight beside him, with their respective consorts flanking them on the outside. To increase the eorl's discomfort, three of Aubrey's personal cyclopian guards were close behind the seated nobles. One carried a crossbow, Gahris noted, an unusual sight among cyclopians. With only one eye, the brutes lacked depth perception and were normally not adept with distance weapons. This one seemed comfortable holding the crossbow, though, and Gahris noted that it had been fitted with a curious device, opposing and angled mirrors, atop its central shaft.

Gahris sighed when he noticed that only a handful of islanders were in attendance this day. He had hoped for a cheering crowd and wished that he had been given the time to assemble one.

But Aubrey was obviously impatient. The viscount was here only so that his pestering consort, Avonese, would stop her incessant nagging.

"Cyclopians?" Avonese whined. "If I wanted to watch cyclopians brawl, I would simply throw a piece of uncooked meat into their midst at Castle Montfort!"

Gahris winced—this wasn't going well.

"Surely you have better to offer than two cyclopians battering each other, Eorl Bedwyr," Aubrey put in, and his look to Gahris was both pleading and threatening. "My cousin Morkney, the duke of Montfort, would be so disappointed to learn that my journey to your island was not a pleasurable one."

"This is not the primary show," Gahris tried to explain against a rising chorus of groans. Finally, the eorl gave up. He signaled to the marshal of the arena, and the man rode out from a side stable and broke up the fight, ordering the two brutes back to the tunnel. The cyclopians gave their customary bow to the eorl's box, then walked away, and were promptly fighting again before they even got out of sight.

The next two combatants, red-haired Katerin and a young lass from across the island, a newcomer to the arena but with promising speed, had barely walked out of the tunnel when both Avonese and Elenia took up cries of protest.

Gahris silently berated himself for not anticipating this. Both women warriors were undeniably beautiful, full of life and full of health. Also, their warrior garb, cut so that they might have full freedom of movement, was something less than modest, and the looks upon the faces of Aubrey and Wilmon showed that they had been cooped up in the company of the two painted "ladies" far too long.

"This will not do!" Avonese cried.

"I do so want to see some sweating man-flesh," Elenia purred, and her ample fingernails drew little lines of blood on Wilmon's arm.

Gahris couldn't tell if it was Wilmon's anticipation of what the sight of sweating man-flesh would do to his eager escort, or if it was simply fear of Elenia that led him to demand that they move on to the next fight.

"We are pressed for time," Aubrey added sharply. "I wish to see a fight, a single fight, among the best warriors Bedwydrin can muster. Surely that task is not beyond the understanding of the eorl of Bedwydrin."

Gahris verily trembled, and it took every ounce of control he could muster to hold him back from throttling the skinny Aubrey. But he nodded his head and signaled to the marshal once more, calling out that it was time for Luthien and Garth Rogar.

On the tiered steps behind the eorl's viewing box, Ethan looked upon his cowed father and the pompous guests, his expression sour.

Both women simultaneously cooed when Luthien and Garth Rogar walked out of the tunnel, side by side, wearing little more than sandals, mailed gauntlets, loincloths, and a collar and bandolier device designed to protect their vital areas.

"Is there a bigger man alive?" Elenia gasped, obviously taken with the flaxen-haired barbarian.

"Is there a handsomer man alive?" Avonese retorted, turning her glower on her companion. She noticed Gahris then, took a deep look at him, then turned back to Luthien, intrigued.

"My son," the eorl proudly explained. "Luthien Bedwyr. And the giant is a Huegoth who floated to our shores as just a boy, as honorable a fighter as any. You will not be disappointed, Viscount."

It was obvious that Avonese and Elenia were in full agreement with the last statement. They continued to gawk and to toss snide comments back and forth, quickly drawing lines.

"The barbarian will crush him down," Elenia remarked.

"Those eyes are too wise to be caught in the primitive webs of a savage," Avonese countered. She jumped up from her seat suddenly and moved to the rail, throwing out her fine cambric handkerchief.

"Luthien Bedwyr!" she cried. "You fight as my champion. Fight well and you will savor the rewards!"

Gahris looked over to Aubrey, stunned by the woman's blunt forwardness and fearing that the viscount would be boiling with rage. It seemed to the eorl that Aubrey was more relieved than angry.

Elenia, not to be outdone, quickly rushed to the balcony and threw out her own kerchief, calling for the Huegoth to come and champion her cause.

Luthien and Garth Rogar walked over and took up the offered trophies, each tucking a kerchief into his belt.

"It shall not be so much as soiled," cocky Luthien said to Avonese.

"Bloodied, yes, soiled, no," Garth Rogar agreed, turning away from giggling Elenia.

Luthien quickly caught up to his opponent as Garth Rogar moved back toward the center of the arena, both of them putting on their helmets. "So the stakes are raised," the young Bedwyr remarked.

Garth Rogar scoffed at him. "You should not be thinking of pleasures with a fight before you," the barbarian said, and as soon as the marshal clapped his hands for the fight to begin, the barbarian charged forward, his long spear thrusting for Luthien's belly and a quick victory.

Luthien was taken off guard by the bold attack. He fell to the side and rolled away, but still took a stinging nick on the hip.

Garth Rogar stepped back and threw up his hands, as if in victory. "And so it is soiled!" he cried, pointing at Avonese's kerchief.

Elenia squealed with joy, oblivious to the dart-throwing gaze Avonese had turned on her.

Now Luthien went on the attack, scrambling forward in a crouch so low that he had to use his shield arm as a third support. His sword whipped across at Garth's legs, but the barbarian hopped back quickly enough. On came Luthien, knowing that if he let up the attack, his opponent, standing high above him, would surely pound him into the dirt.

But Luthien was quick, snapping his sword back and forth repeatedly, keeping Garth Rogar hopping. Finally, the barbarian was forced to stab his spear straight down to intercept a cut that would have cracked his knee. Up came Luthien fiercely, and though he could not realign his sword, he swung hard with his shield, slamming the barbarian in the chest and face.

Garth Rogar staggered backward; lines of blood ran from his nose and one side of his mouth. But he was smiling. "Well done!" he congratulated. As Luthien took an appropriate bow, the barbarian howled and charged back in.

Luthien was ready for the obvious move, though, and his sword flashed across, turning the spear out wide. The cunning Bedwyr rolled in behind the wide-flying weapon, again scoring a hit with his shield—just a glancing blow against Garth Rogar's powerful chest.

The barbarian countered quickly, though, hooking his free arm around the young fighter and driving his knee hard into Luthien's thigh. Luthien stumbled past, and Rogar would have had him, except that the young man was quick enough and wise enough to slice across with his sword, nicking his opponent's knee and stopping the charging giant short.

They squared up again and rushed right back in, fighting for pride and for the love of competition. Sword and spear crossed and parried; Luthien's shield rushes were countered by Rogar's punching fist.

Gahris had never seen his son, and especially Garth Rogar, fight better, and he was positively beaming with pride, for both Wilmon and Aubrey were fully entranced by the action, shouting out cheers for every cunning counter or last-second parry. The men could not match the squeals of Avonese and Elenia, though, as each cheered her champion on. These two were not as familiar with fighting styles as the others and many times thought the fight to be at its end, thinking that one or the other had gained an insurmountable advantage.

But these two fighters were well matched and well trained. Always the appropriate defenses were in place, always the men were balanced.

Garth Rogar started with a spear thrust, but as Luthien's sword parried, the barbarian unexpectedly heaved his weapon up high, taking Luthien's sword with it. Following his own building momentum, Garth lifted a foot for a well-aimed kick, slamming Luthien in the midsection and doubling him over, gasping for breath.

Luthien's shield came up at the last moment to stop the spear's butt end, aimed for his head, but he took another kick, this one on the hip, and went scrambling away.

"Oh, good!" cried Elenia, and only then did Gahris notice the scowl Avonese threw the younger woman's way, and he began to understand that there might be serious trouble brewing.

Sensing the advantage, Garth Rogar roared in, hurling himself at his winded opponent.

Luthien's shield took the spear up high, Luthien ducking underneath and snapping a quick sword cut into the barbarian's lead hand. The mailed gauntlet allowed Garth Rogar to keep his fingers, but he howled anyway for the pain and let go with that hand.

Now Luthien pressed forward, keeping his shield in line as he charged so that Garth could not retract his spear for any parries. His sword cut in from the side, pounding hard against the barbarian's leather bandolier. Garth Rogar winced, but kept his focus, and as Luthien brought the sword back out, then reversed it for a second cut, Garth caught the blade in his mailed fist.

Luthien pressed forward, and Garth got his feet under him enough to press back—just as Luthien had anticipated. Suddenly, the young Bedwyr stopped and backpedaled, and Garth found himself overbalanced. Luthien fell into a backward roll and planted his feet in the barbarian's belly as Garth tumbled over him.

"Oh, send him flying away!" screamed Avonese, and Luthien did just that, pushing out with both feet so that Garth Rogar did a half somersault, landing heavily on his back.

Both men were up in an instant, weapons in hand, eyeing each other with sincere respect. They were weary and bruised, and both knew that they would be wickedly sore the next day, but this was competition at its finest and neither cared.

Across from Gahris, it was Elenia's eyes that were now throwing darts. "Crush him!" she cried out to Garth Rogar, so loudly that her call temporarily halted all the other cheering in the arena, and all eyes, Luthien's and Garth Rogar's included, turned to her.

"It would seem that you have made a friend," Luthien said to the barbarian.

Garth Rogar nearly burst out laughing. "And I would not want to disappoint her!" he said suddenly, and on he came, thrusting his spear. He pulled it up short and whipped it about instead, its butt end ringing loudly off of Luthien's shield. Luthien countered with a straight cut, but the barbarian was out of range. A second spear thrust slipped over Luthien's shield and nearly took his eye out, nicking his helm as he ducked, and the butt end whipped about again, banging both shield and Luthien's back.

That hit stung, but Luthien ignored it, understanding that he had to go to the offensive or be buried under the powerful man's attacks. He started to run with the momentum of the spear, then ducked under it and pivoted about, coming up under Garth's swinging arm. The edge of Luthien's shield hooked under the taller man's armpit, lifting him off balance. Again, Garth Rogar caught Luthien's swinging sword in his hand, but this time, his feet were tangled. When Luthien heaved suddenly, arms and legs wide, the barbarian's spear went flying and Rogar himself fell heavily to the ground.

"Get him! Get him!" Avonese cried.

"Fight back, you oaf!" screamed Elenia.

Luthien was just settling into his stance when Garth Rogar jumped up. Luthien thought Rogar would go for the fallen spear—and he would have let the worthy opponent retrieve it—but Garth, savagery coursing wildly within his barbarian blood, charged instead. Surprised, Luthien got his shield up, and then his whole arm fell numb under the sheer weight of the Huegoth's tremendous punch.

Luthien bounced back a full step, looked in amazement as his shield, one of its straps snapped by the blow, fell from his arm. He just managed to duck a second punch, one that he figured would have hurt him more than any spear could, and leaped back from a third, swinging his broken shield at his opponent as he went to keep the man back.

Garth Rogar smacked the metal shield away and came in, slowing only to dodge a short thrust from Luthien's sword. A second thrust turned him to the side, to Luthien's left, and Luthien's free hand was waiting, snapping a punch into the barbarian's already broken nose.

Garth Rogar tried to fake a smile, but he had to shake his head to clear away the dizziness.

"Do you yield?" Luthien politely asked, and they both heard Elenia's protesting scream from the stands, and Avonese's howls of victory.

Predictably, Garth Rogar charged. At the last instant, Luthien tossed his sword up into the air, right in the barbarian's face. Garth flinched, then jolted to a stop, his own momentum used against him, by a left-right punch combination that would have felled a small bull.

Luthien caught the sword in his left hand, moved it to Garth's neck to force a yield. Ferocious Garth caught its tip, tossed it out wide and clamped his hand on Luthien's forearm.

"Rip his arm off!" Elenia cried. Avonese leaned right across Gahris's lap to hiss at her.

Luthien's muscles flexed as he fell into a clinch with the larger and stronger man. Wilmon, and even Aubrey, scowled a bit at the ensuing sighs of their obviously enchanted consorts.

Luthien held well against Rogar, but knew that the man's sheer weight would soon overwhelm him. He pushed forward with all his might, then took a quick step backward, breaking one hand free, though Garth stubbornly held his sword arm. The combatants exchanged punches; Garth Rogar took a second, and a third, willingly, as he bent to clamp a hand under Luthien's crotch. A moment later, the young Bedwyr was rising helplessly into the air, the angle all wrong for him to get any weight behind a punch—and Garth Rogar's grip on his sword arm remained unrelenting.

Luthien head-butted the barbarian instead, forehead to face. The stunned Garth Rogar heaved him ten feet away, then focused on just keeping his balance. For the barbarian, the world would not stop spinning.

Luthien pulled himself up from the ground and cautiously stalked back in, looking for a clean opening between Garth's wild swings. Luthien was on the verge of exhaustion and feared that a single hit from his powerful enemy would send him spinning to the ground.

He waved his sword all about as he came in slowly, forcing the dizzy barbarian to keep up with its tantalizing movements. The thrust was a feint—Garth Rogar knew that—but so was the following right cross. Luthien pulled up short and fell to the ground, his legs sweeping across, kicking out both of Garth Rogar's knees. Down went the barbarian hard on his back, his breath coming out in one profound blast.

Luthien was up, quick as a cat, but Garth had not the strength to follow. Luthien planted a foot on the fallen man's chest, and his sword tip came to rest on the bridge of Garth Rogar's nose, right between his unfocused eyes.

The screams of Elenia and Avonese were surprisingly similar, but the expressions that each wore after the initial outburst certainly were not.

Gahris was truly pleased by the appreciation, even admiration, stamped upon Aubrey's face, but the eorl's smile disappeared as Avonese again leaned heavily across his lap, looking at the pouting Elenia with sparkling, wicked eyes.

"Pray offer the down-pointing thumb, Eorl Bedwyr," Avonese purred.

Gahris nearly choked. A down-pointing thumb meant that the loser should be killed. That was not the way on the islands: the fights were for sport and training alone!

Elenia cried out in outrage, which only spurred on the evil Avonese.

"Thumb down," she said again, evenly, looking to protesting Elenia all the while. It wasn't hard for Avonese to figure out what Elenia had in mind for the barbarian, and stealing her younger rival's pleasure felt wonderful indeed. "Your son was my champion, he wears my offered pennant, and thus, I am granted the decision of victory."

"But . . ." was all that stammering Gahris managed to get out before Aubrey reached across and put a hand on the eorl's shoulder.

"It is her right, by ancient tradition," the viscount insisted, not daring to displease his vicious companion.

"Garth Rogar fought valiantly," Gahris protested.

"Thumb down," Avonese said slowly, emphasizing each word as she shifted her gaze to look right into Gahris's cinnamon-colored eyes.

Gahris looked past her to see the viscount nodding. He tried to weigh the consequences of his actions at that moment. Avonese's claim was true enough—by the ancient rules, since Luthien had unwittingly agreed to be her champion, she had the right to decide the fate of the defeated man. If he refused now, Gahris could expect serious trouble from Montfort, perhaps even an invading fleet that would take his eorldom from him. Ever was Morkney looking for reasons to replace the often troublesome island eorls.

Gahris gently pushed Avonese aside and looked out to the arena, where Luthien was still poised above the fallen Garth Rogar, waiting for the signal to break and the applause both he and the barbarian so richly deserved. Great was Luthien's astonishment when he saw his father extend his hand, thumb pointing down.

Luthien stood confused for a long while, hardly hearing Avonese's calls for him to finish the task. He looked down at his friend; he could not comprehend the notion of killing the man.

"Eorl Gahris," prompted an increasingly impatient Aubrey.

Gahris called to the arena marshal, but the man seemed as transfixed as Luthien.

"Do it!" vicious Avonese snapped. "Aubrey?"

The viscount snapped his fingers at one of his cyclopian guardsman behind him, the one with the curious crossbow.

Luthien had stepped back by this point and extended his hand to his friend. Garth Rogar had reached up and taken that grasp, starting to rise, when there came the click of a firing crossbow. The barbarian jerked suddenly, clamping tightly on Luthien's hand.

Luthien did not at first understand what had just transpired. Then Garth Rogar's grip loosened, and time seemed to move in slow motion as the proud barbarian slowly slipped back to the dirt.

CHAPTER 3

FAREWELL, MY BROTHER

LUTHIEN STARED AT Garth Rogar in shocked silence, stared at the surprised expression on the flaxen-haired barbarian's rugged and bruised face. Surprised even in death or, perhaps, because of his death.

"Fly, Death!" Luthien wailed, throwing his sword aside and diving down to kneel beside the man. "Be gone from this place, for here you do not belong! Seek an aged man, or an infant with not the strength to survive in this cruel world, but take not this man, this boy, younger than I." Luthien grabbed up Garth Rogar's hand in his own and propped the barbarian's head with his other arm. He could feel the heat leaving Rogar's body, the sweat the barbarian had worked up in the fight becoming clammy. Luthien tried to stammer more protests, but found his tongue caught in his mouth. What might he say to Death, that most callous of spirits which does not care to hear? What use were words when the heat was fast leaving Garth Rogar's young and strong body?

Luthien looked back helplessly to the box, his expression a mixture of confusion and boiling rage. But Aubrey's party, Gahris included, was already gone from sight; further up the stands, Ethan, too, had fled the scene. Luthien's gaze darted all about. Many of the spectators had departed, but some remained, whispering and pointing incredulously to the man lying in the dirt, and the son of Bedwyr leaning over him.

Luthien turned back to Garth Rogar. He saw the back tip of the crossbow quarrel protruding from the man's side, between two ribs, and reached for it tentatively, as if he thought that pulling it free would give Garth Rogar back his breath. Luthien tried to touch the metal shaft, but found that his fingers would not close about it.

A cry made him lift his gaze to see the other warriors fast exiting the tunnel, led by Katerin. She skidded to her knees before the man, and after just an instant, reached up and gently closed his eyes. Her somber gaze met Luthien's and she slowly shook her head.

Up jumped Luthien, roaring, the cry torn from his heart. He looked around wildly, hands clenched at his side, then found a focus to his rage. He tore Avonese's kerchief from his hip and flung it to the ground, then stamped it into the dirt.

"On the death of Garth Rogar, friend and fellow," he began, "I, Luthien Bedwyr, do vow—"

"Enough," interrupted Katerin, rising beside him and taking his arm in hers. He looked at her incredulously, hardly believing that she would interrupt at so solemn a moment. When he stared into her face, though, he saw no apology for her unexpected action, only a pleading look.

"Enough, Luthien," she said softly, in full control. "Garth Rogar died as a warrior by the most ancient and hallowed rules of the arena of our people. Do not dishonor him."

Horrified, Luthien pulled away from Katerin. He stared at his fellows, at the fighters who had trained beside him for these last years, but found no support. He felt as though he was standing in a group of strangers.

And then Luthien ran, across the field and into the tunnel, out into the open area near to the harbor and north along the beach.

"It was unfortunate," Gahris began, trying to downplay the events.

"It was murder," Ethan corrected, and his father looked about nervously, as if he expected one of Aubrey's cyclopian guards to be lurking in the area.

"Strong words," Gahris whispered.

"Often strong is the ring of truth," Ethan said sternly and loudly, not backing off an inch.

"I'll have no more of it," Gahris demanded. Still he looked about, drawing a disdainful glare from his judgmental son. "No more, do you hear!"

Ethan snorted derisively and stared down at this man, this stranger who could be so cowed. He understood Gahris's tentative position quite well, understood the politics of the land. If Gahris took any action against Aubrey, or any of Aubrey's party, then the duke of Montfort would surely retaliate, probably with a fleet of warships. Ethan didn't care, though, and didn't sympathize. To the proud young Bedwyr, some things were worth fighting for, worth dying for.

"And what of the Lady Avonese?" Ethan asked, putting a sarcastic tone on his use of the word "lady."

Gahris sighed, seeming very small to his son at that moment, "Aubrey hints at leaving her behind," he admitted. "He thinks that her influence might be a positive thing for Bedwydrin."

"A new wife for Gahris," Ethan spat out sarcastically. "A spy for Morkney in the house of Bedwyr." His father did not reply.

"And what of this woman who would so readily change consorts?" Ethan asked loudly and venomously. "Am I, then, to call her mother?"

A spark of fury ignited within Gahris, and before he could control the emotion, his hand snapped out and slapped the impertinent Ethan across the face.

Ethan didn't retaliate other than to fix a glare on his father, his striking eyes narrowed.

Gahris had not wanted things to go this far, but there was a danger brewing here, for him and for all the folk of Bedwydrin. In the flash of a passing instant, the white-haired eorl remembered his wife, who died in the great plague, and remembered the free time before that, before Greensparrow. But those times were gone, and the thoughts, like the instant, were passing, stolen by an unrelenting stare that amply reflected what the pragmatic elder Bedwyr knew he had to do.

Luthien looked back from a high bluff toward the north side of the bay as the last lights went out in the town of Dun Varna. He still could not believe the events of this day, could not believe that Garth Rogar, his friend, was dead. For the first time, the sheltered young man tasted the rotten flavor of life under King Greensparrow and, inexperienced in anything beyond the arena, Luthien did not know what to make of it.

Might this be tied to Ethan's perpetually sour mood? he wondered. Luthien knew that Ethan held little respect for Gahris—something that the younger Bedwyr son, who saw his father as a bold and noble warrior, could not understand—but he had always attributed that to a flaw in Ethan's character. To Luthien, Gahris was above reproach, the respected eorl of Bedwydrin, whose people loved him.

Luthien did not know all the ancient rules of the arena, but he did understand that Gahris alone was overseer of the events. Garth Rogar was dead, and his blood was certainly on the hands of Gahris Bedwyr.

But why? Luthien could not understand the reason, the possible gain. He imagined all sorts of wild possibilities—perhaps word had come that the Huegoth barbarians were planning a raid upon Bedwydrin, and it had been learned that Garth Rogar had been acting as a spy. Perhaps Gahris had even uncovered a report that Garth Rogar was planning to assassinate him!

Luthien shook his head and discarded the ridiculous thoughts. He had known Garth Rogar for several years. The noble fighter was no spy and certainly no assassin.

Then why?

"Many in the town are worrying about you," came a quiet voice from behind. Luthien didn't have to turn to know that it belonged to Katerin O'Hale. "Your father among them, I would guess."

Luthien continued his silent stare across the still waters of the harbor toward the darkening town. He did not move even when Katerin came over to stand beside him and took his arm in her own, as she had done in the arena.

"Will you come back now?"

"Vengeance is not dishonor," Luthien replied with a growl. He deliberately turned his head to stare into Katerin's face, though he could barely see her in the gloom of the deepening night.

A long moment of silence passed before Katerin answered.

"No," she agreed. "But proclaiming vengeance openly, in the middle of the arena, against one who names the duke of Montfort as his friend and relative would be a foolish thing. Would you give the man an excuse to kill you, and replace your father, for a moment of outrage?"

Luthien pulled away from her, his anger now showing that he could not honestly disagree.

"Then I make the vow now," he said, "openly to you alone. On the grave of my dead mother, I'll repay he who killed Garth Rogar. Whatever the cost, whatever the consequences to me, to my father, to Bedwydrin."

Katerin could hardly believe what she had just heard, but neither could she rightly berate the man for his honorable words. She, too, burned with helpless rage, feeling like a captive for the first time in her life. She had been raised in Hale, on the open Avon Sea. Her life was spent in danger in small fishing craft braving the swells and the fierce whales, living on the very edge of disaster. But Hale was a private place and a self-sufficient one, rarely visited. Whatever the news of Bedwydrin, or of Eriador and Avon beyond that, Hale was oblivious; and so in their ignorance were the proud folk of Hale free.

But now Katerin had seen the politics of the land, and the taste in her mouth was no less bitter than the taste in Luthien's. She turned the young man toward her fully and moved closer to him, using the warmth of their bodies to ward off the chill winds of the August night.

On the morning winds of the next dawn, the black-sailed ship, proudly flying its pennants of Montfort and Avon, its prow lifting sheets of water high into the crystalline air, charged out of Dun Varna's harbor.

Katerin had returned to her barracks, but Luthien still watched from the wooded ridge. Long indeed would be his travels if he planned to keep his vow of revenge, he realized as the sails diminished. But he was a young man with a long memory, and up there on that ridge, watching the ship depart, Luthien vowed again that he would not forget Garth Rogar.

He would have liked to remain out of Dun Varna for many more days; he had no desire at all to face his father, for what explanation might the man offer? But Luthien was hungry and cold, and the nearest town, where he certainly would be recognized, was fully a day's march away.

He had barely walked through the doors of House Bedwyr when two cyclopians came upon him. "Your father would see you," one of them announced gruffly.

Luthien kept on walking, and nearly got past the two before they crossed their long halberds in his path. The young man's hand immediately went to his hip, but he wasn't wearing any weapons.

"Your father would see you," the cyclopian reiterated, and he reached up with his free hand and grabbed Luthien's upper arm hard. "He said to bring you, even if we have to drag you."

Luthien roughly pulled away and kept his unrelenting stare on the brute. He thought of punching the cyclopian in the face, or of just pushing through the two, but the image of him being dragged into his father's chambers by the ankles was not a pleasant one.

He was standing before Gahris soon after, in the study where Gahris kept the few books his family owned (some of the very few books on all the isle of Bedwydrin) along with his other heirlooms. The elder Bedwyr stood hunched at the hearth, feeding the already roaring fire as if a deep chill had settled into his bones, though it was not so cold this day. Mounted on the wall above him was his most-prized piece, the family sword, its perfect edge gleaming and its golden hilt lined with jewels and sculpted to resemble a dragon rampant with upraised wings serving as the formidable crosspiece. It had been cunningly forged by the dwarves of the Iron Cross in ages past, its blade of beaten metal wrapped tight about itself a thousand times so that the blade only sharpened with use. *Blind-Striker,* it was called, both for its balanced cut and the fact that it had taken the eye of many cyclopians in the fierce war six hundred years before.

"Where have you been?" Gahris asked calmly, quietly. He wiped his sooty hands and stood up straight, though he did not yet turn to face his son.

"I needed to be away," Luthien replied, trying to match his father's calm.

"To let your anger settle?"

Luthien sighed but did not bother to answer.

Gahris turned toward him. "That was wise, my son," he said. "Anger brews rash actions—oft with the most dire of consequences."

He seemed so calm and so logical, which bothered Luthien deeply. His friend was dead! "How could you?" he blurted, unconsciously taking a long stride forward, hands bunched into fists. "To kill . . . what were you . . ." His words fell away in a jumble, his emotions too heated to be expressed.

Through it all, the white-haired Gahris cooed softly like a dove and waved his hand in the empty air. "What would you have me do?" he asked, as though that should explain everything.

Luthien opened his hands helplessly. "Garth Rogar did not deserve his fate!" Luthien cried. "A curse on Viscount Aubrey and on his wicked companions!"

"Calm, my son," Gahris was saying, over and over. "Ours is a world that is not always fair and just, but—"

"There is no excuse," Luthien replied through gritted teeth.

"Not even war?" Gahris asked bluntly.

Luthien's breath came in short, angry gasps.

"Think not of bloodied fields," Gahris offered, "nor of spear tips shining with the blood of fallen enemies, nor turf torn under the charge of horses. Those are horrors that have not yet been reflected in your clear eyes, and may they never be! They steal the sparkle, you see," Gahris explained, and he pointed to his own cinnamon orbs. Indeed, those eyes did seem without luster this August morning.

"And were the eyes of Bruce MacDonald so tainted?" Luthien asked somewhat sarcastically, referring to Eriador's greatest hero.

"Filled with valor are the tales of war," Gahris replied somberly, "but only when the horrors of war have faded from memory. Who can say what scars Bruce MacDonald wore in his heavy soul? Who alive has looked into the eyes of that man?"

Luthien thought the words absurd; Bruce MacDonald had been dead for three centuries. But then he realized that to be his father's very point. The elder Bedwyr went on in all seriousness.

"I have heard the horses charge, have seen my own sword—" he glanced back at the fabulous weapon on the wall "—wet with blood. I have heard the stories—other's stories—of those heroic battles in which I partook, and I can tell you, in all honesty and with arrogance aside, that they were more horror than valor, more regret than victory. Am I to bring such misery to Bedwydrin?"

Luthien's sigh this time was more of resignation than defiance.

"Breathe out your pride with that sigh," Galiris advised. "It is the most deadly and most dangerous of emotions. Mourn your friend, but accept that which must be. Do not follow Ethan—" He broke off suddenly, apparently rethinking that last thought, but his mention of Luthien's older brother, a hero to the youngest Bedwyr, piqued Luthien's attention.

"What of Ethan?" he demanded. "What part does he play in all of this? What has he done in my absence?"

Again Gahris was cooing softly and patting the air, trying to calm his son. "Ethan is fine," he assured Luthien. "I speak only of his temperament, his foolish pride, and my own hopes that you will temper your anger with good sense. You did well in walking out of House Bedwyr, and for that you have my respect. We are given a long rein from the duke of Montfort, and longer still from the throne in Carlisle, and it would be good to keep it that way."

"What did Ethan do?" Luthien pressed, not convinced.

"He did nothing, other than protest—loudly!" Gahris snapped back.

"And that disappoints you?"

Gahris snorted and spun back to face the fire. "He is my eldest son," he replied, "in line to be the eorl of Bedwydrin. But what might that mean for the folk?"

It seemed to Luthien that Gahris was no longer talking to him; he was, rather, talking to himself, as if trying to justify something.

"Trouble, I say," the old man went on, and he seemed very old indeed to Luthien at that moment. "Trouble for Ethan, for House Bedwyr, for all the island." He spun back around suddenly, one finger pointing Luthien's way. "Trouble for you!" he cried, and Luthien, surprised, took a step backward. "Never will stubborn Ethan come to learn his place," Gahris went on, muttering again and turning back to the fire. "Once eorl, he would surely facilitate his own death and bring ruin upon House Bedwyr and bring watchful eyes upon all of Bedwydrin. Oh, what a fool is a proud man! Never! Never! Never!"

Gahris had worked himself into quite a state, pumping his fist into the air as he spoke, and Luthien's first instincts were to go to him and try to calm him. Something held the young man back, though, and instead he quietly left the room. He loved his father, had respected him all of his life, but now the man's words rang hollowly in Luthien's ears—ears that still heard the fateful crossbow click and the pitiful wheeze of Garth Rogar's last breath.

CHAPTER 4

WET WITH THE BLOOD OF A FALLEN ENEMY

WHAT MIGHT HAVE been had the parents of a king not met? What might have been had a hero been cut down in his or her youth by an arrow that whizzed harmlessly past, cracking the air barely an inch away? Often does the simplest chance affect the history of nations, and so it was that August night, when Luthien walked out of House Bedwyr to the stables, where he found Ethan readying a horse, saddlebags stuffed with provisions.

Luthien moved near his brother, eyeing him curiously, letting his expression ask the obvious question.

"I have been sent away," Ethan answered.

Luthien seemed not to understand.

"I am to go to the south," Ethan went on, spitting out every word with disgust, "to travel with the king's soldiers who would go into Gascony and fight beside the Gascons in their war with the Kingdom of Duree."

"A noble cause," replied Luthien, too overwhelmed to consider his words.

"A mercenary cause," Ethan snarled back. "A mercenary cause for an unlawful king."

"Then why go?"

Ethan stopped tightening the saddlebags and turned an incredulous look upon his naive little brother. Luthien just shrugged, still not catching on.

"Because the eorl of Bedwydrin has ordered me to go." Ethan spelled it out plainly and went back to his work.

It made no sense to Luthien, and so he did not reply, did not even blink.

"It will bring honor to our family and to all Bedwydrin, so said Gahris," Ethan went on.

Luthien studied his brother carefully, at first jealous that Gahris had chosen Ethan for the campaign over him. "Would not *Blind-Striker* serve you better if you go for the honor of House Bedwyr?" he asked, noticing the unremarkable weapon sheathed on Ethan's belt.

Again came that disbelieving, condescending look. "Can you be so incredibly blind to the world?" Ethan asked, and he got his answer when Luthien winced.

"Gahris sends me," the elder son went on, "following the whispered suggestions of Aubrey. Gahris sends me to die."

The casual way Ethan spoke struck Luthien more than the words. He grabbed Ethan roughly by the shoulder and spun him away from his horse, forcing his brother to face him squarely.

"I am not his choice for the succession," Ethan spat out, and Luthien, remembering his earlier conversation with his father, could not disagree. "But the rules are clear. I am the eldest son, thus I am next in line as eorl of Bedwydrin."

"I do not challenge your right," Luthien replied, still missing the point.

"But Gahris does," Ethan explained. "And my reputation of disloyalty has gone beyond Bedwydrin, it would seem."

"So Gahris will send you out with the army to win glory and restore your reputation," Luthien reasoned, though he suspected his line of thought was still traveling the wrong direction.

"So Gahris has sent me out to die," Ethan reiterated firmly. "I am a problem to him—even Aubrey has heard of me and understands the difficulties of my potential ascension. Perhaps it is my arrogance, but I do not think Morkney's cousin's only purpose in coming to Bedwydrin was sport."

"You think Aubrey braved the breakers of the Dorsal, came all the way to Bedwydrin, merely to have you sent away?"

"Beyond that, my young brother," Ethan said, and for the first time, a ring of sympathy was evident in his harsh tones. "My young brother, who has never known freedom, who has lived all his life under the rule of Carlisle and Montfort."

Luthien crinkled his brow, now thoroughly confused.

"Aubrey toured the northern islands," Ethan explained. "Caryth, Marvis, Bedwydrin, even the Diamondgate on his return trip, to ensure that all was as it should be in the northland, to help secure Morkney's tethers. Politicians do not take 'holidays.' Ever they work, living to work, to heighten their power. That is their way and their lifeblood. Aubrey came to Bedwydrin in part to deal with me, and also because the duke has no eyes out here. That has been remedied." His work on the mount done, Ethan swung up into the saddle.

"You will have a new mother, Luthien," he went on. "Treat her with respect and fear." He started to walk the horse away, but Luthien, flustered and outraged, grabbed the bridle and held the beast in check.

"One who is known to you," Ethan went on. "One whose pennant you once carried into battle."

Luthien's eyes widened in shock. Avonese? This could not be true! "Never!" he protested.

"On Sunday's morn," Ethan assured him. "The duke has forced Gahris's hand," he explained. "Lady Avonese remains, the perfect spy, to wed Gahris. It is bait, you see, for the fall of the House of Bedwyr. Gahris will bend to the events, or Morkney will have the excuse he desires and will bid Greensparrow to fill the harbor with black sails."

"How can you leave?" Luthien cried out helplessly as all of his sheltered world appeared to be falling down around him.

"How can I stay?" Ethan corrected calmly. "Gahris has given his command." Ethan paused and stared hard at his brother, his intensity offering a calming effect to the excited young man.

"You know little beyond Bedwydrin," Ethan said sincerely. "You have not seen the eyes of the poor children starving in Montfort's streets. You have not seen the farmers, broken in spirit and wealth by demanded taxes. You have not seen the helpless rage of a man whose daughter was taken from him to 'serve' in the house of a noble, or heard the cries of a mother whose child has died in her arms for lack of food."

Luthien's grip on Ethan's saddle loosened.

"I do not accept the world as it is," Ethan went on. "I only know how it should be. And our father, lackey to an unlawful king, has not the strength nor the courage to stand up and agree with me."

Ethan recognized that his blunt accounting was finally beginning to sink into Luthien's naive skull. If he had hit Luthien with a dwarvish maul, he could not have stunned the man any more. Beyond all their differences, Ethan loved and pitied his brother, who had never known life before Greensparrow, the king who had subtly stolen away true freedom.

"Farewell, my brother," Ethan said solemnly. "You are all of my family that I will miss. Keep your eyes to the window and your ears to the door, and above all, beware the Lady Avonese!" A kick of his heels sent his horse leaping away, leaving the perplexed Luthien alone in the yard with his unsettling thoughts.

Luthien did not sleep that night and wandered the grounds alone all the next day, not even harking to a call from Katerin, who saw him from across a field. Again the next night, he did not sleep, thinking of Ethan, of Garth Rogar, of this new view of Gahris.

Most of all, Luthien thought of confronting his father, of calling Gahris out on the accusations Ethan had boldly made. What might the other side of that tale be? he wondered.

But it was a false hope. Ethan's few words had opened Luthien's young eyes, and he did not believe that he could ever close them again.

And so, in the morning of the next day, he went to see Gahris, not to seek any explanation but to put in his own thoughts, to express his anger over the tragedy in the arena and the fact that this Avonese creature was apparently intended to become his mother.

He smiled when he considered how much like Ethan he would sound and wondered if his father would send him away to fight in a distant war, as well.

He entered the study without even knocking, only to find the room empty. Gahris had already left on his morning ride. Luthien started to leave, thinking to go down to the stables and take a horse of his own and ride off in pursuit of the man. He changed his mind almost immediately, though, realizing that Avonese might be riding beside his father, and the last thing in all the world that Luthien wanted was to see that woman.

He made himself comfortable in the study instead, perusing the books on the shelves, even starting a fire in the hearth. He was sitting back in the comfortable chair, feet propped on the desk and book in hand, when the door burst open and a burly guardsman rushed in.

"What are you about?" the cyclopian demanded, waving a trident dangerously. He remained near to the door, though, across the room from Luthien.

"About?" Luthien echoed incredulously, and then his face screwed up even more, for he did not recognize this guard—though he knew all of Gahris's contingent.

"About!" the brute roared back. "What business have you in the private quarters of the eorl and eorless of Bedwydrin?"

"Eorless?" Luthien muttered under his breath, and he nearly choked on the word.

"I asked you a question!" the cyclopian growled, waving its trident again.

"Who in the lava pits of the Five Sentinels are you to ask anything of me?" the young Bedwyr demanded.

"Personal guard of the eorless of Bedwydrin," the one-eyed soldier replied without hesitation.

"I am the son of the eorl," Luthien proclaimed.

"I know who you are, arena fighter," the cyclopian replied, snapping the trident aside. It was only then, as the brute jerked about and revealed a crossbow strapped to its wide back, that Luthien realized the creature's identity. He leaped up from his seat, dropping the book to the desk.

"You were not announced," the cyclopian continued undaunted. "So here you do not belong! Now be gone, before I teach you some of the proper etiquette of nobility!"

The cyclopian clutched the long trident close to its chest and slowly turned toward the door, keeping its bloodshot eye on Luthien for as long as possible.

Luthien stood transfixed, held in place by the enormity of the situation that had been unexpectedly dropped on his shoulders. He had vowed revenge, and now his sworn enemy, whom he had thought long gone on the black-sailed ship, stood before him. But what of the consequences? he had to wonder—and what purpose might be served to Aubrey by leaving this particular cyclopian behind? To leave Avonese behind was one thing—Luthien would not strike down a woman who was no warrior—but to allow this murderous brute to remain on Bedwydrin was beyond Luthien's comprehension. Surely the viscount must have known what would happen. . . .

Ethan's words about bait for the fall of House Bedwyr rang in Luthien's mind, and he knew that his decision now would follow him for the rest of his life.

"You will follow me," the cyclopian remarked, not looking back and giving Luthien a perfect view of the crossbow he had used to murder Garth Rogar.

"Tell me," Luthien began calmly, "did you enjoy killing a human while he lay helpless upon the ground?"

The cyclopian whirled about and faced the young man squarely, an evil smile widening upon its face, showing Luthien an array of pointy and yellow-stained teeth. "I always enjoy killing men," the cyclopian said. "Are you to leave, or learn that for yourself?"

His action purely reflexive, Luthien reached down and grabbed a stone that his father kept on the desk for holding parchments smooth and, in a swift motion, hurled it across the room, where it smacked off the dodging cyclopian's thigh. The creature groaned, then growled and leveled its trident Luthien's way.

"That was not among your brightest actions," Luthien said quietly to himself, taking the moment to realize that he wasn't even wearing a weapon. In stalked the one-eyed brute. Luthien scooped up a wooden chair to use as a shield, but the first powerful thrust of the trident shattered it to kindling and left Luthien scrambling.

He rolled from behind the desk to the hearth and grabbed up a long metal hook used for turning logs. He spun back and put his feet under him just in time to meet the second thrust. Fortunately, the sweeping hook caught the tip of the trident enough to deflect the weapon somewhat to the side, and agile Luthien twisted the other way. Still, he got a painful scratch on the side of his abdomen, a line of blood staining his torn white shirt.

The cyclopian licked its pointy teeth and smiled wide.

"I have no weapon!" Luthien protested.

"That makes it all the more fun," the cyclopian replied, and it started a straight thrust, then reversed its weapon and swung the butt end about in a low arc. Seeing the feint in time, Luthien managed to stop his dodging defense and leap straight up, over the swing. He landed and took one step forward, and poked his fingers straight ahead into the cyclopian's eye.

The powerful backswing of the trident stung the young man again, knocking him aside before he could do any real damage to the large, bloodshot orb, but he had dazed the cyclopian enough to break off combat.

And Luthien knew right where to run.

Back to the hearth he leaped, this time high on the balls of his feet. "You should have finished me while you could!" he cried, and grabbed the dragon-sculpted hilt of the fabulous Bedwyr sword. He laughed and yanked, and pulled the sword free—almost.

Now the cyclopian was laughing—and leveling that wicked trident once more.

Luthien had torn out the hook holding the hilt, but the second hook, near the sword's point, held stubbornly to the wall. The sword was angled far out, but its razor-edge tip was merely digging a line in the stone of the wall. Luthien heaved again to no avail; he rolled about to put all his weight behind the pull, and from that angle, he clearly saw the cyclopian's charge.

He shouted and heaved with all his might, and the sword snapped free of the hook and whipped around and down, smashing hard against the trident's tip just an instant before it would have plunged deeply into his chest. Both combatants were now off balance, their weapons out far too wide for any counter attacks, so Luthien planted one foot against the stonework of the hearth and rushed out at full speed, barreling into his opponent and sending them both tumbling to the floor.

Luthien was up, quick as a cat. He spun and launched a downward cut, but to his amazement, the trident came up and blocked him, the sword blade falling neatly into the groove between two of the weapon's three tips. With a growl, the cyclopian threw him to the side, fully defeating Luthien's attack.

"I am no child in an arena," the one-eye boasted. "I was a commander in the Praetorian Guard!" On the cyclopian came with a series of devilish thrusts and feints, half twists designed to make Luthien duck a second butt-end sweep, followed by reversed movements that again sent the trident straight out in front. The cyclopian worked the long weapon brilliantly, as though it was a small blade, keeping Luthien fully on the defensive.

But neither was the son of Bedwyr some "child in an arena." Luthien's parries were perfect; he reversed his intended dodges as quickly as the cyclopian reversed the attack. Not once did the trident so much as nick him.

Luthien knew that he was in a tough fight, though, and his respect for the cyclopian grew with each close pass. They worked around the room, Luthien, with the shorter weapon, inevitably backing and circling, and the cyclopian quick to press. Then Luthien scrambled behind a divan, an effective shield from the waist down.

He smiled as he easily knocked aside a high thrust, then chopped his blade down atop a lower cut, temporarily pinning the trident to the top of the divan. He could see the frustration building in the one-eye's expression, and he skittered back cautiously when the cyclopian came in a sudden charge, appearing as though it might bull its way right through the small couch.

The cyclopian wisely stopped before it crashed through, for it realized that it would not quickly catch up to the agile Luthien, and knowing that if the couch tangled its feet at all, the cunning young fighter and his sword would surely grab the advantage. The cyclopian then tried to push the piece of furniture aside, but Luthien, understanding that the divan offered him an advantage with his shorter weapon, rushed back in and sliced with the sword, almost taking off the cyclopian's hand and digging a deep slash into the padding of the couch in the process.

"Gahris will not be pleased," Luthien remarked, trying to sound supremely confident.

"Not when he buries his son!" the cyclopian roared, and on the brute came again, a powerful thrust leading the way. The soldier expected Luthien to chop down again, to try and pin the trident to the top of the divan, and if that had happened, the cyclopian intended to barrel through, pushing both Luthien and the couch closer to the wall.

But Luthien dropped straight to a crouch instead, and his parry came in exactly the opposite direction, sword straight across in front of him and going up, not down. Up, too, went the trident, and opportunistic Luthien went up behind the weapons, up and over the divan in a headlong roll. The cyclopian instinctively fell back, trying to realign his weapon, but Luthien came up under his reach, sword leading the way.

Blind-Striker's tip dug into the cyclopian's belly and ran its way up through the creature's diaphragm, cutting at the lungs and heart. The one-eye had the trident up above its head by that time, and angled down at Luthien, and for a horrifying second, Luthien thought the wicked prongs would dive down into him.

Then he saw the light go out of the cyclopian's eye, saw the strength drain from the dying brute's thick muscles. The trident fell to the floor, its dead owner sliding back off of Luthien's sword and falling over it.

Luthien tentatively regained his footing, staring down at the perfectly still cyclopian. His first kill. Luthien did not enjoy the sensation, not at all. He looked at the dead cyclopian and reminded himself many times that this had been the murderer of Garth Rogar, that this brute would have killed him if he had not proven the better warrior. And it was a cyclopian. Sheltered Luthien could not fully appreciate the significance of that fact, but he did understand that cyclopians were not human, in either appearance or temperament. The one-eyes were savage creatures, evil creatures, devoid of love and mercy. This knowledge alone saved the young man from his own conscience at that moment, and allowed Luthien to take heart. A deep breath helped steady the young warrior.

Luthien looked at the bloody sword. Its balance was perfect and its deadly cut incredible. Luthien could not believe how easily *Blind-Striker* had slid through the thick leather coat of the cyclopian and through the creature's body, as well. He had, with a simple cut, chopped more than half a foot into the well-constructed divan, taking out a few boards, he knew, on the way. Holding the sword now, his vow fulfilled, his friend avenged, he felt the blood of his proud ancestors pumping wildly through his veins.

Then Luthien calmed and realized that he had set many events into motion—events that would likely bury him if he remained in Dun Varna. But Luthien wept no tears of pity for his predicament. He had made his choice willingly when he had thrown the stone at the brute and forced the confrontation. There could be no excuses, not in Gahris's cowed eyes, he knew—if all that Ethan had said was true. Luthien now replayed his last meeting with his father, listened to Gahris's words in the new light of Ethan's revelations. His brother had not lied to him.

Luthien could hardly believe how much his life had so abruptly changed, and how it would continue to change as he, now obviously a criminal, made his way far from Dun Varna, far from Bedwydrin. He thought that he must catch up to Ethan on the road, for surely his brother would sympathize with his actions and help him along his way. Luthien cringed. Ethan had probably already reached the ferry to Eriador's mainland. Where would his brother go from there? To Montfort, perhaps? Or all the way around the Iron Cross to Carlisle?

Luthien looked out the room's one small window and could see that the sun was fast climbing in the east. His father would soon return; Luthien would have to find his answers along the road.

He thought of taking the sword—he had never felt such perfect craftsmanship. But *Blind-Striker* was not his, he knew, especially not now. Though he thought his actions justified and honorable, demanded by the death of his friend, in Luthien's young eyes, he had just brought shame upon House Bedwyr. He would not complicate that matter by stooping to common thievery.

He did not wipe the blood from the blade as he carefully replaced it above the hearth. He thought it fitting that Gahris should see what weapon had exacted revenge for the unfair death of Garth Rogar.

CHAPTER 5

WITHOUT LOOKING BACK

LUTHIEN LEFT DUN Varna on the northern road soon after upon his favorite mount, Riverdancer. The steed was a Morgan Highlander, a short-legged, thickly muscled white stallion that could plow through the soft turf of Eriador's perpetually wet ground as well as any beast alive. The Highlander horses had been bred with long, shaggy coats to ward off the chill winds and drizzle. On many Highlanders, this hair was perpetually prickly and snarled, but Riverdancer's coat was smooth as fine silk and glistened with every movement, like the sparkles of a dancing river on a sunny spring day.

Riverdancer carried a heavy load this day, laden with the supplies Luthien would need for the road and, displayed more openly, with fishing gear, including heavy pole-nets. It was not an unusual thing for the young Bedwyr to go off in this fashion, especially considering there had been little training in the arena since the Garth Rogar incident. Certainly few in Dun Varna would expect Luthien to go right back to his fighting.

Few took notice of him as he walked his way through the dirt and cobblestone avenues. He did slow and speak with one man, a captain of a fishing boat, just to ask him what was running north of the bay and whether the sea was calm enough for the pole-nets or if he should try a long line. It was all very cordial, very normal. Just the way Luthien wanted it to be.

When he had gone beyond the bluffs, though, out of sight of the stone-and-thatch houses, he broke Riverdancer into a run. Five miles out of town, he veered down toward the shore to one of his favored fishing spots. There he left his gear, net and pole, and one of his wet boots lying on the *stones* right near the water. Better to give them as many riddles as possible, he thought, though he cringed when he considered his father's pain if Gahris truly thought he had been swept out into the fierce Dorsal.

It couldn't be helped, Luthien decided. Back on Riverdancer, he picked his way carefully among the stones, trying to leave as little visible trail as possible—he sighed deeply when the horse lifted its tail and dropped some obvious signs of passage.

Away from the shore, Luthien turned to the west, riding toward Hale, and then swung back to the south. By early afternoon, he was passing Dun Varna again, several miles inland and far out of sight. He wondered what commotion his actions had brought. What had Gahris and especially Avonese thought when they had gone into the study and found the dead cyclopian? Had Gahris noticed the bloodied sword on the wall?

Certainly by this time somebody had gone north in search of Luthien. Perhaps they had even found his gear and boot, though he doubted that word had gotten back to his father.

Again, the young Bedwyr decided that it couldn't be helped. He had followed the course his heart demanded. In truth, Luthien had only defended himself against the armed cyclopian. He could have stayed in House Bedwyr and been exonerated: even after all that Ethan had told him, Luthien did not believe that his father would turn against him. And so it was not actually fear of the law that sent Luthien away. He only realized that now, passing his home for what might be the very last time. Ethan had brought doubts to him, deep-rooted doubts that made Luthien question the worth of his very existence. What was the truth of the kingdom and the king? And was he truly free, as he had always believed?

Only the road could give him his answers.

The Diamondgate ferry was normally a three-day ride from Dun Varna, but Luthien thought he could make it in two if he pushed Riverdancer hard. The horse responded eagerly, happy for the run, as they charged down the island's central lowlands, and Luthien was far from Dun Varna when he broke for camp. It rained hard that first night. Luthien huddled under his blanket near a fire that was more hiss and spit than flame. He hardly felt the chill and the wetness, though, too consumed by the questions that rolled over and over in his thoughts. He remembered the salty smell of sweet Katerin and the look in her green eyes when they had made love. He should have told her, perhaps.

He did fall asleep sometime not long before the dawn, but he was up early anyway, greeted by a glistening sunny day.

It was a marvelous day, and Luthien felt delight in every bit of it as he mounted Riverdancer and started off once more. Not a cloud showed itself in the blue sky—a rare occurrence, indeed, on Bedwydrin!—and a sense of euphoria came over Luthien, a sense of being more alive than he had ever been. It was more than the sun, he knew, and the birds and animals skittering about on one of the last truly wondrous days before the gloomy fall and chill winter. Luthien had rarely been out of Dun Varna all his life, and then always with the knowledge that he would not be gone for long.

Now the wide road lay before him leading eventually to the mainland, to Avon, even to Gascony and all the way to Duree if he could catch up with his brother. The world seemed so much bigger and scarier suddenly, and excitement welled up in the young man, pushing away his grief for Garth Rogar and his fears for his father. He wished that Katerin was there beside him, riding hard for freedom and excitement.

He was more than two-thirds of the way to the ferry by midday, Riverdancer running easily, as though he would never tire. The road veered back toward the southeast, passing through a small wooded region and across the field just out the wood's southern end. There Luthien came upon a narrow log bridge crossing a strong-running river, with another small forest on the other side.

At the same time, a merchant wagon came out of the trees and upon the bridge from the other end. Its cyclopian driver certainly saw Luthien and could have stopped short of the bridge, allowing the horseman to scramble across and out of the way, but with typical cyclopian bravado and discourtesy, the brute moved the wagon onto the logs.

"Turn about!" the one-eye growled, as its team came face-to-face with Riverdancer.

"You could have stopped," Luthien protested. "I was onto the bridge before you and could have gotten off the bridge more quickly than you!" He noted that the cyclopian was not too well-armed and wearing no special insignia. This brute was a private guard, not Praetorian, and any passengers in the coach were surely merchants, not noblemen. Still, Luthien had every intention of turning about—it was easier to turn a single horse, after all, than a team and wagon.

A fat-jowled face, blotchy and pimpled, popped out of the coach's window. "Run the fool down if he does not move!" the merchant ordered brusquely, and he disappeared back into the privacy of his coach.

Luthien almost proclaimed himself to be the son of the eorl of Bedwydrin, almost drew weapon and ordered the cyclopian to back the wagon all the way to the ferry. Instead he wisely swallowed his pride, reminding himself that it would not be the smartest move to identify himself at this time. He was a simple fisherman or farmer, nothing more.

"Well, do you move, or do I put you into the water?" the cyclopian asked, and it gave a short snap of the reins just to jostle its two-horse team and move them a step closer to Riverdancer. All three horses snorted uncomfortably.

Several possible scenarios rushed through Luthien's thoughts, most of them ending rather unpleasantly for the cyclopian and its ugly master. Pragmatism held, however, and Luthien, never taking his stare off the one-eyed driver, urged Riverdancer into a slow backward walk, off the bridge, and moved aside.

The wagon rambled past, stopping long enough for the fat merchant to stick his head out and declare, "If I had more time, I would stop and teach you some manners, you dirty little boy!" He gave a wave of his soft, plump hand and the cyclopian driver cracked a whip, sending the team into a charge.

It took many deep breaths and a count of fifty for Luthien to accept that insult. He shook his head, then, and laughed aloud, reclaiming a welcome sense of euphoria. What did it count for, after all? He knew who he was, and why he had allowed himself to be faced down, and that was all that truly mattered.

Riverdancer trotted across the bridge and along the road, which looped back to the north to avoid a steep hillock, and Luthien quickly put the incident out of his mind. Until a few minutes later, that is, when he looked back across the river from higher ground down at the merchant's coach moving parallel to him and only a couple of hundred feet away. The wagon had stopped again, and this time the cyclopian driver faced the most curious-looking individual Luthien Bedwyr had ever seen.

He was obviously a halfling, a somewhat rare sight this far north in Eriador, riding a yellow mount that looked more like a donkey than a pony, with an almost hairless tail sticking straight out behind the beast. The halfling's dress was more remarkable than his mount, though, for though his clothes appeared a bit threadbare, he seemed to Luthien the pinnacle of fashion. A purple velvet cape, which flowed back from his shoulders out from under his long and curly brown locks, was opened in front to reveal a blue sleeveless doublet, showing the puffy white sleeves of his silken undertunic, tied tightly at the wrists. A brocade baldric laced in gold and tasseled all the way crossed his chest, right to left, ending in more tassels, bells, and a loop on which to hang his rapier, which was now being held in readiness in one of his green-gauntleted hands.

His breeches, like his cape, were purple velvet, and were met halfway up the halfling's shin by green hose, topped with silk and tied by ribbons at the back of his calf. A huge hat completed the picture, its wide brim curled up on one side and a large orange feather poking out behind. Luthien couldn't make out all of his features, but he saw that the halfling wore a neatly trimmed mustache and goatee.

He had never heard of a halfling with face hair and had never imagined one dressed in that manner, or sitting on a donkey, or pony, or whatever that thing was, and robbing a merchant wagon at rapier point. He pulled Riverdancer down the bank, slipping in behind the cover of some low brush, and watched the show.

"Out of the way, I tell you, or I'll trample you down!" growled the burly cyclopian driver.

The halfling laughed at him, bringing a smile to Luthien's lips as well. "Do you not know who I am?" the little one asked incredulously, and his thick brogue told Luthien that he was not from Bedwydrin, or from anywhere in Eriador. From the halfling's lips, "you" sounded more like "yee-oo" and "not" became a two-syllable word: "nau-te."

"I am Oliver deBurrows," the halfling proclaimed, "highwayman. You are caught fairly and defeated without a fight. I will your lives give to you, but your co-ins and jew-wels I claim as my own!"

A Gascon, Luthien decided, for he had heard many jokes about the people of Gascony in which the teller imitated a similar accent.

"What is it?" demanded the impatient merchant, popping his fat-jowled head out of the coach. "What is it?" he asked in a different tone when he looked upon Oliver deBurrows, highwayman.

"An inconvenience, my lord," the cyclopian answered, staring dangerously at Oliver. "Nothing more."

"See to it, then!" cried the merchant.

The cyclopian continued to stare over its shoulder as the merchant pulled his head into the coach. When the brute did turn back, it came about suddenly and viciously, producing from nowhere, it seemed, a huge sword and cutting it in a wicked chop at the halfling's head. Luthien sucked in his breath, thinking this extraordinary Oliver deBurrows about to die, but quicker than he believed possible, the halfling's left hand came out, holding a large-bladed dagger with a protective basket hilt—a main gauche, the weapon was called.

Oliver snapped the main gauche in a circular movement, catching the sword firmly in its hilt. He continued the fast rotation, twisting the sword, and then with a sudden jerk, sent the weapon flying from the cyclopian's hand to land sticking point-first into the turf a dozen feet away. Oliver's rapier darted forward, its tip catching the top of the cyclopian's leather tunic. The blade bent dangerously, just an inch below the brute's exposed neck.

"Rodent," growled the impudent cyclopian.

The highwayman laughed again. "My papa halfling, he always say, that a halfling's pride is inversely proportional to his height," Oliver replied.

"And I assure you," the halfling continued after a dramatic pause, "I am very short!"

For once, the cyclopian driver seemed to have no reply. It probably didn't even understand what the halfling had just said, Luthien realized, squatting in the brush, trying hard not to burst out in laughter.

"How far do you think my so fine blade will bend?" Oliver asked with a short chuckle. "Now, I have won the day and your precious co-ins and jew-wels."

To Oliver's surprise, though, the single cyclopian guard became six, as soldiers burst out of the coach door and rolled from every conceivable nook in the large wagon, two even coming out from underneath. The highwayman considered the new odds, eased the pressure on his bending rapier, and gave a new finish to his previous thought.

"I could be wrong."

CHAPTER 6

OLIVER DEBURROWS

THE FASHIONABLE HIGHWAYMAN was about eye level with the cyclopian soldiers as he looked at them from atop his yellow mount. He parried a spear thrust from one direction, yanked the bridle to bring his mount back on two legs and swing the beast about just in time to defeat a slashing sword from behind. He was a flurry of activity, but the cyclopian driver, smiling wickedly, pulled out another weapon: a loaded crossbow.

That would have been the end of the legendary (at least in his own mind) Oliver deBurrows, but a short distance away, in the thicket across the river, young Luthien Bedwyr had found his courage and his heart. Luthien had never been fond of the ever-present greedy merchants, placing them in a category just above cyclopians. The halfling was a thief—that could not be denied—but to Luthien so was the merchant. He didn't acknowledge the emotions guiding his actions in that critical moment; he only did as his heart dictated.

He was no less surprised than the cyclopian driver when an arrow, Luthien's arrow, took the brute in the chest and pushed it back down in its seat, the crossbow slipping from its weakening grasp.

If Oliver even saw the shot, he didn't show it. "Yes, do come on, you with one eye who looks so much like the back end of a cat!" he bellowed at one cyclopian, spinning his rapier in such a dazzling (though totally ineffective) display that the cyclopian took two steps back from the yellow mount and scratched its sloped forehead.

Luthien walked Riverdancer out of the thicket and down the steep bank, the strong horse gaining enough momentum to leap out, barely touching the water, crossing with one running stride. Across the field charged Luthien, bow in hand, shooting as he went.

The cyclopians roared in protest. One gabbed a long halberd from the side of the coach and darted out to meet Luthien, then changed its mind amidst the stream of soaring arrows and slipped in behind the coach's horses instead. Oliver, entangled in fending attacks from three different positions, didn't even know what his enemies were yelling about. The halfling did note, though, that the cyclopian now behind his turning mount became distracted.

"Pardon," he said to the brute in front of him, and he hurled his main gauche so that the opponent had to fall back a step, getting tangled but not hurt as it pushed away the halfheartedly tossed weapon. In the same movement, Oliver swooped off his wide hat and placed it over his mount's rump, and the pony responded immediately by rearing up and kicking out, straight into the ribs of the distracted cyclopian behind. Oliver, meanwhile, now saw Luthien, riding and shooting. The composed halfling simply shrugged and turned back to the more pressing situation.

It was still two against one, though, and the halfling found himself immediately hard-pressed, even more so because now he held only one weapon.

Another crossbowman, lying flat on top of the coach, changed its target from Oliver to the newest foe. The cyclopian leveled the weapon, but could not get a clear shot as Luthien bent low to the side of his running horse, using Riverdancer as a shield. The cyclopian fired and missed badly, and Luthien came up high enough to return the shot, his arrow knocking into the wood just below the prone cyclopian's face. Even on the running mount, Luthien managed to reload before the cyclopian, and his second shot, fired no more than twenty feet from the coach, nailed the brute in the face.

Then a halberd was thrust in front of Luthien's face as the next soldier darted out from behind the horse team. The only defense offered to Luthien was to fall back and to the side, right off of Riverdancer. He landed hard, and only by reminding himself through every inch of the brutal tumble that if he did not get right back up he would soon be skewered did he manage to keep his wits about him. He also wisely held onto the bow, and he whipped it across in front as he finally managed to put his feet under him just in time to bat aside the next thrusting attack.

Oliver was able to line up his pony so that both remaining cyclopians were facing him. His rapier snapped back and forth over the pony's low-hung head, intercepting cut after cut. The halfling tried to appear nonchalant, even bored, but in truth he was more than a little concerned. These cyclopians were pretty good and their weapons finely made. Still, Oliver had not survived two decades as a highwayman without a few tricks up his puffy white sleeve.

"Behind you!" he cried suddenly, and one of the cyclopians almost fell for the obvious ruse, almost turned its head to look over its shoulder—not an easy feat when you have only one eye located in the middle of your face!

The other cyclopian kept up its attack without a blink, and the foolish one came back doubly hard as soon as it realized how stupid it looked.

But not only did Oliver guess that the brutes wouldn't fall for the ruse, he hoped they wouldn't. "Behind you!" he cried again, just to egg them on a bit more, just to make them think that he thought they were stupid. Predictably, both cyclopians growled and pressed harder.

Oliver kicked his heels and his yellow pony leaped forward, right between the brutes. So intent were they on their offensive posture, the cyclopians didn't even mark Oliver's swift maneuver as the halfling let go the bridle and rolled off the back end of the pony, turning a complete somersault and landing easily on his feet. The cyclopians swung about as the horse cut between them, and Oliver promptly jabbed his rapier blade deep into the rump of one.

The cyclopian howled and whipped about, and a snap of Oliver's rapier sent the outraged brute's sword falling free.

"Foolish one-eyed sniffer of barnyard animals!" the halfling snorted, holding his hands out wide in disbelief. "I, polite Oliver deBurrows, even told you that it would come from behind!" The halfling then assumed his best fencing posture, free hand on hip. He yelled and leaped forward as if to strike, and the wounded cyclopian turned and fled, howling and fiercely rubbing its stuck butt.

The other cyclopian came on, though, viciously.

"You should be so wise as your friend," Oliver taunted, parrying one swing, ducking a second, and hopping over a third. "You are no match for Oliver deBurrows!"

In response, the cyclopian came on with such a vicious flurry that Oliver was put back on his heels, and though he could have poked his rapier home a dozen times, any offensive strike would surely have allowed the cyclopian a solid hit at him, as well. The creature was strong and its sword nearly as heavy as the halfling, and Oliver wanted no part of that trade.

"I could be wrong," the halfling admitted again, working furiously to keep the brute off of him. He gave a short and sharp whistle then, but the cyclopian took no note of it.

An instant later, Oliver's yellow pony slammed into the brute's back, throwing it facedown on the turf, and the pony continued forward, clambering atop the groaning cyclopian. The curious-looking and curiously trained pony then began hopping up and down, crunching bones with every short jump.

"Have you met my horse?" Oliver asked politely.

The cyclopian roared and tried to rise, but a hoof crushed the side of its face.

Luthien was hurt more than he cared to admit. The wounds wouldn't have been serious, except that he was engaged in a brutal fight at the moment and his head was pounding so badly that he could hardly see straight.

In fact, he saw not one but two halberd tips continually darting his way. He whipped the bow back and forth and backpedaled.

He walked right into a tree, and lost his breath in the surprise. The agile young Bedwyr fell to the side as the cyclopian, thinking him caught, jabbed straight ahead, the wicked halberd tip digging a fair-sized hole in the wood.

Luthien responded with a swing of his own, but he missed and cringed when he heard the bow crack as it struck the tree. He brought it back out in front of him: half of it was hanging by a splinter.

The cyclopian bellowed with laughter; Luthien threw the bow at it. The brute batted it aside and its laugh turned to a growl, but when it began to advance once more, the cyclopian found that its opponent now carried a sword.

Oliver's pony was still dancing atop the groaning cyclopian when the halfling swung into the saddle. He meant to turn about and go help the young man who had come to his aid, but he paused, hearing whispers from inside the coach.

"Shoot him!" he heard a woman say. "Are you a coward?"

Oliver nodded in confirmation, guessing that she was talking to the merchant. Most merchants were cowards, the halfling believed. He hopped to a standing position atop his saddle, turned his pony beside the coach, and stepped lightly onto its roof, nearly tripping over the body of a cyclopian, a long arrow stuck deep into its face. Oliver looked down at his shoe, streaked with the cyclopian's blood, and crinkled his face in disgust. A huge hand shot out suddenly, gabbing the halfling's ankle and nearly knocking him over.

The cyclopian driver held on stubbornly, despite the arrow sticking into his chest. Oliver whipped him atop the head with the side of his rapier blade, and when the brute let go of the halfling's ankle to grasp at its newest wound, Oliver kicked it in the eye. The cyclopian gurgled, trying to scream, and tumbled backward off its seat, falling in a heap behind the nervous horse team.

"Count your luck that you did not mess my fine and stolen clothes," the halfling said to him. "For then I would surely have killed you!"

With a derisive snort, the halfling picked his way to the other side of the coach's roof and knelt down on one knee. A moment later, the plump arms and head of the merchant appeared, holding a crossbow and pointing it in the general direction of Luthien and the last remaining soldier.

Something tapped the merchant on top of his head.

"I do not think that would be such a wise idea," he heard from above. Slowly the merchant turned his head upward to regard the halfling, on one knee still, with his elbow propped against his other knee, green-gloved hand, holding the rapier, against the side of his face, with his index finger tap-tapping against the side of his nose.

"I do not know for sure, of course," the halfling went on casually, "but I think he might be a friend of mine."

The merchant screamed and tried to wheel about and bring the crossbow to bear on this new foe. The rapier snapped suddenly, flashing before the fat man's eyes, and he froze in shock. As soon as his senses recovered and he realized that he hadn't been hit, he tried to finish the move, even going so far as to pull the crossbow's trigger, before he realized that the quarrel was no longer in place along the weapon's shaft, plucked cleanly away by the well-aimed rapier.

Oliver held out his hands and shrugged. "I am good, you must admit," he said. The merchant screamed again and disappeared into the coach, whereupon the woman set upon him, calling him "coward" repeatedly, and many other worse names.

Oliver sat in a comfortable crouch on the roof, enjoying it all thoroughly, and turned his gaze back to the continuing fight.

The cyclopian was working the long halberd fiercely, whipping it to and fro and straight ahead. The young man, to his credit, hadn't been hit, but he was tumbling wildly and snapping his blade all about, apparently unaccustomed to facing so long a weapon.

"You must move straight ahead when he moves ahead!" Oliver called out.

Luthien heard him, but the strategy made no sense. He had fought against spear wielders in the arena, but those weapons were no more than eight feet long. The shaft of this halberd nearly doubled that.

Luthien started forward, as instructed, on the cyclopian's next thrust, and he caught the tip of the halberd on his right shoulder for his effort. With a yelp, the young man fell back, grabbing his sword in his left hand and favoring the stung shoulder.

"Not like that!" Oliver scolded. "Do not thrust in an angle that is complementary to your enemy's line of attack!"

Still hard-pressed, Luthien and the cyclopian paused for an instant to wonder what in the world this curious halfling was talking about.

"Do not line up your body with the enemy's closest tip," Oliver instructed. "Only a silly viper snake would do that, and are you not smarter than a silly viper snake?" The halfling then launched into a long dissertation about the proper methods of parrying long weapons, and of fighting silly viper snakes, but Luthien was no longer listening. A sweeping cut forced him to spin away to the side; a straight thrust for his abdomen had him jerking his rump far out behind him, doubling over. The cyclopian retracted and poked ahead again, thinking he had the young man off balance. He did, indeed, except that Luthien hurled himself facedown to the ground right behind the retracting blade. The halberd's tip as it came jabbing back scratched Luthien's behind but caused no serious damage, and Luthien spun about on the ground and scrambled ahead, grabbing the halberd shaft in his right hand and pulling it down as his sword came whipping up. The long weapon cracked apart.

"Well done!" came the halfling's cry from the top of the coach.

The cyclopian was not unarmed, though, still holding a broken shaft that now effectively served as a spear. Oliver's cheer had barely left his mouth when the one-eyed brute growled and pushed ahead, catching Luthien as he tried to stand. Down went the young man, apparently impaled.

"Oh," the halfling groaned as the roaring cyclopian put his weight behind the spear and began to grind and twist it mercilessly. On the ground, Luthien squirmed and squealed.

Oliver put his grand hat over his heart and lowered his head in respect. But then the cyclopian jerked suddenly and straightened, letting go of his weapon. He stumbled backward several steps and tried to turn, and Oliver saw that he was grabbing his belly, trying to hold in his spilling guts. Back on the ground, Luthien's sword, the top half of the blade bloodied, was sticking straight up. Luthien sat up, tossing the spear aside, and Oliver laughed loudly as he recognized the truth of the matter. Luthien hadn't been impaled; he had caught the cyclopian's blade under his arm and rolled to the side as he fell to disguise the ruse.

"Oh, I do think that I am going to like this one," the halfling said, and he tipped his hat to the victorious Luthien.

"Now, cowardly fat merchant-type, will you admit that you are defeated?" Oliver called, rapping the coach door with his rapier. "You may get out now, or come out at the end of my so fine rapier blade!"

The door creaked open and the merchant came out, followed by a painted and perfumed lady wearing a low-cut-up-high and high-cut-down-low silken crimson gown. The woman eyed the halfling incredulously, but her expression changed when she noticed the handsome young Bedwyr as he walked over to join the group.

Luthien caught her lewd gaze and returned it with an incredulous smirk. He immediately thought of Avonese, and his left hand unconsciously tightened on the hilt of his bloody sword.

Three graceful hops—to the seat, to the horse's rump, and to the ground—brought Oliver down to them, and he walked around the two prisoners. A yank of his free hand took the merchant's belt purse, and a flick of his rapier took the woman's jeweled necklace over her head.

"Go and search the coach," he instructed Luthien. "I did not ask for your help, but I will graciously split the wealth." He paused and thought for a moment, counting kills. At first, he gave Luthien credit for three of the cyclopians, half the enemy, but then he convinced himself that the driver belonged to him. "You defeated two of the six," he announced. "So four of six items are mine."

Luthien stood up straight, indignant.

"You think you get half?" the highwayman balked.

"I am no thief!" Luthien proclaimed. All three—Oliver, the merchant, and the lady—looked about the carnage and the dead and wounded cyclopians lying in the muck.

"You are now," they all said together, and Luthien winced.

"The coach?" Oliver prompted after a long and silent minute slipped past. Luthien shrugged and moved by them, entering the coach. It had many compartments, most filled with food or handkerchiefs, perfume and other items for the journey. After some minutes of searching, though, Luthien found a small iron chest under the seat. He pulled it out to the open floor and hoisted it, then moved back outside.

Oliver had the merchant on his knees, stripped to his underwear and whimpering.

"So many pockets," the halfling explained to Luthien, going through the man's huge waistcoat.

"You may search me," the woman purred at Luthien, and he fell back a step, banging against the coach's open door.

"If you are hiding anything precious under there," the halfling said to her, indicating her skintight, revealing gown, "then you are not half the woman you pretend to be!"

He was laughing at his own joke until he noticed the iron box in Luthien's hands. Then Oliver's eyes lit up.

"I see that it is time to go," he said, and tossed the waistcoat away.

"What about them?" Luthien asked.

"We must kill them," Oliver said casually, "or they will bring the whole Praetorian Guard down upon us."

Luthien scowled fiercely. Killing armed cyclopians was one thing, but a defenseless man and woman, and wounded enemies (even if they were cyclopian) defeated on the field of honor, was something entirely different. Before the young man could begin to protest, though, the halfling moaned and slapped a hand across his face.

"Ah, but one of the one-eyes got away," Oliver said in feigned distress, "so we cannot eliminate all witnesses. It would seem, then, that mercy would serve us well." He looked around at the groaning cyclopians: the driver behind the team; the one trampled into the ground by Oliver's pony, propped on one elbow now and watching the proceedings; the one that Luthien had stabbed still kneeling and holding his belly; and the one that Oliver's horse had sent flying away standing again, though unsteadily, and making no move to come back near the robbers. With the one Oliver had sent running away, rubbing his behind, that left only the dead crossbowman atop the coach.

"Besides," the halfling added with a smirk, "you are the only one who actually killed anybody."

"Take me with you!" the lady screamed suddenly, launching herself at Luthien. She crashed into him, and Luthien dropped the iron box-right on both of his own feet. Inspired by the pain, the overpowering stench of the lady's perfume, and his memories of Avonese, Luthien growled and pushed her back, and before he could think of what he was doing, he punched her right in the face, dropping her heavily to the ground.

"We must work on your manners," Oliver noted, shaking his head. "And your chivalry," he remarked to the merchant, who made not the slightest protest about the punch.

"But that, like the chest of treasure, can wait," the halfling explained. "To the road, my friend!"

Luthien shrugged, not knowing what to do, not even understanding what he had done.

"Threadbare!" Oliver called, a fitting name if Luthien had ever heard one. Oliver's ugly yellow pony trotted around the coach horses and kneeled so that the halfling could better gain his seat.

"Put the chest upon your own horse," Oliver instructed, "and I will go and find my main gauche. And you," he said, tapping the quivering merchant atop the head with the side of his rapier blade. "Count as you would count your own co-ins. And do not stop until you have counted them, every one, a thousand times!"

Luthien retrieved Riverdancer and secured the chest behind the horse's saddle. Then he walked over and helped the woman back to her feet. He meant to offer a sincere apology—this was not Avonese, after all, and he and the halfling had just robbed her—but she immediately wrapped herself around him once more, biting at his earlobe. With great effort (and nearly at the cost of that ear), Luthien managed to pull her back to arm's length.

"So strong," she purred.

"Your lady?" Oliver began, walking Threadbare past the kneeling merchant.

"My wife," the merchant replied sourly.

"A loyal type, I can see," Oliver said. "But then, now we have the money!"

Luthien shoved off and ran away from the woman, getting into his saddle so quickly that he nearly tumbled off the other side. He kicked Riverdancer into a short gallop, seeing the woman running fast after him, and rushed right past Oliver, toward the bridge.

Oliver watched him with amusement, then wheeled Threadbare around to face the merchant and his woman. “Now you may tell all your fat merchant-type friends that you were robbed by Oliver deBurrows,” he said, as though that should carry some significance.

Threadbare reared on his hind legs, and with a tip of his hat, Oliver was off.

CHAPTER 7

THE DIAMONDGATE FERRY

"I AM OLIVER deBurrows," the halfling said, bringing his pony to a trot after the two had put more than a mile behind them. "Highwayman," he added, sweeping his hat off gracefully.

Luthien started to likewise introduce himself, but the halfling was not finished. "I used to say 'highwayhalfling,' " he explained, "but the merchants did not take that so seriously and I had to more often use my rapier blade. To make my point, if you understand my meaning." As he spoke, he snapped the rapier from the loop on his baldric and thrust it Luthien's way.

"I understand," Luthien assured him, gently pushing the dangerous weapon away. He tried to introduce himself but was promptly cut off.

"And this is my fine horse, Threadbare," Oliver said, patting the yellow pony. "Not the prettiest, of course, but smarter than any horse, and most men, as well."

Luthien patted his own shaggy mount and started to say, "Riverda—"

"I do appreciate your unexpected help," Oliver went on, oblivious to Luthien's attempt to speak. "Of course, I could have defeated them by myself—there were only six, you see. But take help where you find help, my papa halfling always say, and so I am grateful to . . ."

"Luth—" Luthien began.

"Of course, my gratitude will not carry beyond the split of the profits," Oliver quickly added. "One in four for you." He eyed Luthien's rather plain dress with obvious disdain. "And that will probably be more wealth than you have ever seen."

"Probably," the son of the eorl of Bedwydrin said immediately, trying to hide his smirk. Luthien did realize, though, that he had left his home without taking much in the way of wealth. He had enough to cross on the ferry and support himself for a few days, but when he had left Dun Varna, he hadn't really thought much beyond that.

"Not in debt, then," Oliver said, barely pausing for a breath, before Luthien, for the fourth time, could offer his name. "But I will allow you to ride beside me, if you wish. That merchant-type was not surprised to see me—and he knew all along that he could have kept me away by showing his six guards openly. Yet he hid them," the halfling reasoned, seeming as if he was speaking to himself. Then he snapped his fingers and looked straight at Luthien so quickly that he startled the young man.

"I do think that he hid the one-eyes in the hopes of luring me in!" Oliver exclaimed. He paused for just an instant, stroking his goatee with one of his green-gloved hands.

"Yes, yes," he went on. "The merchant-type knew I was on the road—this is not the first time I have robbed him at rapier point. I got him outside of Princetown once, I do believe." He looked up at Luthien, nodding his head. "And of course, the merchant-type would have heard my name in any case. So you may ride with me," he offered, "for a while. Until we are beyond the traps this merchant-type has no doubt set."

"You think that the danger is not behind us?"

"I just said that."

Luthien again hid his smirk, amazed at how the little one had just pumped himself up to be some sort of legendary highwayman. Luthien had never heard of Oliver deBurrows before, though the merchants traveling to his father's house in Dun Varna often brought tales of thieves along the road.

"I assure you," Oliver began, but he stopped and looked at Luthien curiously. "You know," he said, seeming somewhat perturbed, "you really should properly introduce yourself when traveling beside someone you have never met. There are codes of etiquette, particularly for those who would be known as proper highwaymen. Ah well," he finished with a great sigh, "perhaps you will learn better in your time beside Oliver deBurrows."

"I am Luthien," the young Bedwyr shouted quickly, before Oliver could interrupt him once more. He wondered if he should, perhaps, go by an alias. But he couldn't think of one at that moment, and he really didn't see the point. "Luthien Bedwyr of Dun Varna. And this is Riverdancer," he added, giving the horse another pat.

Oliver tipped his hat, then pulled up short on his pony. "Bedwyr?" he asked, as much to himself as to Luthien, as though he wanted to hear the ring of the name again. "Bedwyr. This name is not unknown to me."

"Gahris Bedwyr is the eorl of Bedwydrin," Luthien said.

"Ah!" Oliver agreed, pointing one finger up into the air and smiling widely in recognition. That smile went away in an incredulous blink. "Family?"

"Father," Luthien admitted.

Oliver tried to respond, but nearly choked instead. "And you are out here on the road—for sport!" the halfling reasoned. In Gascony, where Oliver had spent most of his life, it was not uncommon for the rowdy children of nobles to get into all sorts of trouble, including ambushing merchants on the road, knowing that their family connections would keep them free. "Draw your sword, you silly little boy!" the halfling cried, and out whipped his rapier and his main gauche. "I so much do not approve!"

"Oliver!" Luthien replied, swinging Riverdancer about to put some ground between himself and the fuming halfling. "What are you talking about?" As the halfling turned his pony to pursue, Luthien grudgingly drew his weapon.

"You bring disgrace to every reputable highwayman in all the land!" the halfling went on. "What need have you of co-ins and jew-wels?" Threadbare sidled up close to Riverdancer, and the halfling, though he was sitting at only about half Luthien's height and could barely reach the man's vital areas, thrust forward his rapier.

Luthien's sword intercepted the weapon and turned it aside. Oliver countered with a rapid series of thrusts, feints and cuts, even slipping in a deceptive jab with the main gauche.

Skilled Luthien defeated every move, kept his balance perfect and his sword in proper defensive posture.

"But it is a game for the son of an eorl," Oliver remarked sarcastically. "He is too bored in his daily duties of cowering his subjects." The thrusts became fiercer still, Oliver apparently going for a kill.

That last line got to Luthien, though, insulted him and insulted his father, who had never acted in such a way. He rocked back in his saddle, letting Oliver play out his fury, then came on with an attack routine of his own, slapping the rapier out wide and swiping his sword across fiercely. Oliver's main gauche intercepted, and the halfling squealed, thinking that he could send Luthien's weapon flying, as he had done to the cyclopian.

Luthien was quicker than that brute, and he turned his blade before Oliver could twist the trapping dagger, nearly taking the main gauche from the halfling's hand and freeing the sword so that it could complete its swing.

Oliver's great hat fell to the ground, and both the halfling and Luthien knew that Oliver's head would have still been inside if Luthien had so desired.

A tug on the reins sent Threadbare back several feet, putting some distance between the combatants. "I could be wrong," the halfling admitted.

"You are wrong," Luthien answered sternly. "You could find fault with Gahris Bedwyr, that I do not doubt. He does not follow his heart if that course would go against the edicts of King Greensparrow, or the duke of Montfort, or any of the duke's many emissaries. But on pain of death, never again speak of Gahris as a tyrant!"

"I said I could be wrong," Oliver replied soberly.

"As for me . . ." Luthien went on, his voice subdued, for he was not sure of how to proceed. What of me? he wondered. What had happened this day? It all seemed a surrealistic blur to the suddenly confused Luthien.

For once, Oliver remained silent and let the young man sort out his thoughts, understanding that whatever Luthien might have to say could be important—both to Oliver and to Luthien.

"I no longer claim any of the rights that accompany the name of Bedwyr," Luthien said firmly. "I have fled my house, leaving the corpse of a cyclopian guardsman behind. And now I have chosen my course." He held his sword up before him, letting its fine blade shine in the sun, though it was still a bit stained with the blood of the merchant's guard. "I am as much an outlaw as are you, Oliver deBurrows," Luthien proclaimed. "An outlaw in a land ruled by an outlaw king. Thus will my sword swing for justice."

Oliver raised his own rapier in like salute and outwardly proclaimed his agreement. He thought Luthien a silly little boy, though, who didn't understand either the rules or the dangers of the road. Justice? Oliver nearly laughed aloud at the thought. Luthien's sword might swing for justice, but Oliver's rapier jabbed for profit. Still, the young man was a mighty ally—Oliver couldn't deny that. And, Oliver mused, lending some credibility to the smile he was showing to Luthien, if justice was truly Luthien's priority, then more of the profits might fall Oliver's way.

Suddenly, the highwayhalfling was beginning to think that this arrangement might not be so temporary. "I accept your explanation," he said. "And I apologize for my too rash actions." He went to tip his hat again, then realized that it was lying on the ground. Luthien saw it, too, and started to move for it, but Oliver waved him back. Leaning low off the side of his saddle, the halfling tipped his rapier low, slipping the point in under the hat. A flick and twist brought the hat spinning atop the rapier's tip as Oliver lifted the weapon. He thrust it up, then jerked his rapier away, and the hat dropped in a spin, landing perfectly atop the halfling's head.

Luthien sat amazed, answering Oliver's smug smile with a shake of his head.

"But we are not safe on the island, fellow outlaw," Oliver said, his expression turning serious. "That merchant-type knew me, or of me, and expected me. He was probably on his way to your own father to organize a hunt for Oliver deBurrows." The halfling paused and snorted. He looked at Luthien and his chuckle became a full-blown laugh.

"Oh, wonderful irony!" Oliver cried. "He goes to the eorl for assistance, while the eorl's own son comes to my assistance!" Oliver's laughter continued to grow, and Luthien joined in, more to be polite than with any real feelings of mirth.

They did not make the ferry that afternoon, as Luthien had hoped. He explained to Oliver that the ferries would not cross the choppy seas at night. In the darkness, the island spotters could not see if any dorsal whales had, come into the narrow channels. A description of the ten-ton man-eaters was all that Oliver needed to be convinced that they should forgo plans to be off the island that same day and set up their camp.

Luthien sat up long into the night in the drizzle beside the hissing and smoking low campfire. To the side, Threadbare and Riverdancer stood quietly, heads bowed, and across the fire, Oliver snored contentedly.

The young man huddled under his blanket, warding off the chill. He still could not believe all that had happened over the last few days: Garth Rogar, his brother, the cyclopian guardsman, and now the attack on the merchant wagon. It remained unreal to Luthien; he felt as if he had fallen into a river of uncontrollable events and was simply being swept along in their tide.

No, not uncontrollable, Luthien finally decided. Undeniable. The world, as it turned out, was not as he had been brought up to expect it to be. Perhaps his last actions in Dun Varna—his decision to leave and his fight with the cyclopian—had been some sort of passage into adulthood, an awakening for the naive child of a noble house.

Perhaps, but Luthien knew that he still had no solid answers. He knew, too, that he had followed his heart both in Dun Varna and when he had seen Oliver's fight with the merchant's guards. He had followed his heart, and out there, on the road, in the drizzle of a chill August night, Luthien had little else to guide him.

The next day was similarly gray and wet, but the companions made good time out of their encampment. Soon the smell of salt water filled their nostrils and put a tang in their mouths.

"If the day was clear," Luthien explained, "we could see the northern spurs of the Iron Cross from here."

"How do you know?" Oliver asked him sarcastically. "Have you ever had a clear day on this island?" The banter was light and so were their hearts (Oliver's always seemed to be!). Luthien felt somehow relieved that day, as though he would find his freedom when he crossed the narrow channel and stepped onto Eriador's mainland. The wide world beckoned.

But first, they had to get across.

From the top of a rocky bluff, the two got their first view of the Diamondgate Ferry, and of the mainland across the narrow channel. The place was called Diamondgate for a small, diamond-shaped isle, a lump of wet black rock in the middle of the channel, halfway between the shores.

Two flat, open barges sat at the ends of long wooden wharves whose supporting beams were as thick as ancient oaks. Off to the side loomed the remains of the older wharves, equally well constructed, their demise a testament to the power of the sea.

The barges, including the two now moored across the channel, had originally been designed and built by the dwarves of the Iron Cross more than three hundred years before, and had been meticulously maintained (and replaced, when the rocks or the currents or a dorsal whale took one) by the islanders ever since. Their design was simple and effective: an open, flat landing for cargo and travelers, anchored at each corner by thick beams that arched up to a central point ten feet above the center of the landing. Here the beams connected to a long metal tube, and through this ran the thick rope that guided the ferry back and forth. A large gear showed on each side of the tube, its notches reaching in through slits along the tube's side. A crank on the deck turned a series of gears leading to these two, which in turn caught the knots on the rope and pulled the ferry along the taut cord's length. The beauty of the system was that, because of the marvelous dwarven gearing, a single strong man could pull the ferry even if it was heavily laden.

But still the crossing was always dangerous. The water this day, as every day, showed white tips on its bouncing waves and abundant rocks, especially near to Diamondgate, where the ferries could dock if they encountered any trouble.

One of the barges was always inoperable, taken down so that its guide rope could be replaced, or when its floor planking needed shoring up. Several dozen men worked long days at Diamondgate just to keep the place in operation.

"They are planning to shut down that one," Luthien, familiar with the operation, informed Oliver, pointing to the barge on the north. "And it seems as if the other is about to leave. We must hurry, or wait perhaps hours for the next barge to cross over." He gave a ticking sound to Riverdancer, and the horse started down the path leading to the landings.

A few minutes later, Threadbare pranced up alongside and Oliver grabbed Luthien's arm, indicating that he should slow the pace.

"But the ferry—" Luthien started to protest.

"There is an ambush about," Oliver explained.

Luthien stared at him incredulously, then looked back to the landing. More than a score of men moved down there, but just a pair of cyclopians, these showing no weapons and appearing as simple travelers waiting to cross. This was not common, Luthien knew, for there were few cyclopians on Bedwydrin, and those were only merchant guards or his father's own. Still, under the edicts of King Greensparrow, cyclopians were allowed free passage as citizens of Avon, and affairs at Diamondgate did not seem so out of place.

"You have to learn to smell such things," Oliver remarked, recognizing the young man's doubts. Luthien shrugged and gave in, moving along the path at as fast a pace as Oliver would allow.

The two cyclopians, and many of the men, spotted the companions when they were about a hundred feet from the landing, but none made any gestures or even called out to indicate that the two might have been expected. Oliver, though, slowed a bit more, his eyes darting this way and that from under the brim of his hat.

A horn blew, indicating that all should move back from the end of the wharf as the barge was about to pull out. Luthien started forward immediately, but Oliver held him in check.

"They are leaving," Luthien protested in a harsh whisper.

"Easy," Oliver implored him. "Make them think that we intend to simply wait for the next crossing."

"Make who think?" Luthien argued.

"You see those barrels along the wharf?" Oliver asked. Luthien swung his gaze about and Oliver squeezed hard on his forearm. "Do not be so obvious!" the halfling scolded softly.

Luthien sighed and subtly looked at the casks Oliver had mentioned. There was a long line of them; they had probably come from the mainland and were waiting for a caravan to claim them.

"They are marked with an X," Oliver remarked.

"Wine," Luthien explained.

"If they are wine, then why do so many have open bungholes?" the alert halfling asked. Luthien looked more closely, and sure enough, saw that every third barrel had a small, open hole in it, minus its bung.

"And if those cyclopians on the landing are simply travelers," Oliver went on, "then why are they not on the departing barge?"

Luthien sighed again, this time revealing that he was starting to follow, and agree with, the halfling's line of reasoning.

"Can your horse jump?" Oliver asked calmly.

Luthien noted that the barge was slowly moving away from the wharf and understood what the halfling was thinking.

"I will tell you when to break," Oliver assured him. "And do kick a barrel into the water if you get the chance as you pass!"

Luthien felt his adrenaline building, felt the same tingling and butterflies in the stomach that he got when he stepped into the arena. There was little doubt in the young man's mind that life beside Oliver deBurrows would not be boring!

They walked their mounts easily onto the boards of the thirty-foot wharf, passing two workers without incident. A third man, one of the cargo workers, approached them smiling.

"Next barge is an hour before the noon," he explained cheerily, and he pointed to a small shed, starting to explain where the travelers could rest and take a meal while they waited.

"Too long!" Oliver cried suddenly, and off leaped Threadbare, Riverdancer charging right behind. Men dove out of the way; the two visible cyclopians shouted and scrambled, producing short swords from under their cloaks. As Oliver had predicted, every third barrel began to move, lids popping off and falling aside as cyclopians jumped out.

But the two companions had gained surprise. Riverdancer sprang past Oliver's pony and blasted past the two cyclopians, hurling them aside. Oliver moved Threadbare to the edge of the wharf, along the row of barrels, and managed to bump more than a few as he rushed by, spinning them into the drink.

The slow-moving ferry was fifteen feet out when Luthien got to the end of the wharf, no great leap for powerful Riverdancer, and the young man held on tight as he soared across.

Oliver came next, sitting high and waving his hat in one hand as Threadbare flew across, coming to a kicking and skidding stop, banging into Riverdancer atop the smooth wooden barge. Back on the wharf, a dozen cyclopians shouted protests and waved their weapons, but Oliver, more wary than his less-experienced companion, paid them no heed. The halfling swung down from his mount, his weapons coming out to meet the advance of a cyclopian that suddenly appeared from among the piles of cargo.

The rapier and main gauche waved in a dizzying blur, a precise and enchanting dance of steel, though they seemed to come nowhere near to hitting the halfling's opponent. The cyclopian gawked at the display, sincerely impressed. But when the flurry was done, the brute was not hurt at all. Its one eye looked down to its leather tunic, though, and saw that the halfling had cut an "O" into it in a fine cursive script.

"I could write my whole name," Oliver remarked. "And I assure you, I have a very long name!"

With a growl of rage, the cyclopian lifted its heavy ax, and Oliver promptly dove forward, running right between its wide-spread legs and spinning about to poke the brute in the rump with his rapier.

"I would taunt you again," the halfling proclaimed, "but I see that you are too stupid to know that you are being taunted!"

The cyclopian howled and turned, then instinctively looked ahead again just in time to see Luthien's fist soaring into its face. Oliver meanwhile had retracted the rapier and rushed ahead, driving his shoulder into the back of the cyclopian's knees. Over went the brute, launched by Luthien's punch, to land heavily, flat on its back. It struggled for just a moment, then lay still.

A splash made Luthien turn around. The cyclopians on the wharf had taken up spears now and were hurling them out at the barge. "Tell the captain to get this ferry moving," Oliver said calmly to Luthien as he walked past. He handed

Luthien a small pouch of coins. "And do pay the man." Oliver walked to the stern of the ferry, apparently unconcerned with the continuing spear volley.

"You sniffers of barnyard animals!" he taunted. "Stupid oafs who poke their own eyes when trying to pick their noses!"

The cyclopians howled and picked up their throwing pace.

"Oliver!" Luthien cried.

The halfling turned to regard him. "They have but one eye," he explained. "No way to gauge depth. Do you not know that cyclopians cannot throw?"

He turned about, laughing, then shouted, "Hello!" and jumped straight up as a spear stuck into the deck right between his legs.

"You could be wrong," Luthien said, imitating the halfling's accent and stealing Oliver's usual line.

"Even one-eyes can get lucky," the halfling replied indignantly, with a snap of his green-gloved fingers. And to prove confidence in his point, he launched a new stream of taunts at the brutes on the wharf.

"What is this about?" an old, weather-beaten man demanded, grabbing Luthien by the shoulder. "I'll not have—"

He stopped when Luthien handed him the pouch of coins.

"All right, then," the man said. "But tether those horses, or it's your own loss!"

Luthien nodded and the wiry old man went back to the crank.

The ferry moved painfully slowly for the anxious companions, foot by foot across the choppy dark waters of the channel where the Avon Sea met the Dorsal. They saw cyclopians scrambling back on the wharf, trying to get the other ferry out of its dock and set off in pursuit. Luthien wasn't too concerned, for he knew that the boats, geared for solid and steady progress across the dangerous waters, could not be urged on any faster. He and Oliver had a strong lead on their pursuers, and Riverdancer and Threadbare would hit the ground across the way running, putting a mile or more behind them before the cyclopians stepped off their ferry.

Oliver joined Luthien beside the horses, limping and grumbling as he approached.

"Are you injured?" a concerned Luthien asked.

"It is my shoe," the halfling answered, and he held his shoe out for Luthien to see. It seemed intact, though quite dirty and quite wet, as if Oliver had just dipped his leg into the water.

"The stain!" Oliver explained, pushing it higher, near to Luthien's face. "When I crossed the roof of the merchant-type coach, I stepped in the blood of the dead cyclopian. Now I cannot get the blood off!"

Luthien shrugged, not understanding.

"I stole this shoe from the finest boarding school in Gascony," Oliver huffed, "from the son of a friend of the king himself! Where am I to find another in this too wild land you call your home?"

"There is nothing wrong with that one," Luthien protested.

"It is ruined!" Oliver retorted, and he crossed his arms over his chest, rocked back on one heel, his other foot tap-tapping, and pointedly looked away.

Luthien did well not to laugh at his pouting companion.

A few feet away, the downed cyclopian groaned and stirred.

"If he wakes up, I will kick him in the eye," Oliver announced evenly. "Twice."

Oliver snapped his glare up at Luthien, whose chest was now heaving with sobs of mirth. "And then I will write my name, my whole name, my very long whole name, across your ample buttocks," the halfling promised.

Luthien buried his face in Riverdancer's shaggy neck.

The ferry was well over a hundred yards out by then and nearing Diamondgate Isle, the halfway point. It seemed as if the friends had made their escape, and even pouting Oliver's mood seemed to brighten.

But then the guide rope jerked suddenly. Luthien and Oliver looked back to shore and saw cyclopians hanging from the high poles that held the ropes, hacking away on the rope with axes.

"Hey, don't you be doing that!" the captain of the ferry cried out, running back across the deck. Luthien was about to ask what problems might arise if the guide rope was cut down behind them when the rope fell free. The young man got his answer as the ferry immediately began to swing to the south, toward the rocks of the island, caught in the current of the channel.

The captain ran back the other way, screaming orders to his single crewman. The man worked frantically on the crank, but the ferry could not be urged any faster. It continued at its snail pace and its deadly swing to the south.

Luthien and Oliver grabbed hard to their saddles and tried to find some secure footing as the ferry bounced in. The boat scraped a few smaller rocks, narrowly missed one huge and sharp jag, and finally crashed into the rocks around a small and narrow inlet.

Cargo tumbled off the side; the cyclopian, just starting to regain its footing, went flying away, smacking hard into the barnacle-covered stone, where it lay very still. One of the other passengers shared a similar fate, tumbling head over heels into the water, coming up gagging and screaming. Threadbare and Riverdancer held their ground stubbornly, though the pony lurched forward a bit, stepping onto Oliver's unshod foot. The halfling quickly reconsidered his disdain over his dirty shoe and took it out of his pocket.

More swells came in under them, grinding the ferry against the stone, splintering wood. Luthien dove to the deck and crawled across, grabbing hold of the fallen man and pulling him back up out of the water. The captain called for his crewman to crank, but then spat curses instead, realizing that with the other end of the guide rope unsecured, the ferry could not possibly escape the current.

"Bring Riverdancer!" Luthien called to Oliver, understanding the problem. He scrambled to the back of the raft and took up the loose guide rope, then looked about, finally discerning which of the many stones would best hold the rope. He moved to the very edge and looped up the rope, readying his throw.

A swell nearly sent him overboard, but Oliver grabbed him by the belt and held him steady. Luthien tossed the rope over the rock and pulled the loop as tight as he could. Oliver scrambled onto Riverdancer's back and turned the horse around, and Luthien came up behind, tying off the rope onto the back of the saddle.

Gently, the halfling eased the horse forward and the rope tightened, steadying the rocking ferry. Oliver kept the horse pressing forward, taking up any slack, as Luthien tied off the guide rope. Then they cut Riverdancer free and the cranking began anew, easing the ferry out of the inlet and back out from the rocks. A great cheer went up from the captain, his crewman, and the four other passengers.

"I'll get her into Diamondgate's dock," the captain said to Luthien, pointing to a wharf around the outcropping of rocks. "We'll wait there for a ferry to come for us from the other side."

Luthien led the captain's gaze back into the channel, where the other ferry, teeming with armed cyclopians, was now working its way into the channel.

"All the way across," the young Bedwyr said. "I beg."

The captain nodded, looked doubtfully to the makeshift guide rope, and moved back to the front of the ferry. He returned just a few moments later, though, shaking his head.

"We have to stop," he explained. "They're flying a yellow flag on the Diamondgate dock."

"So?" put in Oliver, and he did not sound happy.

"They have spotted dorsals in the other side of the channel," Luthien explained to the halfling.

"We cannot take her out there," the captain added. He gave the pair a sincerely sympathetic look, then went back to the bow, leaving Luthien and Oliver to stare helplessly at each other and at the approaching boatload of cyclopians.

When they reached the Diamondgate dock, Luthien and Oliver helped everyone to get off the ferry. Then the halfling handed the captain another sack of coins and moved back to his pony, showing no intention of leaving the boat.

"We have to go on," Luthien explained to the gawking man. They both looked out to the two hundred yards of choppy dark water separating them from Eriador's mainland.

"The flag only means that dorsals have been spotted this morning," the captain said hopefully.

"We know that the cyclopians are very real," Luthien replied, and the captain nodded and backed away, signaling for his crewman to do likewise, surrendering his craft to Luthien and Oliver.

Luthien took the crank and set off at once, looking more to the sides than straight ahead. Oliver remained in the stern watching the cyclopians and the curiously forlorn group they had just left at the dock. Their expressions, truly concerned, set off alarms in the normally unshakable halfling.

"These dorsals," Oliver asked, moving up to join Luthien, "are they very big?"

Luthien nodded.

"Bigger than your horse?"

Luthien nodded.

"Bigger than the ferry?"

Luthien nodded.

"Take me back to the dock," Oliver announced. "I would fight the cyclopians."

Luthien didn't bother to respond, just kept cranking and kept looking from side to side, expecting to see one of those towering and ominous black fins rise up at any moment.

The cyclopians passed Diamondgate, dropping two brutes off as they passed. Oliver groaned, knowing that the cyclopians would inevitably try to cause mischief with the guide ropes once more. But the halfling's fears soon turned to enjoyment. The ropes were suspended quite high over the Diamondgate docks, and the cyclopians had to build a make-shift tower to get anywhere near them. Worse, as soon as the ferry with its cyclopian load had moved out a safe distance, the captain of Luthien's ferry, his crewman, and the other passengers—even the injured one Luthien had pulled from the cold water—set on the two cyclopians, pushing them and their tower over the edge of the wharf and into the dark water.

At Oliver's cheer, young Luthien turned and saw that spectacle and marked it well, though he had no idea then of how significant that little uprising might later prove.

Oliver did a cartwheel, leaped and spun with joy, and came down frozen in place, looking out to the north side, to the open channel and the tall fin—thrice his height, at least—that had come up through the dark waves.

Luthien's smile disappeared as he considered his friend's sudden expression, then shifted his gaze to consider its source.

The dorsal fin sent a high wake in its speeding path, dropped to half its height, then slipped ominously under the water altogether.

Luthien, trying to remember all the advice his local fishermen had ever given to him, stopped the crank, even back-pulling it once to halt the ferry's momentum.

"Crank!" Oliver scolded, running forward, but Luthien grabbed him and held him steady and whispered for him to be quiet.

They stood together as the water around them darkened and the ferry shifted slightly to the south, nearly snapping its guide rope, moved by the passage of the great whale as it brushed under them. When the whale emerged on the other side, Oliver glimpsed its full forty-foot length, its skin patched black and white. Ten tons of killer. The halfling would have fallen to the deck, his legs no longer able to support him, but Luthien held him steady.

"Stay calm and still," the young Bedwyr whispered. Luthien was counting on the cyclopians this time. They were beasts of mountain holes and surely knew little about the habits of dorsal whales.

The long fin reappeared starboard of the craft, moving slowly then, as if the whale had not decided its next move.

Luthien looked behind at the eagerly approaching cyclopians. He smiled and waved, pointing out the tall dorsal fin to them.

As Luthien expected, the cyclopians spotted the great whale and went berserk. They began scrambling all about the deck of their ferry; the one on the crank began cranking backward, trying to reverse direction. A few of the brutes even climbed up to their guide rope.

"Not such a bad idea," Oliver remarked, looking at his own high rope.

Luthien turned his gaze instead to their loyal mounts, and Oliver promptly apologized.

Then Luthien looked back to the great whale, turning now, as he had expected. The cyclopians kept up their frenzy, disturbing the water, inadvertently calling the whale to them.

When the behemoth's course seemed determined, Luthien went back to the crank and began easing the ferry ahead slowly, so as not to attract the deadly whale's attention.

With typical cyclopian loyalty, the cyclopians chose one from their own ranks and threw the poor brute into the water ahead of the approaching whale, hoping that the behemoth would take the sacrifice and leave the rest of them alone.

They didn't understand the greedy nature of dorsal whales.

The black-and-white behemoth slammed the side of the cyclopians' ferry, then, with a flick of its powerful tail, heaved itself right across the flat deck, driving half of the pitifully small craft under water. Cyclopians flew everywhere, flailing and screaming. The dorsal slipped back under the water, but reappeared on the ferry's other side. The whale's head came right out of the water, a cyclopian in its great maw up to the waist, screaming and slapping futilely at the sea monster.

The whale bit down and slid back under, and the severed top half of the one-eye bobbed in the reddening water.

Half a cyclopian would not satisfy a dorsal whale, though. The beast's great tail slapped the water, launching two cyclopians thirty feet into the air. They splashed back in and one was sent flying again; the other was bitten in half.

The frenzy went on for agonizing minutes, and then, suddenly, the dorsal fin appeared again, cutting a fast wake to the north.

"Luthien," Oliver called ominously.

Several hundred yards away, the whale breached, slamming back down into the water, using the jump to pivot about.

"Luthien," Oliver called again, and the young Bedwyr didn't have to look north to know that the whale had found another target.

Luthien realized at once that he could not make the mainland dock, fully fifty yards away. He jumped up from the crank and ran about, thinking, searching.

"Luthien," Oliver said again, frozen in place by the approaching specter of doom.

Luthien ran to the stern of the ferry and called across the water to the shouting people of the Diamondgate dock: "Cut the rope!"

At first, they didn't seem to hear him, or at least, they seemed not to understand, but then Luthien called it again and pointed above himself at the guide rope. Immediately the captain signaled to his crewman, and the agile man put a large knife between his teeth and scrambled up the pole.

Luthien went to stand beside Oliver, watching the whale's approach.

A hundred yards away. Eighty.

Fifty yards away. Luthien heard Oliver muttering under his breath—praying, the young man realized.

Suddenly, the ferry lurched to the side and began a hard swing. Luthien pulled Oliver over to their mounts. Both Riverdancer and Threadbare were standing nervously, nickering and stamping their hooves as if they understood their peril. Luthien quickly tied off the end of the loose rope so that the ferry could not slip down along its length.

The dorsal fin angled accordingly, keeping the pursuit, closing.

Thirty yards away. Oliver could see the whale's black eye.

The ferry was speeding along quite well by then, caught in the deceivingly swift currents, but the whale was faster still.

Twenty yards away. Oliver was praying loudly.

The ferry jolted, skidding off a rock, and when Oliver and Luthien managed to tear their stares from the whale, they realized that they were very near the rock coastline. They looked back just in time to see the dorsal fin veer away, stymied by the shallows.

The companions' relief was short-lived, though, for they were moving at a wild clip, much faster than when they had been cut free near to Diamondgate, and were coming up on a sheer cliff of jagged rock.

CHAPTER 8

A ROAD WELL TAKEN

"GET ON YOUR horse! Get on your horse!" Oliver cried as he mounted Threadbare, holding the reins hard to keep the nervous beast from stumbling.

Luthien followed the command, not really knowing what Oliver had in mind, but with no better plan of his own. As soon as he was astride Riverdancer, he saw Oliver lining up the pony exactly opposite from where the ferry would likely hit, and then the young man began to catch on.

"You must time the jump well!" the halfling called. The ferry lurched suddenly as it grazed across more rocks; the plank furthest aft broke apart and was left drifting in the speeding craft's wake.

"Jump?" Luthien cried back. The approaching wall of stone was only a few feet high, and Luthien held no doubts that Riverdancer could make the leap if they were on solid ground. But the bouncing raft could not be considered solid ground, and even worse, Luthien was not sure of what was on the other side of that wall. He knew what would happen if he did not make the jump, though, and so when Oliver kicked Threadbare into a short run across the ferry, Luthien and Riverdancer followed.

Luthien buried his head in the horse's shaggy mane, not daring to look as he lifted away, propelled by the momentum of the ferry. He heard the explosion of wood on the rocks behind him, knew an instant later that he had cleared the wall.

He looked up as Riverdancer touched down in a short trot on a grassy knoll. Threadbare stood to the side, riderless and with a small cut on her foreleg. For a moment, Luthien feared that Oliver had toppled in the middle of the jump and had been slammed against the stones. Then he spotted the halfling lying in the wet grass and laughing wildly.

Oliver hopped to his feet and scooped up his fallen hat. He looked back to Diamondgate and waved frantically, wanting those who had helped him to know that he and Luthien had survived.

Luthien walked Riverdancer to the edge of the knoll and looked down at the smashed ferry. Twenty yards out, the fierce dorsal whale reappeared, circling the flotsam.

"That was not so bad," Oliver remarked.

Luthien didn't know whether to jump down and punch the halfling, or to throw him into the air in victory. His blood was coursing mightily through his veins, his heart pumping strongly. He felt more alive than ever before, more sheer elation than any victory in the arena could ever have afforded him.

But if Oliver spoke the truth, then what else might the young Bedwyr face beside the halfling? What worse?

Despite his primal joy, a shudder ran along Luthien's spine.

"They are coming to congratulate our quick thinking," Oliver said, drawing Luthien's attention and leading his gaze north along the knoll, back toward the ferry docks on this side of the channel. Two dozen men were running at them, calling out and waving tools.

"To congratulate?" Luthien asked.

Oliver looked down to the smashed ferry. "You think they might want us to pay for that?"

Luthien's shrug sent the halfling running to his mount.

He swung up into his saddle and bowed from a sitting position, sweeping his great hat low along the pony's side. "I do so appreciate your applause," he called to the approaching mob. "But now, I fear, the curtain is closed!"

And off they ran, side by side, the foppish halfling swashbuckler on his ugly yellow pony and the son of Bedwyr on his glistening white stallion.

The next few days proved quite uneventful for the weary companions. They traveled easily south through the Eriadoran farmlands, taking food and lodging where they found it. This was not too difficult, for the farmers of northern Eriador were a friendly folk, and more than willing to share a meal and a place in their barns in exchange for news of the outside world.

Oliver always dominated the conversations on such occasions, telling Luthien and the farmers grand tales of his times in Gascony, telling of adventures far beyond the scope of the "minor inconveniences" he and Luthien had been through since the fight with the merchant wagon.

Luthien listened to all the tales without reply, though he knew that Oliver was three parts bluster and one part truth (and allowing him that formula, Luthien figured, was being generous). The young man saw no harm in the halfling's outrageous claims, and Oliver seemed to entertain the farmers well enough, though none of the farmers were able to provide any information about Ethan. Every morning, when Luthien and Oliver left a farm, they were seen off by an entire family, and sometimes neighbors as well, smiling and waving and calling out for their good fortunes.

Luthien had too much on his mind to worry about any lies or exaggerations the halfling might spout. The young man still could not sort through all of his confusing thoughts and events of the last week, but he knew that he was comfortable with all that he had done. Even when he thought of the cyclopian in his father's house, or the one atop the merchant's wagon, or those in the overturned boat, Luthien held no remorse and took heart that if the identical situation were to come upon him again, he would react in the very same way.

He took heart, too, in his companion. Every day that passed, Luthien found that he liked Oliver's company more and more. This halfling, admittedly a thief, was not an evil person. Far from it. From his actions and the tales of his past (those parts that Luthien decided might have a ring of truth), Luthien could see that Oliver held himself up to some very high principles. The halfling would only steal from merchants and nobles, for example, and despite his suggestions when they had the merchant and his wife helpless on the road, from what Luthien could discern, Oliver was reluctant to kill anything except cyclopians.

And so Luthien, with no idea of how to locate his brother, decided to simply ride along the course beside the highwayhalfling, wherever it might lead, and let the fates guide him.

They moved south for several days, then veered to the east, crossing fields of tall, blowing wheat and high stone walls. "We will go between the mountains," Oliver explained one afternoon, pointing to a wide gap between the main bulk of the Iron Cross and a northern string of peaks. "My boat left me off on the road to Montfort and I have not been this way."

"Bruce MacDonald's Swath," Luthien replied, offering the name given to that particular gap.

Oliver slowed Threadbare and spent a moment in thought. "And will this Bruce MacDonald expect from us a toll?" he asked, putting a protective hand on his jingling pouch.

"Only if he comes from the grave," Luthien replied with a laugh. He went on to explain the legend of Bruce MacDonald, Eriador's greatest hero of old, who drove the attacking cyclopians back into their mountain holes. According to the tales, Bruce MacDonald cut the swath through the mountains, thus crossing more easily and gaining a surprise on the main cyclopian force, who did not expect his army before the spring cleared the mountain passes.

"And now the one-eyes are your friends?" Oliver asked. "We have no cyclopians in Gascony," he bragged. "At the least, we have none who dare to stick their ugly noses out of their dirty mountain holes!" The halfling went on, taking the tale from Luthien, and explained how Gascons dealt with the one-eyed brutes, telling of great battles—far greater, of course, than any Bruce MacDonald might have fought.

Luthien let the halfling ramble and, in fact, faded out of the conversation altogether, considering instead his own retelling of the MacDonald tale and how his blood stirred whenever he spoke of the legendary hero. Suddenly, the young Bedwyr was beginning to understand his own actions and feelings. He knew then why he was not so badly bothered by killing in his father's house. He thought of his feelings for the first cyclopian who had been tossed overboard on the ferry. Luthien had not gone to his aid, but he had rushed to help the man who had similarly been thrown.

Luthien had never realized before how deeply his hatred of cyclopians ran. In realizing the truth, he came to understand Ethan better. He knew then why his brother had quit the arena as soon as the cyclopian guards had been given to Gahris by the duke of Montfort, several years before. A rush of other memories came over the young man as he explored these new emotions: childhood tales he had been told by his father and others detailing the atrocities of the cyclopians before Bruce MacDonald had put them down. Other vicious raids had occurred even more recently, usually against helpless farm families.

Luthien was still deep in his contemplations when Oliver stopped Threadbare and looked all about. The young Bedwyr and his horse continued on, oblivious to the halfling, and would have kept going had not Oliver whistled.

Luthien turned around, eyeing the halfling curiously. Seeing the sincere concern on Oliver's face, he waited until he had walked Riverdancer back beside the yellow pony before he quietly asked, "What is it?"

"You have to learn to smell these things," Oliver whispered in reply.

As if on cue, an arrow cut through the air, well above the companions' heads.

"Cyclopians," Oliver muttered, noting the terrible shot.

Again, as if on cue, the wheat to either side of the road behind them began to shake and whip about and cyclopians crashed out onto the road, riding fierce ponypigs, ugly but muscular beasts that looked like a cross between a shaggy horse and a wild boar.

Luthien and Oliver swung about and kicked their mounts ahead, but out of the wheat came two more cyclopians, one appearing right next to Oliver, and one further down the road.

Oliver reared Threadbare and turned the pony to the side as the cyclopian mount bore down upon him. The intelligent yellow pony kicked out with its forelegs, smacking the cyclopian's arms and sword. Threadbare did no real damage, but did distract the brute, and Oliver, lying low in the saddle, slipped his rapier in under the pony's kicking feet.

The engaged cyclopian never saw the blade coming. It squealed and tried to move away, but the rapier had already done its business. The ponypig continued past Oliver and Threadbare, and Oliver, just to make sure, caught the cyclopian's sword with his main gauche and tossed it away.

The cyclopian was oblivious to that move, though, slumping forward in its saddle, darkness filling its eye.

Further down the road, Luthien angled Riverdancer for a close pass at the charging ponypig. Luthien lifted his sword; the cyclopian leveled a spear.

The one-eye seemed to have the advantage with its longer weapon, and thought it would score a solid hit as the two began their pass.

But Luthien's sword came down, around and inside the tip of the spear. The rolling motion brought the spear out wide, and then high, leaving Luthien's sword across the neck of the snorting ponypig. The young warrior reversed his grip suddenly, turning the blade in line, and its fine edge gashed the cyclopian's forearms and forced the brute to fall back as the two passed.

Luthien kept the pressure firm, forcing the cyclopian right over backward, to land heavily on the dirt road. The brute looked up just in time to see Oliver bearing down on it, and it dropped its face and covered its head with its wounded arms, expecting to be trampled.

Oliver had no time to finish the job, though. With a score of cyclopians bearing down from behind, the halfling could not risk getting tangled in this one's breaking limbs. With a bit of urging, Threadbare cleared the prone cyclopian and thundered on down the road in Riverdancer's wake.

The chase was on, with arrows flying everywhere, and though Oliver's claims about a cyclopian's ability to judge distance were certainly true, the simple rules of chance told both the halfling and Luthien that they were in trouble.

Luthien felt Riverdancer stumble for just a moment and knew that the horse had taken an arrow in the rump. Another bolt came dangerously close, nicking the young man's shoulder.

"Off the road?" Luthien cried out, wondering if he and Oliver should take to the high wheat stalks for cover. Oliver shook his head, though. Horses, even a pony such as Threadbare, could outrun ponypigs on clear ground, but the grunting cyclopian mounts could plow through brush faster than any creature. Besides, the halfling pointed out to Luthien, wheat stalks on both sides of the road were already whipping violently as more cyclopians joined in the chase.

"This merchant-type," Oliver called out, "he really cannot take a joke!"

Luthien had no time to respond, seeing a cyclopian coming out of the tall wheat ahead on his side of the road. He ducked low along Riverdancer's muscled neck and urged the horse forward. Riverdancer lowered his head, too, and gave a short burst of speed. Luthien felt the wind of a waving sword, but he was by the cyclopian too fast for the brute to score a hit.

Then the young man let up a bit and allowed Oliver to catch up beside him. They were in this together, Luthien decided, but he didn't see how either one of them was going to get out of it. More cyclopians were coming out onto the road ahead, and any delay at all would allow those behind the companions to overtake them.

Luthien looked over at Oliver—and nearly laughed aloud, seeing an arrow sticking through the halfling's great hat.

"Farewell!" the young Bedwyr cried, to which Oliver only smiled.

But both of them gawked when they looked ahead once again, for a translucent field of shimmering blue light had appeared on the road before them. Both the halfling and Luthien cried out in surprise and terror, thinking this some sort of devilish cyclopian magic, and tried to turn their mounts aside. Oliver plucked his great hat from his head and held it over his face.

They were too close, their momentum too great, and Riverdancer, and then Threadbare, plunged into the light.

All the world changed.

They were in a corridor of light now, everything appearing dreamlike to Luthien, as though he and Oliver were moving in slow motion. But when the young man looked at the world around or the ground below, he saw that he was moving at tremendous speed—every one of Riverdancer's slow-moving strides took him across great distances.

The corridor of light veered off the road, turning south across the wheat fields, though the passing of the two mounts did not disturb the grain. It was as if they were running in the air, or on a cushion of light, not touching the ground at all, and their mounts' hooves made not a sound. They came upon a wide river and moved across it, above it, without a splash. In a few seconds, the mountains loomed much closer, and then they were speeding up the slopes, crossing ravines as though the great valleys were but cracks in a stone.

A sheer cliff loomed ahead of them suddenly, and Luthien cried out again, though his words were lost behind him as they left his mouth. Straight up the cliff Riverdancer and Threadbare ran, cresting its top a thousand feet up and running across the broken boulder-strewn ground, through a copse of small trees too tightly packed for any horse to pass. Yet they did pass—without shaking a twig or leaf.

Soon Luthien saw another cliff face looming before them, and the light tunnel seemed to end there, with swirling patterns of blue and green dancing on the cliff wall. Before Luthien could even react, Riverdancer crossed into the stone.

Luthien felt the pressure building all about him: an uncomfortable, suffocating feeling. He could not cry out, could not even draw breath in that supremely enclosed place, and he thought he would surely perish.

But then, suddenly and without warning, Riverdancer came through the other side of the rock wall, stepping lightly into a torchlit cave, the horse's hooves clacking loudly on the hard stone.

Threadbare came out right behind, slowed and stopped beside the white horse, and Oliver, after a moment, dared to lower his great hat from his face and look around. He looked behind, too, staring incredulously at the stone wall as the swirling glow dissipated. The halfling turned to Luthien, who seemed as if he was about to speak.

"I do not even want to know," Oliver assured the young man.

CHAPTER 9

BRIND'AMOUR

IT APPEARED TO be a natural cave, somewhat circular and perhaps thirty feet in diameter. The walls were rough and uneven, and the ceiling dipped and rose to varying heights, but the floor was smooth and fairly level. There was one door, wooden and unremarkable, across the way and to the left of the companions. Next to that stood a wooden table with many parchments, some in silvery tubes, some loose but rolled, and others held flat by strangely sculpted paperweights that resembled little gargoyles. Further to the left stood a singular pedestal with a perfect ball of pure and clear crystal resting atop it.

A chair rested against the wall to the companions' right in front of an immense desk with many shelves and cubbies rising above it. Like the table, it was covered with parchments. A human skull, a twisting treelike candelabra, a chain strung of what looked like preserved cyclopian eyes, and dozens of inkwells, vials, and long, feathery quills completed the image and told both friends beyond any doubt that they had come into a wizard's private chambers.

Both dismounted, and Oliver followed Luthien to have a look at Riverdancer's rump. The young Bedwyr breathed a sincere sigh of relief to learn that the arrow had only grazed his valued horse and had not caused any serious wound.

He nodded to Oliver that the horse was all right, then started off toward the intriguing crystal ball while his halfling companion scampered for the desk. "No mischief," Luthien warned, for he had heard many tales of dangerous wizards in his youth and figured that any magician powerful enough to create the light tunnel that brought them here would not be a wise choice for an enemy.

Luthien's wonderment at the strange turn of events only heightened when he looked into the crystal ball. There he was! And Oliver, too, moving about the cave. He saw Threadbare and Riverdancer standing easily, resting from their long run. At first, Luthien thought it was merely a reflection, but he realized that the perspective was all wrong. He seemed to be looking down upon himself from the ceiling.

Over at the desk, Oliver slipped a vial into his pocket.

"Put it back!" Luthien scolded, seeing the halfling's every move within the crystal ball.

Oliver regarded him curiously—how could he know?

"Put it back," Luthien said again when the halfling made no move. He glared over his shoulder.

"Are you so quick to give up such treasures?" Oliver asked, reluctantly taking the small vial from his pocket and holding it up before his eyes. "The ingredients could be most exotic, you know. This is a wizard's house, after all."

"A wizard who saved us," Luthien reminded the thief.

With a deep sigh, Oliver placed the vial back in its place atop the desk.

"Your gratitude is appreciated," came a voice from right beside Luthien. He stared at the empty spot in amazement, then fell back a step as a pattern of the wall seemed to shift. Out from the stones stepped the wizard, his color at first the exact hue of the stone, but gradually reverting to pale flesh tones.

He was old, as old as Luthien's father at least, but held himself straight and with a grace that impressed the young Bedwyr. His thick and flowing robes were rich blue in color, and his hair and beard were white—snowy white, like Riverdancer's silken coat—and flowing all about his shoulders. His eyes, too, were blue, as deep and rich as the robe, and sparkling with life and wisdom. Crow's feet angled out from their corners—from endless hours of poring over parchments, Luthien figured.

When he finally managed to tear his gaze from the robed man, Luthien looked back to see that Oliver was similarly impressed.

"Who are you?" the halfling asked.

"It is not important."

Oliver plucked his hat from his head, beginning a graceful bow. "I am—"

"Oliver Burrows, who calls himself Oliver deBurrows," the wizard interrupted. "Yes, yes, of course you are, but that, too, is not important." He looked at Luthien, as if expecting the young man to introduce himself, but Luthien just crossed his arms resolutely, even defiantly.

"Your father misses you dearly," the wizard remarked, breaking down Luthien's fabricated defenses with a simple statement.

Oliver skipped up beside Luthien, lending support and needing it as well.

"I have been watching the two of you for some time," the wizard explained, slowly moving past them toward the desk. "You have proven yourselves both resourceful and courageous, just the two characteristics I require."

"For what?" Oliver managed to ask. The wizard turned toward him, hand outstretched, and with a shrug to Luthien, the halfling tossed the repocketed vial to him.

"For what?" Luthien asked immediately, impatiently, not wanting to get sidetracked and wanting to keep the dangerous wizard's mind off of Oliver's trickery.

"Patience, my boy!" the robed man replied lightheartedly, seeming not at all offended by the halfling's attempted theft. He stared at the vial for a moment, then offered a smirk at the halfling.

Oliver sighed and shrugged again, then took a similar vial out of his pocket and tossed it to the wizard.

"I always keep spares," the halfling explained to a confused Luthien.

"Several, it would seem," the wizard said, somewhat sharply, holding his hand out once more.

A third sigh came from Oliver, and this time the proper vial was flipped across the room. With a quick glance, the wizard replaced it on the desk and pocketed Oliver's other vials.

"Now," he said, rubbing his hands together and approaching the pair, "I have a proposition for you."

"In Gascony, we do not take well to wizard-types," Oliver remarked.

The wizard stopped and considered the words. "Well," he replied, "I did save your life."

Luthien started to agree, but Oliver cut him off short.

"Bah!" the halfling snorted. "They were only one-eyes. Those we could not outrun would have felt the very wicked sting of my rapier blade!"

The wizard gave Luthien a skeptical look; the young man had no reply.

"Very well," said the wizard. He motioned to the wall and the swirling blue light began anew. "On your mounts, then. It has only been a minute or two. The cyclopians will likely still be about."

Luthien scowled at Oliver, and when the halfling shrugged in defeat, the wizard smiled and dispelled the magical portal.

"I was only bargaining for the best price," the halfling explained in a whisper.

"Price?" balked the wizard. "I just plucked you from certain doom!" He shook his head and sighed. "Very well, then," he said after a moment of thought. "If that is not enough for your service, I will give to you passes into Montfort and information that might keep you alive once you get there. Also, I think that I might be able to convince this merchant you robbed that his continued pursuit of you would not be worth the trouble. And the favor I ask, though undoubtedly dangerous, will not take so long."

"Explain it," Luthien said firmly.

"Over dinner, of course," the wizard replied, motioning to the wooden door.

Oliver rubbed his hands—now the man was talking in terms that he could agree to—and turned for the door, but Luthien stood resolute, arms crossed over his chest and jaw firm.

"I'll not dine with one who will not give his name," the young Bedwyr insisted.

"More for me," Oliver remarked.

"It is not important," the wizard said again.

Luthien didn't blink.

The wizard moved to stand right before him, staring him in the eyes, neither man blinking. "Brind'Amour," the robed man said, and the gravity of his tone made Luthien wonder if he should know that name.

"And I am Luthien Bedwyr," the young man replied evenly, his eyes staring intently as if daring the wizard to interrupt.

Brind'Amour did not, though, allowing the young man the honor of a proper introduction.

The table in the adjoining room was simply spectacular, set for three, including one place with a higher chair.

"We were expected," Oliver remarked dryly, but as he approached the table and saw the display set out, he had no further demeaning comments. Fine silverware and crystal goblets, cloth napkins, and plates fine and smooth were set and ready for the meal. Oliver was, too, judging from the way he hustled over and hopped up into the high seat.

Brind'Amour moved to the side of the room, an artificial chamber with bricked walls, very different from the one they had left behind. He opened several secret cupboards, their doors blending perfectly with the bricks, and brought out the courses—roasted duck and several exotic vegetables, fine wine, and clear, cold water.

"Surely a wizard could have conjured a servant," Luthien remarked after he had taken his seat, "or clapped his hands and let the plates float across to the table."

Brind'Amour chuckled at the notion. "I may have need of my powers later this day," he explained. "The use of magical energy is taxing, I assure you, and it would be a pity indeed if our quest failed because I was too lazy to walk over and bring out the food!"

Luthien let the explanation go at that. He was hungry, and besides, he realized that any important conversation he might now hold with Brind'Amour would only have to be repeated for Oliver's sake. The halfling was practically buried in a bowl of turnips at the moment.

By the time he lifted his glass of wine for a final sip, Luthien had to admit that Brind'Amour had set the finest table he had ever known.

"Perhaps we in Gascony should give another look to our wizard-types," Oliver remarked, patting his fattened belly in whole-hearted agreement with Luthien's thoughts.

"Yes, you could appoint them chefs in every town," Brind'Amour replied with good-hearted sarcasm. "What else would a wizard have to do?" he asked of Luthien, trying to draw the young Bedwyr into the casual conversation.

Luthien nodded but remained distant from the banter as Oliver and Brind'Amour went back and forth, with Oliver recounting the tale of an adventure he had experienced in a wizard's tower, and Brind'Amour adding some detail to Oliver's descriptions and generally nodding and gasping at the appropriately polite places. Now that the meal was done and the formal introductions were at their end, Luthien was anxious to focus on the task at hand. Brind'Amour had saved them from the cyclopians, and passes to Montfort (the last chance he figured he might have of ever catching up with Ethan), as well as getting that merchant off their backs, was a reward the young man could not ignore.

"You mentioned a task," Luthien was finally able to interject. The ease of the conversation disappeared in the blink of a halfling's eye. "Over dinner, I believe you said, but now dinner is over."

"I did not think that I could get my words in above the clamor of an eager halfling guest," Brind'Amour said with a strained smile.

"Oliver is done," the stern and determined Luthien remarked.

Brind'Amour sat back in his chair. He clapped his hands and a long-stemmed pipe floated out of a cubby, lighting as it approached the man, then settling gently into his waiting hand. Luthien understood that the magical display was for his benefit, a subtle reminder that Brind'Amour was in control here.

"I have lost something," the wizard said after several long draws on the pipe. "Something very valuable to me."

"I do not have it," Oliver remarked, clapping his hands.

Brind'Amour gave him a friendly gaze. "I know where it is," he explained.

"Then it is not lost." This time, the halfling's humor did not evoke any appreciative response from Brind'Amour or from Luthien. The young Bedwyr could see the pain on the old man's wizened face.

"It is in a great sealed cave complex not so far from here," he said.

"Sealed?" Luthien asked.

"By myself and several companions," Brind'Amour answered, "four hundred years ago, before the Gascons came to the Avonsea Islands, when the name of Bruce MacDonald was still prominent on every tongue in Eriador."

Luthien started to respond, then stopped, stunned by the implications of what he had just heard.

"You should be dead," Oliver remarked, and Luthien scowled fiercely at him.

Brind'Amour took no offense, though. He even nodded his agreement with the halfling. "All of my companions are long buried," he explained. "I live only because I have spent many years in magical stasis." He waved his hands suddenly, wildly, indicating that he needed a change of subject, that they had gotten off the issue at hand.

Luthien could see that the man was plainly uncomfortable.

"The world might be a simpler place if I was dead, Oliver Burrows," Brind'Amour went on. "Of course, then you two would also be dead," he pointedly reminded them, drawing a tip of the hat from Oliver.

"My task for you is simple," the wizard explained. "I have lost something—you are to go to the caves and retrieve it."

"It?" both friends asked together.

The wizard hesitated.

"We must know what we are looking for," Luthien reasoned.

"A staff," Brind'Amour admitted. "My staff. As precious as anything I own."

"Then how did you come to leave it in this cave?" Oliver wondered.

"And why did you seal the cave?" Luthien added.

"I did not leave it in the cave," Brind'Amour replied rather sharply. "It was stolen from me and placed there not so long ago. But that is another story, and one that does not concern you in the least."

"But . . ." Oliver began, but he quieted as soon as Brind'Amour's dangerous scowl settled on him.

"As for the cave, it was sealed to keep its inhabitants from roaming Eriador," the wizard said to Luthien.

"And what were they?" Luthien pressed.

"The king of the cyclopians and his mightiest warriors," Brind'Amour replied evenly. "We feared that he would ally with the Gascons, since we knew that they would soon be on our shores."

Luthien stared hard at the old man, not sure he believed the explanation. Oliver was even more doubtful. Gascons hated cyclopians more than did Eriadorans, if that was possible, and any potential alliance between the people of the southern kingdom and the one-eyes seemed unlikely at best.

Also, Luthien could not begin to fathom why such extreme measures would have been taken against a race that had been savaged not so long before that. Bruce MacDonald's victory had been complete, bordering on genocide, and as far as the young Bedwyr knew, the cyclopian race hadn't fully recovered to this day.

"Now, with any luck, the cave is uninhabited," Brind'Amour said hopefully, obviously trying to press on past that last point.

"Then why do you not go there and retrieve your so precious staff?" Oliver asked.

"I am old," Brind'Amour replied, "and weak. I cannot hold open the portal from here, my source of power, if I go through the tunnel to that other cave. And so I need your help—help for which you have already been, and will yet be, well paid."

Luthien continued to study the wizard for some time, sensing that what the man had said was not true, or not the whole truth. Still, he had no more specific questions to ask, and Oliver simply sat back in his chair and patted his tummy. They had ridden far that day, fought on the road, and eaten well.

"I offer you now the comfort of warm and soft beds," Brind'Amour promised, sensing the mood. "Rest well. Our business can wait until the morn."

The companions readily accepted, and after a quick check on Threadbare and Riverdancer, who had been put in an empty chamber to the side of the library, they were soon nestled comfortably in featherbeds, and Brind'Amour left them alone.

"Four hundred years old?" Oliver asked Luthien.

"I do not question the words and ways of wizards," Luthien replied.

"But does not this magical stasis intrigue you?"

"No." It was a simple and honest answer. Luthien had been raised among pragmatic and solid fisherfolk and farmers. The only magic prominent at all on Bedwydrin were the herbs of healing women and premonitions of weather conditions offered to the captains of fishing boats by the dock seers. Even those two rather benign magic-using groups made Luthien uncomfortable—a man like Brind'Amour put the young man totally out of his element.

"And I do not understand why a cave holding nothing more than a cyclopian—"

Luthien cut Oliver off with a wave of his hand.

"And who would steal a wizard's staff?" Oliver put in quickly, before Luthien waved his words away once more.

"Let us just be done with this task and be on with our—" Luthien began, and then he paused at an obvious impasse.

"With our what?" Oliver prompted, and wondered, and young Luthien wondered, too.

What would he and Oliver Burrows, who called himself Oliver deBurrows, get on with? Their quest? Their lives? The road to continued thievery and, perhaps, worse?

The young Bedwyr had no answers—either for what would come, or for what had just passed. Ever since the arrival of Viscount Aubrey and his entourage in Dun Varna, Luthien's world had been turned upside down. He had left Dun

Varna in search of his brother, but now he was beginning to get a feel of just how big the world truly was. Over the last couple of days, Oliver had explained to him that ships left the Avonsea Islands for Gascony by a dozen different ports, from Carlisle on the Stratton River to Montfort. And Gascony was a bigger place than Avon, Oliver assured his unworldly companion, with hundreds of cities larger than Dun Varna and scores larger even than Carlisle. And Duree, the land of the war Ethan was supposedly going off to fight, was over a thousand miles south of Gascony's northern coast.

A thousand miles!

How could Luthien hope to catch up to Ethan when he didn't know what course his brother might take?

Luthien never answered Oliver's question; and the halfling, soon snoring contentedly, didn't seem anxious to know.

CHAPTER 10

WHITE LIES?

THE FIRST THING that Oliver and Luthien noticed when they exited Brind'Amour's new magical tunnel was that the cave they had entered was uncomfortably warm. And it was huge. Luthien's torch reflected off of one wall only, the one they had exited, and the two could barely see the crystalline glimmer of the sharp-tipped, long stalactites hanging ominously far above their heads.

There came a flash from behind them, and they turned to see Brind'Amour's portal beginning to shrink. At first, the two scrambled for the light, thinking the wizard meant to desert them. The swirl continued, diminished to the size of a fist, but its light was no less intense.

"He only wishes to make sure that no cyclopians, if they live, could come through," a relieved Oliver remarked.

"Or to make sure that we do not come through until we have found the staff," Luthien added. "He has that crystal ball and will watch our every move."

Luthien moved over to the wall again as he spoke, studying its curious texture. He hadn't been in many caves—only the wizard's and the sea caves along the rocky coast near Dun Varna—but still, this one seemed somehow strange to him. The rock of the walls was coppery in color and rough, as Luthien would expect, but interwoven with it were lines of a darker hue, smooth to the touch.

"Melted ore," Oliver explained, coming to join him. The halfling looked up and all around. "Copper, I would guess. Separated from the stone by some very large heat."

Luthien, too, studied the area. "This must be where the wizards sealed the cave," he decided. "Perhaps they used magical fires to create the avalanche." It seemed to be as much a question as a statement.

"That must be it," Oliver agreed, but he, too, did not sound convinced. He tapped the stone gently with the pommel of his main gauche, trying to gauge its density. From what he could tell, the wall was very thick. That, in turn, led him to the conclusion that something on this side of the wall had caused the heat, but he kept his thoughts private.

"Come along," the halfling muttered. "I do not wish to be in here any longer than is necessary." He paused and looked at Luthien, who was still studying the melted ore, and got the feeling that the intelligent young man's reasoning was following the same trail as had his own. "Not with so many fattened purses awaiting my eager grasp in Montfort," he added a bit too loudly, for echoes came back at him from several directions. His words took Luthien's thoughts from the wall, though, as he had hoped.

No sense in worrying, Oliver believed.

The floor was uneven and dotted by rows of stalagmites, many taller than Luthien. Even though this area was a single chamber, at times it seemed to the two as if they were walking along narrow corridors. Shadows from Luthien's flickering torch surrounded them ominously, keeping them tense, continually glancing from side to side.

They came to a steeply sloping area, and in the open area below they could see that a path had been made through the stalagmites—trampled, it seemed, with great hunks of broken stone scattered all about.

"The traveling will be easier," Luthien remarked hopefully. He gingerly started down the slope, leaning back so far that he was practically sitting down.

Oliver grabbed him by the shoulder and tugged hard.

"Do you not even wonder what broke those things?" the halfling asked grimly.

It was a question that Luthien preferred not to answer, not even to think about. "Come along," was all that he replied, and he resumed his controlled slide to the lower level.

"Wizard-types," Oliver muttered under his breath, and with a last look back to the now-distant wall and the wizard's portal, he shrugged and followed the young man.

When Oliver stopped his descent and looked up once more, he found Luthien standing very still, staring off to the side, looking over one broken stalagmite.

"What . . ." the halfling started to ask, but he got his answer as he came up beside Luthien. Pieces of skeletons lay broken behind the rocky pile. Both the friends looked about nervously, as if expecting some horrid and powerful monster to rush out and squash them.

"Human," Oliver remarked as he moved over to investigate, holding up a skull that showed two eye sockets. "Not cyclopian."

They pieced together three bodies in all, but only two skulls, for the third had apparently been smashed into a thousand pieces. There was little more than whitened bone, but it didn't seem to either of the companions that these corpses had been here for all that long, certainly not four hundred years. One of the legs, buried under some rock, showed ligaments and pieces of skin, and the clothing, though tattered, was not so rotted.

"We might not be the first group Brind'Amour has sent in search of his staff," Luthien remarked.

"And whatever was in here lives still," Oliver added. He looked around at the toppled stalagmites and the crushed skull. "I do not think cyclopians could have done this," he reasoned. "Not even a cyclopian king."

First the melted ore along the wall, then the line of broken rock mounds, and now this. A sense of dread dropped over the companions. Luthien replayed Brind'Amour's words about the cave in his mind. In light of these new discoveries, it seemed to Luthien that the wizard was indeed lying, or not telling the whole truth.

But what could Luthien and Oliver do now? The portal offered them no escape unless Brind'Amour widened it, and Luthien knew that the wizard would not do that until they had recovered his lost staff.

"If the staff is so valuable, then we should expect to find it among the treasures of whatever rules this place," Luthien said determinedly. "And this trail of rubble should lead us to it."

"How fine," Oliver replied.

The trail soon led them out of the vast chamber and they moved down a wide corridor. Both walls were within the area of torchlight then, and they could see the ceiling as well. That offered them little comfort, though, for whatever had come through this passage had not only flattened stalagmite mounds but had broken short the hanging stalactites, as well.

The air seemed to be growing even warmer in here, and the walls shone a deep crimson. After a few hundred yards, the corridor dipped suddenly, turning almost vertical for a few feet, until it widened into a chamber on a more level but still descending slope. Luthien skidded down first, Oliver coming close behind.

They had come to the banks of an underground pool, its still waters shimmering a dull red and orange in the reflections of the light. The torch seemed much brighter in here, for the walls were lined with quartz and other crystals. Across the pool, the companions could see the entrance to another corridor, running generally along the same direction they had been traveling.

Luthien bent low over the water and reached out his hand slowly, tentatively. He could feel the heat of the rising steam, and he dared to gently touch the pool, retracting his hand immediately.

"Why is it so very hot?" Oliver asked. "We are high up in the mountains—there is snow on peaks not so far from here."

"Are we?" Luthien replied, reminding the halfling that they really didn't know where the wizard's tunnel had led them.

Oliver stared at the lake. It was only a hundred feet across and perhaps twice that wide, but it seemed at that moment to be an impenetrable barrier. Perhaps even the end of the road, for it filled the floor of the chamber, and the halfling, who was not so fond of water in the first place, had no intention of swimming across.

"There is a way around," Luthien noticed. He pointed to the left to a ledge running along the wall about ten feet above the water level.

Oliver did not seem thrilled by the prospect of the narrow ledge. He dropped his traveling pack to the ground and fumbled with its straps, ignoring the questions Luthien put his way. A few moments later, the halfling produced a long, thin, almost translucent cord and a three-pointed grappling hook.

The ceiling was not so high in here, no more than thirty feet in most areas, and it was broken and uneven, full of jags and cracks. Oliver put the grappling hook into a spin at the end of the rope, then sent it flying away, high over the lake. It banged against the ceiling, but found no hold and dropped into the water with a resounding *ka-thunk.*

Luthien stared hard at the halfling as the echoes of the splash died away, neither companion daring to move for several seconds.

"I only thought—" Oliver started to explain.

"Get it back," Luthien interrupted, and Oliver began slowly reeling in the line. It came easily, and Oliver explained that he wanted it up on the ceiling so that he could carry the end as he crossed the ledge—in case one of them slipped, or they were forced to get away quickly.

The reasoning seemed sound to Luthien, and it appeared as if Oliver's errant throw had not done any damage. The rope was still coming easily, and the grappling hook couldn't be very far from shore. Then it stopped suddenly, resisting Oliver's strongest tugs.

Luthien and the halfling looked at each other curiously, then Luthien took hold and pulled, too. The rope held fast seeming as though the grappling hook had snared on something along the lake bottom.

"Cut the line and let us be on our way," Luthien offered, and Oliver, though he prized that fine and light cord and hated to lose any part of it, reluctantly reached for his main gauche.

Suddenly the halfling was jerked forward. He instinctively grabbed the rope in both hands, then, realizing that he could not resist the pull and would be taken into the lake, loosened his grasp. Only Oliver's well-made leather gauntlets saved him from serious rope burns as the cord whipped along. The halfling looked back at the coiled and rapidly diminishing pile and began hopping all about, calling for Luthien to do something.

But what could Luthien do? He braced himself and bent low, as if trying to catch the flying rope, but never took the chance, knowing that he could not possibly break its tremendous momentum.

Oliver had started with over a hundred feet of the cord, and it was nearly gone. But then, without warning, the furious pulling suddenly stopped.

The halfling stopped, too, and stood staring at Luthien and at the cord.

"Big fish in this pond," the halfling remarked.

Luthien had no answer, just stood staring out over the lake as the waters flattened to stillness once more. Finally, the young Bedwyr mustered the nerve to reach down and grab the cord. He pulled gently, taking in the rope hand over hand, expecting it to be pulled away again at any moment.

His surprise (and Oliver's, as well) was complete when the grappling hook appeared, covered with brown and red weeds. Luthien lifted it up and cleaned it so that he and Oliver could inspect it. One of the prongs was bent a bit, but it showed no other marks and no sign of flesh or scales or anything else that might indicate what had taken it.

"Big fish who do not so much like the taste of iron," Oliver said with a half-hearted chuckle. "Let us get to the ledge and along our way."

But now Luthien wasn't so sure of that course. He eyed the ceiling and, seeing a spot where two stalactites were joined, forming an inverted arch, he spun the grappling hook above his head.

"Do not lose my so fine rope!" Oliver protested, but before he finished his thought, Luthien let it fly. The hook soared through the gap and came back down on the other side, and when Luthien pulled the cord taut, the hook stuck firmly.

"Now we can go across," Luthien explained.

Oliver shrugged and let Luthien lead the way.

The path along the edge of the lake took them right to the ledge, and soon they were moving steadily, if slowly, along the ledge, ten feet up from the water. The lake remained quiet for a short while, but then Oliver noticed subtle ripples lapping gently against the base of the stone wall.

"Faster," the halfling whispered, but Luthien was already moving as fast as he could. The ledge was no more than a foot wide in many places, and the wall behind it was uneven, sometimes forcing Luthien to arch his back so that he could slip around thick jags.

A moment later, Oliver's urgency was reaffirmed as the two heard the water lapping harder at the base of the wall, and then a spot perhaps thirty feet out from the wall began to churn and bubble.

"What?" Oliver asked incredulously as a column of water rose half a dozen feet into the air, as though something beneath the surface was displacing a tremendous amount of the lake.

And then it smoothed, or seemed to smooth, until the halfling and Luthien realized that they were staring not at the surface of the lake but rather at the curving shell of a gigantic turtle.

The halfling squeaked, and Luthien tried to pick up the pace as the giant glided in. Its head, with a mouth big enough to swallow poor Oliver whole, lifted high out of the water eyeing the scrambling companions dangerously.

Ten feet from the ledge, the head shot forward suddenly on an impossibly long neck. Oliver cried out again and fell back, poking with his rapier. The turtle missed, biting instead a piece of the ledge, and actually chipping the stone!

The great reptilian body turned to keep pace with the halfling. It came forward again, and Oliver started to dodge, but he was grabbed suddenly as Luthien ran back the other way and scooped him into his strong arms.

The ledge was too narrow for such tactics, but Luthien had no intention of even trying to keep his balance. He leaped off and out, just in front of the rushing turtle head, holding tight to Oliver and holding tight to the rope. The turtle whipped its head to the side, but the angle for the snapping maw was not right, and though the head banged hard against Luthien pushing the companions on, the turtle could not bite down.

"Lucky turtle!" Oliver cried, braver now that he was fast swinging out of the monster's reach. "I would make of you a fine soup, such as we have in Gascony!"

They swung in a wide arc, circling close to where they had first come down to the lake, then onward in a loop that took them all the way to the other side. Luthien was no novice with such rope swings; as a boy on Bedwydrin, he had spent his summers swinging out across the sheltered bays near to Dun Varna. He had wisely grabbed the rope up as high as he could before leaping from the ledge, but still the two would have dipped into the water if they had come near to the spot directly below the grappling hook. Only the momentum inadvertently given to them by the banging turtle head saved them from that fate, and still Luthien had to tuck his feet up to keep them clear.

As they rose on the backswing, Luthien slid a bit down the cord, extending their range. He had to let go altogether, taking a screaming Oliver with him, as they fell the dozen feet to splash into the shallow waters near to the yellowish spongy ground on the lake's opposite shore.

Luthien scrambled up first, grabbing the rope and taking it with him as far as its length would allow. He tripped and almost lost it, instinctively swinging it hard toward a cluster of large rocks. Luck was with the young man, for the rope looped about these rocks enough so that it did not slide back into the water. Luthien regained his footing and his composure and went for the rope as Oliver ran past him toward the back exit.

Luthien skidded to an abrupt halt, though, as the turtle's head came back out of the water not so far away. To the young man's utter amazement, the creature opened wide its maw and breathed out a cloud of steam.

Luthien fell back to the ground, saved only by the surrounding boulders that protected him from the full force of the scalding breath. He came up sweating, his face bright red, and ran toward Oliver, who was signaling frantically from the exit. Into the corridor they ran, pausing just inside to look back toward the water.

The pond was still once more, with no sign of the giant turtle.

"My rope?" Oliver asked, looking at the cord, which was securely looped about the rock.

"On the way out," Luthien replied.

"We may need it."

"Then you go get it."

Oliver looked doubtfully at the cord and at the deceptively quiet lake. "On the way out," he agreed, even though both he and Luthien hoped to find a different way back to the wizard's tunnel.

The halfling's demeanor changed considerably when the two companions had put the lake farther behind them. The going was easier on this side, with the cave floors relatively flat and clear of stalagmites and rubble.

"Now we know what caused the problems to those who came before us," Oliver insisted hopefully, even cheerily "And we have left the beast in a lake behind us."

"A lake that we will have to cross once more," Luthien reminded him.

"Perhaps," Oliver conceded, "perhaps not. Once we have found the wizard-type's most valuable staff, he will come to get us, do not doubt."

"Have you considered that the staff might be in the lake?" Luthien had to ask. He did not think this the time for celebration or that all of the dangers had passed.

Oliver did not answer the pragmatic young man directly. He just began muttering about "lying wizard-types" and scoffing at the notion that this cave had been sealed to entrap a cyclopian king. The quiet tirade went on for many minutes as the friends crossed through several unremarkable chambers and adjoining corridors. Oliver even expanded his grumbling to include "merchant-types," "king-types," and several other types that Luthien had never heard of. The young Bedwyr let the halfling ramble, knowing that he really could do little to stop Oliver's momentum.

But the sight that greeted the two as they entered one large, domelike chamber certainly did.

Oliver stood as if stricken, Luthien, too, as the torchlight was reflected back at them from a pile of gold and silver, gems and jewels, beyond anything either of them had ever seen before. One mound of silver and gold was as high as two tall men, dotted with glittering crystals and precious artifacts—goblets and jeweled serving utensils—probably dwarvish in make. As if in a trance, the two moved into the chamber.

Oliver shook the stunning surprise out of his head and ran toward the pile, stuffing his pockets, tossing coins into the air and climbing around with unbridled glee.

"We have come for something specific," Luthien reminded him, "and we will never get out of here carrying much of this."

Oliver didn't seem to care, and Luthien had to admit that this all seemed too good to pass up. There were no other apparent exits from the room, and they had traveled along the most open and easily accessible trail. It seemed that this was either the turtle's hoard—and the turtle showed no indication of following them—or the hoard of a long-dead king, perhaps the cyclopian Brind'Amour had spoken of. But "duty first," Luthien's father had always told him, and that advice seemed pertinent now with so many obvious distractions lying about.

"The staff, Oliver," he called out once more. "Then you can have your play."

From the top of the largest mound of coins, Oliver, the world's happiest thief, stuck his green-gloved thumbs in his ears, waggled his fingers and stuck out his tongue in Luthien's direction.

Luthien was about to scold him once more, but something caught the young man's attention. He noticed a large cloth sack off to the right of where he was standing, on the lower slope of another of the mounds. Luthien was certain that the sack hadn't been there a moment ago.

He looked up the mound, up to the ceiling above it, searching for some perch from which it might have fallen. Nothing was evident. Luthien was not surprised, for if it had fallen, or slid down the mound of coins, he certainly would have heard the movement. With a shrug, he walked the few feet and bent over the sack. He poked at it with his sword, then hooked the weapon into the drawstring, working it back and forth. Convinced that the sack wasn't trapped, Luthien lay his torch on the pile, grabbed the sack's top and pulled it open.

He found a beautiful crimson cape, richer in color, even in the dim torchlight, than anything the young Bedwyr had ever seen. With it was a rectangular piece of wood: two sticks side by side, curving at the ends in opposite directions. As soon as be took the piece out and saw that it was hinged, Luthien recognized it as a bow. He unfolded it, aligned the pieces, and found a pin hanging from a string on it that settled into a central notch and secured the weapon. A small compartment on one end concealed the bowstring of fine and strong gut.

Luthien drew out the silken cape and draped it around his shoulders, even putting up the hood. He picked the sack up next, inspecting it carefully to see if it held any more remarkable items.

It was truly empty, but Luthien then noticed a quiver beneath it, small and sleek and on a belt that would indicate it should be worn on the hip, not on the back. It contained only a handful of arrows. There was one more longer arrow lying next to it, a curious sight indeed, for the last few inches of the shaft, just below the small head, were cylindrical and nearly as thick as Luthien's forearm. Surprisingly, the arrow still seemed somewhat balanced when Luthien picked it up. He studied it more closely and found that the notched end, near the fletching, was metallic, not wood, a counterbalance to the thick end near to the tip. Even with its balance, though, Luthien doubted that he could shoot the weighty and less-than-sleek arrow very far.

"You mean this very same wizard-type's staff?" he heard Oliver shout out, drawing him from his contemplations. "Luthien?"

Luthien pushed back the cape's hood and rushed to the large mound as Oliver slid the oaken staff down its side.

"Ah, there you are," the halfling remarked. He eyed Luthien suspiciously. The young Bedwyr put one arm on his hip, held the strange bow in the other and posed in the new cloak.

Oliver held his hands up, not knowing what he should say. "Now I might play," he replied instead, and he skittered down to the floor some distance to Luthien's left.

Oliver stopped abruptly, staring down at the floor, caught by what appeared to be the shadows of a group of men, their arms held up in front of them as though warding away some danger. Oliver bent to touch the shadowy images, discovering to his horror that they were comprised of ashes.

"You know," the halfling began, standing straight and looking back at Luthien, "in Gascony we have tales of treasures such as this, and every time, they are accompanied by . . ."

The great mound of silver and gold shifted suddenly and fell apart, coins rattling and bouncing to every part of the large chamber. Oliver and Luthien looked up into the slitted eyes of a very angry dragon.

"Yes," the halfling finished, pointing at the great beast, "that is it."

CHAPTER 11

BALTHAZAR

LUTHIEN HAD LIVED his life beside the oceans of the great whales, had seen the bodies of giants taken down from the mountains by his father's soldiers, had nearly been bitten apart by the monstrous turtle in the other room. And he, like every other youth in Eriador and Avon, had heard many tales of the dragons and the brave men who slew them. But none of that could have prepared the young Bedwyr for this sight.

The great wyrm slowly uncoiled—was it a hundred feet long?—and rose up on its forelegs, towering over poor Oliver. Its yellow-green eyes shone like beacons, burning with inner fire, and its scales, reddish gold in hue and flecked with many coins and gemstones, which had become embedded during the beast's long sleep, were as solid as a wall of iron. How many weapons did this monster possess? Luthien wondered, awestricken. Its claws appeared as though they could rend the stone, its abundant teeth gleamed like ivory, as long as Luthien's sword, and its horns could skewer three men in a line. Luthien had heard tales of a dragon's fiery breath. He knew then what had melted the ore in the walls near where he and Oliver had entered, and knew, too, that it wasn't the turtle that had destroyed those stalagmites. The dragon had been there, four hundred years ago, and had taken out its frustration at being imprisoned.

And now it stood before Oliver, seething with rage.

"YOUR POCKETS BULGE WITH MY JEWELS, LITTLE THIEF!" the beast roared, the sheer strength of its voice blowing Oliver's hat to the back of his head.

Oliver unconsciously dropped his hands into his pockets. He kept his wits enough to slip aside from the ashen remains, away from the one spot in this chamber that was relatively clear of dragon treasure.

Luthien stood open-mouthed, amazed that this reptilian beast had spoken. Of course, the dragons of the ancient tales spoke to the heroes, but Luthien had considered that an embellishment on the part of the tale-teller. To hear such a monster, a giant winged lizard, speaking the language of the land was perhaps the most amazing thing of all.

"WELL?" the beast went on, still looking only at Oliver, as though it hadn't yet even noticed Luthien. "DO YOU NOT WISH TO BEG MIGHTY BALTHAZAR FOR YOUR PITIFUL LIFE?"

"I only wish to stare at the magnificence before me," Oliver replied suddenly. "I came in to find, so I thought, only the treasure, and that was magnificent indeed. So very magnificent."

Luthien could hardly believe that the halfling would make any references to the treasure, especially with so much of it obviously in his pockets. He could hardly believe that Oliver found any voice at all in the face of that wyrm!

"But it was not thoughts of your treasure that brought me here, mighty Balthazar," the halfling went on, trying to appear at ease. "It was to beg sight of you, of course. To let my eyes bask in the magnificence of the legend. You have slept away the centuries—there are not so many dragons about these days."

"IF THERE WERE MORE DRAGONS, THEN THERE WOULD LIKELY BE FEWER THIEVES!" the dragon answered, but Luthien noticed that there was some measure of calm in the monster's voice this time, as though Oliver's compliments were having some minor effect. The young Bedwyr had heard, too, of the vanity of dragons—and by the tales, the greater the dragon, the greater its conceit.

"I must humbly accept your description," Oliver admitted, and began emptying his pockets. Coins and jewels bounced on the floor at his feet. "But I did not know that you were still to be about. I only found a turtle—in a lake not so far away. Not so great a beast, but since I have never seen a dragon, I thought that it might be you."

Luthien's eyes widened, as did the dragon's, and the young man thought the wyrm would snap its serpentine neck forward and swallow the halfling whole.

"You can imagine my great disappointment," Oliver went on, before the wyrm could move to strike. "I had heard so very much about Balthazar, but if that turtle was you, then I did not think you worthy of such a treasure. Now I see my error, of course." The halfling stuck his hand deep into a pocket and produced a large gem, as if to accentuate his point, and calmly tossed it onto the nearest pile of treasure.

Balthazar's head swayed back and forth slowly, as if the beast was unsure of how to react. It stopped the motion briefly and sniffed the air, apparently catching a different scent.

"I do not wish to disturb your treasure and did not wish to disturb your sleep," Oliver said quickly, his facade of calm somewhat stripped away. "I only came to look upon you, that I might view the magnificence of a true dragon once in my—"

"LIAR!" Balthazar boomed, and Luthien's ears hurt from the volume. "LIAR AND THIEF!"

"If you breathe at me, you will surely ruin so very much of your gold!" Oliver cried back, skittering to the coin pile. "Am I worth such a price?"

But Balthazar didn't seem too worried about his treasure. It looked to Luthien as if the reptilian beast was actually smiling. It turned its head to put its huge maw directly in line with the halfling and hunched its armored shoulders so that its neck was partially coiled.

Then the beast straightened suddenly and sniffed again, and its great head snapped about—so quickly that the movement stole the strength from Luthien's knees—and dropped its lamplight vision over the young man.

Luthien stood perfectly still, frozen with the most profound terror he had ever known. This was the fabled dragon-gaze, a spellbinding fear that often fell over those who looked into the eyes of such a beast, but like the tales of a dragon's ability to speak, the young Bedwyr hadn't fully appreciated the notion.

He appreciated it now, though. His mind screamed at him to throw aside his weapons and run away, and truly he wanted to, but his body would not move, could not move.

The dragon looked away, back to Oliver, who was staring in Luthien's direction curiously.

"WHO IS WITH YOU?" the beast demanded.

"Not a one," Oliver answered firmly.

Luthien did not understand what they were talking about—they had both just looked right at him!

"LIAR!" Balthazar growled.

"You have already said that," Oliver replied. "Now, what are we to do? I have given back your treasure and I have gazed upon your magnificence. Are you to eat me, or am I to leave and tell all the world what a most magnificent dragon you truly are?"

The dragon backed off a bit, seeming perplexed.

"They have not seen you in four hundred years," Oliver explained. "The tales of Balthazar grow less, do not doubt. Of course, if I were to be gone from here, I could renew the legends."

Crafty Oliver! Luthien thought, and his admiration for the halfling increased a hundredfold in that moment. The mere fact that Oliver could speak under that terrible gaze impressed Luthien, whose own mouth was still cotton dry from fear.

The dragon issued a long and low growl. It sucked in its breath forcefully, straightening Oliver's hat on his head.

"Ah, ah," the halfling teased, wagging a finger in the air before him. "Do not breathe or you will ruin so very much of your gold and silver co-ins."

Luthien could hardly believe it, but the halfling seemed to have this situation in hand. The young man drew strength from that fact and found that he could move his limbs once more.

But appearances could be deceiving when dealing with dragons. Balthazar was weighing the situation carefully, even considering the halfling's offer to go out and spread anew the legend. Such tales would no doubt inspire others to come to the lair, would-be heroes and treasure seekers. The dragon wondered if that might be the way in which it would at last end its imprisonment and be free to fly about the land once more, feasting on whole villages of men.

In the end, though, lazy Balthazar decided that it really didn't want to have to continually wake up and deal with upstart heroes. And Balthazar had already determined that this foppish halfling was a liar and a thief.

The wyrm's head snapped forward, so quickly and terribly that Luthien cried out, thinking Oliver surely eaten. Up came the bow, Luthien nocking the strange arrow as he raised it.

Worldly Oliver, who had studied fighting tactics in the finest schools of Gascony, including tactics used against legendary beasts, was not caught unawares. He dove forward as the dragon's head came down, drawing his rapier as he rolled. When he regained his feet, he prodded the blade straight up, but sighed resignedly as the slender blade bent nearly in half with no chance of penetrating the dragon's armor.

Up reared Balthazar, swishing its great tail, beating its leathery wings so fiercely that the wind from them halted Oliver's advance. Purple cape flying behind him, the halfling squinted against the onslaught and put his free hand on his hat to hold it in place.

That would have been the end of Oliver deBurrows, taken in the bite of a dragon's mouth, but Luthien let fly the arrow, hoping and praying that it was something special.

It arced for the beast, then was deflected by the tremendous wind and seemed as if it would hit nothing but the floor. It never made it that far, exploding unexpectedly in midair.

Rockets squealed and bursts of multicolored sparkles filled the chamber. Balls of sizzling light whooshed out in wobbling lines, one heading straight for Balthazar's face and forcing the dragon to dodge to the side. A red flare rocketed straight up and blew apart with a tremendous, resounding explosion that shook the chamber, rattled the coins and gems and nearly knocked Luthien from his feet.

Balthazar's protesting roar joined in the echoes and squeals.

Oliver had the presence of mind to run off under that cover, thinking quickly enough to bend and scoop Brind'Amour's oaken staff as he passed it. He ran straight for Luthien and would have run by, but the young man reached out and grabbed the staff, which was nearly twice the stumbling halfling's height.

Oliver cried out as if struck, then opened his eyes wide, realizing that it was only Luthien. He willingly gave over the staff and ran on, grabbing the torch, the young man right beside him.

Balthazar roared again as the two exited the chamber, and loosed a line of fiery breath.

Luthien and Oliver were around the corner in time, but deflected flames licked at their backsides and prodded them along; the stone of the corner crackled and melted away. Luthien couldn't resist the urge to look back and see the bared fury of the mighty dragon. Oliver tugged him along fiercely, suspecting that even the slightest delay would put them right in the middle of Balthazar's next flaming blast.

The rocket fanfare continued in the treasure chamber. Above it, the fleeing companions heard the scraping tumult of the dragon's stubborn pursuit.

"THERE IS NOWHERE TO RUN, THIEVES!" Balthazar roared. The great wyrm entered the corridor, claws digging into the stone so that it could pull its huge mass along and breathing forth its deadly breath once more.

Luthien and Oliver were long gone, down the passage and through the next chamber. Luthien thought of turning with the bow and putting a few shots behind him, but he scowled at his own stupidity, wondering what those little arrows were supposed to do against the likes of the armored dragon. He popped the pin out of the bow instead, folded it, and tucked it into his new belt, near the small quiver.

The companions continued to widen their lead, the dragon's bulk working against it in the narrow corridors, but then they came to the one barrier—the underground pool—where Balthazar would have a tremendous advantage.

Luthien started to the right, toward the ledge, though he knew that they could not possibly get all the way along its narrow length before the dragon caught up to them. He saw that the rope was still on this side, still loosely looped about the boulders, and so he turned and went for that instead.

Rope in one hand, Brind'Amour's staff in the other, he climbed the highest rock he could find and bade Oliver to scramble atop his shoulders.

"You will have to get up higher if you wish to swing across!" the halfling pointed out, and Luthien, looking all about for sight of the turtle, handed the staff to the halfling. The young man reached up as high as he could along the rope's length, bent his knees and tensed his legs.

A roar from the corridor behind them launched Luthien into action. He leaped from the rock as high as he could, scrambled hand over hand to get as high a grip on the rope as possible, and tucked his legs under him as he and Oliver swung out over the pool.

They weren't even near the middle when the drag on the trailing rope slowed them and Luthien's legs splashed into the water. Knowing what was to come, the desperate man climbed, hand over hand, to pull himself out of the hot pool, then kept climbing, remembering the awful reach of the giant turtle.

The weight as they came out of the water halted their swing altogether, and the two began to rotate slowly as the rope untwisted.

"I do not so much like this," Oliver remarked.

"Give me the staff," Luthien replied, and the halfling gladly handed it over, using the opportunity of two free hands to scramble a bit higher on Luthien's shoulders. Oliver was already thinking that if the turtle snapped at Luthien, he might be able to leap atop the thing's back and run toward the far shore, then spring out and swim for his life.

He hated the notion of leaving Luthien behind, though, for he had taken a sincere liking to this brave young human.

Luthien, hooking his ankles around the rope and hanging on with one free hand, unexpectedly began to loop himself about the rope, increasing the swing and nearly dislodging Oliver from his shoulders.

"What are you doing?" the halfling demanded.

"At least this will be safe," Luthien answered, and as he came around, he used the momentum of the swing to aid his throw and hurled Brind'Amour's staff toward the far shore. It skipped off the last few feet of water and settled, floating near the bank.

"I thought you meant to try to use the silly thing!" Oliver protested. He ended with a squeal as a loud roar told him that Balthazar was entering the chamber.

"How would I know how to use a wizard's staff?" Luthien quipped back.

"You would not," came an unexpected answer from the shore. The two hanging companions looked over to see Brind'Amour calmly bending over the water to retrieve his valued item. As the rope rotated, the two then saw Balthazar come up to the other shoreline.

"Caught in line between a wizard and a dragon," Oliver remarked. "This is not my very best day."

Luthien grabbed on tight and tried to steady the rope, looking from one powerful adversary to the other. Balthazar issued a long, low growl at the sight of the wizard, and Luthien did not doubt that the dragon remembered well that day four hundred years before, when Brind'Amour and his cohorts had sealed the cave.

"In Gascony, we have always found wizard-types to be amusing, if a bit benign," Oliver remarked, seeming not so optimistic despite Brind'Amour's appearance.

"Go back to your hole!" Brind'Amour called to the wyrm.

"WITH YOUR BONES!" came the not-surprising reply.

Brind'Amour thrust his staff before him, and crackling bolts of black energy shot out from its end. Luthien and Oliver both cried out, thinking that they would be caught in the barrage, but the wizard's bolts arced around them and sizzled unerringly into the dragon and the stones around the beast.

The dragon roared in protest; rocks exploded, and parts of the ceiling fell in, engulfing Balthazar in a cloud of dust and debris.

"In Gascony, we could be wrong," Oliver admitted, and both he and Luthien dared to hope that Brind'Amour had won the day.

Neither of them had dealt with a dragon before. As soon as the energy was expended, the debris settling to the floor, Balthazar reared up and shook himself free of it, looking more angry than ever but hardly wounded. If he had not been so amazed, Luthien would have let go of the rope and let himself and Oliver splash into the protection of the pool, but he was too entranced to move as Balthazar's great head shot forward and his mouth opened wide, sending out a line of white-hot flames.

Brind'Amour had already enacted his next spell, though, and like a great rolling wave, the water between the companions and the wyrm rose up suddenly in a blocking wall.

Fires hissed in protest and clouds of steam rose about the lake. Hot droplets splattered back from the force of the breath, nipping at Oliver and Luthien, who could only close their eyes and hold on.

It went on for what seemed like minutes, Balthazar's unending breath drawing Brind'Amour's powers out to their limits. When Luthien dared to peek out, it seemed to him as though the watery wall was inevitably thinning. Then it fell flat suddenly, and Luthien thought he was surely doomed.

But ended, too, was the dragon's breath, and Luthien could hardly see the massive wyrm through the cloud of thick steam. He heard splashing, though, as Balthazar steadily advanced.

"What are you doing to my rope?" he heard Oliver gasp. He looked at the halfling, then followed Oliver's incredulous gaze to the water and the loose end of the rope. Luthien's eyes widened as well when he saw the spectacle: Brind'Amour had somehow transformed that end of the rope into a living serpent, which was now swimming toward the far bank and the wizard.

The water then churned under the companions—they had almost forgotten about the turtle!

The snake/rope crawled onto the shore and, following Brind'Amour's frantic directions, looped itself about a rock and began to tighten, pulling the companions up at an angle away from the water and the turtle.

Oliver looked back and nearly fainted dead away, staring into the evil and angry eyes of the dragon not more than a dozen feet away. The halfling tried to speak, but got his lips all tied together, and instead began tapping Luthien frantically on the shoulder.

"HELLO, THIEF AND LIAR," Balthazar said calmly. Luthien didn't have to look back to know that he was about to become lunch.

The dragon jerked suddenly; there came a huge splash from below. Oliver looked down as Balthazar looked down—to see the snapping maw of the turtle tightly clamped on the dragon's great leg.

The rope was taut, then, and Luthien began half crawling, half sliding toward the far shore.

Hot water splashed over the companions as the behemoths battled in the lake. The dragon roared and breathed forth and a new cloud of steam joined the first, and the agonized shriek of the startled and wounded turtle cut the air. Luthien finally let go of the rope altogether as they neared the shore and dropped onto the beach, Oliver still clutched tightly to his back and neck.

"Run on!" Brind'Amour prodded them. The wizard understood that the turtle would not last long against the likes of Balthazar. He looked back to the lake one final time, sent forth another black-crackling bolt of energy, and ran after Luthien. Then he produced a magical light, for Oliver had left the still-burning torch on the far bank.

The three had barely exited the chamber, climbing back into the corridor strewn with broken stalagmites, when they heard Balthazar splash ashore, calling out, "THIEVES!" and "LIARS!"

Now the landscape favored the wyrm, with the three companions having to scramble over and around the tumbled blocks. Luthien finally spotted the fist-sized swirl of blue glowing energy, but he heard the dragon right behind them and did not think he had any chance of making it.

Brind'Amour, chanting wildly, grabbed the young man's shoulder suddenly—Oliver's, as well—and all three took off from the ground, flying, speeding for the wall.

Balthazar roared and loosed another line of flames. Oliver screamed and covered his head, thinking that he would smash into the stone. The lights of the tunnel expanded, as if to catch them, and the dragon's breath was licking again at their backsides as they entered the wizard's tunnel.

CHAPTER 12

TALES FROM BETTER DAYS

SMALL WISPS OF smoke rose from their clothes as they tumbled back into the wizard's cave, all three in one ball. Brind'Amour, showing surprising agility, extracted himself first and rose laughing.

"Old Balthazar will be steaming about that one for a hundred years!" the wizard roared.

Luthien eyed him, stone-faced, his stern gaze diminishing the wizard's howls to a coughing chuckle.

"Young Bedwyr," Brind'Amour scolded. "Really, you must learn to laugh when the adventure is at its end. Laugh because you are alive, my boy! Laugh because you stole an item from a dragon's hoard . . ."

"More than one," Oliver corrected, producing several gemstones from his seemingly bottomless pockets.

"All the more reason to laugh!" Brind'Amour cried. Oliver began juggling three of the stones, admiring their glitters in the flickering torchlight, and Brind'Amour raised his fist in a salute to the halfling.

Luthien did not crack the slightest hint of a smile. "Balthazar?" he asked.

"Balthazar?" Brind'Amour echoed.

"You called the dragon Balthazar," Luthien explained. "How did you know?"

Brind'Amour seemed uneasy for just a moment, as though he had been caught in a trap. "Why, I watched you through my crystal ball, of course," the wizard replied so suddenly and exuberantly that Luthien knew he was lying. "The dragon named himself—to Oliver, of course."

"He did," Oliver remarked to an obviously unconvinced Luthien.

"You knew the name before the dragon declared it," Luthien pressed grimly. He heard a clinking sound as Oliver stopped his juggling, one gem falling to the stone floor. And Brind'Amour stopped his chuckling, as well, in the blink of an eye. The atmosphere that only a moment ago seemed to Oliver and the wizard to be a victory celebration now loomed thick with tension. It almost appeared to Oliver that Luthien would strike out at Brind'Amour. "Your tale of a cyclopian king was a lie."

Brind'Amour gave a strained smile. "Dear young Luthien Bedwyr," he began solemnly, "if I had told you that a dragon awaited you at the other end of the magical tunnel, would you have gone through?"

"Very good point," Oliver conceded. He looked up at Luthien, hoping that his friend would just let the whole thing go at that.

"We could have been killed," Luthien said evenly. "And you sent us in there, expecting us to die."

Brind'Amour shrugged, seeming unimpressed by that statement. The wizard's casual attitude only spurred Luthien on. A barely perceptible growl escaped the young Bedwyr's lips; his fists were clenched tightly at his sides.

"Luthien," Oliver whispered, trying to bring him back to a rational level. "Luthien."

"Am I to apologize?" Brind'Amour spat suddenly, incredulously, and his unexpected verbal offensive set Luthien back on his heels. "Are you so selfish?"

Now Luthien's face screwed up with confusion, not having any idea of what the wizard might be talking about.

"And do you believe that I would have allowed the two of you to walk into such danger unless there was a very good reason?" Brind'Amour went on, snapping his fingers in the air in front of Luthien's face.

"And your 'very good reason' justifies the lie and is worth the price of our lives?" Luthien snapped back.

"Yes!" Brind'Amour assured him in no uncertain terms. "There are more important things in the world than your safety, dear boy."

Luthien started to react with typical anger, but he caught a faraway look in Brind'Amour's blue eyes that held his response in check.

"Do you not believe that I grieve every day for those men who went in search of my staff before you and did not return?" the wizard asked somberly. A great wash of pity came over Luthien, as if somehow the gravity of the wizard's words had already touched his sensibilities. He looked at Oliver for support, honestly wondering if he had been caught by some sort of enchantment, but the halfling appeared similarly over-whelmed, similarly caught up in the wizard's emotions.

"Do you know from where a wizard gains his power?" the man asked, and Brind'Amour suddenly seemed very old to the companions. Old and weary.

"His staff?" Oliver answered, a perfectly reasonable assumption given the task he and Luthien had just completed.

"No, no," Brind'Amour replied. "A staff is merely a focus for the power, a tool that allows a wizard to concentrate his energies. But those energies," he went on, rubbing his thumb across his fingertips in front of his face as though he could feel the mysterious powers within his hand. "Do you know where they come from?"

Luthien and Oliver exchanged questioning expressions, neither having any answers.

"From the universe!" Brind'Amour cried abruptly, powerfully, moving both of the friends back a step. "From the fires of the sun and the energy of a thunderstorm. From the heavenly bodies, from the heavens themselves!"

"You sound more like a priest," Oliver remarked dryly, but his sarcasm was met with unexpected excitement.

"Exactly!" Brind'Amour replied. "Priests. That is what the ancient brotherhood of wizards considered themselves. The word 'wizard' means no more than 'wise man,' and it is a wise man indeed who can fathom the complete realities of the universe, the physical and the spiritual, for the two are not so far apart. Many priests do not understand the physical. Many of our recent inventors have no sense of the spiritual. But a wizard . . ." His voice trailed away, and his blue eyes sparkled with pride and that faraway look. "A wizard knows both, my boys, and always keeps both in mind. There are spiritual consequences to every physical act, and the physical being has no choice except to follow the course of the soul.

"Who do you think built the great cathedrals?" Brind'Amour asked, referring to the eight massive structures that dotted the islands of Avonsea. Six were in Avon, the largest in Carlisle and a similar one in Prince-town. The Isle Baranduine, to the west, had only one, and Eriador had one located in Montfort. Luthien had never been into Montfort, but he had passed by the city along the foothills of the Iron Cross. From that perspective, all the buildings of Montfort (and many were large and impressive), and even the one castle of the city, seemed to be dollhouses of children under the long shadows of the towering spires and huge stone buttresses of the massive cathedral. It was called simply the Ministry, and it was one of the greatest sources of pride for the people of Eriador. Every family, even those of the islands, had an ancestor who had worked on the Ministry, and that heritage inspired Luthien to respond now through gritted teeth:

"The people built them," he answered grimly, as if daring Brind'Amour to argue.

The wizard nodded eagerly.

"In Gascony, too," Oliver promptly put in, not wanting his homeland to be left out of any achievement. The halfling had been to Montfort, though, and he knew that the cathedrals of Gascony, though grand, could not approach the splendor of those on the islands. The Ministry had taken the halfling's breath away, and by all accounts, at least three of the cathedrals south of the Iron Cross were even larger.

Brind'Amour acknowledged the halfling's claims with a nod, then looked back at Luthien. "But who designed them?" he asked. "And who oversaw the work, supervising the many hardy and selfless people? Surely you do not believe that simple farmers and fishermen, noble though they might be, could have designed the flying buttresses and great windows of the cathedrals!"

Luthien took no offense at the wizard's words, in full agreement with the logic. "They were an inspiration," he explained, "from God. Given to his priests—"

"No!" The sharpness of the wizard's tone stopped the young man abruptly. "They were an inspiration of the spirit, from God," Brind'Amour conceded. "But it was the brotherhood of wizards who designed them, not the priests who later, with our profound blessings, inhabited them." The wizard paused and sighed deeply before continuing.

"We were so powerful then," he went on, his tone clearly a lament. "It was not so long after Bruce MacDonald had led the rout of the cyclopians, you see. Our faith was strong, our course straight. Even when the great army of Gascony invaded, we held that course. It saw us through the occupation and eventually forced the Gascons back to their own land." Brind'Amour looked straight at Oliver, not judging the halfling but simply explaining. "Your people could not break our faith in ourselves and in God."

"I was told that we had other business to the south," Oliver replied, "and could not keep so many soldiers in Avonsea."

"Your people had no heart to remain in Avonsea," Brind'Amour said calmly. "There was no point, no gain to Gascony. They could never take Eriador, that much was conceded, and with the disarray in the north . . . Well, let us just agree that your king was having little fun in holding the reins about the spirited Avonsea Islands."

Oliver nodded his concession to the point.

"It is ironic indeed that the greatest canker began to grow during the peace that ensued after the Gascons departed," Brind'Amour said, turning his attention back to Luthien. The young Bedwyr got the distinct feeling that this history lesson was almost exclusively for his benefit.

"Perhaps we were bored," the wizard remarked with a chuckle, "or perhaps the lure of the greater powers prodded us on too far. Wizards had always used minor creatures of the lower planes—bane midges and the lesser demons—as servants, calling on them, with their knowledge of other planes of existence, to find answers to those questions we could not discern from within our earthly mantles. Until that time not so long ago, though, our true powers came from the pure energies: fires and lightning, the cold winds of the northern glaciers and the strength of an ocean swell. But then some in the brotherhood, including our present king, Greensparrow"—he spat the name with obvious disdain—"forged evil pacts with demons of great power. It took many decades for their newfound and ill-gotten powers to come to true fruition, but gradually they drove the goodly wizards, like myself, from their ranks." He ended with a sigh and looked down, seeming thoroughly defeated.

Luthien stared long and hard at Brind'Amour, his thoughts whirling down many newly opened avenues. Nothing Brind'Amour had said to him, up until the last couple of sentences, had gone against the precepts he had been taught as a child, the basis for his entire perception of the world. The news that wizards, not priests, had inspired the great cathedrals was only a minor point. But what Brind'Amour had just said rocked the young man profoundly. Brind'Amour had just accused Luthien's king, the man to whom his father owed fealty, of severe crimes—terrible crimes!

Luthien wanted to lash out at the wizard, punch the lying old man in the face. But he held steady and quiet. He felt Oliver's stare upon him and guessed that the halfling understood his turmoil, but be did not return the look. He could not, at that moment.

"My greatest lament," Brind'Amour said softly—and truly, he seemed sincere—"is that the magnificent cathedrals of Avonsea, the dominant structures of every large city in the land, have become so perverted, have become the houses of Greensparrow's eight dukes, the newest generation of perverted wizards. Even the Ministry, which I, Brind'Amour, as a young man, helped to design."

"How old are you?" Oliver asked, but the wizard seemed not to hear.

"Once they stood as a tribute to man's spirituality and faith, a place of holy celebration," the wizard went on, still eyeing Luthien directly. The weight of his tone dissipated the budding rage in Luthien, forced him to hear the man out. "Now they are no more than gathering places where the tax rolls might be called."

The last statement stung, for it rang of truth. Luthien's father had been called to Montfort on several occasions, and he had spoken of walking into the Ministry not to pray or celebrate God but to explain a discrepancy in the tithe sent to Duke Morkney from Bedwydrin.

"But let that not be your concern," Brind'Amour said, his cheery tone obviously forced, "neither of you!"

The way Brind'Amour made the assertion made Luthien wince. The proud young man had a strange feeling that what Brind'Amour had just told him would make a profound difference in his life, would change the very way he looked at the world. What scared Luthien was that he wasn't yet sure what that meant.

"And you both have earned your freedom from my . . . interference and have earned my friendship, whatever that may be worth." The cloud of pained memories had flown clear of the wizard's face. A wistful look came into his eye as he took a moment to fully regard Luthien.

"That cape fits you well," the wizard remarked.

"I found it in the dragon cave," Luthien started to explain, but he stopped, catching the mischievous twinkle in the wizard's blue eyes and remembering the circumstances under which he had come upon the leather sack. "You put it there," he accused.

"I meant to give it to you after you returned with my staff," Brind'Amour admitted. "I would have hated to lose those items—the cape and the folding bow—to Balthazar, as well! But you see, I held faith in you, in both of you, and I thought you might be able to make use of them where you were."

Oliver cleared his throat loudly, interrupting the conversation and drawing looks from both men. "If you could drop us such toys, then why did you not just get us out of there?" the halfling demanded of Brind'Amour. "I had your staff already—it would have been so much easier."

The wizard looked at Luthien but didn't find much support there, for Oliver's line of reasoning had obviously set off some doubts in the young man's mind. "The enchantment was not potent enough," Brind'Amour stammered, trying to figure out how he might begin to explain. "And I didn't know where you were, exactly, and what you might soon be facing."

"Shooting blind?" Oliver asked both incredulously and suspiciously. "Then your aim, it was not so bad."

Brind'Amour began waving his hands, as if to indicate that the companions simply did not understand. "Of course I was able to locate you with a simple spell, though I didn't know where that was, if you understand what I mean. And then to get the items to you was another spell, a fairly simple transference, but certainly no open gate like the one that got you to the lair and got you back from the lair. No, no."

Oliver and Luthien looked at each other, and after a moment, Oliver gave a shrug. Brind'Amour's explanation was acceptable.

"And what of that strange arrow?" Luthien asked, getting back to the original conversation.

"Harmless, really," Brind'Amour said with a chuckle. "I didn't even intend to put it there—it was merely lying beside the belt quiver and just got caught up in the spell! Those types of arrows are called 'fireworks' and were used for celebrations in the happier days before Greensparrow. I must say, you were very resourceful in putting it to such valuable use."

"I was lucky," Luthien corrected. "I had no idea of what the arrow might do."

"Never underestimate the value of luck," Brind'Amour replied. "Was it anything more than luck that brought you to Oliver in his time of need? If not for that chance happening, would the halfling be alive?"

"I had my rapier blade," Oliver protested, drawing out the weapon and holding it directly in front of his face, its side against his wide nose.

Brind'Amour looked at him skeptically and began to chuckle.

"Oh, you have so wounded me!" Oliver cried.

"No, but the merchant's cyclopians surely would have!" the wizard replied with a hearty laugh, and Oliver, after a moment's thought, nodded and replaced his weapon in its sheath, trying futilely to hide his own chuckles.

Brind'Amour's demeanor changed again, suddenly, as he looked at Luthien. "Do not openly wear that cape," he said seriously.

Luthien looked at the shimmering, crimson material cascading down from his broad shoulders. What was the man talking about? he wondered. He wondered, too, what use a cape would be if it could not be worn.

"It belonged to a thief of some renown," Brind'Amour explained. "The bow, too, was his, and those folding bows are outlawed in Avon, since they are the weapons of underground bands, threats to the throne."

Luthien looked at the cape and the bow and continued to ponder the value of such items. Were these gifts Brind'Amour had given to him, or burdens?

"Just keep them away and keep them safe," Brind'Amour said, as if reading Luthien's thoughts. "You might find a use for them, and then again, you might not. Consider them, then, trinkets to spur your memories of your encounter with a dragon. Few in all the world can claim to have seen such a beast, for those that have are likely dead. And that encounter, too, must remain a secret," Brind'Amour said almost as an afterthought, though he seemed deadly serious,

Luthien nearly choked on the request and turned his continuing incredulous look upon Oliver. The halfling put a finger over his pursed lips, though, and shot Luthien a sly wink. The young Bedwyr got the message that worldly Oliver understood this better than he and would explain it to him later.

They said nothing more about the dragon, the gifts, or even about Brind'Amour's history lesson for the rest of that evening. Again, the wizard set a fabulous table before the companions and offered them another comfortable night on the soft beds, which they eagerly accepted.

Brind'Amour came to Oliver later that night, woke him and motioned for him to exit the room. "Watch over him," the wizard explained to the sleepy-eyed halfling.

"You expect great things from Luthien Bedwyr," Oliver reasoned.

"I fear for him," Brind'Amour replied, dodging the question. "Just two weeks ago, he fought friendly jousts in the secure arena of his father's protective home. Now he has become an outlaw, a thief and a warrior . . ."

"A murderer?" Oliver remarked, wondering if Brind'Amour thought the correction appropriate.

"He has killed cyclopians—who meant harm to him, or to you," Brind'Amour replied firmly. "A warrior." He looked back to the closed door of Luthien's room, and he seemed to Oliver a concerned parent.

"He has suffered many adventures all at once," Brind'Amour went on. "Has faced a dragon! That might not seem like much to the likes of Oliver deBurrows—"

"Of course not," the halfling interrupted, and since Brind'Amour was not looking at him, he rolled his eyes, nearly gagging on that claim.

"But no doubt it is traumatic to young Luthien," the wizard finished. "Watch over him, Oliver. I beg you. The very foundation of his world has become, or will likely soon become, as loose sand, shifting under his feet."

Oliver put a hand on his hip and leaned back, putting his weight on one foot, the other tapping impatiently on the floor. "You ask much," he remarked when the wizard turned to regard him. "Yet all the gifts you have offered have been to Luthien, not me."

"The pass into Montfort is more valuable to you than to Luthien," Brind'Amour was quick to point out, knowing Oliver's recent history in the city—and knowing the reputation the halfling thief left behind with some fairly influential merchants.

"I do not have to go into Montfort," the halfling replied casually, lifting one hand before his face to inspect his manicured fingernails.

Brind'Amour laughed at him. "So stubborn!" the wizard remarked jovially. "But would this buy the favor?" From a cupboard to the side of the room, the wizard produced a large leather harness. Oliver's eyes widened as he regarded the device. Among the thieves of any city's alleys, it was commonly called a "housebreaker." Links of leather strapping secured it to a burglar, and other straps—and small pouches, in the case of the more elaborate designs—held many of the tools of the trade.

"This one is special," Brind'Amour assured Oliver. He opened a pouch on one of the shoulder straps, and from it, though it was much too small to hold such an item, took out a curious-looking device: a black, puckered ball affixed to a fine cord. "A cord much finer than the one you were forced to leave in Balthazar's cave," the wizard explained. "And this grapnel will secure itself to the smoothest of walls." To demonstrate, Brind'Amour casually tossed the ball against the nearest wall and pulled the rope tightly. "It will hold three large men," the wizard assured Oliver.

"Three quick tugs," Brind'Amour went on, jerking the rope, "will release the hold." Sure enough, on the third pull, the grapnel popped free of the wall.

Brind'Amour replaced the item and opened another pouch, this one along the harness's belt strap. He held the housebreaker up close to Oliver's face so the halfling could look inside.

Oliver gawked and blinked. The area inside the open flap was much larger than it appeared from the outside—extradimensional, Oliver realized—and within was the most complete set of tools, files and lock picks, fine wire and even a glass cutter, that Oliver had ever seen.

"Just think about the item you desire," Brind'Amour explained. "It will come to your waiting grasp."

Oliver did not doubt the wizard's words, but he dearly wanted to see a demonstration. He held his hand near to the open pouch and silently mouthed, "Skeleton key," then nearly jumped out of his nightshirt when a long-handled key appeared suddenly in his hand.

Recovered from the shock, Oliver turned a devious look on Brind'Amour.

"We have a deal?" the wizard asked, smiling widely.

"I never once thought to walk away from Luthien," Oliver assured the man.

The next morning, as promised, Brind'Amour produced the passes into Montfort—valuable items, indeed. When the three entered the room where Riverdancer and Threadbare had been stabled, they found Brind'Amour's magic already at work. A glowing door swirled upon the wall, the tunnel that would place the friends on the road outside of Montfort.

The farewell was short and friendly, except from Luthien, who remained cautious and suspicious. Brind'Amour accepted the young man's light handshake and tossed a knowing wink at Oliver.

With his crystal ball, Brind'Amour watched the friends as they exited the magical tunnel and stepped onto the road to Montfort. The wizard would have liked to keep his protective gaze over them at all times. He had taken a great chance by giving the cape and bow to young Luthien, and honestly, he did not know whether faith or simple desperation had guided his actions.

Whatever the reason, Brind'Amour had to leave events to the friends now. He could not emerge from his secret cave, not even look out from it in the direction of Montfort, or anywhere that one of Greensparrow's wizard-dukes might sense his magical gaze and trace the energies to the outlaw wizard.

If King Greensparrow even suspected that Brind'Amour was alive, then doom would surely fall over the wizard, and over Luthien and Oliver as well.

Brind'Amour waved his hand and the crystal ball went dark. The hermit wizard walked slowly out of the chamber and to his bedroom, falling listlessly onto his soft bed. He had set the events into motion, perhaps, but now all that he could do was sit by and wait.

CHAPTER 13

MONTFORT

RIVERDANCER SEEMED TRULY glad to be back out on the open road. The shaggy white stallion, coat glistening in the typical morning drizzle, strode powerfully under Luthien. Riverdancer wanted to run, but Luthien kept him in check. The terrain here was more broken than back in the northern fields. They were approaching the foothills of the Iron Cross, and even though they would have the better part of a day's ride to get into Montfort and the rockier mountains, the ground here was strewn with boulders.

"I wish that he had put us closer to the city," Luthien remarked, anxious to see the place. "Though I think Riverdancer could use the run." He patted the horse's muscled flank as he spoke and eased the reins a bit, allowing Riverdancer to spring ahead. Oliver and Threadbare were up beside them again in a moment.

"The wizard, he put us as close as he could," Oliver replied. He noticed Luthien's quizzical look, not unexpected since Oliver was beginning to understand just how sheltered the young Bedwyr truly was. Oliver remembered Brind'Amour's plea to him to watch over Luthien, and he nodded. "Whoever it is that keeps the wizard up in his secret cave is likely in Montfort," he explained.

Luthien thought about it for a moment. "Morkney," he reasoned. Brind'Amour had mentioned that Greensparrow's dukes had been corrupted by demonic powers, as had the king, so the reasoning seemed logical enough.

"Or one of his captains," Oliver agreed.

"Then I should not complain," Luthien said. "Brind'Amour proved a fine friend, and I forgive him his lie about the dragon cave in full—he did come to us in our time of need, after all."

Oliver shrugged in halfhearted agreement. "If he had come sooner, then we might have enjoyed the spoils of a dragon's treasure," the halfling said, and he sighed profoundly at that thought.

"We got our gifts," Luthien replied and patted his saddlebags. He chuckled as he said it, for a cape and folding bow, in truth, did not seem like much of a reward for invading a dragon's lair. But Oliver did not share the young man's mirth, and Luthien was surprised when he looked upon the halfling's cherubic face to see a most serious expression there.

"Do not underestimate that which you have been given," the halfling said solemnly.

"I have never seen such a bow," Luthien began.

"Not the bow," Oliver interjected. "It is valuable enough, do not doubt. But that which I speak of, that which was the greatest gift, was the crimson cape."

Luthien looked at him doubtfully, then looked at his saddlebags as though he expected the cape to slip out and rise up in defense of itself. Truly it was a beautiful cape, its crimson coloring so rich that it invited the eye into its depths and shimmered in the slightest light as though it was alive.

"You do not know, do you?" Oliver asked, and Luthien's expression went from doubtful to curious.

"Did you notice anything so very strange about the dragon's reaction toward you when we were in the treasure cave?" Oliver asked slyly. "And about my own reaction when you met me on the hasty flanking maneuver?"

Hasty flanking maneuver? Luthien pondered for just an instant, but then he realized that to be Oliver's way of saying "desperate retreat." Indeed, Luthien had given some thought to the matter of the halfling's question. In the treasure cave, the dragon had ignored him—even seemed as if it hadn't noticed that Oliver had a companion.

"A dragon's eyes, they are finer than an eagle's," Oliver remarked.

"He never noticed me," Luthien said, knowing that to be the answer Oliver was looking for, though Luthien didn't think as much of that fact as Oliver obviously did.

"Because of the cape," Oliver explained. Luthien was shaking his head before the expected response even came forth.

"But it is true!" Oliver told him. "I, too, did not see you, arid almost ran over you."

"You were intent on the dragon behind you," Luthien rationalized. "And Balthazar was intent on you, especially since your pockets were so stuffed with his treasures!"

"But I did not see you even before we found the dragon," Oliver protested. Now Luthien looked at him with more concern.

"When I first found the staff, I turned about and called down to you," Oliver went on. "I thought you had left or gone behind one of the piles, and only when you pulled back your hood was I able to see you."

"A trick of the light," Luthien replied, but now it was Oliver who was shaking his head.

"The cape is red, but the floor behind you was gray stone and gold co-ins."

Luthien looked back at the saddlebags once more and rubbed his hand across his stubbly chin.

"I have heard of such items," Oliver said. "You will find the cape a handy tool in the streets of Montfort."

"It is the tool of a thief," Luthien said disdainfully.

"And you are a thief," Oliver reminded him.

Luthien held his next thoughts silent. Was he a thief? And if not, what exactly was he, and why was he riding along the road into Montfort beside Oliver deBurrows? The young Bedwyr laughed aloud, preferring that reaction to having to face up to his course thus far. Events had taken him, not the other way around; if Oliver deBurrows called him a thief then who was he to argue?

Montfort came into sight around the next bend, nestled among the rocky cliffs and outcroppings of the northern slopes of the Iron Cross. The companions saw many buildings set in straight rows along the slopes of the foothills and spreading down into the valley, but most of all, they saw the Ministry.

It seemed more a part of the majestic mountains than a man-made creation, as though the hand of God had squared and shaped the stone. Two square-topped towers, each rising more than a hundred feet into the air, flanked the front of the building, and a much taller spire was centered on the back. Huge, arching buttresses lined the sides from the peaked roof to the rows of smaller steeples, accepting the tremendous weight of the stone and channeling it to the ground. Stone gargoyles leaned out from every side of these smaller towers to leer at passersby, and great colored windows depicted a myriad of scenes and free-flowing designs.

Even from this distance, Luthien was overwhelmed by it all, but his spirits never lifted from the ground as he recalled Brind'Amour's lament about the present purpose of the cathedrals. Again the young Bedwyr felt the foundation of his life shifting underneath him, and he almost expected the ground to crack open and drop him into a horrific abyss.

Like most towns near to the wild Iron Cross, Montfort was surrounded by two walls both manned by many grim-faced cyclopians. Two came down to the gate to meet Oliver and Luthien. At first, they seemed suspicious and clutched their weapons tightly, particularly when they glanced upon the outrageous halfling. Luthien expected to be turned away, at the very least, and honestly wouldn't have been surprised if the crossbowmen atop the wall opened fire.

One of the cyclopians moved toward Riverdancer's saddlebags, and Luthien held his breath.

"You have no cause!" Oliver protested firmly.

Luthien glanced at the halfling in disbelief. Certainly he and Oliver might find some trouble if the cyclopian found the folded bow, but that trouble could not compare to the potential repercussions of Oliver's boldness.

The other cyclopian eyed the halfling dangerously and took a step toward him, and was met by Oliver's hand thrusting forward the wizard-forged passes. The cyclopian opened the parchment and looked at it carefully. (Luthien knew that the brute couldn't read it, though, particularly since the pass was upside down at the time.) Still, the cyclopian's expression brightened considerably, and it called its companion to its side.

This cyclopian was smarter, even turned the parchment right-side up after a moment's thought. But the cyclopian's expression, like that of its companion, was soon beaming. The brute looked up to the wall and waved the crossbowmen away, and seemed almost thrilled to let the two riders enter Montfort—the two cyclopians even bowed low as Luthien and Oliver rode past them!

"Oh, this wizard-type, he is very good!" Oliver laughed when they had put the gate behind them. "Very good!"

Luthien did not reply, too entranced by the sheer enormity of Montfort. The largest city the young Bedwyr had ever been in was Dun Varna, and he saw now that Dun Varna could fit into Montfort twenty times over.

"How many people?" he numbly asked Oliver.

"Twenty thousand, perhaps," the halfling replied, and from his tone, Luthien gathered that Oliver was not so impressed.

Twenty thousand people! All of Isle Bedwydrin, a place of five thousand square miles, boasted barely more than a quarter of that. The sheer enormity of Montfort, and the way people were jammed in so tightly together, stunned the young man, and made him more than a little uncomfortable.

"You will get used to it," Oliver assured him, apparently sensing his confusion.

From this vantage point, Luthien noticed an inner wall, anchored at one point by the Ministry, ringing the higher section of the city. Montfort, flanked by many mines rich in various ores, was a prosperous place, but Luthien could see now that, unlike the communities of Bedwydrin, where the wealth was pretty much evenly divided, Montfort was more like two separate cities. The lower areas consisted of many markets and modest houses and tenements, many no more than shacks. As they walked their mounts along the cobblestone streets, Luthien saw children at play with makeshift toys, swinging broken branches like swords or tying sticks together to roughly resemble a doll. The merchants and craftsmen he saw were a hard-working lot, their backs bent under the weight of toil, their hands sooty and calloused. They were friendly enough, though, and seemingly content, tossing a wave or a smile at the two rather unusual visitors.

Luthien didn't have to go up through the inner wall to imagine the types of people he would meet within its confines. Grand houses peeked over the wall, some with spires soaring up into the sky. He thought of Aubrey and Avonese, and suddenly he had no desire to go up into the higher section at all. What he did notice, though, and it touched him as more than a little curious, was that more guards walked the inner wall than both of the outer walls combined.

The young Bedwyr didn't understand it at that time, but what he was getting was his second taste of a society sharply divided by its economic classes.

Oliver led the way into the shadow of a cliff, Montfort's southeastern section, and to a stable. He knew the hands well there, it seemed to Luthien, and tossed the stablemaster an ample pouch of coins. With no bartering and no exchange of instructions, just a friendly greeting and small conversation, Oliver handed over Threadbare's reins and bade Luthien do the same with Riverdancer. Luthien knew how much Oliver cared for his exceptional, if ugly, pony, and so he held no reservations. Oliver had obviously boarded the pony here before to his complete satisfaction.

"On to the Dwelf," the halfling announced when they departed, Luthien carrying the saddlebags over one shoulder.

"The Dwelf?"

Oliver didn't bother to explain. He led on to a seedier section of town, where the eyes of the waifs in the streets showed a hard edge, and where every door seemed to belong to a tavern, a pawn shop, or a brothel. When Oliver turned toward one of these doors, Luthien understood it to be their destination, and in looking at the sign over the place, he understood the name Oliver had given to it. The painting on the sign depicted a sturdy, muscular dwarf and a Fairborn elf, leaning back to butt, each smiling widely and hoisting drinks—a mug of ale for the dwarf and a goblet, probably of wine, for the elf. "THE DWELF, FINE DRINK AND TALK FOR DWARF AND ELF," the words proclaimed, and underneath them someone had scribbled, "Cyclopians enter at your own risk!"

"Why the Dwelf?" Luthien asked, stopping Oliver short of the door.

Oliver nodded down the street. "What do you see at the other taverns?" he asked.

Luthien didn't understand the point of the question. All the places seemed equally busy. He was about to respond when he realized Oliver's intent: all the patrons at the doors to the other bars were either human or cyclopian.

"But you are neither dwarf nor elf," Luthien reasoned. "Nor am I."

"The Dwelf caters to men as well and, mostly, to all who are not men," Oliver explained.

Again, Luthien had a hard time comprehending that point. While there were few Fairborn and even fewer dwarves on Bedwydrin, they were in no way segregated from the general community. A tavern was a tavern, period.

But Oliver seemed determined, and the halfling certainly knew his way around Montfort better than Luthien, so the young Bedwyr offered no further protests and willingly followed Oliver into the tavern.

He nearly choked as he entered, overwhelmed by a variety of smells, ale and wine and exotic weeds the most prominent among them. Smoke hung thick in the air, making the crowd seem even more ominous to Luthien. He and Oliver picked their way through clusters of tables, most surrounded by groups of huddled men, or huddled dwarves, or huddled elves—there didn't seem to be much mingling between the races. Five cyclopians, silver-and-black uniforms showing them to be Praetorian Guards, sat at one table, laughing loudly and casually tossing out insults to anyone near to them, openly daring someone to make trouble.

All in all, it seemed to Luthien as if the whole place was on the verge of an explosion. He was glad he had his sword with him, and he clutched the saddlebags protectively as he bumped and squeezed his way to the main bar.

Luthien began to better appreciate the allure of this place to some of the nonhumans when he saw that many of the bar stools were higher than normal, with steps leading up to them. Oliver perched himself comfortably on one, easily able to rest his elbows on the polished bar.

"So they have not yet hung you, eh, Tasman," the halfling remarked. The barkeep, a rough-looking, though slender character, turned around and shook his head as he looked upon Oliver, who returned the look with a huge smile and a tip of his great hat.

"Oliver deBurrows," Tasman said, moving over and wiping the bar in front of the halfling. "Back in Montfort so soon? I had thought your previous antics would have kept you away through the winter at least."

"You are forgetting my obvious charms," the halfling replied, none too worriedly.

"And you're forgetting the many enemies you left behind," Tasman retorted. He reached under the bar and produced a bottle of dark liquor and Oliver nodded. "Let's hope that they've also forgotten you," the bar-keep said, pouring Oliver a drink.

"If not, then pity them," Oliver replied, lifting his glass as though the words were a toast. "For they will surely feel the sting of my rapier blade!"

Tasman didn't seem to take well to the halfling's cavalier attitude. He shook his head again and stood a glass in front of Luthien, who had retrieved a normal-sized stool to put next to Oliver's.

Luthien put his hand over the mouth of the glass before Tasman could begin to pour. "Just some water, if you please," the young man said politely.

Tasman's steel gray eyes widened. "Water?" he echoed, and Luthien flushed.

"That is what they call light ale on Bedwydrin," Oliver lied, saving his friend some embarrassment.

"Ah," Tasman agreed, though he didn't seem to believe a word of it. He replaced the glass with a flagon topped by the foam of strong ale. Luthien eyed it, and eyed Oliver, and thought the better of protesting.

"I . . . we, will be in need of a room," Oliver said. "Have you any?"

"Your own," Tasman replied sourly.

Oliver smiled widely—he had liked his old place. He reached into a pocket and counted out the appropriate amount of silver coins, then started to hand them over.

"Though I suspect it will need a bit of cleaning up," Tasman added, reaching for the coins, which Oliver promptly retracted.

"The price is the same," Tasman assured him sharply.

"But the work—" Oliver began to protest.

"Is needed because of your own antics!" Tasman finished.

Oliver considered the words for a moment, then nodded as though he really couldn't argue the logic. With a shrug, he extended his arm once more and Tasman reached for the payment.

"Throw in a very fine drink for me and my friend," Oliver said, not letting go.

"Done, and you're drinking them," Tasman agreed. He took the money and moved off to the side.

When Oliver looked back to Luthien, he found the young man eyeing him suspiciously. The halfling let out a profound sigh.

"I was here before," he explained.

"I figured that much," Luthien replied.

Oliver sighed deeply again. "I came here in the late spring on a boat from Gascony," Oliver began. He went on to tell of a "misunderstanding" with some of the locals and explained that he had gone north just a few weeks before in search of honest work. All the while, Tasman stood off to the side, wiping glasses and smirking as he listened to the halfling, but Luthien, who had seen firsthand the reason Oliver, the highway-halfling, had gone north, didn't need Tasman's doubting expression to tell him that Oliver was omitting some very important details and filling in the holes with products of his own imagination.

Luthien didn't mind much, though, for he could guess most of the truth—mainly that Oliver had probably been run out of town by some very angry merchants and had willingly gone north following the caravans. As he came to know the halfling, the mystery of Oliver deBurrows was fast diminishing, and he was confident that he would soon be able to piece together a very accurate account of Oliver's last passage through Montfort. No need to press the issue now.

Not that Luthien could have anyway, for Oliver's tale ended abruptly as a shapely woman walked by. Her breasts were rather large and only partially covered by a low-cut, ruffled dress. She returned the halfling's smile warmly.

"You will excuse me," Oliver said to Luthien, never taking his eyes from the woman, "but I must find a place wherein to warm my chilly lips." Off the high stool he slid, and he hit the ground running, cornering the woman a few feet down the bar and climbing back up onto a stool in front of her so that he would be eye-to-eye with her.

Eye-to-chest would have been a better description, a fact that seemed to bother Oliver not at all. "Dear lady," he said dramatically, "my proud heart prompts my dry tongue to speak. Surely you are the most beautiful rose, with the largest . . ." Oliver paused, looking for the words and unconsciously holding his palms out in front of his own chest as he spoke. "Thorns," he said, poetically polite, "with which to pierce my halfling heart."

Tasman chuckled at that one, and Luthien thought the whole scene perfectly ridiculous. Luthien was amazed, though, to find that the woman, nearly twice Oliver's size, seemed sincerely flattered and interested.

"Any woman for that one," Tasman explained, and Luthien noticed sincere admiration in the gruff barkeep's voice. He looked at the man skeptically, to which Tasman only replied, "The challenge, you see."

Luthien did not "see," did not understand at all as he turned back to observe Oliver and the woman talking comfortably. The young Bedwyr had never looked at women in such an objectified way. He thought of Katerin O'Hale and imagined her turning Oliver upside down by his ankles and bouncing his head off the ground a few times for good measure if he had ever approached her in such a bold manner.

But this woman seemed to be enjoying the attention, however shallow, however edged by ulterior motives. Never had Luthien felt so out of place in all his young life. He continued to think of Katerin and all his friends. He wished that he was back in Dun Varna (and not for the first or the last time), beside his friends and his brother—the brother that Luthien was resigning himself to believe he would never see again. He wished that Viscount Aubrey had never come to his world and changed everything.

Luthien turned back to the bar, staring at nothing in particular, and drank down the ale in a single swig. Sensing his discomfort, Tasman, who was not a bad sort, filled the flagon once more and slid it in front of Luthien, then walked away before the man could either decline the drink or offer payment.

Luthien accepted the gift with an appreciative nod. He swung about on the stool, looking back at the crowd: the thugs and rogues, the cyclopians, itching for a fight, and the sturdy dwarfs, who appeared to be more than ready to give them one. Luthien didn't even realize his own movements as his hand slipped to the pommel of his sword.

He felt a slight touch on that arm, and jerked alert to find that a woman had come over and was half sitting, half standing on the stool Oliver had vacated.

"Just into Montfort?" she asked.

Luthien gulped and nodded. Looking at her, he could only think of a cheaper version of Avonese. She was heavily painted and perfumed, her dress cut alluringly low in the front.

"With lots of money, I would bet," she purred, rubbing Luthien's arm, and then the young man began to catch on. He felt suddenly trapped, but he had no idea of how he might get out of this without looking like a fool and insulting the woman.

A yell cut through the din of the crowd, then, silencing all and turning their heads to the side. Luthien didn't even have to look to know that Oliver was somehow involved.

Luthien leaped from his seat and rushed past the lady before she could even turn back to him. He pushed his way through the mob to find Oliver standing tall (for a halfling) before a huge rogue with a dirty face and threadbare clothing, an alley-fighter sporting a metal plate across his knuckles. A couple of friends flanked the man, urging him on. The woman Oliver had been wooing also stood behind the man, inspecting her fingernails and seeming insulted by the whole incident.

"The lady cannot make up her own mind?" Oliver asked casually. Luthien was surprised that the halfling's rapier and main gauche were still tucked securely in their sheaths; if this large and muscular human leaped at him, what defense could the little halfling offer?

"She's mine," the big man declared, and he spat a wad of some chewing weed to the floor between Oliver's widespread feet. Oliver looked down at the mess, then back at the man.

"You do know that if you had hit my shoe, you would have to clean it," Oliver remarked.

Luthien rubbed a hand across his face, stunned by the halfling's stupidity, stunned that Oliver, outnumbered at least three to one, and outweighed at least ten to one, would invite such a lopsided fight.

"You speak as if she was your horse," Oliver went on calmly. To Luthien's amazement, the halfling then spoke past the man to the woman who had been the subject of the whole argument. "Surely you deserve better than this oaf, dear lady," the halfling said, sweeping off his hat as he spoke.

On came the growling man, predictably, but Oliver moved first, stepping into rather than sidestepping the charge and snapping his head forward and down, a head butt that caught the bullish man right between the pumping thighs and stopped him dead in his tracks.

He straightened, his eyes crossed, and he reached down over his flattened crotch with two trembling hands.

"Not thinking of any ladies now, are you?" Oliver taunted.

The man groaned and toppled over, and Oliver slipped to the side. One of the man's companions was there to take his place, though, with dagger drawn. The weapon started forward, only to be intercepted right over Oliver's head by Luthien's sword and thrown out wide. Luthien's free hand struck fast, a straightforward punch that splattered the man's nose and launched him toward the floor.

"Ow!" Luthien cried, flapping his bruised knuckles.

"Have you met my friend?" Oliver asked the downed man.

The remaining thug came forward, also holding a dagger, and Luthien stopped his flapping and readied his sword, thinking that another fight was upon him. Oliver leaped out instead, drawing rapier and main gauche.

The crowd backed away; Luthien noticed the Praetorian Guards looking on with more than a passing interest. If Oliver killed or seriously wounded the man, Luthien realized, he would likely be arrested on the spot.

A gasp arose as the man lunged with the dagger, but Oliver easily dodged, moved aside, and slapped the man on the rump with the side of his rapier. Again the stubborn thug came on, and again Oliver parried and slapped.

The man Luthien had hit was starting to get up again, and Luthien was about to jump in to meet him, but the woman, charmed by Oliver's attention, was there first. She neatly removed one shoe, holding it up protectively in front of her, seeming the lady all the while. Then her visage turned suddenly savage and she launched a barrage of barefooted kicks on the man's face so viciously that he fell back to the ground, squirming and ducking.

That brought cheers from the onlookers.

Oliver continued to toy with the thug for a few passes, then went into a wild routine, his blades dancing every which way, crossing hypnotically and humming as they cut the air. A step and a thrust brought the main gauche against the man's dagger, and a twist of Oliver's wrist sent the weapon spinning free.

Oliver jumped back and lowered his weapons, looking from the stunned thug to the fallen dagger.

"Enough of this!" the halfling shouted suddenly, quieting the whispering and gasping crowd.

"You are thinking that you can get to the weapon," Oliver said to the man, locking stares with him. "Perhaps you are correct." The halfling tapped the brim of his hat with his rapier. "But I warn you, sir, the next time I *disarm* you, you may take the word as a literal description!"

The man looked at the dagger one last time, then rushed away into the crowd, bringing howls of laughter. Oliver bowed gracefully after the performance and replaced his weapons, gingerly stepping by the original rogue, who was still prone and groaning, clutching at his groin.

Many of the dispersing group, particularly the dwarves, chose a path that took them close enough so that they could pat the daring and debonair halfling on the back—salutes that Oliver accepted with a sincere smile.

"Back five minutes and already there's trouble!" Tasman remarked when the halfling and Luthien returned to their seats at the bar. It didn't seem to Luthien, however, that the man was really complaining.

"But sir," Oliver replied, seeming truly wounded, "there was the reputation of a lady to consider."

"Yeah," Tasman agreed. "A lady with large . . . thorns."

"Oh!" the halfling cried dramatically. "You do so wound me!"

Oliver was laughing again when he returned his gaze to Luthien, sitting open-mouthed and amazed by it all.

"You will learn," Oliver remarked.

Luthien wasn't sure if that was a promise or a threat.

CHAPTER 14

THE FIRST JOB

LUTHIEN THOUGHT "TINY Alcove" the most ridiculous name he had ever heard for a street—until Oliver, leading him through the shabby avenues of dilapidated wooden buildings, turned a corner and announced that they were home. Tiny Alcove was more an alley than a street, barely eight feet wide and shrouded in the shadows of tall buildings whose main entrances were on other fronts.

The two walked down through the gloom of a moonless night, gingerly stepping over the bodies of those drunken men who had not made it to their own doors, or had no doors to call their own. A single street lantern burned in the lane above a broken railing and chipped stairs that led down to an ironbound door. As they passed, Luthien noticed other lights burning within and the huddled shadows of people moving about.

"Thieving guild," Oliver explained in a whisper.

"Were you a member?" Luthien thought the question perfectly reasonable, but the look Oliver gave to him showed that the halfling apparently did not share his feelings.

"I?" Oliver asked imperiously, and he chuckled and walked on, out of the lamplight and into the gloom.

Luthien caught up to him across the lane and four doors down, on the top step of another descending stone stairway that ended in a narrow, but long landing and a wooden door. Oliver paused there for a long, long while, studying the place quietly, stroking his neatly trimmed goatee.

"This was my house," he whispered out of the corner of his mouth.

Luthien did not reply, caught up in the halfling's curious posture. Oliver was tentative, seemed almost afraid.

"We cannot go down there," the halfling announced.

"One must learn to sense these things?" Luthien asked, to which Oliver only smiled and turned, stepping back up to the street level. The halfling stopped abruptly and snapped his fingers, then spun back and whipped his main gauche down the stairs. It hit the door with a loud thump and hung quivering.

Luthien started to ask what the halfling thought he was doing, but the young man was interrupted by a dozen rapid clicking noises, the sound of stone scraping stone, and a sudden hiss. He spun back toward the door, then hopped up next to Oliver as darts ricocheted off the stone stairs. The bottom of the landing burned with a hot fire, and as Luthien stared on in disbelief, a large block of stone slid out from above the doorway, crashing down into the flames.

As though a giant had peeked over the edge of the stairs and puffed out a candle, the flames suddenly disappeared.

"Now we can go down there," Oliver said, and hooked his fingers into his wide belt. "But do watch where you put your feet. The darts were likely poisoned."

"Somebody does not like you," the stunned Luthien remarked, slowly following the halfling.

Oliver grabbed the hilt of the main gauche and gave a great tug, but it did not pull free from the door. "That is only because they never came to know my most charming personality," he explained. He stood straight, hands on hips, and eyed the weapon as though it were a stubborn enemy.

"Too bad you don't have your main gauche," Luthien quipped behind him, seeing his dilemma. "You could disarm the door."

Oliver turned a not appreciative glare on his friend. Luthien reached over the halfling for the stuck dagger, but Oliver slapped his arm away. Before Luthien could protest, Oliver leaped up, grabbed the hilt of the main gauche in both hands, and planted his feet on the door on either side of it.

A heave brought the blade free, and sent Oliver, and Oliver's great hat, flying. He did a backward somersault, landing nimbly on his feet, and caught his hat as he slipped the main gauche back into its scabbard.

"My most charming personality," he announced again, quite pleased with himself, and Luthien, though he hated to admit it to Oliver, was quite pleased as well.

The halfling bowed and swept his arm out toward the door, indicating that Luthien should go first. The young Bedwyr almost fell for it, dipping a similar bow and stepping for the door. He reached for the handle, but then straightened and looked back at Oliver.

"It was your house," he said, stepping to the side.

Oliver brushed his cloak back from his shoulders and boldly strode past Luthien. With a single steadying breath, he yanked the door open. A smell of soot assaulted both the friends, and though the light was practically nonexistent, they could see that the inside wood of the door was blackened. Oliver huffed and took a tentative step over the threshold, then quickly retracted his foot.

A double-bladed pendulum swung past, just inside the door jamb. Its supporting beam creaking, it swung back and forth several times, finally coming to a halt in a vertical position directly centering the door.

"Someone really did not like you," Luthien said again.

"Not true," Oliver quickly replied, and he gave Luthien a mischievous smile. "This trap was my own!" Oliver tipped his hat and gingerly stepped past the pendulum.

Luthien smiled and started to follow, but stopped when he realized the implications of Oliver's game. Oliver had bade him to go first, but the halfling had obviously known about the pendulum trap! Muttering with every step, Luthien entered the apartment.

Oliver was over to the left, fidgeting with an oil lamp. The halfling added some oil and finally got it going, though its glass was gone and its frame had been bent and charred.

Something powerful had hit the place. Every piece of furniture was smashed down and blackened, and the layers of carpets had been burned away to clumps of worthless rags. Smoke hung thickly in the stagnant air, though no traces of any heat remained.

"A magical fireball," Oliver remarked casually. "Or an elvish hot wine."

"Elvish hot wine?"

"A bottle of potent oils," the halfling explained, kicking aside the remains of what looked to have been a chair. "Topped with a lighted rag. So very effective."

Luthien was amazed at how well Oliver seemed to be taking the disaster. Though the light from the battered lamp was dim, it was obvious to Luthien that nothing remained of the place's contents, and obvious, too, that some of those contents had been quite valuable.

"We will find no sleep this night," Oliver said. He opened one of his saddlebags and fished out a plain, less expensive suit of clothing.

"You mean to start cleaning right away?" Luthien asked.

"I do not wish to sleep out in the street," Oliver replied matter-of-factly. And so they went to work.

It took two days of hard labor to clean out the debris and air out the smoke. The friends left periodically during that time, back to the Dwelf for meals, and to the stables to check on their mounts. Each time, they found groups of children hovering about and in their apartment when they returned—curious waifs, half-starved and dirty. Luthien didn't miss the fact that Oliver always brought back a good part of his own meal for them.

Tasman offered them a much-needed bath at the Dwelf that second night, and afterwards, Oliver and Luthien donned their better clothes again and went to the place that they could now rightly call their home.

Bare walls and a rough wooden floor greeted them. Oliver had at least purchased a new lantern, and they had retrieved their bedrolls from the stable.

"Tomorrow night, we begin our furnishing," the halfling announced as he crawled into his bedroll.

"How fare our funds?" Luthien asked, noticing that Oliver's pouches seemed to be getting inevitably smaller.

"Not well," the halfling admitted. "That is why we must begin tomorrow night."

Then Luthien understood, and his expression aptly reflected his disappointment. Oliver wasn't planning on *buying* anything. They were to live the lives of thieves from the outset.

"I had planned a burglary on a certain merchant-type's house," the halfling said. "Before events put me out on the road. The merchant-type's guards remain the same, I am sure, and he has not moved his valuables."

Luthien continued to scowl.

Oliver paused and stared at him, the halfling's mouth turning up into a wry smile. "The life does not please you," he stated as much as asked. "You do not think thieving an honorable profession?"

The question seemed ridiculous.

"What do you know of the law?" Oliver asked.

Luthien shrugged as though the answer should have been obvious—at least as far as stealing was concerned. "To take another man's property is against the law," he answered.

"Aha!" the halfling cried. "That is where you are wrong. Sometimes to take another man's property is against the law. Sometimes it is called business."

"And is what you do 'business'?" the young Bedwyr asked sarcastically.

Oliver laughed at him. "What the merchant-types do is business," he replied. "What I do is enforce the law. Do not confuse the law with justice," Oliver reasoned. "Not in the time of King Greensparrow." With that, the halfling rolled over, ending the conversation. Luthien remained awake for some time, considering the words but uneasy nonetheless.

They made their way across the rooftops of the grand houses in Montfort's upper section, Luthien in his cape and Oliver wearing a tight-fitting but pliable black outfit and the harness Brind'Amour had given him underneath his purple cape. Cyclopians, mostly Praetorian Guards, walked every street, and a couple were up on the roofs as well, but Oliver knew the area and guided Luthien safely.

They came to a waist-high ledge, three stories above the street. Oliver smiled wickedly as he peeked over, then he looked back to Luthien and nodded.

Luthien, feeling vulnerable, feeling like a naughty child, glanced around nervously and pulled his crimson cape up higher about his shoulders.

Oliver took the small puckered ball and the fine line out of his shoulder pouch, stringing the cord through his hands as he went. He popped the unusual grapnel against the ledge and pulled the cord tight.

"Be of cheer, my friend," Oliver whispered. "This night, you learn from the master." Over the side went Oliver, slipping silently down the cord. Luthien watched as the halfling stopped in front of a window, opened another pouch, and took out some small instrument that the young man could not discern. He figured out what it was soon enough when Oliver placed it against the window and cut a wide circle, gently popping out the cut piece of glass. With a quick look around, the halfling disappeared into the room.

As soon as the cord came back out, Luthien slipped over the ledge and eased his way down to Oliver's side.

The halfling held a small lamp, its directional beam focused tightly. Luthien's eyes widened as Oliver shifted that light about the room. Though his father was an eorl, and well to do by Bedwydrin standards, Luthien had never seen such a collection! Intricate tapestries lined every wall, thick carpets covered the floor, and a myriad of artifacts—vases, statues, decorative weapons, even a full suit of plate mail armor—littered the large room.

Oliver placed the lamp on the chamber's sole piece of furniture, a huge oaken desk, and rubbed his plump hands together. He began an inspection, using hand signals to Luthien to let him know what was most valuable. The trick of burglary, Oliver had previously explained, was in knowing what to take, both by its value and its size. One could not go running through the streets of Montfort with an open armload of stolen goods!

After a few minutes of inspection, Oliver lifted a handsome vase of blue porcelain trimmed in gold. He looked at Luthien and nodded, then froze in place.

At first, Luthien didn't understand, and then he, too, heard the heavy footsteps coming down the hall.

The friends got to the window together, Luthien inadvertently stepping on the circle of cut glass that Oliver had laid to the side. Both cringed at the sound of the breakage and looked back nervously to the door. The vase still under his arm, Oliver jumped out to the cord and swung to the side.

Luthien had no time. He looked to the door and saw the handle turn—and only then remembered that the lamp was still perched upon the desk! The young man leaped across the room and blew out the flame, then fell back against the wall and stood perfectly still as two cyclopians entered the room.

The brutes sniffed the air as they moved in, milling about curiously. Only their own lantern offered Luthien any hope that they would not detect the smelly wick of the extinguished lamp. One of the brutes actually sat on the desk barely two feet from Luthien.

Luthien held his breath, put his hand to the hilt of his sheathed sword, and nearly drew it out when the cyclopian turned toward him.

Nearly drew it out, but did not, for the brute, though it was obviously looking right at Luthien, did not appear to notice him at all.

"I do like the pictures of cyclopian victories!" the one-eye laughed to its friend, and Luthien realized that he was standing right in front of a tapestry depicting such a scene. But the cyclopian, though it continued to stare, did not seem to notice any incongruity within the picture.

"Come on," the other cyclopian said a moment later. "No one's here. You heard wrong."

The cyclopian on the desk shrugged and hopped to its feet. It started to leave, but glanced back over its shoulder and stopped suddenly.

Peeking out under the cowl of his hood, Luthien realized that, as chance would have it, the brute had spotted the broken glass. The cyclopian slapped its companion hard on the shoulder, and together they ran to the window.

"The roof!" one of them cried, leaning out and looking up. Again Luthien reached for his sword, but his instincts told him to hold back and avoid a fight at any cost.

The cyclopians ran out of the room, and Luthien went for the window—to be met by Oliver, swinging back in. The halfling slipped down and pivoted on the rope, gave three quick tugs on the line, and hauled in the magical grapnel. He started to set it on the windowsill so that they could slip down to the street, but the sound of more approaching footsteps stopped him.

"No time," Luthien remarked, grabbing Oliver's arm.

"I do so hate to have to fight," Oliver replied, cool as always.

Luthien moved back to the wall, pulling Oliver with him. He flattened his back against the tapestry and opened his cape, indicating that his little friend should slip under its camouflage. Oliver found little choice as the door began to open.

Luthien peeked from under the cowl, Oliver from a tiny opening in the folds, as a wiry man in a nightshirt and cap, obviously the merchant, and several more cyclopians, all bearing lanterns, entered the room.

"Damn!" the man spat out as he looked around and spotted the lamp on the desk, the broken window, and the empty pedestal where the vase had been. He went to the desk at once and fit a key into the top drawer, pulling it open, then gave a relieved sigh.

"Well," the man said, his tone changing, "at least all they took was that cheap vase."

Luthien looked under the neck of his cape, and the halfling, glancing up at him, only shrugged.

"They did not take my statue," the merchant went on, obviously relieved, looking at a small figure of a winged man perched upon the desk. He dropped a hand into the drawer and the friends heard the tinkling of jewels. "Or these." The merchant shut the drawer and locked it.

"Conduct a search of the area," the merchant ordered the cyclopians, "and report the theft to the city watch." He looked back over his shoulder and scowled; both Luthien and Oliver held their breath, thinking they had been bagged. "And see to it that the windows are barred!" the man growled angrily.

Then he left, taking the cyclopians with him, even obliging the friends by locking the room's door behind him.

Oliver came out from under the cloak, rubbing his greedy hands. He went right for the desk—the merchant had conveniently left the lamp sitting upon it.

"That drawer is locked," Luthien whispered, coming up beside the halfling as Oliver fumbled with yet another pouch on the harness. The halfling produced several tools and laid them out on the desk.

"You could be wrong!" he announced a moment later, eyeing Luthien proudly as he pulled open the drawer. A pile of jewels awaited them: gem-studded necklaces and bracelets, and several golden rings. Oliver emptied the contents in a flash, stuffing them into a small sack, which he produced from yet another pouch in the incredible harness. The halfling was truly beginning to appreciate the value of Brind'Amour's gifts.

"Do get the statue," he said to Luthien, and he walked across the room and put the vase back where it belonged.

They waited by the window for half the night, until the clamor of rushing cyclopians outside died away. Then Luthien easily swung the grapnel back up to the roof, and away they went.

The light in the room had been dim, and the friends did not notice the most significant mark they had left behind. But the merchant most certainly did, cursing and wailing when he returned the next day to find that his more valuable items had been stolen. In his rage, he picked up the vase Oliver had returned and heaved it across the room, to shatter against the wall beside the desk. The merchant stopped his yelling and stared curiously at the image on the wall.

On the tapestry, where Luthien had first hidden from the cyclopians, loomed the silhouette of a caped man—a crimson-colored shadow somehow indelibly stained upon the images of the tapestry. No amount of washing could remove it;

the wizard the merchant later hired only stared at it helplessly after several futile attempts.

The crimson shadow was forever.

CHAPTER 15

THE LETTER

LUTHIEN SAT BACK in his comfortable chair, bare feet nestled in the thick fur of an expensive rug. He squirmed his shoulders, crinkled his toes in the soft fur and yawned profoundly. He and Oliver had come in just before dawn from their third excursion into the merchant section this week, and the young man hadn't slept very well, awakened soon after the dawn by the thunderous snoring of his diminutive companion. Luthien had gotten even, though, by putting Oliver's bare foot into a bucket of cold water. His next yawn turned into a smile as he remembered Oliver's profane shouts.

Now Luthien was alone in the apartment; Oliver had gone out this day to find a buyer for a vase they had appropriated three days before. The vase was beautiful, dark blue in color with flecks of gold, and Oliver had wanted to keep it. But Luthien had talked him out of it, reminding him that winter was fast approaching and they would need many supplies to get through comfortably.

Comfortably. The word rang strangely in Luthien's thoughts. He had been in Montfort for just over three weeks, arriving with little besides Riverdancer to call his own. He had come into a burned-out hole in the street that Oliver called an apartment, and truly, after the first day or two of smelling the soot, Luthien had seriously considered leaving the place, and Montfort, altogether. Now looking around at the tapestries on the walls, the thick rugs scattered about the floor, and the oaken desk and other fine furnishings, Luthien could hardly believe that this was the same apartment.

They had done well and had hit at the wealthy merchants in a frenzy of activity. Here were the spoils of their conquests, taken directly or appropriated in trades with the many fences who frequented Tiny Alcove.

Luthien's smile sank into a frown. As long as he looked at things in the immediate present, or in the recent past, he could maintain that smile, but inevitably, the young and noble Bedwyr had to look farther behind, or farther ahead. He could be happy in the comforts he and Oliver had found, but could not be proud of the way he had come into them. He was Luthien Bedwyr, son of the eorl of Bedwydrin and champion arena warrior.

No, he decided. He was just Luthien, now, the thief in the crimson cape.

Luthien sighed and thought back to the days of his innocence. He longed now for the blindness of sheltered youth, for those days when his biggest worry was a rip in his fishing net. His future had seemed certain then.

Luthien couldn't even bear to look into his future now. Would he be killed in the house of a merchant? Would the thieves guild across the lane grow tired of the antics, or jealous of the reputations, of the two independent rogues? Would he and Oliver be chased out of Montfort, suffering the perils of the road in harsh winter? Oliver had only agreed to sell the vase because it seemed prudent to stock up on winter supplies—and Luthien knew that many of the supplies the halfling would stockpile would be in preparation for the open road. Just in case.

A burst of energy brought the troubled young man from his seat. He moved across the small room to a chair in front of the oaken desk and smoothed the parchment on its top.

"To Gahris, Eorl of Bedwydrin," Luthien read his own writing. Gingerly, the young man sat down and took quill and inkwell from the desk's top drawer.

Dear Father, he wrote. He smirked sarcastically to think that, in the span of a few seconds, he had nearly doubled all the writing on the parchment. He had begun this letter ten days ago, if a scribbled heading could be called a beginning. And now, as then, Luthien sat back in the chair, staring ahead blankly.

What might he tell Gahris? he wondered. That he was a thief? Luthien blew a loud sigh and dipped the quill in the inkwell determinedly.

I am in Montfort. Have taken up with an extraordinary fellow, a Gascon named Oliver deBurrows.

Luthien paused and chuckled again, thinking that he could write four pages just describing Oliver. He looked at the small vial on the desk beside the parchment and realized he didn't have that much ink.

I do not know why I am writing this, actually. It would seem that you and I have very little to say to each other. I wanted you to know that I was all right, and doing quite well.

That last line was true, Luthien realized as he gently blew upon the letter to dry the ink. He did want Gahris to know that he was well.

Again came the smile that dissipated into a frown.

Or perhaps I am not so well, Luthien wrote. *I am troubled, Father, by what I have seen and what I have learned. What is this lie we live? What fealty do we owe to a conquering king and his army of cyclopian dogs?*

Luthien had to pause again. He didn't want to dwell on politics that he hardly understood, despite Brind'Amour's emphatic lessons. When the quill ran again over the rough parchment, Luthien guided it in a direction that he was beginning to know all too well.

You should see the children of Montfort. They scramble about the gutters, seeking scraps or rats, while the wealthy merchants grow wealthier still off the labors of their broken parents.

I am a thief, Father. I AM A THIEF!

Luthien dropped the quill to the desk and stared incredulously at the parchment. He hadn't meant to reveal his profession to Gahris. Certainly not! It had just come out of its own accord, the result of his mounting anger. Luthien grabbed the edge of the parchment and started to move to crumble it. He stopped at once, though, and smoothed it out again, staring at those last words.

I AM A THIEF!

To the young Bedwyr, it was like looking into a clear mirror, an honest mirror of his soul and his troubles. The image did not break him, though, and stubbornly, against his weakness, he picked up the quill, smoothed the parchment again, and continued.

I know there is a terrible wrong in the land. My friend, Brind'Amour, called it a canker, and that description seems fitting, for the rose that was once Eriador is dying before our very eyes. I do not know if King Greensparrow and his dukes are the cause, but I do know, in my heart, that any who would ally himself with cyclopians would favor the canker over the rose.

This infestation, this plague, lies thick behind Montfort's inner wall, and there I go in the shadows of night, to take what little vengeance my pockets will hold!

I have wetted my blade in the blood of cyclopians, but I fear that the plague is deep. I fear for Eriador. I fear for the children.

Luthien sat back again and spent a long while staring at his words. He felt an emptiness in his breast, a general despair. "What little vengeance my pockets will hold," he read aloud, and to Luthien Bedwyr, who thought the world should be different, it seemed a pittance indeed.

He dropped the quill on the desk and started to rise. Then, almost as an afterthought, amply wetted the quill's tip with ink and scratched a thick line across the letter's heading.

"Damn you, Gahris," he whispered, and the words stung him profoundly, bringing moisture into his cinnamon-colored eyes.

Luthien was fast asleep on the comfortable chair when Oliver entered the little apartment. The halfling skipped in gaily, a bag of golden coins tinkling at his belt. He had done well with the vase and was busy now thinking of the many enjoyable ways he might spend the booty.

He moved toward Luthien, thinking to wake the young man that they might get to market before all the best items were bought or stolen, but he noticed the parchment lying flat on the desk and slipped quietly that way instead.

Oliver's smile disappeared as he read the grim words, and the gaze he leveled Luthien's way was sincerely sympathetic.

The halfling sauntered over to stand before the troubled young man, forced a smile once more and woke Luthien by jingling the coins in his face.

"Do open your sleepy eyes," the halfling bade cheerily. "The sun is high and the market awaits!"

Luthien groaned and started to turn over, but Oliver grabbed him by the shoulder and, with surprising strength for one so little, turned him back around. "Do come, my less-than-sprightly friend," Oliver bade. "Already this northern wind carries the bite of winter and we have so many things to buy! I will need at least a dozen more warm coats to be properly attired!"

Luthien peeked out from under one droopy eyelid. A dozen more coats? his mind echoed. What was Oliver talking about?

"A dozen, I say!" the halfling reiterated. "So I might properly choose which among them is most fitting for one of my reputation. The others, *ptooey*," he said with a derisive spit. "The others, I discard to the street."

Luthien's face screwed up with confusion. Why would Oliver throw perfectly fine coats out into the street?

"Come, come," the halfling chattered, moving impatiently toward the door. "We must get to market before all the rotten little children steal away the goods!"

The children. Discard the coats to the street indeed! Oliver would throw them out, where those same children Oliver had just complained about, most of them approximately the halfling's size, might pick them up. Luthien had his answer, and the understanding of Oliver's secret generosity gave him the strength to leap out of his chair.

A new spring in his step, a new and valuable purpose, showed clearly to Oliver as they made their way to Montfort's lower central area, a wide and open plaza, lined by kiosks and some closed tents. Corner performers were abundant, some singing, others playing on exotic instruments, others juggling or performing acrobatics. Luthien kept his hand against his purse whenever he and Oliver passed anywhere near these people—the first lesson Oliver had given him about the market plaza was that almost all of the performers used their acts to cover their true profession.

The market was bustling this bright day. A large trading caravan, the last major one of the year, had come in the previous night, traveling from Avon through Malpuissant's Wall and all the way around the northern spurs of the Iron Cross. Most goods came in through Port Charley, to the west, but with the

Baranduine pirates running the straits, the largest and wealthiest of the southern merchant caravans sometimes opted for the longer, but safer, overland route.

The two friends milled about for some time. Oliver stopped to buy a huge bag of hard candies, then stopped again at a clothier's kiosk, admiring the many fur coats. The halfling made an offer on one, half the asking price, but the merchant just scowled at him and reiterated the full price.

The impasse continued for a few minutes, then Oliver threw up his hands, called the merchant a "barbarian," and walked away briskly.

"The price was fair," Luthien remarked, running to catch up with his brightly dressed companion.

"He would not bargain," Oliver replied sourly.

"But the price was already fair," Luthien insisted.

"I know," Oliver said impatiently, looking back at the kiosk. "Barbarian."

Luthien was about to reply, but changed his mind. He had limited experience at the market, but had come to know that most of the goods could be bought at between fifty and seventy-five percent of the obviously inflated asking price. It was a game merchants and buyers played, a bargaining session that, as far as Luthien could tell, was designed to make both parties feel as though they had cheated each other.

At the next stop, another clothier, Oliver and the merchant haggled vigorously over a garment similar to the one the halfling had just passed up. They came to terms and Oliver handed over the money—fully five silver coins more than the other coat had been priced. Luthien thought of pointing this out to Oliver as they walked away with their latest purchase, but considering the halfling's smug smile, he didn't see the point.

And so their morning went: buying, bartering, watching the performers, tossing handfuls of hard candy to the many children running about the crowd. It was truly an unremarkable morning, but one that heightened Luthien's sagging spirits considerably and made him feel that he was doing a bit of good at least.

By the time they were ready to leave, Luthien carried a tremendous sack over his shoulder. Oliver flanked him defensively as they pushed back through the mob, fearing sharp-knived cutpurses. The halfling was turning his head slowly, regarding one such shady-looking character, when he walked headfirst into Luthien's sack. Oliver bounced back and shook his head, then stooped to retrieve his fallen hat. The rogue he had been watching openly laughed, and Oliver thought he might have to go over and inscribe his name on the man's dirty tunic.

"You silly boy," the embarrassed halfling snarled at Luthien. "You must tell me when you mean to stop!" Oliver batted his hat against his hip and continued his scolding until he finally realized that Luthien wasn't even listening to him.

The young Bedwyr's eyes were locked straight ahead in an unblinking stare.

Oliver started to ask what he found so enthralling, but following Luthien's line of vision, it wasn't really very hard for the halfling to figure it out.

The lithe woman was beautiful—Oliver could see that despite the threadbare and plain clothes she wore. Her head was bowed as she walked, her long and thick wheat-colored hair cascading down her cheeks and shoulders—was that the tip of a pointed ear that Oliver saw peeking from within its lustrous strands? Huge eyes, bright and compelling green, peeked out from under those tresses and showed an inner strength that belied her obviously low station in life. She was at the head of a merchant's procession, her sharp-featured master a few paces behind her. Oliver thought the man looked remarkably like a buzzard.

Oliver walked up beside his companion and nudged Luthien hard in the side.

Luthien didn't blink, and Oliver sighed, understanding that his friend was fully stricken.

"She is a slave girl," Oliver remarked, trying to draw Luthien's attention. "Probably half-elven. And that merchant-type would not sell her to you for all the gold in Eriador."

"Slave?" Luthien remarked, turning his confused stare upon Oliver as if the concept was foreign to him.

Oliver nodded. "Forget her now," the halfling explained.

Luthien looked back to find that the woman and her procession had disappeared from sight into the crowd.

"Forget her," Oliver said again, but Luthien doubted that to be an option.

The companions went back to their little apartment and dropped off their goods, then, at Oliver's insistence, went to the Dwelf. Luthien's thoughts lingered on the woman, and the implications of his strong feelings, as they sat by the bar in the familiar place.

He thought of Katerin, as well, the love of his youth. "Of my youth," he mumbled under his breath, considering how curious that thought sounded. He had been with Katerin O'Hale just weeks before, but that life, that innocent existence on Bedwydrin, seemed so far removed to him now, seemed another life in another world, a sweet dream lost in the face of harsh reality.

And what of Katerin? he wondered. Surely he had cared for her, perhaps had even loved her. But that love had not fired him, had not set his heart to pounding, as had the mere glimpse of the beautiful slave girl. He couldn't know, of course, whether that fact should be attributed to honest feelings for the slave, or to the general changes that had occurred in Luthien's life, or to the simple fact that he was now living on the edge of catastrophe. Had all of his emotions been so amplified? And if Katerin walked into the Dwelf at that moment, how would Luthien have felt?

He did not know and could no longer follow his own reasoning. All that Luthien understood was the lifting of his heart at the sight of the fair slave, and that was all he truly wanted to understand. He focused his thoughts on that look again, on the bright and huge green eyes peeking out at him from under those luxurious wheat-colored tresses.

Gradually the image faded, and Luthien again considered his present surroundings.

"Many of the Fairborn are held as slaves," Oliver was saying to him. "Especially the half-breeds."

Luthien turned a fierce look upon the halfling, as though Oliver had just insulted his love.

"Half-breeds," the halfling said firmly. "Half elf and half human. They are not so rare."

"And they are held as slaves?" Luthien spat.

Oliver shrugged. "The pure Fairborn do not think highly of them, nor do the humans. But if you wish to cry tears for any race, my naive young friend, then cry for the dwarves. They, not the elves or the half-elves, are the lowest of Avon's hierarchy."

"And where do halflings fit in?" Luthien asked, somewhat nastily.

Oliver ran his hands behind his head, through his long and curly brown hair. "Wherever we choose to fit in, of course," he said, and he snapped his fingers in Luthien's face, then called for Tasman to refill his empty flagon.

Luthien let the discussion go at that and turned his private thoughts back to the woman and to the issue of slavery in general. There were no slaves on Bedwydrin—at least, none that Luthien knew of. All the races were welcomed there, in peace and fairness, except for the cyclopians. And now, with the edicts coming from Carlisle, even the one-eyes could not be turned away from the island's borders. Cyclopians on Bedwydrin would not find themselves welcomed at every door—even keepers of public inns had been known to tell them lies about no open rooms.

But slavery? Luthien found the whole issue thoroughly distasteful, and the thought that the woman he had spied, the beautiful and innocent creature who had so stolen his heart with just a glance, was a slave to a merchant filled his throat with a bitterness that no amount of ale could wash down.

Several drinks later, Luthien was still sitting at the bar grumbling openly to himself about injustice and, to Oliver's disdain, vengeance.

Oliver elbowed Luthien hard, spilling the meager remaining contents of the young man's flagon down the front of Luthien's tunic. Fuming, Luthien turned a sharp gaze on his friend, but before he could speak out, Oliver was motioning for him to remain silent, and nodding for him to train his eyes and ears to a discussion going on between two roguish-looking men a few stools down.

"It's the Crimson Shadow, I tell ye!" one of them proclaimed. " 'E's back, and Duke Morkney and his thievin' merchants'll get it good, don't ye doubt!"

"How can ye make the claim?" the other rogue asked, waving the notion away. "How long do Crimson Shadows live? What say you, Tasman? Me friend 'ere thinks the Crimson Shadow's come back from the dead to haunt Montfort."

"They seen the shadows, I tell ye," the first rogue insisted. "A slave friend telled me so! And no wash'll take 'em off, and no paint'll cover 'em!"

"There are whispers," Tasman interjected, wiping down the bar in front of the two slovenly rogues. "And if they are true," he asked the first rogue, "would you think it a good thing?"

"A good thing?" the man slurred incredulously. "Why I'd be glad indeed to see those fattened piggy merchants get theirs, I would!"

"But wouldn't your own take be less if this Crimson Shadow hits hard at the merchants?" Tasman reasoned. "And won't Duke Morkney place many more guards on the streets of the upper section?"

The rogue sat silent for a moment, considering the implications. "A good thing!" he declared at last. "It's worth the price, I say, if them fatted swine get what's coming to them!" He swung about on his stool, nearly tumbling to the floor, and lifted his spilling flagon high in the air. "To the Crimson Shadow!" he called out loudly, and to Luthien's surprise, at least a dozen flagons came up in the toast.

"A thief of some renown, indeed," Oliver mumbled, remembering Brind'Amour's description when he had given Luthien the cape and bow.

"What are they talking about?" Luthien asked, his senses too dulled to figure it out.

"They are talking of you, silly thief," Oliver said casually, and he drained his flagon and hopped down from his stool. "Come, I must get you back to your bed."

Luthien sat quite still, staring dumbfoundedly at the two rogues, still not quite comprehending what they, or Oliver, were talking about.

He was thinking of the slave girl, then, all the way home, and long after Oliver dropped him onto his cot.

The second rogue, the doubtful one in the discussion of the Crimson Shadow, watched Oliver and Luthien leave the Dwelf with more than a passing interest. He left the tavern soon after, running a circuitous route along the streets to a secret gate in the wall to the upper section.

The cyclopian guards, recognizing the man but obviously not fond of him, watched him suspiciously as he crawled out the other side. He flashed them his merchant seal and ran on.

He had much to report.

CHAPTER 16

THE PERILS OF REPUTATION

"YOU SHOULD BE thinking of the task at hand," Oliver remarked in uncomplimentary tones as he and Luthien wove their way through the darkened streets toward Montfort's inner wall.

"I do not even think we should be going," Luthien replied. "We have more than enough money . . ."

Oliver spun in front of the young Bedwyr, stopping him with a pointing finger and a vicious scowl. "Never," Oliver said slowly and deliberately. "Never, never say such a stupid thing."

Luthien flashed a disgusted expression and ignored the halfling, but when he tried to continue walking, Oliver grabbed him and held him back.

"Never," Oliver said again.

"When is enough enough?" Luthien asked.

"Bah!" the halfling snorted. "I would steal from the merchant-types until they became pauper-types, giving their riches to the poor. Then I would go to the poor who were no longer poor, and steal the wealth again and give it back to the merchant-types!"

"Then what is the point?" Luthien asked.

"If you were truly a thief, you would not even have to ask," Oliver said, snapping his fingers in Luthien's face, a habit that had become quite regular over the last few days.

"Thank you," Luthien replied without missing a beat, and he forced his way around Oliver.

The halfling stood in the deserted street for some time, shaking his head. Luthien had not been the same since that day a week before in the market. He was thrilled when Oliver had discarded those coats he did not deem appropriate—and the children of Tiny Alcove had fallen upon them like a pack of ravenous wolves—but Luthien's mood had become generally surly, even despondent. He ate little, talked less, and had found an excuse to prevent him from going to the inner section of the city on every occasion Oliver had proposed an excursion.

This time, though, Oliver had insisted, practically dragging Luthien out of the apartment. Oliver understood the turmoil that had come over the proud young Bedwyr, and truthfully, the rapidly growing reputation of the Crimson Shadow added an element of danger to any intended burglaries. Rumors along the seedy streets near Tiny Alcove hinted that many of Montfort's thieves had cut back on activities for a while, at least until the merchants' panic over this Crimson Shadow character died away.

But Oliver knew that it was neither confusion nor fear that held Luthien back. The man was smitten—it was written all over his somber face. Oliver was not coldhearted, considered himself a romantic, even, but business was business. He skittered up beside Luthien.

"If I looked into your ear, I would see an image of a half-elven slave girl," he said, "with hair the color of wheat and the greenest of eyes."

"You aren't big enough to look into my ear," Luthien coldly reminded him.

"I am smart enough so that I do not have to," Oliver quipped in reply. The halfling recognized that this conversation was seriously degenerating, something he did not want with a potentially dangerous job ahead of them, so he jumped out in front again and brought the impatient Luthien to a stop.

"I am not cold to the ways of the heart," the halfling asserted. "I know you are in pain."

Luthien's defenses melted away. "In pain," he whispered, thinking those words a perfect description. Luthien had never known love before, not like this. He could not eat, could not sleep, and all the time his mind was filled, as Oliver had said, with that image of the half-elven woman. A vivid image; Luthien felt as if he had looked into her soul and seen the perfect complement of his own. He was normally a pragmatic sort, and he knew that this was all completely irrational. But for being irrational, it hurt all the more.

"How beautiful is the wildflower from across the field," Oliver said quietly, "peeking at you from the shadows of the tree line. Out of reach. More beautiful than any flower you have held in your hand, it seems."

"And what happens if you cross the field and gather that wildflower into your hand?" Luthien asked.

Oliver shrugged. "As a gentlehalfling, I would not," he replied. "I would appreciate the glimpse of such beauty and hold the ideal in my heart forevermore."

"Coward," Luthien said flatly, and for perhaps the first time since the children had gathered around Oliver's discarded coats, the young Bedwyr flashed a sincere smile.

"Coward?" Oliver replied, feigning a deep wound in his chest. "I, Oliver deBurrows, who am about to go over that wall into the most dangerous section of Montfort to take whatever I please?"

Luthien did not miss Oliver's not-so-subtle reminder that they had more on their agenda this night than a discussion of Luthien's stolen heart. He nodded determinedly to the halfling and the two moved on.

An hour later, the friends managed to find enough of a break in the patrol routes of the plentiful cyclopian guards to get over the wall and up onto a roof in the inner section, along the southern wall under the shadows of great cliffs. They had barely scampered over the lip when yet another patrol came marching into view. Oliver scrambled under Luthien's crimson cape and the young man ducked his face low under the hood.

"So fine a cape," Oliver remarked as the cyclopians moved away, oblivious to the intruders.

Luthien looked about doubtfully. "We should have waited," he whispered, honestly amazed by the number of guards.

"We should be flattered," Oliver corrected. "The merchant-types show us—show the Crimson Shadow—true respect. We cannot leave now and let them down."

Oliver crept along the rooftop. Luthien watched him, thinking perhaps that the impetuous halfling was playing this whole thing too much like a game.

Oliver swung his grapnel across an alley to another roof and secured the line with a slipknot. He waited for Luthien to catch up, looked around to make certain that no other cyclopians were in the area, then crawled across to the other roof. Luthien came next, and Oliver, after some effort, managed to work the rope free.

"There are arrows that bite into stone," the halfling explained as they made their way across another alley. "We must get you some for that bow of yours."

"Do you have any idea of where we are going?" Luthien asked.

Oliver pointed north to a cluster of houses with slanting rooftops. Luthien looked from the halfling to the houses, then back to the halfling, blinking curiously. Always before, the two had hit the southern section. With its flat roofs and the darkness offered by the sheltering mountain walls, it was ideal for burglars. He understood the halfling's reasoning, though; with so many cyclopians in this area, the less accessible houses would not be so heavily guarded.

Still, Luthien could not get rid of a nagging sensation of danger. The less accessible houses were the domains of the richest merchants, even the members of Duke Morkney's extended family. Luthien figured that Oliver knew what he was doing, and so he kept quiet and followed, saying nothing even when the cocky halfling led the way back down to the streets.

The avenues were wide and cobblestoned, but up above them the second stories of the houses were built tightly together. No building fronts were flat, rather they were curving and decorated, with jutting rooms and many alcoves. Teenagers milled about, along with a smattering of cyclopian guards, but between Luthien's cape and the many nooks, the companions had little trouble in avoiding detection.

Oliver paused when they came to one intersection, the side lane marked by a sign that proclaimed it the Avenue of the Artisans. Oliver motioned to Luthien, leading the young man's gaze to a group of cyclopians milling about a block from the intersection and calmly approaching them, apparently in no hurry.

"I'm thinking that tonight we do not go down from a roof," the halfling whispered with a wistful smile, rubbing his eager hands together.

Luthien caught on quickly and eyed the halfling doubtfully. One of the first rules that Oliver had taught him about cat-burglary in Montfort was that the wealthy shops of the inner section were best left alone. The proprietors up here often employed wizards to put up magical wards to watch over their stores. The obvious disinterest of the patrolling cyclopians did lend some hope, but again, that nagging sensation of danger tugged at Luthien.

Oliver grabbed him by the arm and slithered into the avenue. Luthien followed, again trusting the judgment of his more experienced companion. A short while later, the two were standing in the shadows of an alcove between two shops, Oliver admiring the goods displayed in the side panels of their large front windows.

"This one has the more valuable items," the halfling said, speaking more to himself than to Luthien and eyeing the fine china and crystal goblets on display. "But these," he turned about to regard the many pewter figurines and art in the other window, "will be the easier to be rid of.

"And I do so like the statue of the halfling warrior," he remarked. It was obvious that Oliver's mind was made up. He looked all about to make sure that no cyclopians were in the immediate area, then reached under his gray cloak to a pouch on the housebreaker and brought forth the glass cutter.

Luthien stared at the figurine Oliver had noted. It was a fine representation of a halfling in pewter, standing boldly, cape billowing out behind him and sword drawn, its tip to the ground beside bare, hair-topped feet. A fine work indeed, but Luthien couldn't help but notice how it paled compared with the larger, gem-studded statues in the window beside it.

Luthien grabbed Oliver by the arm, just as the halfling placed the glass cutter on the window.

"Who put it there?" Luthien asked.

Oliver looked at him blankly.

"The statue," Luthien explained. "Who put it on such prominent display?"

Oliver looked at him doubtfully, then turned to regard the statue. "The proprietor?" he asked more than stated, wondering why the answer didn't seem obvious to his companion.

"Why?"

"What are you whispering about?" the halfling demanded.

"Bait for a halfling thief?" Luthien asked.

Again Oliver looked at him doubtfully.

"You must learn to smell such things," Luthien replied with a smile, perfectly mimicking Oliver's accent.

Oliver looked back to the statue, and for the first time noticed how out of place it truly seemed. He turned and nodded grimly to Luthien. "We should be leaving."

Luthien felt the hairs standing up on the back of his neck. He leaned out of the alcove, looking one way and then the other, and his expression was grave when he slipped back in beside Oliver.

"Cyclopians at both ends of the lane," he explained.

"Of course," Oliver replied. "They were there all alo—" The halfling stopped in mid-sentence, suddenly viewing things with the same suspicion as Luthien.

"They were indeed," the young Bedwyr remarked dryly.

"Have we been baited?" Oliver asked.

In answer, Luthien pointed upwards. "The rooftops?"

Oliver replaced his tools and had the grapnel out in an instant, twirling it about and letting fly. Once secured, he handed the rope to Luthien and said politely, "After you."

Luthien took the rope and glared at Oliver, knowing that the reason the halfling wanted him to go first was so that Oliver could be hauled up and wouldn't have to climb.

"And do look about before you bring me up," the halfling remarked.

With a resigned sigh, the young man began the arduous task of climbing hand over hand. Oliver snickered when Luthien was out of the way, noticing that the young man's crimson-hued shadow had been left behind on the pewter store's window.

Luthien did not take note of Oliver's movements as he went up, reminding himself that he shouldn't be surprised when he pulled the halfling up a few minutes later to find Oliver carrying a sack filled with china plates and crystal goblets.

"I could not let all our work this night go to waste," the sly halfling explained.

They set off among the steeply pitched rooftops, often walking in gullies between two separate roofs. Unlike the city section near the dividing wall, all the buildings here were joined together, making the whole block one big mountainlike landscape of wooden shingles and poking chimneys. Scrambling along, Luthien and Oliver were often separated, and only luck prevented Luthien from whispering to a shadowy form that appeared in a gully ahead of him.

The form moved before Luthien could speak, and that movement showed it to be several times the size of the halfling.

Cyclopians were on the roofs.

Luthien fell flat on his belly, thanking God once more for his crimson cape. He glanced about, hoping that Oliver would amble up beside him, but had a feeling that the halfling had gone beyond this point along the other side of the angled roof to Luthien's left. He could only hope that Oliver was as wary, and as lucky, as he.

Faced with a dangerous decision, Luthien took out his bow and unfolded it, popping the pin into place. The cyclopian in the gully ahead continued to mill about, apparently not yet sensing that it was not alone. Luthien knew he could hit it, but feared that if the shot was not a clean and swift kill, the brute would bring half the Praetorian Guards in Montfort down upon him.

His decision was made for him a moment later when he heard a cry and a crash, accompanied by the unmistakable sound of a certain halfling's taunts.

Oliver had not been caught unawares. Moving along the gutter over-looking the avenue, the halfling had noted a movement near the peak of the high roof. For a fleeting instant, he thought it to be Luthien, but he realized that his companion was not so stupid as to be up high where he might be spotted a block away.

Oliver then pressed on, looking for a more defensible position. If those were indeed cyclopians up there, they could dislodge him from his precarious perch simply by sliding down the steep roof into him. The halfling came to a break and started to turn right, but stopped, noticing the same cyclopian Luthien was watching. Fortunately, the dull-witted cyclopian hadn't noticed Oliver, and so the halfling ran on along the gutter, taking some consolation in the fact that this next roof was not nearly as steep.

He was hoping that he could get around this roof, too. Then he could swing back around to come at the cyclopian in the gully from the opposite side of Luthien.

He never made it that far.

A cyclopian came at him from over the rooftop, half running, half bouncing its way down, sword waving fiercely. Oliver dropped his sack of booty to the roof and drew rapier and main gauche, settling into a defensive crouch. When the cyclopian came upon him, predictably leading with its outstretched sword, the halfling dodged aside and hooked the blade with his shorter weapon.

He tugged fiercely and the dumb cyclopian, not wanting to lose its weapon, held on stubbornly. Its momentum, coupled with Oliver's tug, proved too much, though, and over the edge the brute pitched, getting a kick in the rump from Oliver as it went tumbling past. The cyclopian yelped through the twenty-five-foot drop, then quieted considerably when it smacked the cobblestones face first. Its arm twisted underneath as it hit, and its own sword drove up through its chest and back to stick garishly into the air.

"Fear not, stupid one-eye," Oliver taunted. He knew he should be quiet, but he just couldn't resist. "Even my main gauche could not now take your precious sword from you!"

Oliver spun about—to see three more cyclopians coming down at him from the rooftop. Figuring to go out in style, the halfling swashbuckler removed his great hat from one of the housebreaker's many magical pouches, slapped it against his hip to get the wrinkles out, and plopped it onto his head.

The cyclopian in the gully jumped straight up at the sound, then shuddered suddenly as Luthien's arrow drove into its back. Luthien started to jump up, thinking to run to Oliver's aid, but he flattened himself again, hearing the distinctive clicks of crossbows from the top of the steep roof to his left.

They were firing blindly, unable to penetrate the crimson cape's camouflage, but they had an idea of where to shoot. Luthien nearly wet his pants as three quarrels drove into the wood, one barely inches from his face.

Luthien was not so blind to the archers, though, seeing their black silhouettes clearly against the cloudy gray sky. He knew that there must be magic in the folding bow (or he must have been blessed with an inordinate amount of luck), for his next shot was too perfect as he shifted to the side and awkwardly fired off the arrow.

One of the cyclopians was jolted upright and tilted back its thick head—Luthien could see the thin black line of his arrow sticking from the creature's forehead. The brute reached up and grabbed the quivering shaft, then fell backward, dead, and slid halfway down the other side of the roof.

The other two cyclopians disappeared behind the roof peak.

Oliver's rapier darted left, then right, his main gauche slashing out to the side, intercepting one attack, his spinning rapier defeating another. Down ducked the halfling as a cyclopian sword swooped over his head.

Then he sneaked in a counter, jabbing his rapier into the leg of one of the brutes just above the knee. The one-eye howled in pain.

"Ha, ha!" Oliver cried, as though the score was a foregone conclusion, hiding his honest surprise that, in his wild flurry, he had managed to hit anything. He brought his rapier up to the brim of his cap in victorious salute, but was put back on his heels, spinning and dodging, even whimpering a bit, as the wounded cyclopian responded with a vicious flurry of its own.

The halfling felt his heels hanging over open air. His blades went into another blinding spin, keeping the cyclopians at bay long enough for him to skitter along the roof's edge. The maneuver allowed him to regain secure footing, though the cyclopians kept pace every step, and the halfling quickly came to the realization that fighting with three-to-one odds, with his back leaning out over a long drop, was not such a smart thing to do.

The two cyclopians, their crossbows reloaded, popped up over the roof peak again. They glanced all about, cursing the crafty thief and his concealing cloak, then fired at the spot where they suspected Luthien had been.

Luthien, having slipped around the roof, looked up the slope, past the dead cyclopian, to the backs of his remaining adversaries. Up came the bow and he let fly his arrow, hearing the grunt as one of the brutes caught it full in the back. The other cyclopian regarded its companion curiously for just a moment, then snapped its terrified gaze about. It scrambled up the last few steps of the roof and leaped over the peak, but took Luthien's next flying arrow right in the belly.

Groaning, the brute disappeared over the peak.

Luthien readied another arrow, amazed, for the cyclopian that had taken the shot in the back staggered down the peak at him. The brute picked up momentum and speed with every stride, and Luthien soon realized that it was running completely out of control, blinded by pain and rage. It fell far short of Luthien and slid down to the roof's rough shingles on its face.

Oliver's only saving grace was the fact that the three cyclopians had never learned to fight in harmony. Their lumbering strikes did not complement each other, and for Oliver, it seemed more as though he was fighting one fast, long-armed opponent than three.

Still, the halfling was in a precarious position, and it was only the cyclopians' clumsiness, and not his own skills with the blade, that gained him a temporary advantage. One of the brutes lunged forward only to be intercepted by the cyclopian standing beside it, also lunging forward. The two got tangled together, and one actually fell on its rump to the roof. The third cyclopian, also coming straight forward in a thrusting maneuver, became distracted, turning its gaze to the side.

Oliver's main gauche took the weapon from the brute's hand.

"What will you do now?" the halfling taunted his disarmed opponent. The cyclopian stared dumbfoundedly at its empty hand as though it had been betrayed.

The angry brute snarled, curled its fingers, and punched out, and Oliver, caught by surprise, barely ducked in time. The halfling had to bend at the waist, then wave his arms frantically to regain his balance. He came up straight and slashed across with his shorter blade, forcing the advancing cyclopian back at the last desperate instant.

"I had to ask," Oliver scolded himself.

His slip had given the edge back to the cyclopians, all three standing straight and untangled once more. The one who had lost its sword grinned wickedly, drawing out a long curved dagger.

Oliver was back on his heels in an instant. "This is not going well at all," he admitted, and gave a profound sigh.

One of the brutes lunged for him again, and Oliver's rapier turned the attack aside. Then, to Oliver's surprise, the cyclopian kept going forward, pitching right off the ledge—and Oliver noticed an arrow sticking from its back. The halfling glanced up past the cyclopians to see Luthien running over the peak, bow in hand and readying another arrow.

"I love this man," Oliver said, sighing.

One of the cyclopians charged up to intercept Luthien before he could ready another arrow.

Luthien shrugged and smiled agreeably, dropping the bow to the roof and whipping out his sword. In came the brute, standing somewhat below the young man, and down snapped Luthien's blade, diagonally across the cyclopian's sword.

Luthien brought his sword back up, turning it as he went so that its tip sailed further ahead, nicking the cyclopian on the cheek. Up came the cyclopian's blade as well, stubbornly aimed for Luthien's chest.

But Luthien was quick enough to bring his sword ringing down on the thrust once again, this time turning his blade under his own arm as he slapped the cyclopian's sword out to the side. Continuing the subtle twist of the wrist, Luthien straightened his elbow suddenly, snapping the sword tip ahead.

The cyclopian grimaced and took a quick step back, sliding Luthien's blade out of its chest. It looked down to the wound, even managed to get a hand up to feel the warmth of its spilling blood, then slumped facedown on the roof.

The cyclopian remaining against Oliver, wielding only the dagger, used sheer rage to keep the halfling on the defensive. It sliced across, back and forth, and Oliver had to keep hopping up on his toes, sucking in his ample stomach as the blade zipped past. The halfling held his rapier out in front to keep the cyclopian somewhat at arm's length and kept hurling taunts at the brute, goading it into making a mistake.

"I know that one-eye is not a proper description," the halfling said, laughing. "I know that cyclopians have two eyes, and the brown one on their backsides is by far the prettier!"

The brute howled and whipped its arm above its head, cutting down with the dagger as if it meant to split Oliver down the middle. In stepped the halfling and up came his arms in a cross above his head, catching and cradling the heavy blow, though his little legs nearly buckled under the tremendous weight.

Oliver spun about to put his back toward his opponent, which further extended the cyclopian's arm and forced the brute to lean forward. Before the cyclopian could react, Oliver reversed his grip on his main gauche and brought it swinging down, like a pendulum, to rise behind him and move in the general direction of the cyclopian's groin.

Up went the squealing cyclopian on its toes and higher, and Oliver aided the momentum by bending at the waist and throwing his weight backward into the brute's rising shins.

Then the cyclopian was flying free, turning a half somersault. It hit the cobblestones flat on its back and lay very still.

"It is not so bad," Oliver called after it. "While you are down there, you might retrieve your sword!"

"More are coming," Luthien started to explain as he joined Oliver by the sack of booty. He understood his point was moot when Oliver reached into the sack, drew out a plate and whipped it sidelong up the roof. Luthien turned about to see the spinning missile shatter against the bridge of a cyclopian's nose as the beast came over the peak.

Luthien looked back to Oliver in disbelief.

"That was an expensive shot," the halfling admitted with a shrug.

Then the two were running along the uneven roofs, and when they ran out of rooftops, they descended to the street. They heard the pursuit—so much pursuit—and found themselves surrounded.

Oliver started for an alcove, but Luthien cut him off. "They will look down there," the young man explained, and instead, he put his back against the plain wall to the side of the shadowy alcove's entrance.

Oliver heard cyclopians turning into the lane all about him and promptly dove under the folds of the cloak.

As Luthien had predicted, the one-eyes flushed out every alcove in the area, then many ran off, grumbling, while others began checking all the houses and shops nearby. It was a long, long while before Luthien and Oliver found the opportunity to run off again, and they cursed their luck, seeing that the eastern horizon was beginning to glow with the onset of dawn.

Soon they found cyclopians on their trail again, particularly one large and fast brute that paced them easily. With the rising sun, they couldn't afford to stop and try to hide again, and they found the situation growing more and more desperate as the stubborn beast on their heels called out directions to its trailing and flanking companions.

"Turn and shoot it! Turn and shoot it!" Oliver shouted, sounding as winded and exasperated as Luthien had ever heard him. Luthien thought the reasoning sound, except for the fact that he did not have the time to turn around for any kind of a shot.

Then the city's dividing wall was in sight across Morkney's Square, a wide plaza centered by a tremendous fountain and flanked by many craft shops and fine restaurants. The square was quiet in the early light; the only movements were that of a dwarf chipping away at a design on the newly built fountain and a few merchants sweeping their store fronts, or setting up fruit and fish stands.

The friends ran past the seemingly ambivalent dwarf, Oliver taking the effort to quickly tip his hat to his fellow short-fellow.

The large cyclopian came running right behind, howling with glee, for it was sure that it could get the little one, at least, before Oliver got over the wall.

The distracted cyclopian never saw the dwarf's heavy hammer, only saw the stars exploding behind its suddenly closed eyelid.

Oliver looked back from the wall, grabbed Luthien and bade him do likewise. They nodded their appreciation to the dwarf, who didn't acknowledge it, just patiently reeled in his hammer (which was on the end of a long thong) and went back to his work before the other cyclopians flooded the square.

Back at their apartment, the morning bloom in full, Luthien grumbled considerably about how dangerously close they had come that day, while Oliver, fumbling in his sack, grumbled about how many of the plates and goblets he had broken in their wild flight.

Luthien eyed him with disbelief. "How could you even think of stealing anything at that time?"

Oliver looked up from the sack and shot Luthien a wistful smile. "Is that not the fuel of excitement and courage?" he asked, and he went back to his inspection, his frown returning as he pulled a large chip of yet another plate out of the sack.

The halfling's mouth turned up into that mischievous smile again a moment later, though, and Luthien eyed him curiously as he reached deeply into his sack.

Oliver shot Luthien a sly wink and took out the pewter figurine of a halfling warrior.

CHAPTER 17

OUTRAGE

THE FRIENDS SPENT the next few days in or near their apartment, making small excursions to the Dwelf mostly to hear the chatter concerning the mysterious Crimson Shadow. The last daring hit, raiding two shops and taking out several cyclopian guards in the face of an apparent conspiracy of several merchants, had heightened the talk considerably, and Oliver thought it prudent, and Luthien did not disagree, that they lie low for a while.

Oliver accepted the self-imposed quarantine in high spirits, glad for the rest and thrilled to be a part of the growing legend. Luthien, though, spent most of the days sitting quietly in his chair, brooding. At first, Oliver thought he was just nervous about all the attention, or simply bored, but then the halfling came to understand that Luthien's sorrows were of the heart.

"Do not tell me that you are still thinking of her," Oliver remarked one rare sunny day. The halfling had propped the door half open, letting the remarkably warm September air filter into the dark apartment.

Luthien blinked curiously when he looked at Oliver, but it didn't take the young man long to realize that Oliver had seen through his sad frown.

He looked away quickly, and that nonverbal response told Oliver more than any words ever could.

"Tragic! Tragic!" the halfling wailed, falling into a chair and sweeping his arm over his eyes dramatically. "Always this is tragic!" His movements shifted the chair, knocking it against a pedestal, and Oliver had to react quickly to catch the pewter halfling figurine as it started to tumble to the floor.

"What are you speaking of?" Luthien demanded, not in the mood for any cryptic games.

"I am speaking of you, you silly boy," Oliver replied. He paused for a few moments, dusting off the pedestal and replacing his trophy. Then, with no response apparently forthcoming, he turned a serious expression upon Luthien.

"You have been searching for the meaning of life," Oliver stated, and Luthien eyed him doubtfully. "I only lament that you choose to find it in the form of a woman."

Luthien's expression became a fierce scowl. He started to respond, started to rise up from his chair, but Oliver waved a hand at him absently and cut him off.

"Oh, do not deny it," the halfling said. "I have seen this very thing too many times before. Courtly love, we call it in Gascony."

Luthien settled back down in the chair. "I have no idea of what you are talking about," he assured Oliver, and to emphasize his point, he looked away, looked out the partially opened door.

"Courtly love," Oliver said again, firmly. "You have seen this beauty and you are smitten. You are angry now because we have not returned to the market, because you have not had the opportunity to glimpse her beauty again."

Luthien bit hard on his lip, but did not have the conviction to deny the words.

"She is your heart's queen, and you will fight for her, champion any cause in her name, throw your cloak over a puddle of mud in her path, throw your chest in front of an arrow racing toward her."

"I will throw my hand into your face," Luthien answered seriously.

"Of course you are embarrassed," Oliver replied, seeming not at all concerned, "because you know how stupid you sound." Luthien looked at him directly, an open threat, but still the halfling was undeterred. "You do not even know this woman, this half-elf. She is beautiful, I would not argue, but you have imagined everything, every quality you desire, as part of her, when all you really know is her appearance."

Luthien managed a slight chuckle; the halfling was right, he knew. Logically, at least, Luthien was acting ridiculous. But he couldn't deny his feelings, not in his heart. He had seen the green-eyed half-elf for perhaps a minute, and yet that vision had been with him ever since, in waking hours and dreams alike. Now, discussed openly in the bright air of a shining morning, his obsession sounded ridiculous.

"You seem to possess a great deal of knowledge on this subject," Luthien accused, and Oliver's mouth turned up into a wistful smile. "Personal knowledge," Luthien ended wryly.

"Perhaps," was the strongest admission Oliver would offer.

They let it go at that, Luthien sitting quietly and Oliver busying himself in rearranging the many trophies they had acquired. Luthien didn't notice it, but many times that morning, Oliver's expression would brighten suddenly, as though the halfling was reliving fond memories, or Oliver would grimace in heartfelt pain, as though some of the memories were, perhaps, not so pleasant.

Sometime later, Oliver tossed his winter coat across Luthien's lap. "It is ruined!" he wailed and lifted up one sleeve to show Luthien a tear in the fabric.

Luthien studied the cut carefully. It had been made by something very sharp, he knew, something like Oliver's main gauche, for instance. The weather had been unseasonably warm the last few days, even after sunset, and as far as Luthien could remember, the halfling had not worn this coat at all. Curious that it should be torn, and curious that Oliver should find that tear now, with the sun bright and the air unseasonably warm.

"I will throw it out to the greedy children," the halfling growled, hands on hips and face turned into one of the most profound pouts Luthien had ever witnessed. "Of course, this weather will not hold so warm. Come along, then," he said, grabbing his lighter cloak and moving for the door. "We must go back to market that I might buy another one."

Luthien didn't have to be asked twice.

They spent the day in the bustling market, Oliver perusing goods and Luthien, predictably, watching the crowd. The thief of the young man's heart did not show herself, though.

"I have found nothing of proper value," Oliver announced at the end of the day. "There is one merchant-type who will be in a better bargaining mood tomorrow, though. Of this much, I am sure."

Luthien's disappointment vanished, and as the young man followed his halfling friend out of the market, his expression regarding the halfling was truly appreciative. He knew what Oliver was up to, knew that the halfling was truly sympathetic to his feelings. If Luthien had held any doubts that Oliver's lecture concerning "courtly love" was founded in personal experience, they were gone now.

They went through a similar routine at the market the next day, breaking for lunch at one of the many food kiosks. Oliver carried on a light conversation, mostly about the shortcomings of merchant-types: winter was near at hand and he had found little luck in reducing any of the prices for warm coats.

It took the halfling some time to realize that Luthien wasn't listening to him at all and wasn't even eating the biscuit he held in his hand. The halfling studied Luthien curiously and understood before he even followed the young man's fixed stare across the plaza. There stood the half-elven slave girl, along with her merchant master and his entourage.

Oliver winced when the half-elf looked up from under her wheat-colored tresses, returning Luthien's stare, even flashing a coy smile the young man's way. The worldly halfling understood the implications of that response, understood the trials that might soon follow.

Oliver winced again when the merchant, noticing that his slave had dared to look up without his permission, stepped over and slapped the back of her head.

The halfling jumped on Luthien before he even started to rise, blurting out a dozen reasons why they would be foolish to go over to the merchant at that time. Fortunately for the halfling, several of the people nearby knew him and Luthien from the Dwelf and quickly came over to help out, recognizing that trouble might be brewing.

Only when a group of Praetorian Guards came over to investigate did the fiery young Bedwyr calm down.

"All is well," Oliver assured the suspicious cyclopians. "My friend, he found a cock'a'roach in his biscuit, but it is gone now, and cock'a'roaches, they do not eat so much."

The Praetorian Guards slowly moved away, looking back dangerously with every step.

When they were out of sight, Luthien burst free of the many hands holding him and stood up—only to find that the merchant and his group had moved along.

Oliver had to enlist the aid of the helpful men to "convince" Luthien, mostly by dragging him, to go back to the apartment. But after the helpful group had gone, the young Bedwyr stormed about like a caged lion, kicking over chairs and banging his fists on the walls.

"I really expected much better from you," Oliver remarked dryly, standing by the pedestal to protect his treasured halfling warrior figurine from the young man's tirade.

Luthien leaped across the room to stand right in front of the halfling. "Find out who he is!" the young Bedwyr demanded.

"Who?" Oliver asked.

Luthien's arm flashed forward, snapping up the figurine, and he cocked his arm back as if he meant to throw the statue across the room. The sincerely terrified expression on Oliver's face told him that the halfling would play no more coy games.

"Find out who he is and where he lives," Luthien said calmly.

"This is not so smart," Oliver replied, tentatively reaching for the figurine. Luthien jerked his arm up higher, moving the trophy completely out of the little one's reach.

"It might even be a trap," Oliver reasoned. "We have seen that many merchant-types wish us captured. They might suspect that you are the Crimson Shadow, and might have found the perfect bait."

"Bait like this?" Luthien replied, indicating the statue.

"Exactly," Oliver said cheerily, but his bright expression quickly descended into gloom when he realized Luthien's point. The previous danger hadn't stopped Oliver from lifting the bait from the hook.

The halfling threw his hands up in defeat. "Lover-types," he grumbled under his breath, storming out of the apartment and pointedly slamming the door behind him. But Oliver was truly a romantic, and he was smiling again by the time he climbed the stairs back to the street level.

CHAPTER 18

NOT SO MUCH A SLAVE

"I CANNOT TALK you out of this?" Oliver asked when he returned late that afternoon to find Luthien pacing the small apartment anxiously.

Luthien stopped and fixed a determined stare upon the halfling.

"Stealing co-ins and jew-wels is one thing," the halfling went on. "Stealing a slave is something quite different."

Luthien didn't blink.

Oliver sighed.

"Stubborn fool," the halfling lamented. "Very well, then. We are in some luck, it would seem. The merchant-type's house lies in the northwestern section of town, just south of the road to Port Charley. There are not so many guards up there and the wall has not yet even been completed about these new houses. Lesser merchant-types, mostly. But still they will have guards, and you can be death-sure that, in stealing a slave, you will put Duke Morkney and all of his Praetorian Guards on our tail. When we go . . ."

"Tonight," Luthien clarified, and again, the defeated halfling sighed.

"Then tonight might be our last night in the hospitable city of Montfort," Oliver explained. "And we will be on the road with winter licking at the backs of our boots."

"So be it."

"Stubborn fool," Oliver grumbled, and he moved across the floor to his bedroom and slammed the door behind him.

They got to the alley beside the merchant's house, a fine two-story L-shaped stone structure with many small balconies and windows, without incident. Oliver continued to express his doubts and Luthien continued to ignore him. The young man had found a purpose in life, something that went beyond discarding winter coats where the poor children of Tiny Alcove might find them. He thought himself the proverbial knight in shining armor, the perfect hero who would rescue his lady from the evil merchant.

He never thought to ask if she needed rescuing.

The house was quiet—all the area was quiet, for few thieves bothered to come this way and thus few guards patrolled the streets. A single candle showed through one of the house's windows, on the short side of the "L." Luthien led Oliver to the wall of the darker section, the main section.

"I cannot talk you out of this?" Oliver asked one final time. When Luthien scowled at him, he tossed his magical grapnel, which caught above a balcony and just below the roof. This time Oliver went first, fearing to let the anxious Luthien up on that balcony without him. The way the young man was behaving, Oliver feared he would crash through the doorway, slaughter everybody in the house, then walk up to the Ministry, woman in arms, and demand that Duke Morkney himself pronounce them married!

The halfling made the balcony and slipped over to the door. Confident that no one was about, he came back to the rail to signal for Luthien to follow.

Oliver wasn't really surprised to see the young Bedwyr already halfway up and climbing furiously.

He would have hissed out a scolding at his impetuous companion, but something else caught the halfling's attention. Looking across the courtyard to a window showing the flicker of a candle, Oliver saw a woman—the beautiful slave, he knew from her long tresses, shining lustrously even in the dim light. The halfling watched curiously as the woman tucked that hair up under a black cap, then picked up a bundle, blew out the candle, and moved for the window.

Luthien's hand came over the top of the railing and the young Bedwyr began to pull himself up. He was stopped as he straddled the railing by the smiling halfling, Oliver motioning for him to look over his shoulder.

A makeshift rope, a line of tied bedsheets, hung from window to ground, and a lithe form, dressed in gray and black, similar to Oliver's thieving clothes, nimbly made its way down.

Luthien's lips tightened into a grimace. Some thief had dared to break into the house of his love!

Oliver didn't miss the expression and understood where the anger was coming from. He put a hand on Luthien's shoulder, turning the young man to face him, then put a finger over his pursed lips.

The lithe form dropped to the ground and slipped off into the shadows.

"Well?" Oliver asked, indicating the rope.

Luthien didn't understand.

"Are you going back down?" the halfling asked. "We have no more business here."

Luthien looked at him curiously for a moment, then blinked in amazement and snapped his gaze across the small courtyard. When he looked back to Oliver, the halfling was smiling widely and nodding.

Luthien slid down the rope, and Oliver followed quickly, fearing that the young man would run off into the night. Oliver's humor about the unexpected turn of events faded quickly as he began to understand that even though this slave was apparently not what she appeared to be, this might be a long and difficult evening.

The halfling hit the ground, gave three tugs to retrieve his grapnel, and ran off after Luthien, catching the man two blocks away.

Luthien stood at a corner, peeking around the stone into an alley. Oliver slipped in between his legs and peeked around from a lower vantage point.

There stood the half-elven slave—there could be no doubt now, for she had removed the cap and was shaking out her wheat-colored tresses. With her were two others, one as tall as Luthien but much more slender, the other the woman's size.

Luthien looked down at Oliver at the same time the halfling turned his head to look up at Luthien.

"Fairborn," the halfling mouthed silently, and Luthien, though he had little experience with elves, nodded his agreement.

Luthien let Oliver, more versed in the ways of trailing, lead as they followed the group to the richer section of Montfort. The young Bedwyr could not deny the obvious, but still he was surprised when the three elves slipped into a dark alley, set a rope and quietly entered the second-story window of a dark house.

"She does not need your help," Oliver remarked in Luthien's ear. "Leave this alone, I beg."

Luthien could not find the words to argue against Oliver's solid logic. The woman did not need his help, so it appeared, but he would not, could not, leave this alone. He pushed Oliver away and kept his gaze locked on the window.

The three came back out in a short time—they were efficient at their craft—one of them carrying a sack. Down to the alley they went, and the slave woman gave a deft snap of the rope that dislodged the conventional grappling hook.

Oliver dove into the fold of Luthien's cape, and Luthien fell back motionless against the wall as the three came rushing out, passing barely five feet from the friends. Luthien wanted to reach out and grab the half-elf, confront her there and then. He resisted the urge with help from Oliver, who apparently sensing his companion's weakness, had prudently grabbed a tight hold on both of Luthien's hands. As soon as the three elven thieves were safely away, Oliver and Luthien took up the chase all the way back to the northwestern section.

The three parted company in the same place they had met the other two taking the sack and the slave heading back for her master's house.

"Leave this alone, I beg," Oliver whispered to Luthien, though the halfling knew beyond doubt that his plea was falling on deaf ears. Luthien didn't have to trail the woman now, knowing her destination, so he slipped ahead instead. He ducked behind the last corner before the merchant's house, melted under the folds of his cape and waited.

The woman came by, perfectly silent, walking with the practiced footsteps of a seasoned thief. She moved right past the camouflaged Luthien, glanced both ways along the street and started across.

"Not so much a slave," Luthien remarked, lifting his head to regard her.

He nearly jumped out of his boots at the sheer speed of the half-elf's movements. She whipped about, a short sword coming out of nowhere, and Luthien shrieked and ducked the metal blade clicking off the stone above his head. Luthien tried to move to the side, but the woman paced him easily, her sword flashing deftly.

In the blink of an eye, Luthien was standing straight again, his back to the wall, the tip of a sword at his throat.

"That would not be so wise," came Oliver's comment from behind the woman.

"Perhaps not," came a melodic, elven voice from behind the halfling.

Oliver sighed again and managed a glance over his shoulder. There stood one of the woman's companions, grim-faced, sword in hand and its tip not so far from the halfling's back. A bit to the side, further down the alley, stood the other female, bow in hand, an arrow trained upon Oliver's head.

"I could be wrong," the halfling admitted. He slowly slid his rapier back into its sheath, then even more slowly, allowing the elf to watch his every move, reached for a pouch and produced his hat, fluffing it and plopping it on his head.

The woman's green eyes bored into Luthien's stunned expression. "Who are you to follow me so?" she demanded, her jaw firm, her expression grave.

"Oliver," Luthien prompted, not knowing what he should say.

"He is a stubborn fool," the halfling gladly put in.

Luthien's expression turned sour as he regarded his loyal companion.

The woman prodded slightly with the sword, forcing Luthien to swallow.

"My name is Luthien," he admitted.

"State your business," she demanded through gritted teeth.

"I saw you in the market," the young man stammered. "I . . ."

"He came for you," Oliver put in. "I tried to tell him better. I tried!"

The woman's features softened as she regarded Luthien, and a note of recognition came into her eyes. Gradually, she eased her sword away. "You came for me?"

"I saw him hit you," Luthien tried to explain. "I mean . . . I could not . . . why would you allow him to do that?"

"I am a slave," the woman replied sarcastically. "Half-elven. Less than human." Despite her bravado, a certain tinge of anger and frustration became evident in her tone as she spoke.

"We are standing in the street," the male elf reminded them, and he motioned for Oliver to get back into the alley. To the halfling's relief, the thief put up his sword and the other one eased her bowstring back and removed the arrow.

The half-elf bade Luthien to follow, but hesitated as he walked by, looking curiously at the shadowy image he had left behind on the wall. Smiling with a new perspective, she followed Luthien into the alley.

"You are all half-elven," Oliver remarked when he had the moment to study the three.

"I am full Fairborn," the woman with the bow answered. She looked at the male, an unmistakable connection between them. "But I do not desert my elven brethren."

"The Cutters," Oliver remarked offhandedly, and all three of the elven thieves snapped their surprised looks upon him.

"A notorious thieving band," Oliver explained calmly to Luthien, who obviously had no idea of what was going on. "By reputation, they are all of the Fairborn."

"You have heard of us, halfling," the woman with Luthien said.

"Who in Montfort has not?" Oliver replied, and that seemed to please the three.

"We are not all elves," the half-elven woman answered, looking back over her shoulder at Luthien, a look that truly melted his heart.

"Siobhan!" the male said sternly.

"Do you not know who we have captured?" the woman asked easily, still looking at Luthien.

"I am Oliver deBurrows," the halfling cut in, thinking that his reputation had preceded him. To Oliver's disappointment, though, none of the three even seemed to take note that he had spoken.

"You have left a curious shadow behind," Siobhan remarked to Luthien. "Out in the street. A crimson shadow."

Luthien looked back that way, then turned to Siobhan. and shrugged apologetically.

"The Crimson Shadow," the male half-elf remarked, sounding sincerely impressed. He slid his sword completely away then, nearly laughing aloud.

"And Oliver deBurrows!" the halfling insisted.

"Of course," the male said offhandedly, never taking his gaze from Luthien.

"Your work is known to us," Siobhan remarked, her smile coy. Luthien's heart fluttered so badly he thought it would surely stop. "Indeed," she continued, looking to her friends for confirmation, "your work is known throughout Montfort. Truly you have put the merchants on their heels, to the delight of many."

Luthien was sure that he was blushing a deeper red than the hue of his cape. "Oliver helps," he stuttered.

"Do tell," the deflated halfling muttered under his breath.

"I would have thought you a much older man," Siobhan went on. "Or a longer-living elf, perhaps."

Luthien eyed her curiously. He remembered Brind'Amour's words that the cape had belonged to a thief of high renown, and it seemed that Siobhan had heard of the cape's previous owner, as well. Luthien smiled as he wondered what mischief the first Crimson Shadow might have caused in Montfort.

"It grows late," remarked the elven woman from further down the alley. "We must go, and you," she said to Siobhan, "must get back inside your master's house."

Siobhan nodded. "We are not all of the Fairborn," she said again to Luthien.

"Is that an invitation?" Oliver asked.

Siobhan looked to her companions, and they, after a moment, nodded in reply. "Consider it so," Siobhan said, looking back directly at Luthien, making him think, in the secret hopes of his heart, that the invitation was more than to join the thieving band.

"For you and for the esteemed Oliver deBurrows," she added, her tone revealing that extending the invitation to Oliver, however kindly phrased, had come more as an afterthought.

Luthien looked over her shoulder to Oliver, and the halfling gave a slight shake of his head.

"Consider it," Siobhan said to Luthien. "There are many advantages to being well connected." She flashed her heart-melting smile one last time, as if confirming to the stricken Luthien that she had more than a thieving agreement in mind. Then, with a nod to her departing companions, she started across the street toward her impromptu rope.

Luthien never blinked as he watched her graceful movements, and Oliver just shook his head and sighed.

CHAPTER 19

IN HALLOWED HALLS

FEIGNING INTEREST, DUKE Morkney leaned forward in his wooden chair, his skinny elbows poking out of his voluminous red robe, hands set on his huge desk. Across from him, several merchants spoke all at once, the only common words in their rambling being "theft" and "Crimson Shadow."

Duke Morkney had heard it all before from these same men many times over the last few weeks, and he was truly growing tired of it.

"And worst of all," one merchant cried above the tumult, quieting the others, "I cannot get that damned shadow stain off of my window! What am I to reply to the snickers of all who see it? It is a brand, I say!"

"Hear, hear!" several others agreed.

Morkney raised one knobby hand and thinned his lips, trying to bite back his laughter. "He is a thief, no more," the duke assured them. "We have lived with thieves far too long to let the arrival of a new one—one that conveniently leaves his mark—bother us so."

"You do not understand!" one merchant pleaded, but his face paled and he went silent immediately when Morkney's withered face and bloodshot amber eyes turned upon him, the duke scowling fiercely.

"The commoners may help this one," another merchant warned, trying to deflect the vicious duke's ire.

"Help him what?" Morkney replied skeptically. "Steal a few baubles? By your own admission, this thief seems no more active than many of the others who have been robbing you of late. Or is it just that his calling card, this shadowy image, stings your overblown pride?"

"The dwarf in the square . . ." the man began.

"Will be punished accordingly," Morkney finished for him. He caught the gaze of a merchant at the side of his desk and winked. "We can never have too many dwarvish workers, now can we?" he asked slyly, and that seemed to appease the group somewhat.

"Go back to your shops," Morkney said to them all, leaning back and waving his bony arms emphatically. "King Greensparrow has hinted that our production is not where it should be—that, I say, is a more pressing problem than some petty thief, or some ridiculous shadows that you say you cannot remove."

"He slipped through our trap," one of the merchants tried to explain, drawing nods from three of the others who had been in on the ambush at the Avenue of the Artisans.

"Then set another trap, if that is what needs be done!" Morkney snapped at him, the duke's flashing amber eyes forcing the four cohorts back a step.

Grumbling, the merchant contingent left the duke's office.

"Crimson Shadow, indeed," the old wizard muttered, shuffling through the parchments to find the latest word from Greensparrow. Morkney had been among that ancient brotherhood of wizards, had been alive when the original Crimson Shadow had struck fear into the hearts of merchants across Eriador, even into Princetown and other cities of northern Avon. Much had been learned of the man back in those long-past days, though he had never been caught.

And now he was back? Morkney thought the notion completely absurd. The Crimson Shadow was a man—a long-dead man by now. More likely, some petty thief had stumbled across the legendary thief's magical cape. The calling card might be the same, but that did not make the man the same.

"A petty thief," Morkney muttered, and he snickered aloud, thinking of the tortures this new Crimson Shadow would surely endure when the merchants finally caught up to him.

"I work alone," Oliver insisted.

Luthien stared at him blankly.

"Alone with you!" Oliver clarified in a huffy tone. The halfling stood tall (relatively speaking) in his best going-out clothes, his plumed chapeau capping the spectacle of Oliver deBurrows, swashbuckler. "It is very different being a part of a guild," he went on, his face sour. "Sometimes you must give more than half of your take—and you may only go where they tell you to go. I do not like being told where to go!"

Luthien didn't have any practical arguments to offer; he wasn't certain that he wanted to join the Cutters anyway, not on any practical level. But Luthien did know that he wanted to see more of Siobhan, and if joining the thieving band was the means to that end, then the young Bedwyr was willing to make the sacrifice.

"I know what you are thinking," Oliver said in accusatory tones.

Luthien sighed deeply. "There is more to life, Oliver, than thievery," he tried to explain. "And more than material gain. I'll not argue that joining with Siobhan and her friends may lessen our take and our freedom, but it might bring us a measure of security. You saw the trap the merchants set for us."

"That is exactly why you cannot join *any* band," Oliver snapped at him.

Luthien didn't understand.

"Why would you so disappoint your admirers?" Oliver asked.

"Admirers?"

"You have heard them," the halfling replied. "Always they talk of the Crimson Shadow, and always their mouths turn up at the edges when they speak the name. Except for the merchant-types, of course, and that makes it all the sweeter."

Luthien shook his head blankly. "I will still wear the cape," he stammered. "The mark . . ."

"You will steal the mystery," Oliver explained. "All of Montfort will know that you have joined with the Cutters, and thus you will lower your budding reputation to the standards of that band. No, I say! You must remain an independent rogue, acting on your own terms and of your own accord. We will fool these silly merchant-types until they grow too wary, then we will move on—the Crimson Shadow will simply disappear from the streets of Montfort. The legend will grow."

"And then?"

Oliver shrugged as if that did not matter. "We will find another town—Princetown in Avon, perhaps. And then we will return to Montfort in a few years and let the legend grow anew. You have done something marvelous here, though you are not old enough to understand it," the halfling said. It seemed to Luthien that this was about as profound and intense as he had ever heard Oliver. "But you, the Crimson Shadow, the one who has fooled the silly merchant-types and stolen their goods from under their fat noses, have given to the people who live on the lower side of Montfort's wall something they have not had in many, many years."

"And that is?" Luthien asked, and all the sarcasm had left his voice by this point.

"Hope," Oliver answered. "You have given hope to them. Now, I am going to the market. Are you coming?"

Luthien nodded, but stood in the room for several minutes after Oliver had departed, deep in thought. There was a measure of truth in what the halfling had said, Luthien realized. By some trick of fate, a chance gift after a chance meeting with an eccentric wizard, and that after a chance meeting with an even more eccentric halfling, he, Luthien Bedwyr, had found himself carrying on a legend he had never heard of. He had been thrust into the forefront of the common cause of those who had been left out of King Greensparrow's designs for wealth.

"A peasant hero?" remarked the young man who was not a peasant at all. The furious irony, the layers of pure coincidence, nearly overwhelmed Luthien, and though he was truly confused by it all, an unmistakable spring was evident in his step as he ran out to catch up with Oliver.

The day was cold and gray—typical for the season—and the market was not so crowded. Most of the worthy goods had been bought or stolen and no new caravans had come in, or would for many months.

It didn't take long for Luthien and Oliver to wish that more people were at the plaza. The two, particularly Oliver, were quite a sight, and more than a few cyclopians, including one who wore a thick bandage around his bruised skull, took note of the pair.

They stopped at a kiosk and bought some biscuits for lunch, chatting easily with the proprietor about the weather and the crowd and anything else that came to mind.

"You should not be out here," came a whisper when the proprietor shuffled away to see to another customer.

Luthien and Oliver looked at each other, and then at a slender figure, cloaked and hooded, standing beside the kiosk. He turned to face them more squarely and peeked up from under the low hood, and they recognized the male half-elf they had met the previous night.

"Do they know?" Oliver asked quietly.

"They suspect," the half-elf answered. "They'll not openly accuse you, of course, not with witnesses about."

"Of course," Oliver replied. Luthien continued to stare off noncommittally, not wanting to give away the secret conversation and not understanding much of what the half-elf and Oliver were talking about. If the brutish cyclopians suspected him and Oliver, then why didn't they simply walk over and arrest them? Luthien had been in Montfort long enough to know that the law here required little evidence to haul someone away—gangs of Praetorian Guards were commonplace in the area near to Tiny Alcove and usually left with at least one unfortunate rogue in tow.

"There is news," the half-elf continued.

"Do tell," Oliver started to say, but he quieted and looked away as a group of cyclopians ambled past.

"Not now," came the half-elf's whisper as soon as the cyclopians had moved off a short distance. "Siobhan will be behind the Dwelf at the rise of the moon."

"We will be there," Oliver assured him.

"Just him," came the reply, and Oliver looked over at Luthien. When Oliver turned his curious glance back the half-elf's way, he found that the thief had moved along.

With a sigh, the halfling turned back again, toward Luthien and the open plaza, and then he understood the half-elf's sudden departure. The cyclopian group was returning, this time showing more interest in the pair.

"My papa halfling, he always say," Oliver whispered to Luthien, "a smart thief can make his way, a smarter thief can get away." He started off, taking Luthien's arm, but was forced to stop as the cyclopians rushed in suddenly, encircling the pair.

"Cold day," one of them remarked.

"Buying the last things for winter?" asked another.

Oliver started to respond, but bit back his retort as Luthien broke in suddenly, looking at the cyclopian directly.

"That we are," he replied. "Montfort's winter is colder for some than for others."

The cyclopian didn't seem to understand that remark—Oliver wasn't sure that he did, either. Though Oliver didn't know it, his last remarks at the apartment had put a spark into the young Bedwyr, had touched a chord in Luthien's heart. He was feeling quite puffed at this moment—feeling the part of the Crimson Shadow, the silent speaker for the underprivileged, the purveyor of coats for cold children, the thorn in the rich man's side.

"How long've you been in Montfort?" the brute eyeing Luthien asked slyly, fishing for clues.

Now Oliver stepped forward and wrapped his arm about Luthien's waist forcefully. "Since the day my son was born," the halfling proclaimed, to the wide-eyed stare of Luthien. "Alas, for his poor mother. She could not accept the size of this one."

The cyclopians looked at each other in confusion and disbelief. "He's your father?" the one addressing Luthien asked.

Luthien draped his arm about Oliver's shoulders. "My papa halfling," he answered, imitating Oliver's thick accent.

"And what business—" the cyclopian began to ask, but a comrade of his grabbed his arm and interrupted, motioning for him to drop the matter.

The cyclopian's fierce scowl diminished as he glanced around the marketplace. Dozens of men, a couple of dwarves, and a handful of elves were watching intently—too intently—their faces grim and more than one of them wearing a dirk or short sword at his belt.

The cyclopian group was soon on its way.

"What happened?" Luthien asked.

"The cyclopians just met people who have found their hearts," Oliver answered. "Come along and be quick. The Cutter was right—we should not be about this day."

■ ■ ■

"Kiss me." Her melodic tones caught the young man off guard, and the unexpected request nearly buckled his knees.

Luthien froze in place, staring blankly at Siobhan, having no idea of what to do next.

"You want to." She stated the obvious.

"I came because I was told that there was some news," Luthien informed her. He wished that he hadn't said that as soon as the words left his mouth; what a stupid time to be changing the subject!

The half-elf seemed even more alluring to poor Luthien as she stood in the silver moonlight in the shadowy alley behind the Dwelf. She gave a coy smile and pushed her long tresses back from her fair face. Luthien glanced back over his shoulder, as though he expected Oliver to be standing nearby watching him. The halfling had gone into the Dwelf and told Luthien to meet him there when he finished his business with Siobhan.

Luthien looked back to see that Siobhan's smile had already disappeared without a trace.

"The dwarf—" she began grimly, but she stopped suddenly as Luthien leaped up to her and kissed her full on the lips. The embarrassed young man hopped back immediately, searching Siobhan's expression for some hint of a reaction.

But it was Luthien, and not Siobhan, who seemed most ill at ease. The half-elf only smiled and shook the hair back from her face, seemingly composed. "Why did you ask me to do that?" Luthien asked bluntly.

"Because you wanted to," Siobhan replied.

Luthien's proud shoulders slumped visibly.

"And I wanted you to do it," Siobhan admitted. "But I thought we should be done with it."

"Be done with it?" Luthien echoed. That did not sound promising.

Siobhan took a deep breath. "I only thought that you and Oliver should know . . ." she began to explain. She paused, as if the words were hard to come by.

Luthien was beginning to get more than a little alarmed. "Know what?" he prompted, and stepped toward Siobhan, but she put up a defensive hand and took a step back.

"The dwarf," she went on. "The dwarf who helped you in Morkney Square. He has been taken by the Praetorian Guard and locked in a dungeon to await trial."

Luthien's expression went grave, his hands clenched anxiously at his sides. "Where?" he asked determinedly. Siobhan had no doubt he meant to run off that very moment and rescue the dwarf.

Her helpless shrug, accompanied by a sincere expression, thoroughly deflated him. "The Praetorian Guards have many dungeons," she said, shaking her head. "Many dungeons. The dwarf will be tried in the Ministry on the morrow, along with so many others," Siobhan quickly added. "He will be sentenced to the mines, no doubt."

Luthien didn't understand. He stood in quiet thought for a moment, trying to sort some things out, then looked curiously at Siobhan. How could she possibly know about the dwarf in Morkney Square? he wondered, and it seemed as if she was reading his thoughts, for that coy smile returned to her face.

"I told you there were benefits to being well connected," she said, answering his unspoken question. "And I thought that you should know."

Luthien nodded.

Almost as an afterthought, Siobhan added, "The dwarf, Shuglin by name, knew that he would be caught, of course."

"Was he part of your band?"

Siobhan shook her head. "He was a craftsman and no more."

Luthien nodded knowingly, but he didn't *know* anything at all. Why would this craftsman dwarf help him, fully understanding that he would likely be captured and punished?

"I must be going," Siobhan said, looking up at the position of the moon.

"When will I see you again?" Luthien asked anxiously.

"You will," Siobhan promised, and started to fade into the shadows.

"Siobhan!" Luthien called, more loudly than he had intended, his desires getting the best of his judgment. The fair maiden stepped back near to him, an inquisitive look on her face.

Staring into the green glow of her eyes, Luthien could not find any words. His expression said it all.

"One more kiss?" she asked. She barely had the words out before Luthien was up against her, his lips soft against hers.

"You will see me again," she teased again, pulling back. And then she was gone, a shadow among the shadows.

"It is all a game," Oliver complained when he and Luthien were walking home later that night, the young man with a few too many ales in him. "Surely you are not so stupid that you cannot understand that."

"I do not care!" It was a determined statement, if a bit slurred.

"Dwarves are always being accused, tried, and sentenced to hard work in the mines," Oliver went on stubbornly. "Legal and unarguable slavery. That is how Montfort has become so wealthy, can you not see?"

"I do not care."

Oliver was afraid Luthien would say that.

Before the next dawn, the two companions were creeping along the city's dividing wall at the base of the Ministry. They got over the divider easily enough, and Oliver, knowing the routine, positioned them in the shadows of the cathedral's northern wing: a transept, one of two armlike sections of the long building that gave it the general shape of a cross. Few buildings were close to the cathedral on this side, forming an open plaza. "We must go in the west end," Oliver explained, peeking around the edge of the huge transept wall, and he told Luthien to put away the cape.

Luthien did as instructed, but he was hardly conscious of the act. This was the closest he had been to the Ministry, and how small the young Bedwyr felt! He looked straight up the side of the building's wall to the tremendous flying buttresses and many gargoyles hanging out over the edge to look down upon puny humans such as he. Ominous and imposing was Montfort's Ministry in the growing light of predawn.

Soon after the sun came up, the plaza was buzzing with many people, merchants and craftsmen, and quite a few Praetorian Guards, as well. Luthien noted that many of the people had brought their children along with them.

"The last day of the week," Oliver explained, and Luthien nodded, realizing that another week, and the whole month of September, had indeed passed them by. "Tax day. They bring their children in the hope of mercy." Oliver's ensuing snicker showed that he did not think mercy a likely thing for any of them.

They waited inconspicuously behind the transept as the Ministry's tall and narrow oaken doors were unlocked and opened at the west end, and the procession made its way into the giant structure, one group at a time. Burly cyclopians stood to either side of the doors, asking questions, herding the men and their families as they would sheep.

Oliver pulled Luthien further back into the shadows of the wall as a caravan of ironbound wagons rolled up to the side door in the middle of the transept's north-facing wall, another impressive portal, though not as huge as the cathedral's towering western doors. Many Praetorian Guards came out of the cathedral to meet the transported prisoners—four men, three women, and two dwarves, all dressed in loose-fitting gray robes, mostly open at the front. Luthien recognized the one who had helped him and Oliver immediately, from the dwarf's bushy blue-black beard poking out under the cowl of his robe, and by his clothes, the same sleeveless leather tunic he had been wearing that morning in Morkney Square.

"Shuglin," the young Bedwyr mouthed silently, remembering the name Siobhan had told him.

He motioned to Oliver, but the halfling held him back firmly. Luthien threw a plaintive look at the halfling.

"Too many," Oliver mouthed, and pointed to a structure across the plaza from the prisoner wagons. Luthien noticed several forms milling about this smaller building and a couple sitting on the cobblestones like the beggars who were more common to the city's lower section. They were fully cloaked, their faces hidden, but scrutinizing them more closely now, Luthien understood his partner's concern.

Each one of them was broad-shouldered like a warrior, or like a cyclopian.

"Do they expect us?" Luthien whispered in Oliver's ear.

"It would be an easy trap," the halfling replied. "An easy way to be rid of a growing problem. Perhaps they understand how stupid you can be."

Luthien glared at him, but standing beside that tremendous structure, the day brightening around them, the streets and cathedral teeming with Praetorian Guards, Luthien couldn't honestly refute the halfling's insult. He didn't want to leave, but instead wondered what in the world he might do.

When he looked back at Oliver, his expression went from crestfallen to curious. The halfling had tucked his dark jacket, his black shoes and his hat away in pouches, had rolled his pant legs up even higher, and was in the process of slipping into the printed dress of a young girl. That done, Oliver produced a horsehair wig, long and black (where he had gotten that, Luthien had no idea), then wrapped veils about his head, strategically covering his mustache and goatee.

Good old Oliver, Luthien thought, and he had to fight hard to keep his laughter from bursting forth.

"I am your virgin daughter, merchant-type," the halfling explained, handing Luthien a pouch that jingled with coins. Luthien opened it and peeked in, and his eyes went wide to see that the coins were gold.

Oliver took him by the arm and led him boldly around the corner of the transept. They gave the prisoner wagons and the cyclopians a wide berth, moving near the center of the plaza as they made their way up to the Ministry's western door.

That western wall held Luthien's attention all the way to the door. It was not flat, but rather filled with niches, and in these were beautiful, brightly painted statues. These were the figures of Luthien's religion: the heroes of old, the shining lights of Eriador. He noted that they had not been maintained of late, their paint chipping and peeling, and the nests and droppings of many birds evident in nearly every niche.

The young Bedwyr was beginning to work himself into quite a state, but Oliver's unexpected outburst broke into his private thoughts.

"I told you that we would be late, Papa!" the halfling wailed in a high-pitched voice.

Luthien glanced incredulously the halfling's way, but straightened immediately and eyed the two amused cyclopian guards. "Are we too late?" he asked.

" 'E's afraid of the mines for missing the tax call," one of the brutes remarked, and it blinked lewdly as it regarded Oliver. "Or might be that Morkney'll take his little daughter." The wicked laughter that followed made Luthien want to go for his hidden sword, but he held steady.

Oliver nudged him hard, and when he looked at the halfling, Oliver motioned fiercely for the pouch.

Luthien nodded and grabbed a few gold coins. He'd owe Oliver dearly for this; he knew how hard it was to part the halfling from his ill-gotten gains!

"Are you sure that I am late?" Luthien asked the cyclopians. They looked at him curiously, their interest apparently piqued by his sly tone.

Luthien looked up and down the near-empty plaza, then inched his coin-filled hand toward them. The dimwitted cyclopians caught on.

"Late?" one asked. "No, you're not late." And the brute stepped aside and drew open one of the tall doors, while its companion eagerly scooped up the bribe.

Luthien and Oliver entered a small and high foyer, barely a five-foot square, with doors similar to the outside pair looming directly before them. They both breathed easier when the cyclopians shut the outside doors behind them, leaving them alone for the moment.

Luthien started to reach for the handle of an inside door, but Oliver stopped him and put a finger to pursed lips. They moved their ears against the wood instead, and could hear a strong baritone voice calling out names—the tax roll, Luthien realized.

They had come this far, but what were they to do now? he wondered. He looked to Oliver, and the halfling nodded in the direction over Luthien's shoulder. Following the gaze, Luthien noticed that the foyer was not enclosed. Ten feet up the middle of both side walls were openings leading straight in, to concealed corridors that ran south along the front wall of the structure.

Out came the magical grapnel, and up they went. They passed several openings that led onto a ledge encircling the cathedral's main hall, and came to understand that this corridor was the path used by the building's caretakers to clean the many statues and stained-glass windows of the place.

They went up a tight stairway, and then up another, and found a passage leading to an arched passageway that overlooked the cathedral's nave fully fifty feet up from the main area's floor.

"The triforium," Oliver explained with a sly wink, apparently believing that they would get a good view of the proceedings in relative safety.

They were fifty feet up from the floor, Luthien noted, and barely halfway to the network of huge vaulting that formed the structure's incredible roof. Again the young Bedwyr felt tiny and insignificant, overwhelmed by the sheer size of the place.

Oliver was a couple of steps ahead of him by then, and turned back, realizing that Luthien wasn't following.

"Quickly," the halfling whispered harshly, drawing Luthien back to the business at hand.

They scampered along the back side of the triforium wall. On the front side of the passageway, centering every arch, was a relatively new addition to the cathedral, a man-sized, winged gargoyle, its grotesque and horned head looking down over the ledge, looking down upon the gathering. Oliver eyed the statues with obvious distaste, and Luthien heartily concurred, thinking the gargoyles a wretched stain upon a holy church.

They crept along quietly to the corner of the triforium, where the passageway turned right into the southern transept. Diagonally across the way, Luthien saw the pipes of a gigantic organ, and beneath them the area where the choir had once stood, singing proud praises to God. Now cyclopians milled about in there.

The altar area was still perhaps a hundred feet away, tucked into the center of a semicircular apse at the cathedral's eastern end. The bulk of this apse was actually in Montfort's lower section, forming part of the city's dividing wall.

Luthien's eyes were first led upward by the sweeping and spiraling designs of the apse, up into the cathedral's tallest spire, he realized, though from this angle, he could not see more than halfway up the towering structure. He shook his head and looked lower to the great tapestries of the apse, and to the altar.

There, Luthien got his first good look at the infamous Duke Morkney of Montfort. The old wretch sat in a comfortable chair directly behind the altar, wearing red robes and a bored expression.

At a podium at the corner of the apse stood the roll-caller, a fierce-looking man flanked by two of the largest cyclopians Luthien had ever seen. The man read a name deliberately, then paused, waiting for the called taxpayer—a tavern owner in the lower section whom Luthien recognized—to shuffle out of one of the high-backed wooden pews in the nave and amble forward with his offering.

A sour taste filled Luthien's mouth when the summoned man handed a bag of coins over to a cyclopian. The merchant stood, head bowed, while the bag was emptied onto the altar, its contents quickly counted. The amount was then announced to Morkney, who paused a moment—just to make the merchant sweat, Luthien realized—then waved his arm absently. The merchant verily ran back to his pew, gathered up the two children who had come in with him, and scooted out of the Ministry.

The process was repeated over and over. Most of the taxpayers were allowed to go on their way, but one unfortunate man, an old vendor from a kiosk in the market, apparently had not given enough to suit the greedy duke. Morkney whispered something to the cyclopian at his side, and the man was promptly dragged away. An old woman—his wife, Luthien assumed—leaped up from a pew, wailing in protest.

She was dragged off also.

"Pleasant," Oliver muttered at Luthien's side.

About halfway through the tax call, two hours after Luthien and Oliver had found their high perch, Morkney raised one skinny hand. The man at the lectern stepped down and another took his place.

"Prisoners!" this new caller yelled, and a group of cyclopians rose and stepped out from the first pew, pulling the chained men, women, and dwarves along with them.

"There is our savior," Oliver remarked dryly, noting the bushy-haired dwarf. "Have you any idea of how we might get near to him?"

The obvious sarcasm in Oliver's tone angered Luthien, but he had no response. To his dismay, it seemed that the halfling was right. There was nothing he could do, nothing at all. He could see at least two-score cyclopians in the cathedral and did not doubt that another two-score were nearby, not counting the ones in the wagons beyond the door of the north transept. That, plus the fact that Morkney was reputedly a powerful wizard, made any plan to spring Shuglin seem utterly ridiculous.

Charges were read and the nine prisoners were given various punishments, various terms of indenture. The four men would accompany a caravan to Princetown—likely to be sold off to the army once they reached the Avon city, Oliver informed Luthien. The three women were sentenced to serve as house workers for various merchants, friends of the duke—Oliver did not have to explain their grim fate. And the dwarves, predictably, were given long terms at hard labor in the mines.

Luthien Bedwyr watched helplessly as Shuglin was pulled away down the north transept and out the side door to a waiting wagon.

The tax call soon began anew, and Oliver and the fuming Luthien made their way back along the triforium to the hidden corridor and down to the ledge overlooking the foyer. They let one released merchant go out, then slipped down into the small narthex. Oliver retrieved his grapnel and slipped it away, then adjusted his veils and motioned for Luthien to lead the way.

The cyclopian guards made some nasty comment as the "merchant" and his virgin daughter stepped between them, but Luthien was hardly listening. He didn't say a word all the way back to Tiny Alcove, and then paced the apartment like a caged dog.

Oliver, still in his maiden's garb, remarked that midday was almost upon them and the Dwelf would soon be open, but Luthien gave no indication that he heard.

"There was not a thing you could do!" Oliver finally shouted, hopping up to stand on a chair in Luthien's pacing path so that he could shout in the man's face. "Not a thing!"

"They took him to the mines," the burdened young man remarked, turning back on his heels and ignoring the ranting halfling. "Well, if they took Shuglin to the mines, then I go to the mines."

"By all the virgins of Avon," Oliver muttered under his breath, and he sat forcefully down in the chair and pulled the long black hair of his wig over his eyes.

CHAPTER 20

THE VALUE OF A KISS

OLIVER AND LUTHIEN waited for more than an hour, crouched among a tumble of boulders in the rocky foothills just a quarter of a mile outside Montfort's southern wall, overlooking the narrow trail which led to the mines. Riverdancer and Threadbare, glad to be out of the city, grazed in a small meadow not far away. Oliver had explained that the slaver wagon would not leave the city until the tax calls were completed—in case Morkney found some other "volunteers" who preferred to work in the mines rather than pay their heavy tithes.

Luthien had planned to hit the wagon here, long before it got to the mine; Oliver knew better.

The young Bedwyr's expression fell considerably when the wagon came bouncing along, escorted by a score of cyclopians riding fierce ponypigs.

"Now can we go to the Dwelf?" the weary halfling asked, but from the determined way angry Luthien stormed off to retrieve his mount, Oliver guessed the answer.

They trotted along the road a good distance behind the wagon, but sometimes catching sight of it far ahead on the rocky trail as it came out along an open ledge.

"This is not so smart a thing," Oliver said many times, but Luthien didn't reply. Finally, with more than three miles of trail behind them, the halfling stopped Threadbare. Luthien went on for about twenty yards, then turned Riverdancer about and looked back accusingly at his friend.

"The dwarf—" he began, but stopped immediately as Oliver threw his hand up. The halfling sat with his eyes closed, his head tilted back, and it seemed to Luthien that he was sniffing the air.

Threadbare leaped at Oliver's command, crashed through the brush at the side of the road and disappeared. Luthien eyed Oliver incredulously for just a moment, then heard the rumble of rushing ponypigs not so far up the road.

He had no time to escape to where Oliver had gone! Head down over the horse's thick mane, Luthien kicked Riverdancer into a dead run, back toward Montfort. A mile passed before he found a place where he could get off the road, and he and his horse skidded into a shallow gully and banged roughly off a stone wall. Luthien dropped from the saddle and grabbed Riverdancer's bridle, trying to soothe and quiet the nervous beast.

He needn't have worried, for the cyclopian band passed by at a full gallop, the thunder of their heavy mounts and the empty wagon bouncing behind them burying any other sounds.

After a few deep breaths, Luthien walked Riverdancer back to the road, waited a moment to make sure that all the one-eyes had passed, then galloped back the other way. He found Oliver right where he had left him.

"Is about time," the halfling complained. "We must get to the dwarf before they bring him to the lower mines. Once he is down there . . ." Oliver didn't bother finishing the thought, since Luthien was long past him by then.

The mine entrance was little more than an unremarkable hole in the side of a mountain, its sides propped with heavy timbers. The friends tethered their horses far to the side of the trail and crept to a vantage point behind some brush. They saw no cyclopians milling about; saw no movement at all.

"It is not well guarded," Luthien remarked.

"Why would it be?" Oliver asked him.

Luthien shrugged and started out from their hiding place. Oliver grabbed his arm, and when he looked back, the halfling directed his gaze along the mountain wall to another opening at the right of the mine entrance.

"It could be the barracks," the halfling whispered. "Or it could be where they keep the prisoners before they send them down."

Luthien looked from one entrance to the other. "Which one?" he finally asked, turning back to Oliver.

Oliver held his hands out wide and finally pointed to the main mine. "Even if this dwarf, Shuglin, is not in there, that is the way they must get him down."

Luthien moved up to the wall, Oliver right behind. He put the cowl of his crimson cape low and inched along, pausing at the entrance. The tunnel was dark, very dark, and Luthien had to pause until his eyes adjusted to the gloom. Even then, he could hardly make out the shapes within.

He lifted a fold in his cloak and Oliver scooted under, then Luthien inched his way around the corner and into the mine. They went around one bend—a side passage broke off to the right, possibly leading to tunnels within the other mine opening. Further down the passageway they were traveling, though, they saw the flicker of a torch and heard the footsteps of approaching cyclopians.

Into the side passage the friends skittered, taking up a position so they could continue to watch down the tunnel. Luthien had his bow out and assembled in an instant, while Oliver, flat on the floor, peeked around the corner.

The torchlight grew; two cyclopians rounded the next bend, talking lightly. Oliver held two fingers up in the air for Luthien to see, then kept his hand up high, ready to signal the attack.

Luthien drew back his bowstring. The light intensified, as did the sound of heavy cyclopian footsteps. Oliver's hand snapped down and Luthien leaped by the prone halfling into the tunnel, bow bent and arrow ready to fly.

The cyclopians were barely a dozen feet away, leaping wildly in surprise.

Luthien missed.

He could hardly believe it, but as one of the cyclopians jumped and twisted in fright, its arm waving high, his arrow sliced in below the creature's armpit, grazing it but doing no real damage.

Luthien stood staring blankly, holding his bow as if it had deceived him. On came the growling cyclopians, and if Oliver hadn't slid out to intercept, Luthien would have surely been cut down.

Rapier and main gauche whipped in a wild dance, Oliver scoring a wicked hit in the ribs of the closest brute and nicking the second before they even realized he was there.

The wounded cyclopian, weapon arm tight against its side, clubbed at the halfling with its torch. Its companion fell back a step, then came on, throwing curses and waving a heavy club.

Oliver rolled left, back toward the tunnel. Luthien, sword drawn, dove ahead behind the halfling. The club wielder, its bulbous eye following Oliver's movement, gawked in surprise as the young man's sword exploded into its chest.

Oliver came up short, halfway through the roll, and fell forward instead, inside the arc of the down-swinging torch. The halfling's rapier plunged ahead once, and then again, and the cyclopian staggered backward, eyeing little Oliver with sheer disbelief.

Then it fell dead.

Taking only the moment to put out the torch (and for Oliver to ask, "How did you miss?"), the two friends moved on more urgently now. Soon more torchlight loomed up ahead.

The tunnel ended at a ledge forty feet above the floor of a large, roughly oval chamber. Five cyclopians were in here and, to the friends' relief, two dwarves, including one with a bushy, blue-black beard and a sleeveless leather tunic. Both were shackled at the wrists and ankles, surrounded by their cyclopian captors. The group stood near the opposite end of the chamber in front of a large hole cut into the floor. Suspended above the hole was a block and tackle, with one thick rope going to a cranking mechanism on the chamber's floor at the side of the hole and two other ropes disappearing beneath the floor.

One cyclopian leaned over the hole, loosely holding the side rope and looking down, while another worked the crank.

Luthien crouched and nocked another arrow, but Oliver looked at him doubtfully, pointing to one side and then the other of the well-lit room. At least three tunnels came into this chamber at the floor level.

Luthien understood the halfling's concerns. This higher region of the complex was likely for the guards, and those three tunnels, and the one Luthien and Oliver had just come down, might quickly fill with cyclopians at the first sounds of battle.

But Luthien did not miss the significance of the crank. Those two ropes supported a platform, he figured, and once Shuglin and the other dwarf went down, they would be lost to him forever.

The cyclopian leaning over the hole nodded stupidly and called down. The brute was answered by another cyclopian, and then another, not far below the rim.

The first cyclopian jerked suddenly, then fell headlong into the hole. Four other cyclopians, seeing the arrow in their companion's back, looked across the room and up to the ledge, to see Luthien fire off another arrow, then take a rope from Oliver. The arrow skipped harmlessly off the cranking mechanism, but the cyclopian working it fell back and shrieked.

Oliver, his adhering grapnel set against the ceiling far out from the ledge, jumped onto Luthien's back and as soon as Luthien packed his folding bow away, the two swung down, crimson and purple capes billowing behind them. Luthien angled the jump toward the crank: the most important target, he figured.

Oliver's calculations in setting the grapnel were not far off, and Luthien let the halfling down as they came to the low point of the swing, the halfling falling the last three feet to the floor, landing in a headlong roll, one somersault after another.

Luthien continued on toward the cyclopian near the crank. The young Bedwyr kicked out, trying to knock the brute aside, but he went up too high as he passed, kicking at empty air when the cyclopian ducked. The brute's distraction cost it dearly, though, for when it looked back down, it saw Oliver, or more specifically the tip of Oliver's rapier, coming toward it. The fine blade pierced the cyclopian's belly and sliced upward into its lungs, and it fell aside, gasping for breath that would not come.

Luthien, spinning in tight circles from the momentum of his kick, swung right over the shaft. As he had figured, he saw a large platform holding half a dozen yelling cyclopians fifteen feet below the rim. But the far edge of the hole was still out of reach when his momentum played out and the rope began its inevitable swing the other way—where three armed cyclopians waited.

Luthien wisely jumped free, flailing his arms wildly. He banged his shin hard against the lip of the shaft and nearly fell in. With a groan and a roll, he cleared the drop and regained his footing, drawing his sword. With a quick look, he rushed to the far side of the rim. One of the cyclopians went for the halfling; the others shoved past the dwarves and went to the corner to meet the circling Luthien.

And all of them were screaming for help, screaming that "the Crimson Shadow" was upon them!

"I see the biggest came for me," Oliver remarked, and he wasn't idly bantering. The brute facing him was among the largest and ugliest cyclopians Oliver had ever seen. Worse still, the cyclopian wore heavy padded armor—Oliver doubted that his rapier could even get through it—and wielded a huge double-bladed battle-ax.

Down came the weapon in an overhead chop, and Oliver darted forward, rolling right through the brute's widespread legs. He looked back to see sparks flying as the weapon took a chunk of stone out of the floor.

Oliver dove and rolled back the other way as the cyclopian roared and swung about. Then they were facing each other squarely again, Oliver with his back to the crank and the shaft beyond.

Luthien charged in bravely, daring the odds. These two brutes were also well armored, and they wielded fine swords that accepted the heavy hits of the young Bedwyr's first flurry and turned his blade aside.

Luthien lunged straight forward; a sword chopped his blade's tip to the stone, while the other brute thrust ahead, forcing Luthien to twist violently to the side to avoid being impaled. He got his weapon back in line quickly and slapped the stubborn cyclopian's sword away, then countered viciously.

But the attack was again defeated.

Oliver's rapier jabbed into the front of the cyclopian's armor three times in rapid succession, but the blade only bent and would not penetrate. The halfling had hoped to tire the heavy-muscled brute, but it was he who was soon panting, diving this way and that to avoid the mighty battle-ax.

He glanced all about, searching for a new tactic, a chink in the cyclopian's armor. What he found instead was a ring of keys tagged onto the brute's belt. Instinctively, the halfling glanced over at Luthien, and continued to watch the young man out of the corner of his eye, waiting for the right moment.

Luthien was hard-pressed but fought back valiantly, fiercely, keeping the cyclopians in place. Looking past his adversaries, he saw the two dwarves untangle themselves from the chain that hooked them together at the ankles, saw them line up, and could guess well enough what they had in mind.

Luthien's sword snapped left and right, left and right, routines easily defeated, but demanding his opponents' complete attention.

The charging dwarves hit the cyclopians in the back of the legs, heaving them forward.

Luthien's sword snapped right, turning down the blade of that brute. The young Bedwyr then spun fast to the left, tucking his shoulder so that the cyclopian would not ram him and so the brute would slip behind him. And Luthien's sword flashed left, not only defeating the attack of that stumbling cyclopian, but knocking its sword to the stone.

He heard Oliver call out his name and spun around once more, jamming an elbow into the ribs of the cyclopian behind him and knocking the unfortunate brute down the shaft. Then Luthien rushed forward out of the tumbling cyclopian's desperate reach.

In one fluid motion, Oliver's rapier darted at his adversary and slipped to the side, through the loop of the key ring. Out to the right went the blade, snapping the keys from the jailor's belt, then high and back to the left, the key ring slipping free and flying through the air.

Into Luthien Bedwyr's waiting hand.

Luthien slid down to the floor, knowing the most important shackle to be the one binding the dwarves together. He was lucky—the second key fit—and the lock clicked open, and Luthien jumped back up to meet the remaining cyclopian, its sword back in its hand.

For all the advantage the friends had apparently gained, though, none were breathing easier. Torchlight flickered from two of the side tunnels, and yells and heavy footsteps echoed down one. The soldiers on the platform below the room were not content to sit back and wait, either. A one-eyed face came above the lip, and then another to the side; the brutes were climbing the guide ropes.

The jailor roared to see its keys go flying away and on the monster came, its huge ax thrashing back and forth. Oliver twisted and darted, making no attempt to get a weapon up to block the battle-ax, knowing that either of his blades would be snapped in half or taken from his hand by the sheer force of the jailor's blows.

The ax chopped down, and Oliver skipped left, near the crank. Up he hopped, atop the spindle and heavy rope. Then he hopped straight up again, desperately tucking his little legs under him as the ax swished across. The powerful cyclopian broke its momentum in mid-swing and curved the ax up high, over its head.

Down it came, and Oliver leaped and rolled to the right. The ax smashed onto the spindle, bit hard into the rope. The dimwitted jailor blinked in amazement as the frayed hemp unraveled and snapped, then watched helplessly as the rope's severed end soared off toward the block and tackle, and the platform (and a dozen cyclopians) fell away!

"I do thank you," Oliver remarked.

The jailor roared and swung about, overbalancing with the unbridled strength of the blow. The cyclopian never came close to hitting the halfling, though, for Oliver was on his merry way back toward the crank even as the ax came across the other way. Up again, Oliver poked straight out, his rapier's tip scoring a hit into the cyclopian's big eye.

The blinded jailor slashed wildly, this way and that, banging his ax off the stone, off the crank. Oliver tumbled and rolled, thoroughly enjoying the spectacle (as long as the ax didn't get too near to him!), and gradually, by calling out taunts, he managed to get the jailor near the edge of the hole.

On a nod from Oliver, Shuglin barreled into the backside of the jailor, launching the brute over the side.

"Should've kept the ax," the dwarf grumbled as the jailor, and the battle-ax, plummeted from sight.

One on one, Luthien had little trouble in parrying the vicious strokes of his cyclopian adversary. He let the one-eye play out the rage of its initial attack routine and gradually turned the tide against it, setting it on its heels with one cunning thrust after another.

Understanding that it could not win, the beast, with typical cyclopian bravery, turned and fled—to join its companions who were then entering the chamber from the side passages.

And so the forces faced off for several tense seconds, the cyclopian ranks swelling to a dozen or more. Oliver looked back into the shaft doubtfully, for it dropped out of sight into the gloom and he did not even have his grapnel and line. Luthien managed to get the shackles off of Shuglin, then went to work on the other dwarf, while Shuglin ran over and retrieved the sword from the first cyclopian Oliver had killed.

Still the cyclopians did not advance, and Luthien understood that they were allowing their enemies to prepare themselves only because they expected more reinforcements to enter the room.

"We must do something," Oliver reasoned, apparently having the same grim thoughts.

Luthien slipped his sword in its scabbard and took out his bow, popping it open, pinning it, and setting an arrow in one fluid motion. The cyclopians understood then what this man with the curious stick was doing, and they fumbled all over themselves trying to get out of harm's way.

Luthien shot one in the neck, and it went down screaming. The others screamed, too, but they did not run for cover. Rather, they charged before Luthien could set another arrow.

"That was not what I had in mind," Oliver remarked dryly.

In the ensuing tumult, the desperate companions did not hear the twang of bowstrings, and all four of them looked on curiously as several of the charging brutes lurched weirdly and tumbled to the stone. Seeing arrows protruding from their backs, the friends and the cyclopians looked back to the room's ledge and saw a handful of slender archers—elves, probably—their hands moving in a blur as they continued to rain death on the cyclopians.

The one-eyes scrambled and fled, many running with one or two arrows sticking from them. In response, arrows and spears came whistling out of the side passages, and though Oliver's claims about a cyclopian's lack of depth perception held true once more, the sheer numbers of flying bolts presented a serious problem.

"Run on!" came a cry from the ledge, a voice Luthien knew.

"Siobhan," he said to Oliver, pulling the halfling along as he made for the wall.

Luthien grabbed Oliver's rope and gave three quick tugs, releasing the magical grapnel from the ceiling. Siobhan's group already had one rope down to them, and Shuglin's companion grabbed on and began climbing swiftly, hand over hand. An arrow thunked into the dwarf's heavily muscled shoulder, but he only grimaced and continued on his determined way.

Luthien set Oliver's rope, heaving the grapnel onto the wall up beside the ledge, and he handed the rope over to Shuglin. The dwarf bade Oliver to grab on to his back, and up they went, Luthien shaking his head in amazement at how quickly the powerful dwarf could climb.

A spear skipped across the stone between Luthien's legs; cyclopians came out of all three passages, the lead ones carrying large shields to protect them from the archers on the ledge.

Luthien had wanted to wait and let Shuglin and Oliver get off the rope, not knowing how much weight the small grapnel would support, but he had run out of time. He leaped up as high as he could, grabbing the rope (and tucking its end up behind him), and began pulling himself up, hand over hand, trying to steady his feet against the wall so that he could walk along.

It wasn't as easy as the powerful dwarves made it look. Luthien made progress, but he would have surely been caught, or prodded by long spears, except that Shuglin shrugged Oliver off as soon as they made the ledge, and he and his dwarven companion took up the rope and began to methodically haul it in.

Arrows whizzed down past Luthien's head, and even more alarmingly, arrows and spears came up from below. He felt a bang against his foot and turned his leg to see an arrow sticking from the heel of his boot.

Then rough hands grabbed his shoulders and he was hauled over the ledge, and on the group ran. They passed several dead cyclopians, including the two Luthien and Oliver had killed, and came out of the tunnel, hearing that the cyclopians had gained the ledge behind them and were once again in pursuit.

"Our horses are there!" Luthien explained to Siobhan, and she nodded and kissed him quickly, then pushed him along to catch up with Oliver. She and her Cutter companions, along with Shuglin and the other dwarf, went the other way, disappearing into the brush.

"I cannot believe they came for us," Luthien remarked as he caught up to the halfling, Oliver with one foot already in Threadbare's stirrup.

"You must be a good kisser," the halfling answered. Then Threadbare leaped away, Riverdancer pounding right behind, back out onto the road.

The cyclopian horde exited the mine, howling with outrage, but all they heard was the pounding of hooves as Luthien and Oliver charged away.

CHAPTER 21

UNWANTED ATTENTION

LUTHIEN CASUALLY WALKED into the Dwelf sometime after Oliver, as the halfling had instructed. Oliver had grown very cautious in the week since the escape at the mines and had gone out of his way so that he and Luthien were not viewed as an inseparable team. Luthien didn't really understand the point; there were enough halfling rogues in this area of Montfort to more than cover their tracks. If the Praetorian Guard was searching for a human and his halfling sidekick, they would have dozens of possibilities to sift through.

Luthien didn't argue, though, thinking the halfling's demands were prudent.

The Dwelf was packed, as it had been every night that week. Elves and dwarves, halflings and humans filled every table—except one. There in the corner sat a group of cyclopians, Praetorian Guards, brimming with fine weapons and wearing grim, scowling expressions.

Luthien pushed his way through the crowd and found, conveniently, an empty stool at the bar near Oliver.

"Oliver!" he said, overly excited. "So good to see you again! How long has it been? A month?"

Oliver turned a skeptical look upon the exuberant young man.

"You were both in here the night before last," Tasman remarked dryly, walking past.

"Oops," Luthien apologized, giving a weak smile and a shrug. He looked around at the throng. "The crowd is large again this night," he remarked.

"Good gossip brings them in," Tasman replied, walking past the other way and sliding an ale across the counter to Luthien as he went off to see to another thirsty customer.

Luthien hoisted the mug and took a hearty swig, then noticed Oliver's profound silence, the halfling wearing an expression which showed him to be deep in contemplation.

"Good gossip—" Luthien started to say. He was going to ask what the patrons might be talking about, but in just deciphering the small patches of conversation he caught out of the general din about him, he knew the answer. They were talking about the Crimson Shadow—one scruffy-looking human even shuffled his drunken way near the cyclopians' table and muttered, "The Shadow Lives!" and snapped his fingers under their noses. One of the brutes started up immediately to throttle the rogue, but its comrade grabbed it by the arm and held it firmly in place.

"There is sure to be a fight," Luthien said.

"It will not be the first this week," Oliver replied glumly.

They remained in the Dwelf for more than an hour, Luthien taking in all the excited chatter and Oliver sitting with a single ale, mulling over the situation. A general chorus of dissatisfaction sounded behind every story, and it seemed to Luthien as if the legend he had become had given the poor of Montfort a bit of hope, a rallying point for their deflated pride.

His step was light when Oliver left the Dwelf, signaling him to follow.

"Perhaps we should stay a while," Luthien offered when they walked out into the crisp night air. "There may be a fight with the cyclopians, and the brutes are better armed than the Dwelf's patrons."

"Then let the patrons learn their folly," Oliver retorted.

Luthien stopped and watched the halfling as Oliver continued on his way. He didn't know exactly what was bothering Oliver, but he understood that it probably had something to do with the increased attention.

Oliver was indeed worried, fearful that this whole "Crimson Shadow" business was quickly getting out of control. It did not bother the halfling to hear the populace speaking out against the tyrannies of Morkney and his pompous merchant class—those wretches had it coming, the halfling figured. But Oliver did harbor a thief's worst fear: that he and Luthien were attracting too much unwanted attention from powerful adversaries. The halfling loved being the center of attention, oftentimes went out of his way to be the center of attention, but there were reasonable limits.

Luthien caught up to him quickly. "Have you planned an excursion into the upper section this night?" the young man asked, and it was plain from his tone that he hoped Oliver had not.

The halfling turned his gaze upon Luthien and cocked an eyebrow as if to mock the question. They had not pulled any jobs since springing Shuglin, and Oliver had explained that they likely wouldn't go into the upper section again for at least a month. He knew why Luthien was asking, though.

"You have plans," he stated as much as asked. Oliver could guess the answer readily enough. Luthien was ready for another tryst with Siobhan.

"I will meet with the Cutters," Luthien answered, "to check on Shuglin and his companion."

"The dwarves fare well," Oliver said. "Elves and dwarves get on well, since they share persecution at the hands of the humans."

"I just want to check," Luthien remarked.

"Of course," Oliver said with a wry smile. "But perhaps you should come this night back to the apartment. The air is chill and the Dwelf will likely see trouble before the moon is set."

The deflated look that washed over Luthien nearly pulled a burst of laughter from Oliver's serious expression. Oliver didn't harbor any intentions of keeping Luthien from his meeting, he just wanted to make the young man squirm a bit. In the halfling's view, love should never be an easy thing: sweeter tasting is the forbidden fruit.

"Very well," the halfling said after a long and uncomfortable moment. "But do not be out too late!"

Luthien was off and running, and Oliver did chuckle. He smiled all the way back to the apartment, his worries brushed aside by his romantic nature.

Candles burned long into the night in the private chambers of Duke Morkney's palace. A group of merchants had demanded an audience, and the duke, so busy with the approaching end of the trading season, could find no time to accommodate them earlier in the day.

Morkney could easily guess the topic of this meeting—all of Montfort was buzzing about the break at the mines. Morkney was not so concerned with the news—this wasn't the first time a prisoner had escaped, after all, and it wouldn't likely be the last. But these merchants, standing before the duke's fabulous desk, their grim features set with worry, obviously were more than a little concerned.

The duke sat back in his chair and listened attentively as the merchants complained and whined, their stories always connected to this mysterious Crimson Shadow figure.

"They're painting red shadows all over my store!" one man grumbled.

"And mine," two others said at the same time.

"And nearly every street in Montfort bears the words 'The Shadow Lives!' " offered another.

Morkney nodded his understanding; he, too, had seen the annoying graffiti. He understood, too, that this Crimson Shadow wasn't doing the painting. Rather, others were taking up the call of this mysterious figurehead; and that, Morkney was wise enough to realize, was more dangerous indeed.

He listened to the rambling merchants for another hour, politely, though he heard the same stories over and over again. He promised to take the matter under serious consideration, but secretly, Morkney was hoping that this minor annoyance would simply go away.

King Greensparrow was complaining again about the size of Montfort's tithe, and by all the words of the local seers, the winter would be a cold one.

And so the duke of Montfort was more than a little relieved when the captain of his Praetorian Guard interrupted his breakfast the next morning to inform him that the wagon caravan which had set out for Avon—the caravan carrying the four men who had been sentenced the same day as the dwarf, Shuglin—had been attacked on the road.

The captain of the guard produced a tattered red cloak, its material taking on the darker hue of dried blood in many places.

"We got the bloke," the cyclopian said. "No more Crimson Shadow. And we got the halfling 'twas said to be traveling in the shadow's shadow! And seven others"—he held up six fingers—"that were with them."

"And the caravan?"

"On its merry way," the cyclopian replied happily. "I lost four, but we got two more prisoners now, and the Crimson Shadow and the halfling're dead and dragging by ropes behind."

Morkney took the torn cloak and promised the soldier that he and his troops would be properly rewarded, then dismissed the cyclopian and found that his breakfast suddenly tasted better.

Later, though, on a sudden discomforting hunch, Morkney took the torn cloak into his private study. He searched his library for a specific tome, then fumbled through his desk drawers to find the proper components for a spell. The Crimson Shadow had left telltale signs behind him on his thieving adventures, silhouettes magically created against walls and windows, and by Morkney's reasoning, this cloak was likely the source.

The duke sprinkled exotic herbs and powders over the tattered cloth and read the enchantment from his book. The components eerily glowed a silvery blue hue, then went dark.

Morkney waited quietly for another minute, then another. Nothing happened. The bloodstained cloak was not magical and had never been enchanted.

Like the vandals painting walls throughout the city, this attempted raid had not been the handiwork of the real Crimson Shadow, but rather the lame attempt of an upstart glory-seeker.

Duke Morkney settled back into a large chair and put his old and shaky hand up to his chin. The Crimson Shadow was fast becoming a real problem.

▪ ▪ ▪

The Dwelf was subdued that day and that night, sobered by news that a halfling named Stumpy Corsetbuster and a human rogue by the name of Dirty Abner had been killed out on the road east of Montfort. The Crimson Shadow was dead, said the rumors—rumors that Oliver deBurrows did not seem so unhappy to hear when he entered the tavern to join Luthien sometime after sundown.

"Yep, the Crimson Shadow's no more, so it's said," Tasman remarked to them, filling their mugs.

It occurred to Luthien that the barkeep's expression was not in accord with the gravity of his words. And how long had it been, Luthien wondered, since Tasman had asked him or Oliver for any payment? Or were free drinks a benefit of renting an apartment from the barkeep?

Tasman walked away to see to another customer, but he let his stare—his knowing stare, Luthien realized—linger long on the young man and the halfling sitting beside him.

"A pity about Stumpy," Oliver remarked. "A fine halfling-type, with a fine fat belly." As with Tasman, though, Luthien didn't think Oliver's emotions agreed with his words.

"You're not bothered by this," the young man accused. "Some men—and your fine halfling-type—are dead."

"Thieves are killed every day in Montfort's streets," Oliver remarked, and he looked directly into Luthien's cinnamon-colored eyes. "We have to consider the benefits."

"Benefits?" Luthien nearly choked on the word.

"Our money will not last the winter," Oliver explained. "And I do not like the prospects of wandering the open road with so cold snowflakes coming down around me."

Luthien figured it out. He settled back over his mug of ale, his expression forlorn. The whole affair left a sour taste in his mouth.

"Now if we could only coax your remarkable cape to stop leaving its mark behind," Oliver added.

Luthien nodded grimly. There was a price in all of this less-than-honorable life, he decided, a price paid for by his conscience and his heart. People had died in the name of the Crimson Shadow, impersonating the Crimson Shadow, and now he and Oliver would use that grim fact for their benefit. Luthien drained his mug and motioned for Tasman to get him another.

Oliver tugged on his arm and nodded to the Dwelf's door, then whispered that they would be wise to take their leave.

A group of Praetorian Guards entered the tavern, smug looks on their ugly faces.

Soon after Luthien and Oliver got back to their apartment, a fight erupted in the Dwelf. Three men and two cyclopians were killed, many others wounded, and the Praetorian Guards were driven back into the upper section.

Duke Morkney was again awake late that night. Midnight was the best hour for what he had in mind, the time when magical energies were at their peak.

In his private study, the duke moved to one wall and slid a large tapestry aside, revealing a huge golden-edged mirror. He settled into a chair directly in front of it, read from a page in another of his magical tomes and tossed a handful of powdered crystal at the glass. Almost immediately, the reflections in the mirror disappeared, replaced by a swirling gray cloud.

Morkney continued his arcane chant, sending his thoughts—thoughts of the Crimson Shadow—into the mirror. The gray cloud shifted about and began to take form, and Morkney leaned forward in his chair, thinking that he would soon learn the identity of this dangerous rogue.

A wall of red came up suddenly across the mirror, blotting out everything within its enchanted confines.

Morkney's eyes widened in amazement. He took up the chant again for nearly an hour, even sprinkled the mirror several more times with the valuable crystalline powder, but he could not break through the barrier.

He went back to his desk and the pile of books and parchments he had pored over all day. He had found several references to the legendary Crimson Shadow, a thief who had terrorized the Gascons in their days of occupation. But these written tidbits were as vague as the clues left by the man now wearing the mantle. One reference had spoken of the crimson cape, though, and told of its magical dweomer designed to shelter its possessor from prying eyes.

Morkney looked back to the red mirror; apparently the cloak could shelter its possessor from magical prying, as well.

The duke was not too disappointed, though. He had learned much this night, gaining confirmation that the rogues on the road were impostors and that the real Crimson Shadow was indeed still alive. And wise Morkney, who had lived through centuries, was not too upset that the cloak had blocked his scrying attempt. He could not get the image of the Crimson Shadow into his mirror, but perhaps he could locate someone else, some tear in this crafty thief's disguise.

CHAPTER 22

BAIT

OLIVER WENT INTO the Dwelf alone a couple of days later. As usual, the place was crowded, and as usual, most of the talk centered on the continuing antics of the Crimson Shadow. One group of dwarves at a table near the bar where Oliver was sitting whispered that the Crimson Shadow had been killed out on the road, trying to free four enslaved men. The muscular, bearded dwarves lifted their flagons in toast to the memory of the gallant thief.

"He's not dead!" a human at a nearby table protested vehemently. "He pulled a job last night, he did! Got himself a merchant on the way." He turned to the other men at the table, who were nodding in complete agreement.

"Skewered the bloke right 'bout here," one of them added, poking a finger into the middle of his own chest.

Oliver was not surprised by any of the outrageous claims. He had witnessed similar events back in Gascony. A thief would rise to a level of notoriety and then his legend would be perpetuated by imitators. There was more than flattery involved here; often lesser thieves could pull jobs more easily, frightening their targets by impersonating a notorious outlaw. Oliver sighed at the thought that someone had died playing the Crimson Shadow, and the possibility that he and Luthien, if caught, might now be charged with murdering a human merchant did not sit very well. Pragmatically, though, all the talk was good news. Imitators would blur the trail behind Oliver and Luthien; if the merchant-types thought the Crimson Shadow dead, they would likely relax their guard.

The contented halfling tuned out the conversations and took a look around the Dwelf, searching for a lady to court. The pickings seemed slim this night, so Oliver went back to his ale instead. He noticed Tasman then, standing a short distance down the bar, wiping out glasses and eyeing him grimly. When Oliver returned the look, the wiry barkeep eased his quiet way down to stand before the halfling.

"You came alone," Tasman remarked.

"Young Luthien cannot control his heart," Oliver answered. "He goes again this night to meet with his love—a moonlight tryst on a rooftop." The halfling spoke wistfully, revealing that he was beginning to approve of the lovers. Oliver was indeed a romantic sort, and he remembered his days back in Gascony when he had left one (at least) broken heart behind him in every town.

Tasman apparently was not sharing the halfling's cozy feelings. His expression remained grim. "He'll be back at the apartment soon, then," he said.

"Oh, no," Oliver began slyly, misunderstanding Tasman's meaning. As he continued to study the grim-faced barkeep, Oliver began to catch on.

"What do you mean?" he asked bluntly.

Tasman leaned over the bar, close to Oliver. "Siobhan, the half-elf," the barkeep explained. "She was taken this day for trial in the morning."

Oliver nearly fell off his stool.

"She was accused for the escape at the mines," Tasman explained. "Her merchant master walked her into Duke Morkney's palace this very afternoon—apparently she didn't even know that she was to be arrested."

Oliver tried to digest the information and to fathom its many implications. Siobhan arrested? Why now? The halfling could not help but think that the half-elf's professional relationship with the Crimson Shadow had played a part in this. Perhaps even her personal relationship with Luthien had come into play. Was the wizard-duke onto Luthien's true identity?

"Some are even saying that she's the Crimson Shadow," Tasman went on, and Oliver winced at hearing that, certain then that Siobhan's arrest was no simple coincidence. "They're sure to be asking about that in the Ministry tomorrow morning."

"How do you know all this?" the halfling asked, though he realized that Tasman had keen ears and knew many things about Montfort's underworld. There was a reason that Oliver and Luthien had enjoyed free drinks and meals for the last weeks. There was a reason that wise Tasman seemed as amused as Oliver by the many tales of phony Crimson Shadows.

"They're making no secret of it," the toughened barkeep replied. "Every tavern's talking about the half-elf's arrest. I'm surprised that you hadn't heard of it before now."

Suspected thieves were arrested almost every day in Montfort, Oliver knew, so why was this one being made so public?

Oliver thought he knew the answer. The word "bait" kept popping into his mind as he skittered out of the Dwelf.

■ ■ ■

Oliver lost his "little-girl" smile as soon as he and Luthien walked between the Praetorian Guards outside the Ministry's great front doors the next morning. In the foyer, the halfling looked disdainfully at his disguise, wondering why he kept winding up in this place. Of course, Oliver had known the night before, when he had told forlorn Luthien of Siobhan's arrest, that he would find himself in the Ministry once more.

But he didn't have to like it.

"We might be causing her harm," Oliver reasoned, and not for the first time, as he set the magical grapnel on the passageway's entrance high above the room. Luthien took the rope in hand and verily ran up the wall, then hoisted Oliver behind him.

"Morkney might only suspect that she has knowledge of the Crimson Shadow," Oliver went on when he got into the hidden passage. "If we are caught here this day, it could weigh badly on the one you love." To say nothing of how it would weigh on the two of them! Oliver reasoned, keeping the thought private. The flustered halfling pushed the long black hair of his wig out of his face and roughly rearranged his printed dress, which had gotten all twisted up in the climb.

"I have to know," Luthien answered.

"I have seen many traps baited like this before," Oliver said.

"And have you ever left a love behind?" Luthien asked.

Oliver didn't answer and made no further remarks. The question had stung, for Oliver had indeed left a lover behind—a halfling girl of eighteen years. Oliver was very young, living in a rural village and just beginning his career as a thief. The local landowner (the only one in town worth stealing from) could not catch up to Oliver, but he did find out about the halfling's romance. Oliver's lover was taken and Oliver had run off, justifying his actions as in his lover's best interest.

He never found out what happened to her, and many times, in hindsight, he wondered if his "tactical evacuation" had been wrought of pure cowardice.

So now he followed Luthien up to the higher levels, as they had gone on their first excursion into the great cathedral. Oliver noticed that there seemed to be more cyclopians about this day than on that previous occasion, and many more villagers, as well. Morkney was planning a show, the halfling mused, and so the wicked duke wanted an audience.

Oliver grabbed Luthien by the shoulder and bade the man to put on the crimson cape—and Oliver wrapped his own purple cape over the print dress, and plopped his hat, which had gotten more than a little rumpled, atop his head—before they crept out onto the gargoyle-lined triforium fifty feet up from the floor.

They went out quietly and without interruption, ending at the corner of the south transept, where Luthien crouched behind a gargoyle, Oliver behind him.

The scene was much the same as the first time the friends had ventured into the majestic building. Red-robed Duke Morkney sat in a chair behind the great altar at the cathedral's eastern end, appearing quite bored as his lackeys called the tax rolls and counted the pitiful offerings of the poor wretches.

Luthien watched the spectacle for only a moment, then focused his attention on the front pews of the cathedral. Several people were sitting in line, wearing the gray hooded robes of prisoners and guarded by a group of cyclopians. Only one was a dwarf, yellow haired, and Luthien sighed in relief that it was not Shuglin. Three others were obviously men, but the remaining three appeared to be either younger boys or women.

"Where are you?" the young Bedwyr whispered, continuing his scan through long minutes. One of the forms in the prisoner line shifted then, and Luthien noted the end of long wheat-colored hair slipping out from under her hood. Instinctively, the young man edged forward as if he would leap off of the ledge.

Oliver took a tight hold on Luthien's arm and did not blink when the young man turned to him. The halfling's expression reminded Luthien that there was little they could do.

"It is just as it was with the dwarf," Oliver whispered. "I do not know why we are here."

"I have to know," Luthien protested.

Oliver sighed, but he understood.

The tax rolls went on for another half hour, everything seeming perfectly normal. Still, Oliver could not shake the nagging feeling that this was not an average day at the Ministry. Siobhan had been taken for a reason, and spreading the news about the arrest had been done deliberately, the halfling believed. If Shuglin had been arrested to send a clear message to the Crimson Shadow, then Siobhan had been taken to lure the Crimson Shadow in.

Oliver looked disdainfully at Luthien, thinking how much the young man resembled a netted trout.

The man calling the roll at the lectern gathered up his parchments and moved aside, and a second man took his place, motioning for the Praetorian Guards to prepare the prisoners. The seven gray-robed defendants were forced to stand and the man called out a name.

An older man of at least fifty years was roughly pulled out from the pew and pushed toward the altar. He stumbled more than once and would have fallen on his head, except that two cyclopians flanking him caught him and roughly stood him upright.

The accusation was a typical one: stealing a coat from a kiosk. The accusing merchant was called forward.

"This is not good," Oliver remarked. The halfling nodded toward the merchant. "He is a wealthy one and likely a friend of the duke. The poor wretch is doomed."

Luthien's lips seemed to disappear into his frustrated scowl. "Is anyone ever found innocent in this place?" he asked.

Oliver's reply, though expected, stung him profoundly. "No."

Predictably, the man was declared guilty. All of his belongings, including his modest house in Montfort's lower section, were granted to the wealthy merchant, and the merchant was also awarded the right to personally cut off the man's left hand that it might be displayed prominently at his kiosk to ward off any future thieves.

The older man protested weakly, and the cyclopians dragged him away.

The dwarf came out next, but Luthien was no longer watching. "Where are the Cutters?" he whispered. "Why aren't they here?"

"Perhaps they are," Oliver replied, and the young man's face brightened a bit.

"Only to watch, as are we," the halfling added, stealing Luthien's glow. "When thieves are caught, they are alone. It is a code that the people of the streets observe faithfully."

Luthien looked away from the halfling and back to the altar area, where the dwarf was being pronounced guilty and sentenced to two years of labor in the mines. Luthien could understand the pragmatism of what Oliver had just explained. If Duke Morkney believed that a thieving band would try to come to the rescue of one of its captured associates, then his job in cleaning out Montfort's thieves would be easy indeed.

Luthien was nodding his agreement with the logic—but if that was truly the case, then why was he perched now, fifty feet above the Ministry's floor?

It worked out—and Oliver was sure that it was no coincidence—that Siobhan was the last to be called. She moved out of the pew, and though her hands were tied in front of her, she proudly shook off the groping cyclopians as they prodded her toward the lectern.

"Siobhan, a slave girl," the man called loudly, glancing back to the duke. Morkney still appeared bored with it all.

"She was among those who attacked the mine," the man declared.

"By whose words?" the half-elf asked sternly. The cyclopian behind shoved her hard with the shaft of its long pole-arm, and Siobhan glanced back wickedly, green eyes narrowed.

"So spirited," Oliver whispered, his tone a clear lament. He was holding firmly to Luthien's crimson cape then, half-expecting the trembling young man to leap down from the ledge.

"Prisoners speak only when they are told to speak!" the man at the podium scolded.

"What worth is a voice in this evil place?" Siobhan replied, drawing another rough shove.

Luthien issued a low and guttural growl, and Oliver shook his head resignedly, feeling more than ever that they should not be in this dangerous place.

"She attacked the mine!" the man cried angrily, looking to the duke. "And she is a friend of the Crim—"

Morkney came forward in his chair, hand upraised to immediately silence his impetuous lackey. Oliver didn't miss the significance of the movement, as though Duke Morkney did not want the name spoken aloud.

Morkney put his wrinkled visage in line with Siobhan; his bloodshot eyes seemed to flare with some magical inner glow. "Where are the dwarves?" he asked evenly.

"What dwarves?" Siobhan replied.

"The two you and your . . . associates took from the mines," Morkney explained, and his pause again prodded Oliver into the belief that this entire arrest and trial had been put together for his and Luthien's benefit.

Siobhan chuckled and shook her head. "I am a servant," she said calmly, "and nothing more."

"Who is the owner of this slave?" Morkney called out. Siobhan's master stood from one of the pews near the front and raised his hand.

"You are without guilt," the duke explained, "and so you shall be compensated for your loss." The man breathed a sigh of relief, nodded and sat back down.

"Oh, no," Oliver groaned under his breath. Luthien looked from the merchant to the duke, and from the duke to Siobhan, not really understanding.

"And you," Morkney growled, coming up out of his chair for the first time in the two hours Oliver and Luthien had been in the Ministry. "You are guilty," Morkney said evenly, and he slipped back down into his seat, grinning wickedly. "Do enjoy the next five days in my dungeons."

Five days? Luthien silently echoed. Was this the sentence? He heard Oliver's groan again and figured that Morkney was not quite finished.

"For they will be your last five days!" the evil duke declared. "Then you will be hung by your neck—in the plaza bearing my own name!"

A general groan rose from the gathering, an uneasy shuffling, and cyclopian guards gripped their weapons more tightly, glancing from side to side as if they expected trouble. The sentence was not expected. The only time during Morkney's reign that a sentence of death had ever been imposed was for the murder of a human, and even in such an extreme case, if the murdered human was not someone of importance, the guilty party was usually sentenced to a life of slavery.

Again the word "bait" flitted through Oliver's thoughts. His mind careened along the possible trials he and his cohort would soon face, for Luthien would never allow such an injustice without at least a try at a rescue. The halfling figured that he would be busy indeed over the next five days, making connections with the Cutters and with anyone else who might help him out.

The distracted halfling figured differently when he looked back to Luthien, standing tall on the ledge, his bow out and ready.

With a cry of outrage, the young Bedwyr let fly, his arrow streaking unerringly for the chair and Duke Morkney, who glanced up to the triforium in surprise. There came a silvery flash, and not one arrow, but five, crossed the opening to the north transept. Then came a second flash, and each of those five became five; and a third, and twenty-five became a hundred and twenty-five.

And all of them continued toward the duke, and Luthien and Oliver looked on in disbelief.

But the volley was insubstantial; the dozens of arrows were no more than shadows of the first, and all of them dissipated into nothingness, or simply passed through the duke as he leaned forward in his chair, still grinning wickedly and pointing Luthien's way.

Luthien felt himself an impetuous fool, a thought that did not diminish when he heard Oliver's remark behind him.

"I do not think that was so smart a thing to do."

CHAPTER 23

TELL THEM!

LUTHIEN FELL BACK from the ledge as the gargoyle statue writhed to life. He whipped his bow across, breaking it on the creature's hard head, and started to call out for Oliver. But he soon realized that the halfling, now with his great hat upon his head, was already hard-pressed as the sinister statues all along the triforium animated to the call of their wizard master.

"Why do I always seem to find myself fighting along a ledge?" the halfling whined, ducking a clawed hand and jabbing ahead—only to sigh as his slender rapier bowed alarmingly, barely penetrating the gargoyle's hard skin.

All gathered in the cathedral had, by this time, learned of the tumult along the arched passageway. Cyclopians shouted out commands; the duke's man at the lectern called for the "death of the outlaws!" and then made the profound mistake of altering his cry to, "Death to the Crimson Shadow!"

"The Crimson Shadow!" more than one curious commoner shouted from the pews, pointing anxiously Luthien's way. The timing was perfect for the young Bedwyr, for at that moment, he landed a clean strike on the gargoyle, his sword slashing down across the creature's neck and biting deep into the hard wing. Luthien bulled ahead and the gargoyle fell from the ledge, flapping its wings frantically, though with the wound, it could not sustain itself in the air and spiraled down to the floor.

"The Crimson Shadow!" more people called out, and others screamed in terror as they came to recognize the living gargoyle.

Chased by two of the winged monsters, Oliver skittered behind Luthien to the edge of the corner where the triforium turned into the south transept. Frantically the halfling fumbled out his grapnel and rope, but he did not miss the significance of the growing tumult below.

Luthien's sword sparked as it cut a ringing line across one gargoyle's face. The young Bedwyr fought fiercely, trying to hold the powerful creatures at bay. He knew that he and Oliver were in trouble, though, for more monsters were coming along the arched passageway from the other way, and still others had taken wing and were slowly drifting across the open area of the transept.

Cyclopians were fast organizing down below, trying to corral the increasingly agitated crowd—many people, gathering their children in their arms, had run screaming for the western doors. One cyclopian reached for Siobhan and promptly got kicked in the groin. The other brute flanking her had even less luck, taking an arrow in the ribs (shot from somewhere back in the pews) as it tried to grab ahold of the fiery half-elf.

And still other people stood staring blankly, pointing to the triforium and calling out for the mysterious thief in the crimson cape.

Oliver, rope and grapnel free by then, did not miss the significance of it all.

"Yes!" he cried as loudly as he could. "The Crimson Shadow has come! Your hour of freedom is upon you, good people of Montfort."

"For Eriador!" Luthien cried, quickly catching on to the halfling's plan. "For Bruce MacDonald!" In lower, more desperate tones, he quickly added, "Hurry, Oliver!" as the gargoyles pressed ahead.

"Brave people of Montfort, to arms!" shouted the halfling, and he sent his grapnel spinning above his head and launched it to the base of the vaulting above and out a bit from the triforium. "Freedom is upon you. To arms! Now is the moment for heroes. Brave people of Montfort, to arms!"

Luthien groaned as a heavy gargoyle arm clubbed him across the shoulders. He went with the weight of the blow, spinning into a stumbling step and falling over Oliver. Scooping the halfling in one arm, the young Bedwyr wrapped himself about the rope and leaped out.

The spectacle of Luthien and Oliver, crimson and purple capes flying behind them, swinging from the triforium, sliding down the rope inexorably toward the altar and the tyrant duke, replaced panic with courage, gave heart to the enslaved people of Montfort. Fittingly, a merchant with a large bag of coins, his taxes for the day, struck the first blow, smacking that same bag across the face of the nearest Praetorian Guard and laying the cyclopian out. The mob fell over the brute, one man taking its weapon.

Near to the side, another cyclopian was pulled down under a thrashing horde.

And from the back, Siobhan's allies, the Cutters, drew out their concealed weapons and bows and drove hard into a line of charging cyclopians.

Siobhan's accuser rushed around the podium, dagger in hand, apparently meaning to strike the half-elf down. He changed his mind and his direction, though, as the dwarven prisoner barreled forward to the half-elf's side. Down the north transept went the man, screaming for Praetorian Guards.

Siobhan and the dwarf glanced all about, saw their jailor go down near one of the front pews, and rushed for the spot, seeking the keys to their shackles.

Oliver and Luthien got more than halfway to the floor, and to the apse, before they were intercepted by a gargoyle. Luthien let go his hold on Oliver and freed up his sword hand, hacking wildly as the rope spun in a tight circle.

Oliver understood their dilemma, understood that more gargoyles were coming in at them. By the halfling's estimation, even worse was the fact that they were hanging in the air, open targets for the angry wizard-duke. The halfling looked to the floor and sighed, then gave three sharp tugs on the rope.

The gargoyle latched on to Luthien, and all three dropped the fifteen feet to the floor. On the way down, the halfling kept the presence of mind to scramble above the gargoyle, even to put the tip of his main gauche against the engaged creature's scalp, and when they hit, the force of the landing drove the weapon right through the animated monster's head.

Luthien was up first, whipping his sword back and forth to keep the nearest cyclopians at bay. Intent on him, the brutes didn't react to an approaching group of men, but the gargoyles flying down found good pickings. One man was lifted into the air, his head wrapped in gargoyle arms, his hands of little use against the hard-skinned monster.

All the nave was wild with the riot, all the people fighting with whatever weapons they could find, and many calling out, "The Crimson Shadow!" over and over.

Duke Morkney clenched his bony fists in rage when the troublesome Oliver and Luthien dropped into the throng, and he stopped the chanting that would have sent a bolt of energy out at the duo. When he looked around, Morkney realized that focusing on the two might not be so wise; the people in the cathedral far outnumbered his cyclopians, and to the duke's surprise, quite a few of them had apparently brought in weapons. Morkney's gargoyles were formidable, but they were not many, and they were slow to kill.

Another arrow whistled the duke's way, but it, too, hit his magical barrier, multiplying and diminishing in substance, until the images were no more than mere shadows of the original.

Morkney was outraged at the riot, but he was not worried. He had known that this scenario would come to pass sooner or later, and he had prepared well for it. The Ministry had stood for hundreds of years, and over that time, hundreds, mostly those who had helped construct the place or had donated great sums to the church, had been interred under its stone floor and within its thick walls.

Duke Morkney's thoughts slipped into the spirit world now, reached out for those buried corpses and called them forth. The Ministry's very walls and floor shuddered. Blocks angled out and hands, some ragged with rotting skin, others no more than skeletal remains, poked out.

"What have we started?" Luthien asked when he and Oliver got out of the immediate battle and found a moment to catch their breath.

"I do not know!" the halfling frankly admitted. Then both fell back in horror as a gruesome head, flesh withered and stretched thin, eyeballs lost in empty sockets, poked up from a crack in the floor to regard them.

Luthien's sword split the animated skull down the middle.

"There is only one way!" Oliver shouted, looking toward the apse. "These are Morkney's creatures!"

Luthien took off ahead of the halfling. Two cyclopians intercepted. The young Bedwyr's sword thrust forward, then whipped up high and to the side, taking one of the brutes' swords with it. Luthien followed straight ahead, his fist slamming the cyclopian in the face and knocking it over backward.

Down Luthien dropped, purely on instinct, barely ducking the wicked cut of the second brute's blade. He turned and slashed, disemboweling the surprised cyclopian.

Oliver came by him in a headlong roll, somehow launching his main gauche as he tumbled, the dagger spinning end over end and nailing the next intercepting Praetorian Guard right in the belly. The brute lurched and howled, a cry that became a gurgle as Oliver's rapier dove through its windpipe.

Luthien barreled past Oliver, throwing the dying guard aside. Another cyclopian was in line, its heavy sword defensively raised before it.

Luthien was too quick for the brute. He slashed across, deflecting the cyclopian's sword to his left, then continued the spin, turning a complete circuit and lifting his foot to slam the brute in the ribs, under its highflying arm. The cyclopian fell hard to the side. It was stunned, but not badly wounded. It did not come back at Luthien and Oliver, though. Rather, it scrambled away to find someone easier to fight.

The friends were at the altar, at the edge of the apse, with no enemies between them and Duke Morkney, who was now standing before his comfortable chair.

Oliver went under the altar, Luthien around to the left. The duke snapped his arm out toward them suddenly, throwing a handful of small pellets.

The beads hit the floor all around the altar and exploded, engulfing the friends in a shower of sparks and a cloud of thick smoke. Oliver cried out as the sparks stung him and clung to his clothes, but he kept the presence of mind to dart under Luthien's protective cape. Choking and coughing, the two pushed their way through—only to find that Duke Morkney was gone.

Oliver, always alert, caught a slight motion and pointed to a tapestry along the curving wall of the apse. Luthien was there in a few quick strides and he tore the tapestry aside. He found a wooden door, and beyond it, a narrow stone stairway rising inside the wall of the Ministry's tallest tower.

Siobhan and the eight Cutters in the cathedral split ranks, each going to a different area to try and calm the frenzied mob, to try and bring some semblance of order to the rioting citizens. One of the Cutters tossed the half-elf his bow and quiver, then drew out his sword and rushed two cyclopians. Only one was there to meet the charge, though, as Siobhan quickly put the bow to good use.

The cyclopians were not faring well, but their undead and gargoyle allies struck terror into the hearts of all who stood before them.

One woman, using her walking stick as a club, knocked the head off a skeleton, and her eyes widened in shock as the disgusting thing kept coming at her. She would have surely been killed, but the dwarven prisoner, free of his shackles, slammed into the headless thing and brought it down to the floor under him, thrashing about and scattering the bones.

Siobhan looked all about and saw a woman and her three children trying to duck low under a pew as a gargoyle hovered above them, slashing with its claws. The half-elf put an arrow into the gargoyle, then another, and as the monster turned toward her, a group of men leaped up from the pews and grabbed it, pulling it down under their weight.

Siobhan realized that any way she ran would be as good as another; the fighting was throughout the nave. She headed for the apse, thinking to find Luthien and Oliver and hoping for a shot at Duke Morkney. She emerged from the throng just as the tapestry swung back behind her departing lover and his halfling sidekick.

The stair was narrow and curving, circling the tower as it climbed, and Luthien and Oliver were afforded a view only a few feet in front of them as they ran upward in pursuit of the duke. They passed a couple of small windows with thick stone sills sporting small statues, and Luthien prudently kept his sword in line with these, expecting them to writhe to life and take up the fight.

About seventy steps up, Luthien pulled up short and turned to regard Oliver, who was distracted as he continued to coil the line of his magical grapnel. Luthien bade him to hold a moment and listen carefully.

They heard chanting not so far ahead on the winding stair.

Luthien dove flat to the stone and tried to pull Oliver down behind him. Before the startled halfling could react, there came a rapid series of explosions rocketing down the stairs, a bolt of lightning ricocheting off the stone. It sizzled past—Luthien felt its tingling sting along his backbone—and then it was gone. Luthien looked up, expecting to find Oliver's blackened body.

The halfling was still standing, trying to straighten his disheveled hat and fix the broken orange feather.

"You know," he said nonchalantly, "sometimes is not so bad to be short."

Luthien jumped up and on they ran, the young Bedwyr leaping two stairs at a time, trying to get at the duke before he could cause more mischief.

Luthien could not ignore the deep gouges in the stone wall at every point where the bolt had struck, and he wondered then what in the world he was doing. How had it come to this? How was it that he, the son of the eorl of Bedwydrin, was now chasing a wizard-duke up the tallest spire of Eriador's greatest building?

He shook his head and charged on, without a clue.

Around the endless spiral, the young Bedwyr's eyes widened in surprise and terror, and he ducked, crying out as a heavy ax chipped the stone above his head. Two cyclopians blocked the stairs, one behind the other.

Luthien pressed quickly with his sword, but the cyclopian had a large shield and the advantage of the higher ground, and the young Bedwyr had little to hit at. More dangerous was the cyclopian's ax, chopping down whenever Luthien got too near, forcing him back on his heels, driving him back down the stairs.

"Fight through!" Oliver cried behind him. "We must get to the wizard-type before he can prepare another surprise!"

Easier said than done, Luthien knew, for he could not offer any solid attacks against his burly and well-protected foe. On even ground, he and Oliver would already have dispatched the two cyclopians, but in the stair, it seemed utterly hopeless to Luthien.

He was even considering turning back, joining the ruckus in the nave, where he and Oliver could at least do some good.

An arrow skipped off the wall above Luthien's head, angled upward. The cyclopian, shield down low to block the continuing sword blows, caught it full in the chest and staggered backward.

Up came the brute's shield reflexively; Luthien didn't miss the opportunity to thrust his sword into the cyclopian's knee. The brute fell back on the stairs, helpless, and the second cyclopian promptly took flight.

Oliver's flying dagger got the other monster in the back, two steps up.

Luthien had finished off the first cyclopian and the second turned with a howl—just in time to catch a second rebounding arrow.

Luthien and Oliver figured it out as Siobhan came around the bend behind them.

"Run on!" Oliver bade Luthien, knowing that the lovesick young man would likely stop and make sweet eyes at their rescuer for eternity. To Luthien's credit, he was already in motion, bounding past the fallen brutes and up the winding stair. "We must get to the wizard-type . . ."

"Before he can prepare another surprise!" Luthien finished for him.

They put two hundred steps behind them, and Luthien's legs ached and felt as though they would buckle beneath him. He paused for a moment and turned to regard his halfling friend.

"If we wait, the wizard-type will have a big boom waiting for us, I am sure," Oliver said, brushing the thick wig hair back from his face.

Luthien tilted his bead back and took a deep breath, then ran on.

They put another hundred steps behind them and then saw the unmistakable glow of daylight. They came to a landing, then up five more stairs to the very roof of the tower, a circular space perhaps twenty-five feet in diameter that was enclosed by a low battlement.

Across from them stood Duke Morkney, laughing wildly, his voice changing, growing deeper, more guttural and more ominous. Luthien leaped to the platform, but skidded to a quick stop and looked on in horror as the duke's body lurched violently, began twisting and bulging.

And growing.

Morkney's skin became darker and hardened to layered scales along his arms and neck. His head bulged weirdly, growing great fangs and a forked and flicking tongue. Soon Morkney's face resembled that of a giant snake, and great curving horns grew out from the top of his head. His red robes seemed a short skirt by then, for he was twice his original height, and his chest, so skinny and weak before, was now massive, stretching his previously voluminous robes to their limits. Long and powerful arms reached out of those sleeves, clawed fingers raking the air as the duke continued his obviously agonizing transformation.

Drool dripped off the front of the serpentine face, sizzling like acid as it hit the stone between the monster's three-clawed feet where Morkney's boots lay in tatters. With a shrug, the beast brushed free of the red robe, great leathery wings unfolding behind it, its black flesh and scales smoking with the heat of the Abyss.

"Morkney," Luthien whispered.

"I do not think so," Oliver replied. "Perhaps we should go back down."

CHAPTER 24

THE DEMON

"I AM MORKNEY no more," the beast proclaimed. "Gaze upon the might of Praehotec and be afraid!"

"Praehotec?" Luthien whispered, and he was indeed afraid.

"A demon," Oliver explained, gasping for breath—from more than the long run up the stairs, Luthien knew. "The clever wizard-type has lent his material body to a demon."

"It is no worse than the dragon," Luthien whispered, trying to calm Oliver and himself.

"We did not beat the dragon," Oliver promptly reminded him.

The demon looked around, its breath steaming in the chill October air. "Ah," it sighed. "So good to be in the world again! I will feast well upon you, and you, and upon a hundred others before Morkney finds the will to release me to the Abyss!"

Luthien didn't doubt the claim, not for a minute. He had seen giants as large as Praehotec, but nothing, not even Balthazar, had radiated an aura as powerful and as unspeakably evil. How many people had this demon eaten? Luthien wondered, and he shuddered, not wanting to know the answer.

He heard movement on the steps behind him and glanced back just in time to see Siobhan come up onto the lower landing, bow in hand.

Luthien took a deep breath and steadied himself. In his love-stricken heart, it seemed as if the stakes had just been raised.

"Come with me, Oliver," he said through gritted teeth, and he clutched his sword tightly, meaning to charge into the face of doom.

Before the halfling could even turn his unbelieving stare on his taller friend, Praehotec reached out a clawed hand and clenched its massive fist.

A tremendous wind came up suddenly from over the battlement to their left, assaulting the companions. At the same moment, Siobhan let fly her arrow, but the gust caught the flimsy bolt and tossed it harmlessly aside.

Luthien squinted and raised an arm defensively against the stinging wind, his cape and clothes whipping out to the right, buffeting Oliver. The halfling's hat pulled free of his head; up it spiraled.

Instinctively, Oliver leaped up and caught it, dropping his rapier in the process, but then he was flying, too, bouncing head over heels in a soaring roll. As he came back upright, he went high into the air, right over the battlement. Stunned Oliver was fully a dozen feet out from the ledge when Praehotec's snakelike face turned up into a leering grin and the demon released the wind.

Oliver let out a single shriek and dropped from sight.

Crying out for his lost friend, Luthien charged straight in, sword slashing viciously. Siobhan's arrows came in a seemingly continuous line over his head, scoring hit after hit on the beast, though whether or not they even stung the great Praehotec, Luthien could not tell.

He scored a slight nick with his sword, but the blade was powerfully batted away. Luthien dropped to one knee, ducking a slashing claw, then came right back to his feet and hopped backward, sucking in his belly to avoid the demon's swiping arm.

An arrow nicked Praehotec's neck and the demon hissed.

In came Luthien with a straightforward thrust that cut the fleshy insides of the demon's huge thigh. The young Bedwyr whipped his head safely to the side as the fanged serpent head rocketed past, but a swiping claw caught him on the shoulder before he could regain his balance, gouging him and heaving him aside.

He kept the presence of mind to slash once more with his blade as he fell away, scoring a hit on Praehotec's knuckle.

Luthien knew that last cut had hurt the demon, but he almost regretted that fact as Praehotec turned on him, reptilian eyes flaring with simmering fires of rage.

He saw something else, then, a flicker in the demon's fiery eyes and a slight trembling on the side of the beast's serpentine maw.

An arrow razored into the demon's neck.

That flicker and trembling came again, and Luthien got the feeling that Praehotec was not so secure in this material body.

The demon straightened, towering above Luthien, as if to mock his suspicions. It shifted its furious gaze, and from its eyes came two lines of crackling red energy, joining together inches in front of the demon's face and sizzling across the tower's top to slam into Siobhan, throwing her back down the stairs.

Luthien's heart seemed to stop.

▪ ▪ ▪

Hanging from the tower's side, Oliver plopped his hat on his head once more. The thing was on fairly straight, but the wig underneath it had turned fully about, and the long black tresses hung in front of his face, obscuring his vision. His legs and one hip ached from his swinging slam into the stone, and his arms ached, too, as he clung desperately to the rope of his magical grapnel.

The horrified halfling knew that he could not simply hang there forever, so he finally found the courage to look up, shaking the hair out of his face. His grapnel—that beautiful, magical grapnel!—had caught a secure hold on the curving stone, but it was not close enough to the tower's rim for the halfling to climb over it, and Oliver didn't have nearly enough rope to get down the side to the street below.

He spotted the depression of a window a bit above him and to his left.

"You are so very brave," he whispered to himself, and he brought his legs up under him and stood out from the wall. Slowly, he walked himself to the right, then, when he figured that he had the rope stretched far enough, he half ran, half flew back to the left, like a pendulum. Diving at the end of his swing, he just managed to hook the fingers of one hand over the lip of the window, and with some effort, he wriggled himself onto the ledge.

Oliver grumbled as he considered the barrier before him. He could break through the stained glass, but the window opening was crossed by curving metal that would certainly bar his entrance to the tower.

The grumbling halfling glanced all about, noticed that a crowd was gathering down below, many pointing up his way and calling out to their compatriots. In the distance, Oliver could see a force of Praetorian Guards making their way along the avenues, coming to quell the rioting in the cathedral, no doubt.

The halfling shook his head and straightened his hat, then gave three quick tugs to release the grapnel. He might be able to set the magical thing below him and get down the tower in time to escape, he realized, but to his own amazement, the halfling found himself swinging the item up instead, higher on the wall and near to another window.

Bound by friendship, Oliver was soon climbing, to the continuing shouts of the crowd below.

"Sometimes I do not think that having a friend is a good thing," the halfling muttered, but on he went, determinedly.

Inside the cathedral, the riot had turned into a rout. Many cyclopians were dead and the remaining brutes were scattered and under cover, but the crowd could not stand against Morkney's horrifying undead brigade and the wicked gargoyles. The Cutters worked to herd the frantic people now, to put them together that they might bull their way to an entrance.

All that mattered to the rioters at this point was escape.

The cyclopians seemed to understand, the gargoyles, too, and whichever way the mob went, barriers were thrown up in their path.

And the horrid undead monsters dogged their every step, pulling down those who were not fast enough to dodge the clawing, bony hands.

A primal scream of outrage accompanied Luthien's bold charge. The young Bedwyr wanted only to strike down this foul beast, caring not at all for his own safety. Two clawed hands reached out to grasp him as he came in, but he worked his sword magnificently, slapping one and then the other, drawing oozing gashes on both.

Luthien ducked his shoulder and bore in, slashing, even kicking, at the huge monster.

The demon apparently understood the danger of this one's fury, for Praehotec's leathery wings began to flap, lifting the creature from the tower.

"No!" Luthien protested. He wasn't even thinking of the dangers of letting Praehotec out of his sword's range; he was simply enraged at the thought that the murderous monster might escape. He jumped up at the beast, sword leading, accepting the inevitable clawing hit on his back as he came in close.

He felt no pain and didn't even know that he was bleeding. All that Luthien knew was anger, pure red anger, and all of his strength and concentration followed his sword thrust, plunging the weapon deep into Praehotec's belly. Smoking greenish goo poured from the wound, covering Luthien's arm, and the stubborn young Bedwyr roared and whipped the sword back and forth, trying to disembowel the beast. He looked Praehotec in the eye as he cut and saw again that slight wavering, an indication that the demon was not so secure in the wizard's material form.

Praehotec's powerful arm slammed down on his shoulder, and suddenly, Luthien was kneeling on the stone once more, dazed. Up lifted the demon, wings wide over Luthien like an eagle crowning its helpless prey.

From somewhere far away, the young Bedwyr heard a voice—Siobhan's voice.

"You ugly bastard!" the half-elf growled, and she let fly another arrow.

Praehotec saw it coming, all the way up to the instant it drove into the beast's reptilian eye.

Siobhan! Luthien realized, and instinctively the young Bedwyr braced himself and thrust his sword up above his head.

Praehotec came down hard, impaling itself to the sword's crosspiece. The demon began to thrash, but then stopped and looked down curiously at Luthien.

And Luthien looked curiously at his sword, its pommel pulsing with the beating of the beast's great heart.

With a roar that split stone and a violent shudder that snapped the blade at the hilt, Praehotec flung itself back against the parapet.

Siobhan hit it with another arrow, but it didn't matter. The demon thrashed about; red and green blood and guts poured down the creature.

Luthien stood tall before it, fought away his dizziness and pain and looked into the eyes of the monster he thought defeated.

He recognized the simmering fires a moment too late, tried to dodge as lines of red energy again came from the demon, joining in a single line and blasting out.

Luthien went tumbling across the tower top, and Siobhan once more disappeared from sight, this time to roll all the way to the bottom and land hard on the lower landing, where she lay, groaning and helpless.

Luthien shook his head, trying to remember where he was. By the time he managed to look back across the tower, he saw Praehotec standing tall, laughing wickedly at him.

"You believe that your puny weapons can defeat Praehotec?" the beast bellowed. It reached right into the garish wound in its belly and, laughing all the while, extracted Luthien's slime-covered blade. "I am Praehotec, who has lived for centuries untold!"

Luthien had no more energy to battle the monster. He was defeated; he knew that, and knew, too, that if Greensparrow had indeed made such allies as Praehotec, as Brind'Amour had claimed, and as Morkney had apparently proven true, then a shadow might indeed soon cover all of Eriador.

Luthien struggled to his knees. He wanted to die with dignity, at least. He put one foot under him, but paused and stared hard at the monster.

"No!" Praehotec growled. The demon wasn't looking at Luthien; it was looking up into the empty air. "The kill is rightfully mine! His flesh is my food!"

"No," came Duke Morkney's voice in reply. "The sweet kill is mine!"

Praehotec's serpentine face trembled, then bulged weirdly, reverting to the face of Duke Morkney. Then it returned to Praehotec, briefly, then back to Duke Morkney.

The struggle continued, and Luthien knew that the opportunity to strike would not last long. He staggered forward a bit, trying to find some weapon, trying to find the strength to attack.

When he glanced back across the tower top, he saw not Praehotec but Duke Morkney's skinny and naked body, the duke bending low to retrieve his fallen robe.

"You should be dead already," Morkney said, noticing that Luthien was struggling to stand. "Stubborn fool! Take pride in the fact that you fended off the likes of Praehotec for several minutes. Take pride and lie down and die."

Luthien almost took the advice. He had never been so weary and wounded, and he did not imagine that death was very far away. Head down, he noticed something then, something that forced him to stand straight once more and forced him to remember the losses he had suffered.

Oliver's rapier.

To Duke Morkney's mocking laughter, the young Bedwyr stepped over and picked up the small and slender blade, then stood very still to find his balance and stubbornly rose up tall. He staggered across the tower top, toward his foe.

Morkney was still naked and still laughing as Luthien staggered near, rapier aimed for the duke's breast.

"Do you believe that I am not capable of defeating you?" the duke asked incredulously. "Do you think that I need Praehotec, or any other demon, to destroy a mere swordsman? I sent the demon away only because I wanted your death to come from my own hands." With a superior growl, Morkney lifted his bony hands, fingers clawed like an animal, and began to chant.

Luthien's back arched suddenly and he froze in place, eyes wide with shock and sudden agony. Tingling energy swept through him, back to front and right out of his chest. It seemed to him, to his ultimate horror, that his own life energy was being sucked out of him, stolen by the evil wizard!

"No," he tried to protest, but he knew then that he was no match for the powers of the wicked duke.

Like a true parasite, Morkney continued to feed, taking perverse pleasure in it all, laughing wickedly, as evil a being as the demon he had summoned.

"How could you ever have believed that you could win against me?" the duke asked. "Do you not know who I am? Do you now understand the powers of Greensparrow's brotherhood?"

Again came the mocking laughter; the dying Luthien couldn't even speak out in protest. His heart beat furiously; he feared it would explode.

Suddenly, a looped rope spun over the duke's head, drawing tight about his shoulders. Morkney's eyes widened as he regarded it, and he followed its length to the side to see Oliver deBurrows, crawling over the battlement.

The halfling shrugged and smiled apologetically, even waved to the duke. Morkney growled, thinking to turn his wrath on this one, thinking that he was through with the impudent young human.

The instant he was free, Luthien jerked straight, and the motion brought the deadly rapier shooting forward, its tip plunging into the startled duke's breast.

They stood face to face for a long moment, Morkney staring incredulously at this curious young man, at this young man who had just killed him. The duke chuckled again, for some reason, then slumped dead into Luthien's arms.

Down below, in the nave, the gargoyles turned to stone and crashed to the floor, and the skeletons and rotting corpses lay back down in their eternal sleep.

Oliver looked far below to the now huge crowd and the large force of Praetorian Guards coming into the plaza beside the Ministry.

"Put him over the side!" the quick-thinking halfling called to Luthien.

Luthien turned curiously at Oliver, who was now scrambling all the way over the battlement and back to the tower's top.

"Put him over the side!" the halfling said again. "Let them see him hanging by his skinny neck!"

The notion horrified Luthien.

Oliver ran up to his friend and pushed Luthien away from the dead duke. "Do you not understand?" Oliver asked. "They need to see him!"

"Who?"

"Your people!" Oliver cried, and with a burst of strength, the halfling shoved Morkney over the battlement. The lasso slipped up from the duke's shoulders and caught tight about his neck as he tumbled, his skinny, naked form coming to a jerking stop along the side of the tower a hundred feet above the ground.

But the poor people of Montfort, under this one's evil thumb for many years, surely recognized him.

They did, indeed.

Out of the north transept came the victorious mob from the cathedral, taking their riot to the streets, sweeping up many onlookers in their wake.

"What have we done?" the stunned young Bedwyr asked, staring down helplessly at the brutal fight.

Oliver shrugged. "Who can say? All I know is that the pickings should be better with that skinny duke out of the way," he answered, always pragmatic and always opportunistic.

Luthien just shook his head, wondering once more what he had stumbled into. Wondering how all of this had come to pass.

"Luthien?" he heard from across the tower top, and he spun about to see Siobhan, leaning heavily on the battlement, her gray robe in tatters.

But smiling.

EPILOGUE

The snow lay thick along the quiet streets of Montfort, nearly every street lined with the red stains of spilled blood. Luthien sat atop the roof of a tall building in the lower section, looking out over the city and the lands to the north.

The people of Montfort were in full revolt, and he, the Crimson Shadow, unwittingly had been named their leader. So many had died, and Luthien's heart was often heavy. But he gathered strength from those who savagely fought on for their freedom, from those brave people who had lived so long under tyranny and now would not go back to that condition, even at the price of their lives.

And, to Luthien's amazement, they were winning. A powerful and well-armed cyclopian force still controlled the city's inner section beyond the dividing wall, protecting the wealthy merchants who had prospered under Duke Morkney. Rumors said that Viscount Aubrey had taken command of the force.

Luthien remembered the man well; he hoped the rumors were true.

The fighting had been furious in the first weeks following the duke's death, with hundreds of men, women, and cyclopians dying every day. Winter had settled in quickly, slowing the fighting, forcing many to think merely of keeping from freezing or starving. At first, the cold seemed to favor the merchants and cyclopians in their better quarters within the city's higher section, but as time went on, Luthien's people began to find the advantage. They controlled the outer wall; they controlled any goods coming into the city.

And Siobhan's group, along with a number of ferocious dwarves, continued to wreak havoc. Even now, plans were being laid for a full-scale raid upon the mines to free the rest of Shuglin's enslaved people.

But Luthien could not shake his many doubts. Were his actions truly valuable, or was he walking a fool's parade? How many would die because he had chosen this course, because at that fateful moment in the Ministry, the Crimson

Shadow had been revealed and the people had rallied behind him? And even with their astonishing initial victories, what hope could the future hold for the beleaguered people of Montfort? The winter would be a brutal one, it seemed, and the spring would likely bring an army from Avon, King Greensparrow's forces coming to reclaim the city.

And punish the revolutionaries.

Luthien sighed deeply, noticing another rider galloping out from Montfort's northern gate, riding north to spread the news and enlist help—in the form of supplies, at least, from nearby villages. There was word of some minor fighting in Port Charley to the east, but Luthien took little heart in it.

"I knew you would be up here," came a voice from behind, and Luthien turned to see Oliver climbing up onto the roof. "Surveying your kingdom?"

Luthien's scowl showed that he did not think that to be funny.

"Ah, well," the halfling conceded, "I only came to tell you that you have a visitor."

Luthien cocked a curious eyebrow as a woman climbed over the roof's edge. Her eyes were green as Siobhan's, the young Bedwyr realized, somehow surprised by that fact, but her hair was red, fiery red. She stood tall and proud, holding something wrapped in a blanket before her, locking stares with her old friend.

"Katerin," Luthien whispered, hardly able to get words out of his suddenly dry mouth.

Katerin walked across the roof to stand before the man and handed him the item.

Luthien took it gingerly, not understanding.

His eyes went wide when he slipped off the blanket and saw *Blind-Striker,* his family's treasured sword.

"From Gahris, your father and the rightful eorl of Bedwydrin," Katerin O'Hale explained, her tone stern and determined.

Luthien looked searchingly into her green eyes, wondering what had happened.

"Avonese is in chains," Katerin said. "And there is not a living cyclopian on Isle Bedwydrin."

Luthien found breath hard to come by. Gahris had followed his lead, had taken up the war! The young man glanced all about, from the smiling Katerin, to the smiling Oliver, to the snow-covered rooftops of the quiet city.

He was faced with a decision then, Luthien knew, but this time, unlike the many events that had led him to this fateful point, he was making it consciously.

"Go out, Oliver," the young man said. "Go out and tell the people to take heart. Tell them that their war, the war for their freedom, has begun." Luthien again locked stares with the proud woman from Hale.

"Go out, Oliver," he said again. "Tell them that they are not alone."

ABOUT THE AUTHOR

R.A. Salvatore's first book, *The Crystal Shard*, was published in 1988; in 1990 his third novel, *The Halfling's Gem,* hit the *New York Times* bestseller list. Since then he has written more than sixty novels, which have sold more than thirty million copies worldwide. In addition, Salvatore has numerous game credits, making him one of the most important figures in modern epic fantasy. Among his books are numerous titles in the saga of dark elf Drizzt Do'Urden, the Coven series, the Crimson Shadow trilogy, and many more.

Salvatore spends a good deal of time speaking to schools and library groups, encouraging people, particularly young people, to read. He enjoys a broad range of literary writers, from James Joyce to Dante and Chaucer, and counts among his favorite genre literary influences Ian Fleming, Arthur Conan Doyle, Fritz Leiber, and J. R. R. Tolkien. Salvatore makes his home in Massachusetts, with his wife, Diane, and their dogs. His gaming group still meets on Sunday nights.

He is currently working on more novels set in the Demon wars and Dark Elf series.

THE CRIMSON SHADOW

FROM OPEN ROAD MEDIA

OPEN ROAD
INTEGRATED MEDIA